Last Out at Roaring Water Bay

by

Eddie Rampling

Eddie Rampling is hereby identified as author of this
work in accordance with Section 77 of the Copyright, Designs
and Patents Act 1988

This book is published by
Grosvenor House Publishing Ltd
28–30 High Street, Guildford, Surrey, GU1 3HY.
www.grosvenorhousepublishing.co.uk

A CIP record for this book
is available from the British Library

ISBN 1-905529-43-0

AUTHOR'S NOTE

Within the context of this story it is mentioned that a Japanese submarine the I-52 was sunk by the Allies in the Atlantic in 1944. This is a true historical event and cannot be related to my imagination. Yet this wartime incident did provide me with the inspiration to develop and fantasize an intriguing piece of skulduggery and the introduction of my treasure seeker anti-hero Shackleton (Shacks) Speed. This is my first complete novel which I thoroughly hope the reader will enjoy.

Yet as I put my finishing touches to this piece of work there is something that disturbs me about a writer delving deep into an unlimited imagination to create a story. That maybe one day that piece of speculation spat out from the writer's brain could uncannily relate to hidden truths that are out there waiting to be discovered. After all what is fiction but a dream? Sometimes dreams can come true and who knows maybe this is the time? Maybe this is the story?

CHAPTER ONE

Down in a shallow gully at the far end of windswept Berkshire field is where my life changed without even consulting me. It happened precisely the moment when the metal detector sent a signal into my headphones indicating the buried object and even then I never sensed that anything was wrong. To me it was just another day, another casual venture hopeful of a successful treasure piece because that was what I excelled in, finding things that made money. What I wasn't prepared for, and something I would never have envisaged, is that somewhere along my road to unforeseen bedlam there was the possibility I might have to kill someone.

But I didn't know all that when I eased the spade into the soil, put the detector down to one side, slipped the headphones down around my neck and turned over the grassy clump of dirt with high expectancy, when I saw what I had uncovered, the whole event had started and there was no turning back.

For one fleeting moment of disappointment I actually felt as if I had been conned. Instead of the anticipated antiquity I stood there staring at a length of rotting braided flex. It can happen that way sometimes, but not usually to me. In frustration I ripped the cable from the ground and as I did a fist of skeletal knuckles burst out from the soil.

My gut reaction had me rearing away expecting the stench of decaying flesh when there was none to smell before my insatiable curiosity coaxed me to continue digging. I worked carefully clearing the soil from around the hand bones, burrowing deeper into the slope until I had revealed the corpse's head and left shoulder. Judging by the rotting leather skullcap, flying tunic, glare goggles, the oxygen equipment and mouth inflatable life jacket, it was obvious now I had found the remains of a wartime pilot still harnessed inside the shattered bubble canopy which suggested the pilot never got the chance to escape.

I stood back and gestured a quick military style salute. My, "welcome home, Mister," was greeted by the unnerving movement of the skeleton's head rolling slowly sideways as the loose soil fell way which allowed something to fall from behind the glare goggles and dangle there. They were the pilot's identity tags. I leaned over and took them gently in one hand and made an effort to clean the metal with spit and finger rubbing, struggling at first because the indentations on the tag were so faint by years of corrosion. Eventually one word showed clearly, 'Craven'. I let the tags fall back and stepped away from the body.

I didn't spend too much time pondering if Craven was a first or second name because I had no intention to make this my problem. I wiped my soiled hands across my trousers, took the mobile phone from my jacket pocket and called the owner of the land.

"Tommy...Yes it's me, Shacks. Come down to the far field as quickly as you can...Don't ask questions, mobiles cost money. I'm down in a gully...Look for where the cows are...No I'm not in any trouble, but hurry anyway."

As I slipped the phone back into my pocket I noticed something held in the skeleton's hand that the flex was attached to. Now I was well aware of the implications for desecrating a war grave but my inquisitive nature, which has got me into deep trouble in the past, had me prising the finger bones apart and removing the device. It was a push button mechanism seized with corrosion and beyond usage when I tried to press the trigger. It had to have operated something special so I began tracing where the flex went, gently easing the cable from the crumbling peaty soil, eager to find the source before Tommy arrived.

It finally disappeared into a wooden surround which disintegrated when I pulled it from the soil, exposing a corroded camera and without doubt I knew I had found a reconnaissance plane. With no hesitation I snapped the flex from the camera, crouched down onto one knee, slipped the rucksack from my shoulder, took out a large polythene bag and placed the camera inside. I had the package back into the rucksack quicker than a Harrods shoplifter.

I got to my feet when I heard the clanging of Tommy's ancient tractor as it approached the top of the gully. He was on foot when I caught sight of him peering down. He had his dog beside him, a strange looking beast he named Winston, a cross between a Labrador and a Staffordshire bull terrier and despite the reputation of a half fighting dog, Tommy insisted he was a loveable four-legged character and he wouldn't hurt a fly. I believed him. Nonetheless this was a situation when no dog could be trusted.

I said to Tommy, "Come down! But leave the dog up there I don't want the mutt running around the countryside with a bone clamped in his mouth."

Tommy looked rather puzzled. "Winston hasn't got a bone!" He finally said.

"He will have if he comes down *here*."

Still puzzled, Tommy finger signalled and told Winston to sit and stay, then he began a slow descent, his arms spread out for balance not wanting the indignity of a slip onto his arse. I was amazed how agile he was for his age.

Tommy Bickermass had told me he was seventy two years old and the deep cut lines criss-crossing his leathery face verified his age. His day attending the farm began so early that it was rumoured he was solely responsible for waking up the crack of dawn before the cockerel even thought about it. He was dressed in his usual flashy woman pulling attire, a grubby flat cap, green checked tweed jacket covering a black satin waistcoat and a stained shirt. His brown cord trousers he had tucked into a pair of knee cap length Wellington boots that flopped when he walked. The thick curls of hair showing from beneath his hat was a mixture of yellow streaks mingling with grey and white, the yellow strands caused by the application of Grecian 2000, so he assured me.

When he saw the grisly remains he startled. His grey eyes popped out and most noticeably a peculiar shade of white varnished his red mottled complexion. Composing himself with a puff of his cheeks, he said, "Blimey!" then added something really stupid. "Is the bugger dead?"

I looked to the heavens in dismay. "He's been buried there for years on the strength of it!" I said sarcastically.

Tommy tilted back his flat cap to scratch an imaginary itch. He shook his head in disbelief and said solemnly, "Know who the bugger is?"

"My guess he's a veteran of world war two. R.A.F. fighter pilot judging by the flying wings insignia badge on his tunic."

I thought it wise not to mention the camera or my theory of a reconnaissance plane. I had my reasons, the less others knew the less chance of yours truly getting into serious trouble. And then I noticed a strange trance like look in Tommy's eyes. I thought he was on the verge of a heart attack and quickly asked him if he was okay.

His silence annoyed me.

"Well, are you alright?!" I snapped at him.

Finally, in a slow drawl he said, "I can't believe it!"

"Believe what exactly?"

Tommy got a little excited. "That Billy Banter was right after all!"

"Who might Billy Banter be if you don't mind me asking?"

"Oh he's a bit of a strange fellow, a bit slow in the brain. I've known him since we were kids. He was harmless and never bothered anyone. Aye, I remember it all now. Late summer it was, during the war. You'd find Billy running through the long grass pretending to be a fighter plane. He spent hours doing it. Then one day he came up with an incredible tale that he had shot a plane down and it had crashed in these parts. I mean, it wasn't surprising nobody took notice of strange boy who hadn't all the cogs in his brain working correctly. And now this turns up. He still lives around here. I suppose I should tell him he was right after all but I doubt he'd remember me."

"Well if someone had believed him it's just possible the pilot's life might have been saved," I said accusingly. "Instead he perished, trapped in his cockpit. No doubt he suffocated to death."

Tommy hit back. "Bugger off, Shacks! You make it sound so gruesome. We weren't to know. We were just kids."

"Well you can make amends now. I'll trust you to call the local constabulary to get this mess sorted."

One of Tommy's eyebrows arched. "Are you not stopping?"

"Frigging hell I'm out of here! I might have found it but I can't take any credit. The authorities and I don't exactly complement each other when it concerns digging up the countryside whether it's for a dead body or the crown jewels."

Tommy winked at me. "So you were never here then?"

"That's right. Besides, why share the coverage you'll get. You'll be hailed a national hero in the papers."

Tommy's face gleamed at the thought of fame. "My name will be in the papers?" A huge smile appeared as I nodded in agreement, then his face dropped and he said with sadness in his voice, "Don't suppose the bracelet turned up?"

I took a plastic bag from my jacket pocket and handed it to him. Tommy eyes brightened as he examined the soiled contents inside the bag. "You found it!"

"Two hours ago, middle field. I thought I'd continue scanning the rest of the fields while I was in the vicinity so I can eliminate it from my map references. Good job too. Or else this poor saviour of our wretched country would have rotted into total oblivion, never to receive an honourable burial."

Tommy gripped the bracelet tightly. "Well, the pilot will get his funeral and I've got this back. It means a lot to me. You're a good un' Shacks."

"I know." I said smartly.

I collected my equipment, hitched a ride on the tractor back to the farm, threw the gear into the boot of my car and headed for London, where my first stop was at a photography shop situated on the corner of Lambeth Road and Kennington Road. Larry 'the lens' Lazerow was the proprietor, a friend of mine. I plonked the camera I'd got from the crash site on the counter with the instruction, "develop that if you can Lens!", and watched the astonishment creep across his Barbadian face. Before he had the time to protest I had dashed from his shop leaving a trail of words in my wake, "Sorry, Lens. In a rush, important engagement," and went home expecting only good things to happen.

CHAPTER TWO

The next time I stumbled across the crashed plane was five days later while at home in a quiet suburb of Hammersmith having breakfast and shuffling through the morning paper. I came across Tommy's smiling face on page four in the middle of a quarter sized spread under the heading:

'LOST IN ACTION WAR HERO'S BODY FOUND IN FARMER'S FIELD.'

Tommy's account of the discovery was fascinating. He began by stating that his trusty dog actually made the find, which had accounted for the severe disturbance around the wreck. I had to congratulate Tommy as that was improvisation at its best. In fact his entire description of the event was a masterful piece of fictitious nonsense with a few truths mixed into the conversation with the reporter, and so realistic, I would have been proud to call it mine. Strange, I thought, the old sod never gave me the impression he could be such a lying bastard. There was no mention of my presence at the crash site so I had to be thankful that at least he had got something right if not truthful.

As I read on I became concerned. The name of the exhumed pilot didn't match the name I saw on the identity tags that hung around the skeletons neck. The Ministry of Defence had released the name Flying Officer Derek Rowland which was a ridiculously long way from the name *Craven* I had seen. Someone, for whatever reason, had made an outstanding gaff along the process of identification and unfortunately, nowadays, you just can't get the right staff.

Then it struck me. Frigging hell! They're going to bury the wrong man in the wrong grave and if the truth is revealed then a lot of people were going to be really pissed off! I should have got straight on the phone to complain about the incompetence of the misprint. I should have, but I wasn't about to counter-sign my admission that I had been present at the crash site. I shrugged my shoulders as I contemplated another cock-up in the statistics of British history and finished breakfast, which was just as well because the rap on the front door thundered through my hallway like an echo through the dingy vaults of a medieval castle.

I wasn't expecting anyone and I detest door-call merchants, so I ignored the intrusion rather hoping that whoever it was would go away and leave me alone. It didn't work. The thumping on the solid oak door had me convinced that the annoyer could only have achieved such force by using a sledgehammer. By the time I got to the door and opened it aggressively I was in the mood to ring someone's neck.

I was about to remonstrate but was taken aback by the strange appearance of the two callers. Ugly was a better description. Tall, slim men dressed in smart dark silk suits who gave me the impression that they liked to scare people. From their slicked back black hair, down to their highly polished shoes, both men had strikingly similar features. They could have easily been mistaken for twins, but they weren't. The slightly taller of the two had jagged scars running up the sides of his nose as if some deranged person had tried to permanently detach it from his face. I also noticed his left hand was bandaged and by the clinical cleanness of the material it had been bound recently.

I put their ages as early forties. Both had a shoulder deformity, a severe stoop developed by poor posture and beady dark eyes that stared unblinkingly. Both had aquiline noses above funny shaped mouths and their protruding thyroid cartilages gave the illusion of them having bent necks. In my opinion, sit the two men on the branch of a leafless tree in a savannah in Africa and they would quite easily pass as a pair of black African vultures waiting patiently for their next meal to die.

I wasn't about to die and since I don't have much respect for people who supposedly represent authority, I said snappily. "Can I help?"

The scar-less one on the left side of me reacted first by flipping open a warrant card in front of my face and said just as quickly, "Detective Inspector Filbert, Ministry of Defence Police. You are

Mister Shackleton Speed?" He wasn't asking, he was telling me in anticipation of my instant denial.

He never gave me the time to study his credentials properly because he whipped the card back into his pocket. I didn't protest mainly because I was thinking aloud and there could have been a number of reasons why the M.o.D. should be stood on my doorstep, but I had only one, a particular field in Berkshire came to mind. In the hope of distracting them, I said, "I'm too old to join the Forces. If it's recruitments you require try further down the road, plenty of younger fodder there."

Frustrated expressions glared back at me as they shuffled forward in a way I considered threatening. I stood my ground as any true gladiator would.

Filbert's eyes flickered which I took as a sign of controlled anger. "This is not about availability for recruitment, Mister Speed. We are here on a more serious matter."

I deliberately arched my eyebrows. "Just how serious are you talking and why should it concern me?"

"It's a criminal matter involving a war grave being desecrated, to be precise, and it does concern you!"

I stabbed my forefinger into my chest. "Are you accusing me?"

Filbert smiled thinly. "I don't see anyone else stood beside you, Mister Speed. Perhaps we should go inside to discuss things or would you prefer we went down to the local police station where you will be cautioned?"

I should have been stronger and told them both to 'sod off' back to where they escaped from. I should have, but a refusal might highlight my guilt because they were on my doorstep for one thing only, and Tommy Bickermass had dropped me deep in it as I had told no one else that I'd been present at the crash site.

I let them in, closed the front door and took them into my study but didn't shut the door fully nor did I offer them a chair. I remained standing too and looked Filbert straight in the eye.

"I'm afraid I'm not ghoulish enough to visit graveyards," I said calmly, though I had a funny feeling the crafty bastards were recording the conversation as I noted a slight bulge in Scar-face's breast pocket which I guessed was a voice recorder ready to catch the unsuspecting confession. "Have you considered juvenile vandals?"

Filbert seethed. "I'm not referring to just any graveyard, Mister

Speed. If you read the papers you might be aware of the recently discovered Spitfire in the Berkshire countryside."

"Yes," I said. "I was reading the story when you interrupted my peaceful relaxation." Casually I asked, "What's it got to do with me?"

"It has everything to do with you, Mister Speed."

My mind was ticking over fast. *Frigging hell, Tommy, just how deep have you got me in?* "And what might that be?" I asked

Filbert didn't hesitate as he struck for my jugular. "The ministry don't appreciate the interference of non-commissioned aviation archaeologists vandalizing war crash sites."

I expressed surprise. "No I don't think they would."

"That's right, Mister Speed! So why did you steal a piece of the craft's equipment which would be vital for us in identifying the full facts of the wreck?"

It was difficult keeping a straight face with such directness.

"Try impressing me with a better accusation!"

Filbert's eyes flickered again. "Oh I can fully understand your denial as you are nothing more than an ignorant souvenir hunter. But you have something that belongs to us and by removing it from the crash site contravenes the War Graves Act."

My brow furrowed. "I have no idea what you're talking about."

Filbert smiled as he talked. "Butter would have trouble melting in your mouth, Mister Speed." I had to accept he wasn't in any way dissuaded by my plea of innocence as he pressed on. "You have stolen a vital piece of equipment from the crash site. We want it back!"

I have a well rehearsed ploy to always act thick in circumstances where accusations can get you into a lot of bother and I'm rather proud of my thespian aptitude. "What stolen equipment is that, considering I wasn't even there?"

"You are a very fluent liar, Mister Speed!"

"It happens to be the truth."

Filbert shook his head in disappointment "Don't insult our intelligence, Mister Speed. We don't derive situations from pure guesswork. We probe deeply. We have to when dealing with unscrupulous scum whose intention is to scavenge off the dead. Locating petty grave robbers like you hardly tests the versatility of our organization."

"Steady on!" I snapped. "I invited you into my home in good

faith. Not to be accused of something that doesn't concern me in the slightest. I was going to offer you a drink, but you can forget that!"

Filbert bared his teeth. "We're not here to socialize, Speed-," he soon dropped the niceties of Mister-"we are here to get to the bottom of this matter. We know you was there at the crash site mentioned, plundering a war grave. We want the piece of equipment you took. Cooperate and we will drop any impending charges of theft."

"There is nothing to drop. I took nothing. Who told you I was there?"

"Your name was mentioned."

"And my accuser was?"

"That's strictly confidential."

"Then I'm afraid you've got the wrong Shackleton Speed."

Filbert smiled sinisterly. "I don't think so. The Shackleton Speed we require is a metallurgist."

I slowly shrugged my shoulders, wondering how the hell he knew that. "So I've a qualification. Been checking on me?"

Filbert went on. "Renowned for plundering the land for lost treasure with a metal detector."

"It's a hobby enjoyed by thousands of others."

"Owner of a Roadster, 500K Mercedes Benz."

"So I have one in the garage."

"It was seen in Berkshire," he snapped.

"There's more than one on the road," I countered.

I couldn't help but shrivel inside knowing Tommy's narration had been far more detailed than I had anticipated. Owning up now would only get me in deeper bother, so I decided to allow them to do the speculating and I'll continue the denials. I was no novice on the subject of *digging my way out of shit* and neither was I about to change.

At that moment Scar-face began mooching around the study desk and shelves, much to my annoyance, as he cast an investigative eye around the room, probably deciding to make himself useful instead of standing there with his finger up his arse. He began touching items which angered me, especially when his greasy hands picked up a picture frame of my late parents for closer inspection and the unceremonious way he roughly replaced it. With the tip of his forefinger he flicked loose papers and envelopes giving me the impression he was memorizing all that caught his eye.

I said meaningfully. "Break anything and I'll frigging sue your department!"

Scar-face directed a searing glare at me. In a deep drawl he said, "I suggest you start giving the right answers or else you might not be around to enjoy your luxuries."

I had no reason to doubt his threat and I suppose it could have been quite frightening to a weaker minded person. But I don't succumb to threats and neither do I scare easily. I snubbed my nose up at him in defiance and said, "If you want to carry on wiping your grubby hands on my belongings I suggest you show me a search warrant!?"

Which I knew never existed. So cockily I said, "You don't have one?"

Scar-face's complexion went purple. Within a few minutes of our paths crossing I'd managed to make his gut ache. Yet as I observed his instant transition I began to have my doubts over his authenticity as a ministry official as I had never seen a person of authority deliver the face of a deranged madman as he did. I kept a close watch on him or at least I thought I had done until I realized much later what the crafty bastard had done.

As the situation stood they lied better than I did because there was one outstanding flaw in their story. Tommy never saw me take anything from the wreck and neither did I tell him I had. I think they were guessing that anything was taken at all. Now was probably the right time to find out before I threw them out.

I said, "Even though I wasn't where you say I was, what is it that I have stolen?"

Filbert sneered. "Forgot already? It's the reconnaissance camera."

"Oh I see! Now let me get this straight. A plane crashes from a great height and probably disintegrated on impact over sixty years ago and you still expect to pick up all the pieces?" I shook my head. "I don't think that is possible."

I still couldn't sway Filbert. "You must think we are very gullible people, Speed. You dug it from the wreck and stole it!"

I had no intention of falling into any verbal trap. "Look! You may have the incapability to find something but you can't blame innocent people. Now if you're absolutely convinced there is something out there to find I'll lend you my metal detector if you can't afford one!"

They ignored my last remark but their confused minds were thinking.

I decided to call their bluff. "Otherwise," I expressed stone faced, "if I'm under suspicion then arrest me now because I'm beginning to get bored with your wild accusations." I paused for an answer. "So what is it to be, handcuffs or are you two going to hold hands and skip away back to Whitehall?"

I expected a backlash and Scar face didn't disappoint as he bared a set of chipped, horribly stained teeth and snarled his words. "Arrogance can get you seriously hurt, Shackleton Speed."

At least he respected my name. But I was ready for him.

Filbert stepped between us. I suppose I should be thankful for his intervention as it certainly prevented a lot of damage to my furniture. He smiled thinly. "Fortunately for you, Speed, we have matters far more important than yours. But don't assume this is the end. Next time the search warrant will be intact and pinned to your forehead for closer inspection."

There was no need to usher them to the door with the assistance of my faithful defensive baton. They left without even a glance back. I watched their departure with anticipation as they climbed into a black saloon and sped away. I had no doubt I would see them again. Not that I wished to, but it seemed inevitable.

If I had been gifted with the ability of hindsight and the magical gift of manipulating time I would have used both extensively because the next three hours became my ultimate nightmare. I didn't know it then but things were changing dramatically, how dramatically was beyond my imagination, and certainly well beyond my control.

It started late in the afternoon when the telephone rang. Before I even had the chance to lift the receiver it stopped ringing and within seconds my mobile phone hummed its favourite tune. My, "hello", was engulfed by a hype of hysteria that savaged my eardrum.

"He's dead, Shacks! For Christ's sake he's dead!"

At first I'd trouble understanding who the emotional voice belonged to. Then it clicked. "Tim! Is that you?"

"Who the fuck do you think it is, Shacks?" There was a stifled sob mixed with his anger.

"Calm down, Tim, I'm struggling to understand what you're saying. Take a deep breath before you talk."

I heard the intake of breath. "It's Uncle Tommy!"

"What about him?" I asked calmly.

"He-he's been found dead."

My blood drained as the invisible hand grabbed hold of my heart and ripped it from my chest. My voice stiffened. "When did this happen?"

I heard another sharp intake of breath. "Yesterday afternoon. The farm hand found him floating in the slurry tank."

I had to think about that. "Do you mean the large steel tank full of cow shit that you have to climb a ladder to get a look in?" I asked incredulously.

"I think so, Shacks…oh for Christ's sake he's dead. Shacks…he's fucking dead!

I was trembling. "Tell me what happened?"

"No one knows for sure, Shacks. Police reckon he must have been stood on the gantry at the top of the tank and probably lost his footing and fell in. Reckon, for an old man it would have been like trying to swim in porridge, the more he struggled the more he sank. Oh hell, Shacks, it's too horrible to think about."

"Are you saying that Tommy drowned in cow shit?" I didn't mean to sound corny or disrespectful.

"So the police say. Benny, the farm hand, he found him. Said he saw Tommy's hat near the tank. He climbed up to have a look and noticed the usually crusted topped slurry had been broken. He saw something half submerged and when he hooked it with a pole,"-I heard a faint sniffle-"he pulled Uncle Tommy to the surface."

"Frigging hell that must have been a shock for Benny?"

Another sniffle, "He's devastated. They had to sedate him"

"It doesn't surprise me."

"Me too, Uncle Tommy was like a father to him. All Benny could say over and over was Tommy never climbed onto the tank gantry, never!"

"So what's going to happen now?"

"The police are still investigating the incident, but they're adamant that it was a terrible accident…Christ, Shacks, why should such a nice man die that way."

I exhaled a huge breath. I couldn't agree with Tim more. I could think of a number of people I'd rather hear about dead than poor Tommy Bickermass. It was ironic though, the hero one minute, dead the next. There is no justice in life and fate has such a pathetic way of running its business.

As for the appropriate condolences I have to admit I'm useless in such delicate situations. I said, "Can I do anything, Tim?"

"No, Shacks. Everything is being done. Some of the family are already there. I knew you'd want to know about the tragedy before you heard it elsewhere."

"I appreciate that."

"I'm going over later today. I'll ring you when I know more."

"Okay, Tim."

"You will be at his funeral, won't you Shacks?"

"Of course I will. He was a friend of mine too."

I was visibly shaking when I turned the mobile off.

I slumped down onto the sofa and leaned back staring blankly at the ceiling while I trawled the term tragic accident through my head. I found it difficult to believe Tommy was stupid enough to have fallen in a tank of shit. In the six months I had known him, in my opinion, he was a chap who had all his wits about him. Even Benny had said, 'he never climbed up to the gantry', so that made the theory of accident seem vulnerably weak. Why the hell don't the police keep an open mind once in a while and listen to people who know people? But they don't. They just plough on regardless with numerous theories and none are near the full truth until it's too late.

Deep down inside I felt miserable. Tommy was such a likeable chap and would be missed. Yet the more I thought about his death, the more guilty I felt, as if I'd been partly responsible. I'm not psychic nor would I pretend to be, but I had this awful feeling something was terribly wrong.

I began thinking of the two ministry men standing on my doorstep. I wondered how much they knew about Tommy's death. They had obviously been at the farm at some stage. And what an idiot I'd been because I had failed to double check or verify their credentials before allowing them access. Come to think of it, Scarface didn't even show any credentials and neither did he reveal his name. From the moment they showed up everything had started to rot to the core. Perhaps they had contributed to Tommy's fall into the slurry tank? They had managed to get him to reveal my name. They may have tried to scare him into telling the location of the camera and had threatened to throw him into the slurry. Perhaps Tommy had struggled too much and had fallen in. Or maybe they had pushed him?

I spent the next ten minutes trying to answer questions that only a reliable witness present at the farm could answer. But what is certain they knew about the camera. Yet if they were genuine ministry men eager to retrieve government property why did they leave so easily without making more of a fuss? It didn't make sense!

Then it clicked. Why indeed did they leave so easily? Suddenly I was sat upright staring towards the study as I remembered Scar-face messing around with my belongings, being too nosey. It was shortly after when they went.

I jumped up and dashed to the study. I looked around where Scar-face had mooched through my belongings and other various papers that he had disturbed. I checked the bureau and scanned the book shelves. I noticed he had shifted the telephone to a different angle. Then I realised something was missing.

The sad bastard had lifted my telephone pad!

I was wondering why when I had visions of the photography shop where I'd left the camera. My heart raced as I thought of the dreadful possibility that I may have put Lens's life in jeopardy. Hurriedly I rang the shop, feeling clammy as I waited impatiently for the phone to be answered. Palpitations increased and the blood flow made me perspire even more and only eased when Lens finally raised the receiver and went through the motions of announcing the name of the business in his laid back West Indian voice.

"Dis' is Larry's photographic agency, Larry speaking."

He must have thought I'd flipped when I asked him if he was okay because I had never asked him that before. For an eerie few seconds he didn't answer though I could hear him breathing.

"Frigging hell, speak to me you dumb bastard!" I angrily snapped.

"Hey Shacks, man!" his voice finally drifted through. "Stay cool. Hard to take in, man, cos I didn't realize you'd a heart!"

"Listen to me," I pushed on. "Has anyone asked about the camera I gave you?"

There was a pause and I well imagined his wide eyes rolling in their sockets with sheer panic. "Shacks, is da damn thin' hot?"

"No! Remember I told you I dug it from the ground."

"Yeah, man, but whose ground? No, don't say, man, I'd only have illusions of piss smelling prison walls and sloppy dinners and nasty shit stabbers molesting my cute arse. Definitely don't say, man, I wanna sleep at night not toss and turn with da guilt of stealing."

"Lens, you're avoiding my question! Has anyone asked? Think Lens. It's important!"

"No ones asked, man."

"Are you sure?"

"Yeah, I'm sure, man."

I relaxed knowing Lens was safe but he said damningly, "Which brings me ta say dis camera is a complete bag of mutilated crap."

"Frigging hell, Lens, I wasn't considering displaying the thing. Did you manage to retrieve anything worthwhile or not?"

"Scrap, that's what I got. In a thousand twisted pieces now. I had ta go in with the surgical expertise of a brain surgeon ta remove da film. Rubber gloves, dissecting tool, da works, man"

"Stop pissing about!"

"Okay man!" he finally conceded and raced through his findings. "Found four pictures which I masterly extracted from da middle of da roll. Da rest, I'm afraid, a complete waste of my effort, water-marked beyond recognition."

"I'm amazed you saved that many, if any at all."

"Shacks, you know me: miracles I can do in weeks, impossibilities, dhey take a few days. Da pictures are in da post."

"Great! What do I owe you?"

"Da usual, Shacks, Chinese meal and all da beer I can take. Throw in a loose woman. An' anythin' else you might want to add, like a few weeks in Las Vegas."

"Don't want much then!" I quipped.

"With spending money!" he added

At that moment I clearly heard the chink of the photography shop doorbell interfere with Len's voice over the telephone. Lens hurriedly said. "Got ta go, Shacks, paying customers," and after a low whistle, he added, "Hell man, dhey a couple of weirdoes! Last time I saw a pair like these I was watching wild life in Africa and dhey were devouring the carcass of some half eaten Lion spoils." Then I heard him speak to whoever had entered the shop before his voice faded away from the receiver.

At first I wondered what Lens was talking about when he mentioned *Africa* and *Lion spoils,* until my brain registered. By then Lens had already replaced his receiver and I was shouting into a tunnel of emptiness. "Lens, Lens! Get out of there!"

I quickly redialled. It rang a few times and went dead. My pulse began throbbing. I dialled once more, whispering the words, "pick up the phone, Lens, pick up the phone!", as I waited. All I received was the tinny echo of a discontinued line.

I slammed the receiver down and sprinted for my car keys and was in the Roadster driving hard and furious, breaking every road rule in the book. I didn't frigging care how dangerous I drove, though I hoped no police car would try to halt my progress because I was in no mood to stop.

I hit the accelerator harder, the engine growling as I rammed through the gears. I tore down street by street, overtaking like a stupid boy-racer, tyres screeching as I negotiated tight bends, ignoring blaring car-horns and the probable and deserved fingered gestures. But I wasn't looking who I passed on the road. I was too focused driving to save a friends life.

On reaching Lambeth Road I seethed as the traffic was at a standstill. I could see a police roadblock ahead. In the distance I saw the large plume of black smoke rising above the buildings. Fire engines were at the scene and in action. More were on the way. I pulled the Roadster into the side of the road, got out and began running between vehicles as I headed towards the fire. My frantic running had me gasping for breath. My lungs hurt. The taste of acrid smoke tainted my mouth. Then my stride stiffened when I realized the photography shop was on fire. I stopped and stared in disbelief. I shouted out, "Lens!", and continued running towards the building.

My progress came to an abrupt halt when a policeman's huge hand slapped into my chest. "Sorry sir! He said strongly, assertively. "You must step back. There's danger of an explosion."

He got his timing right as a muffled bang blew out one of the shop windows and a mixture of shattered glass and a mushroom of orange black smoke bombarded the fire-fighters. Instinctively we both ducked even though debris never reached us. The explosion only made me more determined. I had to save Lens from the inferno and I attempted to pass my holder and get to the burning premises only for the policeman to begin wrestling me to the ground to stop me. Again I shouted out Lens's name. Two, three times I called, still grappling with the policeman. I never went to ground. Some inner strength kept me on my feet, pushing hard, struggling for freedom from his powerful grip.

Then he had his face in front of mine. "Is there someone in there?" he quickly asked, shaking me to get me focused and staring into my eyes for a definite answer. "Is there still someone inside the building?"

"The proprietor," I snapped. "Larry Lazerow. He got out, didn't he?"

I will always remember the policeman's expression of uncertainty. I shivered as he spoke. "Nobody showed. Are you sure he was in there!?"

"Yes!" I answered sharply, controlling the anger swelling up inside. "I spoke to him only twenty minutes ago on the telephone. The line went dead so I came straight here. Please tell me he got out?"

I have never witnessed a policeman panic before. In fact I'd never seen one more scared than I was. I don't think it was due to the heat of the fire when I saw beads of sweat leak from beneath his helmet and trickle down his face. I knew then Lens never got out and the inferno had consumed him. Uncontrollably my legs shook and buckled. I found myself sat on the kerbside with my head in my hands listening to the policeman shouting to the chief fire officer that there might be a casualty inside the building.

It took the fire brigade an hour to quell the ferocious fire, and perhaps another thirty minutes before the fire team could ensure a safe passage for the inevitable forensic team. I wasn't particularly clock watching as another hour passed before the fire team returned with a bulging body bag. What contents I'd left in my stomach ended on the street floor between my legs.

"Excuse me, sir!" the same policeman addressed me.

I looked up, fearing the worst. Expressions tell a great deal and the policeman's hadn't changed for the better.

"Was it Larry?" I asked, then wondered why as the policeman probably didn't even know him.

"I believe it was hard to tell, Sir. It wasn't exactly in identifiable condition."

My head dropped back into my hands.

"I will require your name and address, Sir, as there will be the need for a statement at some stage of the investigation."

I nodded and squeaked out the relevant details. Not that I really wanted to, he just wouldn't let me leave until I had. I couldn't recall where I went next, some bar, didn't remember the name. I drank until the Vodka numbed my brain.

I later discovered that they identified the charred body of Larry Lazerow not by any physical part of his anatomy but by the gold ring he had pieced through the end of his foreskin. Larry said the girls adored it.

CHAPTER THREE

It was not by choice that I found myself in mourning twice as I sat there at home thinking and drinking while trying to understand what had hit me. I blamed myself for Len's death mainly for failing to reach him in time. But should I be chastised as I was in no position to prevent the unpreventable? And had he died by sinister hands as I strongly believe? And what about the two sad bastards from the MoD, had they arrived at the photography shop that fatal day? If they had it wasn't difficult to imagine how easily Lens would have succumbed when threatened. He was too much of a nice guy. He detested violence. He couldn't even fight his way out of a wet paper bag. His resistance to an assault would have been nonexistent because he probably never thought he was going to die in his own shop. My head began to hurt. Yet what really nailed my brain was why should anyone want to commit murder for a piece of scrap camera?

Yes the camera was definitely the link. The deaths of both Tommy and Lens had been no freak accidents I was sure. Killing someone to make it look like an accident had been practiced since the first lawman arrived.

It was alright speculating what happened. My biggest problem would be convincing the police what had happened and for them to begin a murder enquiry. I soon got my chance.

I was summoned to Kennington Road Police station on a wet and miserable morning. On principle I'm not normally cooperative with the police, but on this occasion I had to reassure myself that the police fully understood the seriousness of what was going on right under their noses. And if they had already done their job thoroughly I'm sure the evidence accumulated would be sufficient to arrest the culprits and for me to identify.

I approached the desk sergeant with noticeable apprehension, told him who I was, and he made a phone call upstairs. Waiting, I glanced around. Police stations, wherever situated in the world, always gave me the feeling of uneasiness, mainly because I had frequented quite a few in my time in order to defend myself against false accusations, but that's another dozen or so stories.

I was shown to an interview room shortly followed in by the interviewer who introduced himself as Detective Constable Stevens. He was a tall, young, fresh looking chap with well groomed dark hair and had a lean strong build. He had a determined look and gave me the distinct impression that he could go a long way through the police ranks. The more I studied him, the more I concluded he was just another ambitious copper who would ignore common sense to get a prosecution.

He smoothed his trousers down with his hands and sat down looking at his papers then to me. He said, "You are Mister Shackleton Speed?"

I nodded confirmation. "Yes, that's right."

"I'm sorry to drag you down to the station on such a horrible rainy day-," he sounded sincere but his eyes betrayed him, "and I hope not to detain you any longer than necessary." He coughed lightly to clear his throat. "Now I'm led to believe you actually spoke to Mister Lazerow shortly before his unfortunate death. Is this correct?"

"Yes, by telephone." I said irritably.

He wrote it down. Then he looked at me with a powerful stare that made me shift uncomfortably in my chair. "You seem apprehensive, Mister Speed?"

"I'm tired. It's hard to accept the death of a friend."

Stevens nodded in agreement. "I quite understand. Ah-," he glanced at his notes, "the telephone conversation with Mister Lazerow, anything special you discussed?"

"Just to say he'd completed some work for me."

"Work of any importance?"

"No!" I was getting a bit peeved.

"How did he sound to you over the phone?"

"How he sounded? I'm not following."

"Did he sound distressed or was there anything else out of the ordinary?

I should have realized sooner what he was suggesting but my

mind had other ideas that nowhere matched the Detective's. "No he sounded like he always sounded, happy and content."

His eyes flicked up. "So what induced you to dash over to the proprietor's premises collecting speeding tickets?"

"The line went dead without warning."

The eyes still probed. "You redialled?"

"Yes."

"What occurred?"

"No dialling tone, just a dead line. I panicked."

"You panicked?"

"I worried about him! Has this anything to do with his murder?"

I hit a nerve in the Detective's back teeth as he sat up straight, but I could see he disagreed with me. "I'm sorry, but I think there's been a misunderstanding. This is not a murder inquiry I'm conducting."

For a moment I *was* speechless. I recovered. "It's not? Then why–."

"Are you here?" He interrupted.

I detest having my sentence anticipated and finished. "Well, yes!"

He smiled weakly. "This is to establish the last known movements of the deceased and the state of his mental health in preparation for the report destined for the Coroner's office. Every minute detail has to be established for a correct verdict in court."

"So there's nothing suspicious about the way he died?"

"Not that we are aware of. Fire investigators pinpointed the probable cause of the fire was by a small explosion of chemicals relating to the processing of photographs. They concluded that the owner of the photography shop, Mister Lazerow, probably mixed the wrong chemicals which created an explosive reaction that ignited flammable material."

I jumped straight down his throat in protest. "That can't be right! Larry never made mistakes! His expertise in photography was legendary."

The Detective was having none of it. "The fire investigators confirm this by where the body was positioned and the intensity of the blaze. They are extremely professional in their field, I assure you, Mister Speed."

"Well they've got it wrong this time! Larry could do his job with his eyes closed and three parts pissed."

"So he drank a lot too?"

Typical police twister, I wanted to tell him and simultaneously expressed disgust at his accusation. "Not during the working week and that's truthful. What I said was a figure of speech. I was trying to emphasize that Larry was careful beyond being careful. Mistakes are unthinkable. Someone else started that fire!"

"I know you're upset-."

"I'm not upset!" I interrupted.

He tried to allay me. "I know the difficulty when losing a good friend."

"I've got over that! It's what you're trying to tell me that upsets me. It just doesn't add up. I knew Larry inside out and he wouldn't be that clumsy."

"It's evident how you feel, but I can categorically state the forensic fire team are extremely confident with their finding. I'm not saying they were hundred percent brilliant but they're usually pretty close. I can vouch for their competence."

"I'm not disputing their forensic skills. What I'm trying to say is Larry Lazerow does not make those mistakes. He was too damn *good* at his job. The fire was caused by someone else and made to appear as an accident!"

The policeman's eyebrows lifted. "Then perhaps you can throw some light over the proceedings, Mister Speed? You seem to have very strong opinions on the matter. Do you have any notions to support your theory?"

"I know two men entered the shop while he was in conversation with me. The fire started shortly after that."

"These two men, are you referring to customers?"

"More than customers, they were from the Ministry of Defence."

"How did you know considering it was a phone call?"

"Larry told me before the line went dead." I had to lie.

"Why should the MoD want to call upon, Mister Lazerow?"

My brain went into constructive overdrive as I concocted what I considered to be a decent enough story. "Are you aware of the recent discovery of a war plane in Berkshire?"

He nodded. "I read it in the papers."

I went on to explain everything, eradicating myself from the scene, of course. "Well the farmer who owned the land where the plane crashed asked Larry to take some photographs of him standing near the wreck so Tommy, that's Tommy Bickermass the farmer in question, could put the pictures in his scrapbook."

"Put pictures into a scrap book." He sounded incredibly bored.

"Yes. To capture the memories so he could show his grand-children." Sarcastically, I added, "It's what normal families usually do!"

"To show grand-children crashed planes?"

I wondered if he ridiculed everyone he interviewed. As big as he was he needed a good slap and I was certainly strong and fit enough and certainly in the mood to do just that. But somehow I didn't rate my chances of exiting the building without the assistance of a stretcher if I did. Instead I gave him something else to mix into his thin dossier for the Coroner.

I said, "What about Tommy Bickermass, he has also died in mysterious circumstances."

He looked disappointed with me. "Mister Speed, please. Surely you're not implying the MoD had something to do with both deaths?"

"That's precisely what I'm saying."

"Why, Mister Speed?" The slight conviction in his tone suggested he took me seriously but I was only kidding myself.

"How the frigging hell should I know why!" I barked. "That's what I believe."

A noticeable smirk appeared on the Detective's face. "It's hardly in the best interest of the MoD to exterminate people because of an old fighter plane being dug up. This country wants to recover all its dead heroes not get rid of new ones. Being paranoid isn't going to solve very much. Life is full of unlucky people making fatal mistakes, which are usually very costly to themselves."

"I'm not being paranoid." I protested. "I suppose the two ministry men pestering me at home were a figment of my imagination, especially when they accused me of vandalizing the wreck-." I could have shrivelled up like a prune at that moment knowing what I said. I quickly added, "Even though I wasn't even there!"

He was on to my gaff. "You *weren't*?"

"No, I wasn't. And I have no idea why they thought that I was there."

Stevens scratched the end of his nose. "Do you have any names for these ministry people?"

"I only caught one, a Detective Inspector Filbert."

I assumed I'd triggered something because the Detective suddenly stood and said, "Excuse me for a moment." And he promptly left the room as if he was bursting for the toilet.

Twenty minutes the slimy bastard kept me waiting. Being isolated in a police station within four tight walls, no windows and a whining wall-fan that irritated me to the point of insanity can be tediously daunting. The wait certainly tested my patience because I found myself drumming my fingertips hard upon the table with no true rhythmical beat but I did take a peek at his notes. When he finally returned he had in his hand a fresh paper file which he placed onto the table. As he sat down I noticed his accusing stare had become a permanent feature on his face.

I said enthusiastically, "Got something already?"

Slowly, deliberately, he said, "I've been in contact with the MoD. They state, categorically, that there are no impending or further investigations regarding the crash site in question. They assure me all normal procedures have been carried out and completed. The pilot's body was exhumed in readiness for a military funeral. The crash site has been logged and is now a protected area. As for a Detective Inspector Filbert, you might be interested to know, he retired from the ministry ten years ago and would have gladly made the journey to see you if he'd been able to get out of his wheelchair. So I'm afraid, whoever came knocking on your door, Mister Speed, it certainly had nothing to do with M.o.D. Perhaps you have been infuriating someone else?"

I didn't answer. My glare at him was sufficient enough.

He opened the folder and fleetingly glanced through the contents. I could tell by the gleam in his eye that he had found something incriminating against me. "This should interest you, Mister Speed!"

"Oh!"

"My-my-you have been extremely busy." I wanted to loose myself when he began rhyming off extracts concerning my scrapes with the law. "What is this printed here! Eleven court appearances in front of the judge concerning non-declaration of treasure trove."

"Does it not mention that I was acquitted eleven times?" I said defensively.

He detested my interruption. "*And,*" his voice raised, "neither has your exploits escaped the attention of Interpol. It seems that you have been plying your infamous trade among the scallywags in the black market labyrinths of Amsterdam, Brussels, Hamburg, and other various seedy parts of Europe. Yes, Mister Speed, this suggests to me you have been a very *busy* man."

The smarmy bastard, I thought. So I dug a few English antiquities from the ground and sold them on in Europe. What's the big fuss? It's not my fault the highest bidder happens to be in Amsterdam or Brussels or Hamburg.

Again I was on the defensive, I said, "You'll find all the allegations are untrue. Is there a point to all this? Only I thought the reason for coming here today was to discuss Larry Lazerow's demise. Not if I've been a bad boy in the past!"

"Most definitely there's a point, Mister Speed," his tone was sharper now, "It's a warning really, to stay away from the crash site."

"There's no law against looking," I said stubbornly.

"I was referring to the use of a metal detector because if I get word that anything goes missing I'll make sure the next conviction against you will stick forever. Is that clear?"

I stood and looked him straight in the eye with the strong urge to tell the sad bastard he was a week too late, but I resisted the temptation and made for the door only for the Detective to stop me in my tracks.

"There is one more thing, Mister Speed."

I didn't bother to turn and face him. Over my shoulder I said, "Yes."

"It's advisable that you refrain from spreading rumours concerning your inappropriate theories, especially to the newspapers, until after the Coroners verdict. But remember, Mister Lazerow died as a consequence of his own misfortune and nothing else."

I was halfway through the door when he added: "Please convey my condolences to Mister Lazerow's family. Good day, Mister Speed."

I left sharply before I said something I would never regret.

Frigging hell! I was mad when I walked out from the police station. I had gone there in the hope of persuading them they had a murder enquiry on their hands and instead it turned into an inquisition.

As I drove away my anger blurred my concentration. In a better frame of mind I might have noticed the black Mercedes slipping in behind the Roadster sooner than I did. It was difficult to see who the occupants were because the car had tinted windows but something told me the vultures were circling their intended prey. I prepared myself mentally, my sweaty palm hovering over the gearlever in readiness for a racing gear change in case of a sudden attack. They weren't going to catch me out as easily as they caught Larry or Tommy. With every manoeuvre I made, I double checked the rear view mirror in an attempt to see if it was the two bogus M.o.D. officials, but as I turned another corner the car didn't follow and I was alone again. I detest the word 'paranoia'. It suggests madness and a need to be dragged off to the nearest asylum, but before I'm certified, I wanted answers to questions buzzing around inside my head and I was determined to get them regardless of which feet I had to squash.

I also had to rethink my strategy because I wasn't going to get any help from anyone.

CHAPTER FOUR

I never went to the inquest on Lens's death as my attendance would have had no bearing on the outcome. Accidental was firmly planted in the minds of everyone and any interference from me would change nothing. Naturally I was pensive as to why I still walked this crazy wretched earth still in one piece and the only conclusion I had is they hadn't finished with yet. The sensible solution would be for me to go into hiding. Loose myself amid other tourists in some over-crowded resort. Hell I was kidding myself! That was the easy way out. I wanted to kick arse. I wanted to avenge Lens's death. But my most disturbing thought centred on how far I would be willing to go to have my revenge.

I began to devise a plan and where I should start. Okay, I realized I'm no super sleuth, nor did I pretend to be. I could hire a private detective but I didn't want to be responsible for sending a person into the unknown regardless how professional he was. Besides when it came to chasing answers I'd spent the last ten years finding lost treasure and gained the skill of outwitting the treasure trove department, all of which, puts me in a position of not being a com-plete novice after all.

I knew my situation wasn't favourable. I was a one man army with no fire-arms experience and up against-. What was I up against? Two men of unscrupulous character insisting I hand over a battered camera, for starters. That frigging camera!

That was my start, the camera! I went to retrieve the mail I'd thrown unceremoniously into the waste-bin by the study door and sifted through the pile. I could tell Lens's handwriting straight away when I selected the A5 size brown envelope, ripped open the seal and studied the contents. I was looking at four black and white pho-tographs of poor quality and water-marked around the edges. All four showed a surfaced submarine with what appeared to be a plume of smoke coming from its stern.

I went down to the plush comfort of my cellar studio and placed each photograph in turn onto the enlargement projector and examined them on the screen. The submarine was near a rocky shoreline, and though I'm not an expert on the war, I could just make out the symbol of the Rising Sun on the conning tower, and the faint lettering I-52. All it confirmed was a Japanese submarine in dire trouble. More significantly, why should a Japanese submarine be the focus of attention by a British plane within striking distance of, what I presumed to be, a European shoreline? It all seemed a bit weird especially when the Japanese did all their fighting in Asia, though if my memory served me right, I recalled supply liaisons between the Germans and Japanese. But they were usually conducted out in the Atlantic or in or around the security of German held ports and territory. Perhaps the shoreline was German? Whatever it all meant I couldn't make head or tail of it, yet these photos were redeemed to be worth taking a man's life. I placed the pictures in the wall safe where nothing less than a nuclear bomb would extract them.

The following day I was back in Berkshire for Tommy Bickermass's funeral. There is a saying, 'that you suddenly realize you're getting old by the number of funerals you attend', and I suppose my sudden increase of two rather made my thirty-five years feel more like seventy. I never bothered attending the church service just the burial itself. The whole occasion was a quiet funeral for a nice quiet man who lived for nothing more than the chance to make an honest crumb. I felt as if I had let him down.

I never mentioned to any of the congregation about my suspicions of how Tommy died. Perhaps I should have but I didn't, mainly because they were upset enough. If I began spreading dodgy presumptions amongst family and friends and they turned out to be untrue, I could imagine my arrival in these parts again would be repelled by the barrel of a twelve bore shotgun or a pitchfork up my backside.

It was the moment when the priest mentioned *dust to dust* that I heard Tommy's dog, Winston, pining for his master. I noticed the poor beast had a nasty looking wound just above the left eye. I waited until after the service and asked Tommy's daughter, Debbie, how Winston had acquired the wound.

"Nobody seems to know," she said sombrely, her eyes red, still the odd floating tear ready to seep and trickle down her cheek. "They found him hiding in the barn covered in blood. The vet had to put three stitches in a deep cut. But once he was patched up he was fine."

While I gave the dog a sympathetic pat, I said, "Have you ever heard of Billy Banter? I recall Tommy-sorry, your father-mentioning his name after he found the plane wreck."

Debbie gave me a strange look. "Yes I do. But that isn't his real name; it's Billy Slade. Why do you want know, if you don't mind me asking?"

"It goes back to when they were kids during the war. According to your father, Billy witnessed the war plane crashing in the field."

Her lips pursed. "I've never heard that story."

"Well actually there was no story to tell because no one believed Billy at the time. I think he deserves to know he was right after all. Do you know of his whereabouts?"

"Yes, of course. He lives in a nursing home at the far side of the village. It's an old converted mansion called 'Three Trees'." She gave me a suspicious look. "You do know he has limited intelligence, learning difficulties?"

"As a matter of fact I do, your father told me."

"Well, Mister Speed-."

"Please, call me Shacks."

"Well Shacks, to be honest I don't think he could even remember the war years, I doubt he can remember what he did yesterday."

"I have to try. It's what your father wanted. He was going to tell Billy himself."

Suddenly Winston caught my eye. The poor blighter seemed nervously twitchy. He began growling, not loudly. He bared his fangs, stretching the lead until he was almost strangled, his eyes focused on the stone church wall. She was struggling to hold his advance.

I said, "The dog's edgy."

"I don't know what's got into him?" She sounded embarrassed. "I've never seen him act so strange."

I followed Winston's glare and saw nothing, but I had a funny feeling he was having the same paranoia that I was experiencing. His antics though gave me a wonderful idea.

"What's going to happen to Winston?" I asked seriously.

She paused before answering obviously having a number of

options going through her mind. "Probably stop with us. My father would have wanted that."

"I'd like to look after him." I humbly offered. "Only for a while until everything has been finalized."

She gave the proposal a thought, gave me that strange look again, and shrugged her shoulders. "I can't see why not," she finally said. "I must confess I'm a little reluctant to keep him at my house. I'm actually allergic to animal hairs. Be sure to take care of him well."

I said I would and assured her I'd keep in touch.

She was alarmed. "Are you not coming back to farm? There's food and drink laid on."

It hadn't been my intention to stay longer than planned, but I couldn't refuse her desperate look. "Of course, I am."

"And you can collect Winston's dog bowls and biscuits while you're there."

Nice! I thought as she handed me the dog lead.

"You might as well get used to handling him," she told me.

So I headed back to the Roadster with an obedient animal by my heels, but I did observe the dog's continued interest in the stone wall although he never fought me to head in that direction. But more importantly, Winston would be an ally and a wonderful early warning system to sniff out the enemy when I couldn't see them. I'm sure he wouldn't let me down in that department.

As I gazed out of the farmhouse window I saw young Benny going about his daily business taking the herd in for milking. I guess the young farmhand found it strange to be without the old man about the place. I only wished it had all been a bad dream and for Tommy to come wandering out of the cow shed wearing the same clothes as when I last saw him...

Debbie disrupted my thoughts when she offered me a sandwich, which I politely declined. I wasn't particularly hungry but I did accept the offer of a sweet sherry.

When the chance came I slipped away from the crowd and took the opportunity to see where everything had happened. I found the slurry tank where Tommy died and I was about to climb the vertical steel rung ladder when something caught my eye. I reached down and picked up a large, rusty adjustable spanner which was concealed by overgrown, weedy grass at the base of the tank. As I examined the tool I noticed at the tip of the adjustable jaws a small piece of, what I assumed it to be, dried skin with a few strands of short black hair. It never occurred to me when I picked the spanner up that I might have just contaminated possible finger-prints of the previous holder because I was sure that Winston would have gone berserk if I had shown him what had clobbered him.

I dropped the spanner and climbed to the top of the tank. The gantry was about two metres long and a metre wide and plenty of space to hold three men! There was nothing much else to see. The tank had been emptied but the smell of cow shit still lingered and suddenly I felt sick. I went back to the farmhouse and found Debbie to say I was leaving and went to see Billy Slade.

I found Three Trees mansion and drove the obligatory ten miles an hour along the driveway and parked near the main entrance of a 1920 red brick building. I took a carry bag from the rear seat and told Winston to guard the car, which he seemed to understand. I got out and approached the large oak door and rang the doorbell. A nubile girl with her hair in plaits, dressed in a white tunic answered. I asked to see the matron of the establishment. She smiled pleasantly and ushered me inside and through another set of coloured glass doors and told me to wait in the main hall. Immediately the hospital smell infiltrated my nostrils. I felt dizzy. Frigging hell, how I had hated that odour since childhood and the memories of my first real encounter with a syringe the size of a javelin. I suppose at my age the squeamishness should have disappeared. I was still a coward.

The matron, a peroxide blond of about fifty, greeted me with a face like thunder and a bite as bad as her bark. She didn't appear to take kindly to my intrusion into her highly efficiently run nursing home and greeted my request with open hostility when I asked if I could spend time with Billy Slade.

"It's very unusual for Billy to receive visitors, in fact, it's nonexistent."

"As I explained, Matron, a friend of Billy's from his childhood days has recently died. The funeral was this morning. The deceased left me instructions that I was to pass on this present-," I showed her what I had in the carry bag, "-and to convey a message to him, an important and confidential message."

Talk of death seemed to soften her up. "Very well, Mister-ah-?"

"Shackleton Speed."

"Very well, Mister Speed, but you must patient with Billy as he sometimes struggles to understand." She pointed the way. "Through the lounge and out of the French windows, you will find Billy at the bottom of the garden on his favourite bench overlooking the wheat fields. Please don't walk on the grass, keep to the gravel pathways."

The old chap I approached appeared normal as he gazed skyward. I wondered if he was perhaps deaf when he didn't even acknowledge my arrival. He had tight cropped white hair and a sunken mouth. He was dressed in a thick, blue woolly jumper that was tucked into the waist of a pair of grey baggy trousers, which was tightly secured by a leather belt and doubly secured by a pair of red braces. None of what I saw inspired me with confidence and I wondered if I was doing the right thing being here.

"Hello, Billy!" I said pleasantly.

He turned to me.

"My name is Shacks."

He smiled displaying a set of gums. His, "hello", came out slow.

Suddenly he got to his feet and began wobbling slowly up and down the pathway with his arms outstretched and between rasping the sound of engine noises he shouted out, "I...like...planes."

Embarrassed by his strange antics I said. "Come back to land, Billy, I want to talk to you." I did feel a bit of an idiot saying that and hoped no one was watching at the time.

He sat down exhausted, and in between catching his breath he spoke wearily. "I was a pilot...you know...during the war...against the Germans."

I played along but wondered why. "Yes I know you were. It is about during the war that I want to talk to you."

"Oh...heard then...I was a pilot?"

"Yes, Billy, I heard."

"I...like...planes!"

"Yes, Billy, I know you do."

I reached into the bag and retrieved a metal replica of a Spitfire plane and showed it to him. Billy was delighted. He reached for it but I drew it away from his grasp. I said, "It's yours, Billy, if you listen and concentrate on what I'm going to ask you. Okay?"

He understood and nodded enthusiastically, panting heavily, his tongue hanging out like a hungry dog eagerly anticipating a large bone from his master.

I deliberately talked slower so he could fully absorb what I was saying. "Think back when you were a young boy during the war. Remember the war Billy? A plane, just like this one in my hand, crashed in the local fields. Remember that, when you were a little boy?"

The vacant stare on his face didn't quite instil confidence and perhaps Debbie had been right to warn me I'd be wasting my time. But prevail I must because illiterate Billy was all I had to go on. I pressed him again. "Remember telling people that you saw the crash. No one believed you, did they, Billy?"

"I was…a pilot! No one believed…I was…a pilot."

I was beginning to show my frustration, especially in my voice. "I believe you, Billy. You were an excellent pilot, but do you remember the frigging plane!?"

I probably overdid the anger part because he stared at me like a frightened child. I sighed heavily, extremely disappointed. My tactical approach was failing badly. Overall my experience in dealing with a person like Billy was nil. It had been a long shot anyway, and though I hate the word defeat, it was pointless pursuing something that led nowhere. I gave Billy the replica plane and suddenly his eyes brightened. At least I would leave him in a happy mood, though I would be dragging my feet for the rest of the day.

"It's like the one…that got shot down." Billy suddenly said without any prompting.

I tried not to show too much excitement but inside I was bursting at the seams.

"What do you mean, Billy?"

Billy tapped the replica with his finger. "There…there were…two of these planes. Have you…got another one for me?"

"No Billy, I'm sorry but I'll bring you another one next time I come to see you. Would you like that?"

Billy's head was nodding so hard I thought it was attached to a rubber neck.

"But first I'd like to know why there were two planes. What were they doing?"

Billy's face went blank. I assumed it must be his expression when thinking hard. Finally he said: "One was…chasing…the other one."

Now he was beginning to interest me.

Billy suddenly put his hand to his mouth sniggering. "I use to play…chasing. I chased…all the girls, kissed them…when I caught them."

"Yes, Billy I bet that was good fun. Now forget about girls we can talk about them later. Now remember the planes. What do you mean by the planes *chasing each other*, were they playing chasing games? Perhaps they were having fun too? Maybe they were fooling about, to show their flying skills." I demonstrated with flat hands.

"Oh no...I saw it...I was in my...plane, flying...through the field. I was only...a small plane. No one could see me. I saw it happen. I was scared...I hid in the grass. The plane...behind the other one...it had its guns...shooting bullets...rat-tat-tat-tat-tat. The plane...it made the other one...crash. I watched it...it came down from the sky...smoke coming...from its tail." He demonstrated the entire scene with the replica Spitfire quite convincingly.

"Are you sure, Billy? It was a long time ago."

"It was...on fire...I never...saw it again." He smiled impishly, "I set fire...to my paper airplanes. They don't like me doing that." His face saddened. "They shout at me...for being a naughty boy...send me to bed early...with no supper. I've stopped doing it...now. I like my supper!"

I looked at him incredulously and wondered if this was the right place for Billy!

He glanced at me with speculative eyes. "You believe me...don't you?"

"You must understand, Billy, it sounds ludicrous to someone who never saw those two planes. Two friendly Spitfires battling against each over the skies of England when effectively they should be fighting Germans, it doesn't make any sense."

Poor Billy, he never understood a word I said. He was happy manipulating the replica plane and rasping the sound of an attacking Spitfire.

As for Billy's account of that day it was so far fetched it wasn't surprising no one believed an illiterate boy during the war. If just one person had taken the time to verify Billy's story I would not have found the wreck, nor find myself in the precarious position of looking over my shoulder every five minutes waiting for the inevitable hit-man. I left Billy flying the replica.

Before leaving Three Trees I had a quiet word with Matron about the possibility that Billy might have other visitors, nasty reporters trying to make a fast pound or two. I told her of the plane that had been recently discovered, and how Billy and the deceased had seen it crash during the war. I suggested that if uninvited callers insisted on speaking to Billy she had them removed from the premises immediately. She looked waspish and I knew she would oblige.

"Don't you worry, Mister Speed, Billy won't be pestered by anyone. Will you be coming again to visit, Billy?"

In all honesty I'd no reason to ever see Billy again. "Yes, of course I shall." I had never found lying hard to do.

On the way back to London I found a nice eating place with a quiet corner where I could unravel the complexity of the entire situation so far and chew over a piece of skulduggery. Why would a R.A.F. Spitfire shoot another Spitfire from the sky? It was too ludicrous to comprehend. Perhaps what Billy saw was an incident of friendly fire, a regular occurrence during wartime night-fights, but not during daylight? Unless the pilot needed spectacles, it's a mistake that couldn't be made. Perhaps Billy had got the identification wrong and it had been a German plane that shot down the Spitfire. Overall it meant nothing conclusive to me. Then in reality could I trust the mind of Billy Slade?

CHAPTER FIVE

I entered the London Imperial War Museum late afternoon determined to find out all I could about Craven. The curator, a grey haired, grey winged moustached chap who went by the title of Flying officer Captain Wright, retired, was keen to help.

As I approached him looking lost, he said, "Can I be of assistance, Sir?"

"Pilots missing in action during the second world," I asked. "Is it possible to view the records?"

"Of course you can, Sir. Are you a journalist, Mister-ah?"

I never told him my name and he didn't push for it.

"What makes you think that?"

He tapped the side of his pock marked nose. "This tells me a lot, Sir."

I gestured with my finger how right he was.

The curator walked along the corridor in military fashion and funny as it might sound I found myself walking in the same manner. He ushered me to a desk, pottered around the bookshelves, moments later plonked a thick hardback book in front of me. "If he's missing in action,"-he tapped the book-"his name will be listed."

I thanked him and he left me to dwindle through the pages.

There were two Cravens unaccounted for during the war. I could forget about the rear gunner on a Lancaster Bomber and concentrate on Wing Commander Ralph Craven, and an impressive number of honours that followed his name. I took out a pad and pen and began making notes of importance. After gaining enough material to write a short novel I went back to the curator. "Is there any information on the particular missions the pilots were involved in before going missing?'

The curator expressed surprise. "Now there's a first. Not a usual request." He shook his head unfavourably. "But I'm afraid that's impossible. Such information falls within the classified format and can only be obtained directly from the Ministry of Defence. For that you'll require an appointment, and more appropriately, security clearance."

There ended my day at the museum because it was one appointment I wouldn't be making and with my reputation I'd be lucky to even stand outside the main gate without getting clobbered by a police truncheon.

Outside I checked the notes I'd jotted down. During the war Craven had been stationed at R.A.F. Duxford. It seemed a favourable place and it was open to the public, so the following morning I drove straight to Cambridgeshire.

I knew I hadn't been followed because I took a route around London that even a professionally organized surveillance team from MI5 couldn't follow, never mind the intelligible mind of a London cabbie. I also thought I was in for a relaxing day.

*

When I arrived at R.A.F. Duxford my timing put me in the middle of a spectacular Air Show. I watched an old Bi-plane groan across the sky as I made my way along the pathway. But I was more interested in the airfield's own museum. Once inside the building I didn't have a clue exactly what I was looking for, rather hoping that if there was anything significant it would immediately jump out and catch my attention. I concentrated on glass framed photographs scattered around the walls and came across a collection that showed the resident pilots stationed at Duxford in the autumn of 1943.

There was one particular photograph that attracted me, a large group photograph listing all the pilot's names and ranks which I studied carefully. Finally, figuratively speaking, I came face to face with Wing Commander Ralph Craven standing proudly in the centre of the group and all pilots ready for action in their fatigues and customary flying jackets. I would never have thought that such a handsome face had once lined the skeleton I found.

From the way he portrayed himself he appeared to be a very confident person, which you would expect from a leader of men. He was noticeably young. In fact they were all noticeably young. No one, I guessed, above the age of twenty-four. I wrote down every name listed on the photograph. I wondered how many were still alive with whom I could talk to. Then it struck me and a sudden chill glided down the curve of my spine as I contemplated that just maybe one of the men in the photograph with Craven might be his murderer and if I was to confront the alleged killer straight to his face he might decide to kill me on the spot.

Then I had to asked myself what harm could a man do when he was probably in his eighties, also taking into consideration he might be dead, wheel chair bound, or simply lapsed into dementia that he couldn't recall the last time he had a shit, never mind shoot someone in the frigging back.

With the collection of names safe in my notebook, I went outside to speculate everything while watching the air-show without too much enthusiasm until I caught sight of an elderly chap who marvelled and applauded every manoeuvre the planes made. He obviously knew a great deal about the relics so I decided I'd pinch some of his knowledge. I moved through the crowd and stood beside him.

"Marvellous old rust buckets," I said, as any true admirer would.

"Old rust buckets!" he countered as strong as his hoarse throat would let him.

I pointed skywards as a Spitfire roared overhead followed by a second plane which I had no chance of identifying in a month of Sundays.

He scowled at me and replied acidly, "They're more than rust buckets, lad." His voice warbled as he talked. "Those magnificent 1030 hose-power machines helped save England from certain destruction during war, lad, and don't you forget it!"

"Oh don't get me wrong. I'm not ridiculing the crafts," I said reassuringly. "But for comfort, compared to modern planes, they must have felt like carpet handbags."

I touched a nerve with that one.

"They weren't built for comfort, lad." He scowled, "Fighting machines, that's what they were. The finest in their time and as fast as they come; swift, so manoeuvrable it could turn on a sixpence."

"You obviously know a lot about them?"

"Know lad! During the war I happened to be part of the ground crew that kept those beauties air worthy when they were needed. 'Erks', we were nicknamed but we were a skilled bunch with it. When those battle battered Spits returned we would work through the night to patch them back up again in readiness for the next flight."

"So you were actually stationed here during the war?"

"Aye lad, I was."

"The war certainly kept you busy."

"Aye, it did that, lad, and more. In a short space of time, when the V12 Rolls Royce Merlin engines became the power of the Spitfire, we had to become experts, didn't have time to be taught the intricate workings of those engines. 'Erks had to quickly require the skills to repair stressed skin, split flaps, hydraulics, pneumatics, and the electrics; some wage packet if you could do all that nowadays! Aye lad, needless to say those wonderful crafts didn't require much love and care to fight. They were awesome fighters."

Now I was very interested. "What about the pilots themselves, did you get know any of them?"

"Sure I did. They came and went for various reasons. The war took a lot of good young men. Didn't exactly socialize with them, didn't have the time for niceties, too busy."

"Are any of the pilots still alive today?"

"Hard to say, lad, but I wouldn't count on any of them holding a pilots licence anymore." His chuckle of laughter was drowned by the sound of an ancient plane rattling overhead.

I smiled along with him and said, "I wasn't looking for flying lessons."

"Aye, I know, lad, just having a bit of a laugh."

"There is one pilot I am interested in who was stationed here during the war. Wing Commander Ralph Craven. Do you remember that name?"

His saggy eyes lit up. "Now that chap I do recall! What a nice considerate man he was. Always had a kind word to say and he made sure we had piping hot mugs of tea and lashings of toast when we grafted during the cold nights. Sometimes he would stay with us in the hangars while we worked, reminiscing on the good days before the outbreak of war. Then one day he never came back, missing in action. That was the problem with the damn war, a pilots life seemed more expendable than most."

"Yes, I'm already aware of Ralph Craven's fate. I'm more interested in talking to anyone who flew with him."

"Are you related to him, lad?"

"He was my Grandfather."

His jawbone drooped. He was most humbly apologetic. "How tactless of me, I never thought to-."

43

I butted in. "Really, there's no problem, honestly! It was all a long time ago." Frigging hell, I was beginning to sound so sincere I began to believe every bit of bullshit I spoke. I now knew how a thespian feels when he plays a character so believable he has problems distinguishing what was fictional and what was reality. It was a strange feeling to have.

"Do you know of anyone?" I prompted him.

As the rusty cogs of his brain clanged into a blank memory the air above exploded into a mass of pandemonium when two modern fighter planes zoomed across the sky and blasted my eardrums to the point of insanity that I wanted to scream. As for the old man remembering ex-patriots it was probably a long shot. Then again I was desperate for anything.

I could have sworn I heard a ting echo from between his ears just a second before he got all excited and raised a finger.

"Group Captain Bane!" he suddenly bellowed above the racket.

Stooping with the noise of the jets overhead, I said, "Who?"

"Group Captain Bane; that's the name of the bloke I saw here two years ago. Had trouble with his legs and relied on a pair of walking sticks. I remember him well now. One of the surviving pilots of the campaign."

I suddenly felt deflated. "Two years is a long time, might be dead by now?"

"I doubt it. He struggled to walk but he didn't half look youthful for his age, made me feel like his father. We were gossiping like two old women. He knew his planes alright. As a matter of interest, he said he made the trip every year from Yorkshire, though I only ever saw him that one time, two years ago."

"Yorkshire is a big place on the map, did the chap relate to any specific area where he lived?"

He shook his head slowly. "He did mention the place. I can't quite recall."

"Try to remember," I said, struggling to control my frustration.

Then he suddenly snapped his fingers. "Gaggle-something! Gagglestone. No...not Gagglestone." His face creased with thought. Seconds seem like minutes. "Giggle-something. Yes, that sounds more like the place he lived." I could feel the heat of his brain going into uncontrollable overdrive, then, he was alive and spurting. "I've got it! Giggleswick! That's the name of the place in Yorkshire."

"Positive it was Giggleswick?"

"Yes, yes, I'm sure he mentioned that name."

His confidence seemed weak so I prompted him more. "Is that in reference to Giggleswick near, Settle?"

He looked at me vacantly. "If you say it's there. To be truthful I've never been to the place."

I made my excuses for not stopping, thanked him for the information and left the commotion and fuss of the air show with more enthusiasm in my step than I had an hour ago. Strangely, I was beginning to enjoy my days as a detective that I was seriously considering it as an occupation. A private dick! Shackleton Speed P.I. Yes I was seriously thinking along that line yet it's funny how ideas can change so dramatically and suddenly they don't seem fun anymore.

As I approached the Roadster I was too intent on cursing Winston as he bounced insanely around the car's interior that I never noticed it nor heard it above the roar of aircraft engines hurtling across. Some detective I would make because there was good reason for the dog's madness but I didn't see it until it was almost too late.

I caught a glimpse of the rampaging steel out of the corner of my eye as it hurtled towards me. I jumped and twisted in one movement and scaled the bonnet of a blue car a tenth of a second before the large van smashed into the side frame of the vehicle precisely where my legs and midriff would have been. So violent the crash, the van shunted the car clear of its path. The impact sent me sprawling from the bonnet and as I crunched to the ground I rolled onto my knees and heard the van accelerate away as erratically as it had approached.

I had been lucky. A few bumps and the inevitable bruises later but I was still in one piece and was quickly up on my feet watching the back end of a battered white van leaving the scene. I attempted to make a mental note of the registration but I was wasting my time because the van didn't have one. The only visible identification I saw was on the rear door which bore the impoverish scrawl of 'wash me' highlighted in the dirt.

By the time I'd considered giving chase the frigging van had disappeared from the car-park and could have taken a number of routes to escape. I cursed my incompetence for not being more alert and cursed even more that they had managed to follow my trail so easily when I had taken all the trouble to prevent such a thing occurring.

I hand brushed the dust from my clothing while I glanced around for any witnesses to the serious attempt on my life and found precisely none. The incident made me over cautious as I approached the Roadster. At least Winston looked pleased that I was still in one piece.

I suppose it was my lawful duty to alert someone to the mess of smashed vehicles but that would have taken up valuable time, explanations, statements and other useless boring details in reference to insurance purposes. It was time I didn't have and I considered that anyone who can afford to drive a top of the range car would hardly struggle to compensate their loss.

I quickly got into the Roadster and patted Winston. "Good boy! You certainly scared them off good and proper."

I sat there for a moment, mainly to gather my senses and to get my breath back, yet I couldn't help wondering how they easily found me. Then I had this ridiculous, unimaginable thought. I got out of the car and began a search of the exterior of the Roadster for some sort of tracking device. Checked under the bonnet, probed under the wheel hubs, finger searched along the underside of the body, onto my hands and knees looking under the car. I found nothing but grime. I checked if the boot had been forced, it hadn't. Finally I came upon something that wasn't in the price when I bought the vehicle.

I didn't know if I should be pleased or disappointed when I found a small black device attached to the inside of the exhaust tail pipe. I found it was magnetic as I forcibly pulled it free. It gave no indication of being a tracking device, no blips, no sign of an L.E.D., no audible sounds of operation, but I had to assume it was because I didn't put it there. I reattached the device to another vehicle and drove away from Duxford as quickly as possible heading north.

CHAPTER SIX

Yorkshire in early summer is without contradiction a splendid piece of English countryside, green and fresh. In comparison to the appalling air pollution across London, here I could fill my lungs to double their usual size without collapsing into an asthmatic heap.

Finding Group Captain Josh Bane in the village of Giggleswick had all the adventurous excitement of scouring a tatty directory inside a piss smelling telephone kiosk. I rang him first to explain my predicament and the urgency to discuss the recent discovery of the crashed Spitfire. He agreed without fuss. I suspected he was a little lonely and needed the company and would have probably agreed to anything.

Sweet-pea cottage, where Josh Bane lived, was awash with an abundance of flowering colour and fragrance. I followed the narrow brick pathway and rapped my knuckles on the solid oak wood door. It took him a while to answer and when he finally did the door creaked opened and I saw a frail bent man clutching a Zimmer frame. If he had appeared youthful to others two years ago then something had savaged his complexion to a gauntly sick grey, and without being too distasteful or unkind, I found him just before the grim reaper did.

It was hard to imagine this white haired bony old man capable of commanding the skies of Britain during the war. His suspicious watery, grey eyes scanned me with inescapable apprehension.

I smiled to reassure him I wasn't the enemy. "Hello, Mister Bane. Shackleton Speed. I rang a little while ago."

Then a slight glow of life brightened his eyes. "Ah, yes, yes, young man! Come in," he beckoned, his voice slow and slightly hoarse, yet within that mixture of an aged larynx there was the educated posh tone of an ex-Cambridgeshire man.

I said, "It's good of you to see me at such short notice."

"I'm always one for a good chat, young man. Can you squeeze past the old Zimmer chariot and head straight on, to the sun lounge. I've got a pot of tea and some digestive biscuits already on the table."

The door closed behind me and I walked slowly through, trying to avoid being nosey, an almost impossible thing to do in a strangers home. I heard Josh Bane scraping along after me, his bout of genuine asthmatic breathing sounding as if a stalking dragon followed my every footstep.

On reaching the sun lounge a faint flow of fresh air brushed my face and rustled the leaves of various pot plants that spread and towered filtering the sun-light entering the room. I was impressed with the spectacular rear view of the rolling hillside.

As he shuffled into the room, I said, "Very pleasant in these parts."

"Yes, we've been lucky these past years with Yorkshire summers."

Josh Bane puffed out his cheeks as he eased himself into one of the cushioned basket chairs placed around the pine coffee table. "Sit yourself down, young man, can't have guests standing about. If you would be so kind and pour the tea, my shaky hands never seem to fill a cup properly anymore."

The chair creaked as I made myself comfortable. I talked while I poured. "When I phoned you confirmed that you were stationed at Duxford air field during the war?"

I noticed colour returning to his cheeks as he reminisced. "Indeed I was, young man. 66 Squadron based at Duxford fighter command." His tired eyes widened. Those were exciting times, dangerous, but exciting nevertheless. I flew a Spitfire."

He was obviously proud of his past and he would have surely brought out his ribbon of war medals to prove it, if his legs had been more stable. I handed him a cup and took a taste of mine while observing the old boy, noticing his hands shook slightly as he slurped his drink

Josh Bane nodded towards the table. "Help yourself to biscuits they're very nice dipped in tea."

I politely declined as I wasn't particularly peckish, though, I knew if I'd allowed Winston inside the cottage he'd have scoffed the lot without introduction. I said, "Do you recall Wing Commander Ralph Craven?"

"Ralph Craven! Indeed I do. Never forget the chap. Ralph Craven was an outstanding Officer. The type of comrade you wanted beside you in those bitter times of conflict. A strong willed chap, as I remember, admirably respected amongst the men. In comparison to the other pilots under my command, I could trust him totally with anything." Then he expressed sadness. "Alas…one day he went out on a mission and never returned. He was listed as 'lost in action'."

"You obviously knew him better than most?"

"He's the kind of chap you never forget. What has he to do with the fighter plane found recently?"

"It was his body still strapped in the cockpit."

He nearly choked on his drink when I said that.

He swallowed hard, coughed and said, "Absolutely impossible young man! I might be old and withered but my eyes are still pretty damn good. The newspaper I read categorically stated the pilots name as Flying Officer Derek Rowland, missing in action since 1943."

"They were wrong. Or the wrong information was given out."

His face reddened in anger. "I very much doubt that, young man!" Then he calmed, and the red blobs on his cheeks disappeared. "Don't let your tea get cold."

I took another sip. "That's what I found strange. The name given in the papers didn't correspond with the identification tag still attached around the neck of the pilot's remains. To be blunt, they buried the wrong man in the wrong military grave. I should know I found the wreck with my metal detector. I clearly saw the name Craven."

His right eyebrow arched. "A farmer and his dog discovered the wreck."

"That's not strictly true. I thought in my best interest someone else should take the credit."

Josh Bane tapped the side of his wrinkled nose. "This tells me you're not quite telling me everything, are you, young man?"

I didn't really want to alarm him in anyway, so I said, "There isn't much to say."

He just screwed up his eyes at me. "I'm listening, young man!"

"Well-to be honest, I make a living out of selling things I find buried in the ground. I won't bore you with details of what I've achieved over the years, but put it this way, if the Tower of London still housed hardened criminals who didn't hand over treasure trove material, I'd be locked up forever. As for the crashed plane in Berkshire, I took the reconnaissance camera from the wreck."

"That's damned despicable! Robbing war graves is against the Law! You're going to get into a lot of trouble."

"I'm already in a lot of trouble, but I didn't take anything that belonged to the pilot. I can assure you. All I took was a rusty old camera that without doubt would have been dumped for what it was worth, or so I thought. Now it seems the camera is worth killing for."

His cup and saucer rattled violently. "Whatever do you mean by *killing for*?"

"Well two people I knew who had knowledge of the camera have already died because of it."

"Good gracious young man! You must inform the police straight away."

I shook my head as I went on, "I've already tried to tell the police. They laughed in my face and accused me of inciting trouble. Both incidents were dismissed as terrible and unfortunate accidents."

"Were they accidents?"

"Not in my eyes. Both killings were made to look like accidents, that I'm certain. Naturally I want to discover the truth so I can shove it back up police noses."

Josh Bane got a little flustered. "I can't see how I can possibly help you!"

I finished my tea and placed the cup and saucer onto the table. "There's a tremendous amount you can help me with. Beginning with the day Wing Commander Craven went missing, I need to know everything that happened. It's important."

"It was such a long time ago."

"My integrity depends on it."

"I'll try, young man, but my accuracy may stray a little."

"Anything will be worthwhile,"

He grinned cheekily. "Do you want me to start with what he had for breakfast?"

I suppose he was trying to lighten a serious issue and I probably should have at least smiled, but I was too exhausted and uptight to bother. I said, "If it assists remembering the day then by all means."

He seemed disappointed by my casualness. "I was cracking a joke, young man. To help kick start my tired brain into action."

I cooperated with a nod and smile.

Then he irritated me when he leaned forward and placed his cup and saucer shakily down on the table and then leaned back into his chair in one continual movement of incredible slow motion as if he was preparing for a nap.

"Now then," he finally began, "from what I can recall the mission was of the utmost importance-." He suddenly stopped as if he had said something wrong.

"Is there a problem?" I asked.

"Well I'm not too sure, young man. I'm a little concerned if I'm still governed by the official secrets act." (I was about to say, 'I doubt it'), when he said: "No, no, no, impossible. Damn silly of me! Especially with all the documentaries they slap on the television nowadays. Now as I was saying. The mission, from what I can remember, was of the utmost importance and was referred to Duxford fighter command by the War Office. At the briefing we were told of an operation involving British Intelligence and the American Atlantic fleet who were tracking a Japanese submarine attempting to rendezvous with a German U-boat in mid-Atlantic to exchange cargo. Although it wasn't mentioned at the briefing, the rumours soon spread that the submarine was carrying 200 tons of gold bullion to assist the Germans financially to continue the war in Europe.

"Naturally with all the German codes broken, they tracked the Japanese submarine, I think it was the I-52, along its entire route from the Southern hemisphere to the Atlantic and the Germans from their U-boat base. Using ships modified into small aircraft carriers, the Americans launched their attack and caught the Japanese submarine and sunk it to the bottom of the sea.

"As a matter of interest there was a documentary on the subject shown on the television involving American treasure seekers who were convinced the sunken sub still had gold aboard. Treasure seekers pretending that the historical intrigue of the lost submarine held precedence over the importance of finding gold bullion; cods-wobble! But as it was, to add insult to injury, the greedy sods never found any gold and probably never will. Serves them right too!"

"Now you've mentioned it I do remember the programme," I said. "But do I hear a little animosity in your voice?"

"You must understand, young man, disturbing the dead serves no purpose at all. Bloody treasure seekers are a pain in the arse. (For a split second I wondered if he was having a go at me.) The Japanese may have been the enemy but they were still true warriors willing to die for what they believed, and a lot of brave men died that day."

I hurried him along. "So what was your squadron's mission?"

"Be patient young man! I'm coming round to that." He coughed to clear his throat. "While the Americans were playing war games in mid-Atlantic chasing submarines for real, R.A.F. Duxford command had been given a pointless exercise of trying to locate a second Japanese submarine. The Allies were reacting to an independent intelligence source that came from deep inside Japan. The information received told of the mysterious departure of another submarine displaying the same prefix I-52 which set sail at precisely the same time as the first, but from a different port, its destination, supposedly, was German held territory.

"Naturally the Allies suspected that the information regarding the second submarine was a diversion. Nevertheless, the search for the second submarine went ahead. Duxford was chosen mainly because our squadron of Super-marine Spitfires had been previously redesigned for the purpose of long flights to protect Bomber Command on their raids over Germany." He went into a tediously boring explanation of the intricate modifications done to the crafts. I tried to look interested, "Anyway, the operation was given the code-name 'Huggermugger'. The operation involved reconnaissance flights as far wide as the Spitfires fuel tanks would take them; the North Atlantic; the North Sea, searching for a ghost submarine. In all truth it was like trying to find a needle down a dark passageway at the height of the blackout period. There were no reports of any sighting whatsoever."

"Not quite that difficult to find needles if you look in the right places," I said as I took the photographs from my inside jacket pocket and gave them to him for inspection.

He looked long and hard at the photographs. Finally, he said, "The qualities bad. Where did you get these from?"

"The camera I took from Ralph Cravens wrecked plane."

His eyes illuminated. "This is amazing, young man."

"I thought they'd be of interest to you."

"Quickly now-," he pointed to a small writing desk sat in a corner-, "there is a magnifying glass in the top drawer. Can you get it for me, please?" There was excitement in his voice, a new lease of life.

I did as he asked and watched him as he became absorbed in the photographs, meticulously scanning every millimetre, talking as he scanned. "This submarine carries the identification I-52. The shape alone tells me it is the design of a Japanese submarine, and one that's in some considerable trouble."

"Could that be the mysterious submarine that set sail the same time as the Atlantic bound sub?"

He looked up. "You did say these photographs came from the crash site?"

"Positive."

"Well there can be no doubt." He handed the photographs back to me and I put them away inside my jacket while I watched his face twist in deep thought. "Are you sure it was Ralph Craven's name on the tag?"

"I only saw Craven, but I have checked records to confirm it,"

Josh Bane looked horrified. "I wonder if 'Sniffer' saw the submarine. I recall he never mentioned anything when he landed back at the Duxford other than to report he had a spot of engine trouble and lost sight of Ralph over the Welsh Mountains."

"Who's Sniffer?" I asked curiously.

"Squadron Leader Dillon 'Sniffer' Deveron, as I knew him. Besides being Ralph's wing protector that day, he was better known for his arse licking when in the company of senior officers. Admittedly, he was a damn good pilot, but boy, could he shift up to the higher command's backsides when he got the chance. It didn't surprise me when he continued his service in the Air Force after the war finished."

"Trustworthy type of chap, was he?"

"In what way do you define trustworthy?" The look in his eyes told me he was suspicious with my line of questioning.

"Would you trust him with your life?" I tried not to sound dramatic.

"In war time you had no choice but to trust your comrades."

"How well did you know him?"

"Personally, you mean?"

I nodded.

"I had never met him before the war, and I hardly spent time leisurely with him at the airfield. In combat, it doesn't pay to get too friendly because a pilots life only lasted day by day."

"What about the flight path Ralph Craven flew that day?"

"Ah-well, that's difficult to say. But I think his flight path would have taken him as far as out into the Atlantic via the coast of Ireland, circle round to go over the North Sea. It's hard to be precise."

"And this Squadron Leader Deveron, he also took the same route?"

"As I told you, young man, Deveron was Ralph's escort. His job was to protect Ralph's plane if he came under hostile fire, say from the submarines gun cannons or even a marauding German fighter. It was virtually impossible to defend the craft and snap pictures at the same time. And even if the task of doing both was mastered, it didn't make any difference to a converted reconnaissance plane because the craft didn't carry any weapons."

Now that did interest me. "So Craven wouldn't have been able to defend himself if he had to?"

"Yes, that's correct, young man, totally vulnerable. It took a brave man to fly reconnaissance, especially on those lonely flights across Europe and into enemy territory. The Spitfire MK X1 had a Merlin 60 series engine. It was incredibly fast and powerful and speed was the essential defence for reconnaissance flights, speed and larger fuel tanks. Even then the power of the Merlin engine wasn't fast enough with the excess weight the Spitfire carried. A directive came from the high command to strip the craft of every conceivable item the Spitfire didn't need to achieve that speed. All weapons, radio equipment, everything that wasn't bolted down was dismantled and disregarded. The Spitfire became a shell."

"Would there be any reason for any other craft to fly with the two pilots?"

"No. Not unless they defied orders."

I took a deep breath and asked, "Would Deveron be crazy enough to shoot down a Spitfire?"

Josh Bane stared at me in astonishment, his mouth half open trying to say something. He swallowed hard and said, "Are you implying that Deveron *caused* Ralph to crash by shooting his plane out of the sky? Is that what you're saying?"

He was certainly good at reading the lines on my face. I nodded encouragingly. "That is my assumption."

"Deveron left him to die?"

"Yes."

"Perish the thought!" By the anger in his voice I think if he had been strong enough he would have thrown me out of his house without my feet touching the ground. He ranted on, "A man doesn't become Chief Air Marshall Sir Dillon Deveron, and the rest of the lettering to follow, on the pretence of being a traitor to his country."

"I have a witness who watched the entire sequence on that fateful day. The witness saw a Spitfire open its guns on another Spitfire, the plane crashed but no one believed the witnesses story." I considered it inadvisable to mention the mental state of my star attendee.

"No, no. It sounds too incredible to comprehend. There must be a mistake! Where was this person at the time?"

"Close by the crash site, in another field."

"That's still a good distance to be positively sure."

"The witness didn't hesitate when describing the attack."

"No-no-young man, I cannot accept such an accusation. I shouldn't even be discussing the matter with you. Do you realise the consequences of such a treacherous act?"

"At the time he would have been hanged," I said, casually.

"Hung, drawn and quartered, more like." He started shaking his head and thundered on. "But that's unthinkable! What possible reason should Deveron want to do such an awful act on a fellow brother in arms?"

"The rumour of gold bullion sounds a feasible reason."

His expression froze. "It's preposterous! It's inconceivable to accuse a good man who fought hard for his country."

"I don't think so. Greed can affect us all. According to the documentary concerning the discovery of the I-52, the salvage team found no gold on the Atlantic submarine. Let us assume that the apparent decoy submarine, and the photographs confirm its existence, carried the real cargo on board. Sounds daft I know, but it's feasible. Now wouldn't a hoard of gold bullion turn a man into a madman?"

Josh Bane nodded in agreement. "Make me think twice I suppose. But for Christ's sake, young man, Deveron was a war hero. If there was gold to be found why should he want to continue in the R.A.F.?"

"He couldn't find the wreck, that's why! It crashed at such a speed it buried deep into the soft earth, lost from sight. The summer grasses were high, could easily camouflage the craft. Then it became a matter of time. Summers came and went, the plane lost forever. But that didn't deter Deveron. Richness beyond belief drove him on in his pursuit. The search for the plane became his career. With every discovered crash site he could have monitored the situation. His only problem was time itself. The search became years, a lifetime, in fact. Now that's changed, the plane has been found, and let me tell you, a lot of undesirables are hot in pursuit of it now, and believe me they are willing to kill for it."

Josh Bane absorbed the story thoughtfully. "It is a very scary situation you have fallen into, young man. I still feel you should put the matter into the hands of the police."

"I don't think so. They treat me like a crackpot now."

"I must confess, though, I do find it rather difficult to imagine a man in his eighties, as Dillon Deveron will be now, running amok and killing people for alleged gold he believed at the time to be nonexistent, as we all did while serving at Duxford. Okay the pictures prove the existence of another submarine. It does not prove there is gold bullion on board. Would you kill on those pretences? Would you risk the probable wrath of British justice if you were wrong? Have the dishonour of such a cowardly act splattered over every newspaper in the country."

I didn't give him an answer because I felt I was right.

He carried on. "I don't suppose the likes of Dillon Deveron would either. Can you imagine an old man, held high in esteem within the military, how he would feel to be accused of such a despicable thing? And the threat of prison pushed into his haggard face for good measure, I think the shock would kill him before they had chance to cart him away."

I suppose it was fair to assume Dillon Deveron could be in the same position as Josh Bane and is probably scuttling around with the aid of a Zimmer frame. Hardly killer potential if that's the case. But anyone can give orders. One phone call would be enough and no one could excuse Deveron from guilt, at least not until I'd confirmed his innocence.

"Have you seen Deveron recently?"

Josh Bane appeared flabbergasted. "Surely you're not thinking of asking him to his face?"

"I haven't decided."

"Well I'm sorry but I can't help you."

"You won't reveal where he is?"

"Oh-no-no, I don't even know where he is and neither do I know if he's still alive. I've seen him on occasions many years ago at the odd reunion and at Remembrance Day. As for his present whereabouts, I've no idea at all!"

There was nothing more to know so I eased from the chair, smiled, and said, "I must press on back to London. I've a lot to do.

You've been a tremendous help and I appreciate the time you have given me. No need to get up, I'll see myself out."

Josh Bane's gaunt sunken face had me worried. I'd seen that type of expression before, that traumatized look of a man witnessing a convicted criminal on his way to the electric chair. The thought made me shiver.

"Take care, young man," he said kindly. "Intuition tells me you're turning over a barrowful of rotting maggots. Finding that submarine might favour your quest for the truth, it might also be your death warrant."

"I'll be okay!" I assured him, though he didn't look convinced.

"That might be so, young man. I only hope that when I pick up a paper in the future I'll being reading the greatest gold find ever, though I pray I don't read your name in the obituaries column instead."

I rather hoped he was joking, but he wasn't. He may have put the curse of death on me, but in the meantime he had given me a lead to the whereabouts of one elusive submarine, which without doubt, would stir interest among the natives, especially the ones I was after.

I drove back to London with an overactive mind and a bad headache and the bruises from my early clash now beginning to take shape. I also needed sleep. As I drove through the night I glanced across at Winston. Nothing seemed to stop the wretched hound from sleeping. He'd flaked out on the seat the moment I turned the engine. I also made an astonishing discovery. I never realized dogs snored, and with such an annoying effect, which at least prompted me not to drop asleep while driving.

As I approached home I was just in the middle of a yawn when I suddenly realized something was missing. There were no street lights on. The road was darker than the deepest depths of an abandoned coalmine. Not just that, none of my security lights came on as I turned the Roadster into the driveway. The dark played havoc with my vision and taking into consideration there was no breeze that evening, I could have sworn the shrubbery began to move as I drove up to the garage door.

CHAPTER SEVEN

The bushes had stopped moving by the time I switched off the engine and stepped from the car. It didn't require psychic powers to realize that I had hostile company especially when Winston shot out from the car to be by my side. He was agitated but controlled and neither did he bark or growl. He waited patiently. I think his intention was to allow the danger to come out into the open. The dog obviously knew more than I did because the ploy worked and from the shadows of the shrubbery stepped two beady-eyed vultures in the shape of the man who had stolen the identity of Filbert and his bogyman minder.

They failed to notice Winston tucked in behind my left leg as they rapidly approached. The anxiety I had when I got out of the car dispersed the moment I prepared myself for the inevitable attack.

"You're frigging trespassing!" I said strongly.

I heard the double click a second after I felt Winston's body tense against my leg. Although no switchblades were shown or swished in a frantic arc of rage as they neared us, the distinct positioning of their hands hanging limply by their sides told me all I needed to know.

Winston reacted far quicker than I did. The moment the bogyman's hand twitched, the speed of the dog latched on the striking wrist and I had parried Filbert's upward strike and caught the blade hand. The instinct for survival produces a tremendous amount of inner strength and energy. My heart raced and the muscles pumped as I hit him with every thing I had: head, hands, knees and feet, and not necessarily in that order. Ten years since I threw a punch in anger and I hadn't lost my touch. It was vicious and frantic but I didn't cease the bombardment until I heard the sound of the blade crashing to the floor. Then I hit him again with a flurry of body punches before finishing off with a terrific uppercut that dropped him to the floor with a crunching thud. He groaned then silenced but he never moved.

I quickly switched my attention to the fracas behind me. Winston had his fangs buried in the side of his face with the savagery of a pit bull dogfight. I thought of intervening but changed my mind when human screams of agony ghoulishly crept through the night air and my hand wasn't going anywhere near the action.

I turned back to Filbert, knelt down beside him and grabbed him by the hair and yanked his head up. His eyes were groggy and I didn't care. I wanted some answers.

"Right you piece of shit! Start by telling me your proper employer? And don't give me the verbal diarrhoea *the Ministry* because I know differently." I shook his head hard to wake him up. "Talk shit breath!"

Suddenly Winston's piece of meat broke free and began running down the driveway with the dog snapping at he heels with every stride. I let Filbert's head hit the ground and got to my feet to watch the pursuit. I made the wrong move. Stupidly I had given Filbert the chance to scarper, which he did, straight through the shrubbery and scaled the garden wall running in the same direction as his companion.

I cursed loudly and gave chase. I would have caught him if a car hadn't raced down towards us, screeched to a crawl, allowing Filbert to scramble into the rear door before the car roared past me with Winston in pursuit of the tailpipe.

I whistled the dog back from a pointless chase and gave him a pat for his gallant effort. "Good boy. Sure showed the sad bastards who's the boss." And he promptly spat out half an ear. "Didn't like the taste, hey boy! Never mind, I've a juicy piece of meat in the fridge that's far more appetising than bits of scum."

I watched until the red tail-lights of the car disappeared and was about to turn back to the house when I was startled by a beckoning voice from the shadows across the road.

"Mister Speed, I presume?"

"Depends who wants me!"

The stranger approached. I was ready to repel another attack and so was Winston. But we both held back on noticing he had his hands half raised to show he carried nothing to endanger us.

"You're certainly a hard man to track down," he said, slightly out of breath.

He was a tall, bulky chap, which was about as much as I could make out in the dark. He continued. "I've been waiting your return for hours. I'd dropped to sleep in my car down the road." He gesticulated to some parked vehicles thirty metres away. "The commotion woke me up."

"Well-I'm really sorry about *that*," I said sarcastically.

"We need to talk."

I wasn't in the mood to talk or listen. I said, "It's late and I'm rather tired, and as you have probably observed, I'm pretty agitated. So fuck off!"

The stranger took a step back and said, "I fully intend to after the spectacle I've just witnessed. Yet if you can spare the time, I must speak with you on urgent matters. I appreciate the situation is momentarily inconvenient, so I posted my credentials through your letterbox. You can give them back to me later."

He was certainly a calm character.

"Why should I want to talk to you?"

"Well-I can put a name to your attackers, for starters." He had my attention. "But since you're in such a bad mood, and obviously in need of sleep, perhaps we can meet later today. I'll treat you to breakfast, around ten. You'll find me at the establishment called, 'The Greaseless Grill'. Do you know it?"

"King's Road," I said.

"That's the one." He gave a flick type wave and disappeared down the road.

Before going inside I inspected the security lights. I wasn't surprised to discover that they had been vandalized beyond repair and I guessed the street lamps had suffered the same treatment.

Once inside the house I studied the stranger's credentials. They were impressive so I had no excuse not to accept that Detective Inspector Dan Hamer was from the Ministry of Defence Police. There was a telephone number and the extension number to establish if the details matched the visitor, which, after some sleep, I rang. Everything about him was confirmed. Fate had brought us together, and I wasn't about to ignore my destiny.

*

'The Greaseless Grill', serves a gourmet breakfast equal to any of the top restaurants in London, everything cooked to absolute perfection.

Fresh crisp bacon, perfect yellow eggs, large flat mushrooms in a delicious sauce, cooked tomatoes, and toast that melts in the mouth. All swilled down the gullet with a pot of proper brewed tea, no dry tasting paper tea bags, just pure leaves. It's an expensive place to eat and always busy and I was going to enjoy it immensely because I wasn't paying.

Detective Inspector Dan Hamer was sat at a table drinking coffee when I arrived. The daylight did him no favours. By the deep age lines cut into his face, I guessed he was in his fifties. His physique bordered a person whose love affair with the gymnasium had all but gone. He wasn't grossly fat by any means, but the loss of a few pounds of flesh would improve him tremendously.

Hamer half rose from the comfort of his chair for the courtesy shake of hands. He had a strong grip. I estimated his height to be around five feet eleven inches tall that carried his plump figure adequately. There were patches of grey running through his neatly trimmed brown hair. He had deep set hazel coloured eyes, a slightly bent nose, and a strong square chin that I reckon could take a good punch.

"Glad you accepted the offer, Mister Speed. Please, sit down."

As he re-seated I gave him back his credentials. "I did check them."

He smiled thinly. "I would have been disappointed if you had-n't."

As I sat down and pulled the chair in, I said, "I don't usually accept offers from strangers but I've always been weak minded when someone offers me free food and hopefully some interesting answers."

"We'll get to the questions and answers in a moment, Mister Speed. I don't wish to put you off a delicious breakfast."

I accepted that.

My first impression of Hamer had me thinking I was dealing with a polite chap, but first impressions mean nothing as everyone is polite when they want something.

"I gather those two Neanderthals didn't return last night?" he seemed concerned.

"No. I've good internal security anyway. I always feel safe in my bed, unless, of course, they were in possession of a tank, then I might have sweated a little."

Hamer nodded his approval. "Good. I must say you certainly look in better shape after a few hours sleep. And how is your dog?"

"Winston you mean? He's fine."

"Is that the dog's name! Is he about?"

"He's at home, sleeping. I thought the other diners might not appreciate his ravenous appetite and slobbering jowls when he eats, if I had brought him along."

"He's an incredible animal and a cleverly vicious one too! That was some display last night. I'm glad I stayed on the opposite side of the road."

"He's not usually vicious."

"Indeed! I only wish some of the men under my command had the same bite as your dog."

"He's not actually mine. He belongs to a friend of mine. I'm just looking after him for a while."

"I'd say that he was looking after you, Mister Speed. And he's an unusual breed."

"He's cross bred between a Labrador and a Staffordshire-Bull Terrier."

He nodded. "That accounts for his ferociousness in battle."

"He's a softy at heart, he just detests anyone attacking his friends, as you duly witnessed."

On queue breakfast arrived. The aroma drifting from the plate forced me to swallow saliva quickly before it excreted down the sides of my chin. I was famished and tucked in heartily asking the appropriate questions in-between mouthfuls.

"How come your card landed through my letterbox, I've already had a bad experience with the ministry police."

Hamer stopped chewing. "I gather from those two thugs last night? Well they certainly don't work for the ministry."

"I did have doubts about them."

"What did they want?"

"They thought I had something that belonged to them."

"Have you?"

"Never found out. So who are they?"

"A couple of horrors, Mister Speed, though it was pretty dark last night to be one hundred percent sure of their identity. As I stand, I'm afraid uncertainty outweighs certainty. Nevertheless, if it's them, then you are dealing with two dangerous men."

"Just how dangerous are we talking?"

"Well let me put it this way, usually their victim dies. Their names are Damian Love and Theodore Hate. Very similar characters and often mistaken for brothers, though I assure you they are nothing of the kind. For recognition purposes your opponent was Love and the dog tackled Hate. Love is the mouthpiece of the two. Not to be underestimated as his brutality is on equal terms with Hate. Where they descended from or what nationality they are, I'm not sure.

He leaned forward. "They make a living out of killing people," he whispered and withdrew talking normally. "They have no preference as long as someone pays them. Their usual application to a victim is to carve them up as a butcher does with a cow carcass. They escape justice with relative ease. Never any witness to their crime. They are usually efficient bastards, their targets wrapped up, sealed, and delivered, until that is, they met a more resilient opponent in you, Mister Speed, and Winston, of course."

"You seem to know a lot about them?"

"I should do, especially when it concerns an incident in Cyprus five years ago when a British army sergeant was murdered on the orders of a Turkish Mafia boss. Okay it turned out the slimy toad sergeant was up to no good, and we were on to him, but he was knifed to death before we got to him. We knew the two characters Love and Hate were the hired executioners, only we couldn't prove it, end of the investigation. The army officer is flown home, military funeral and nothing more is said. Another unsolved tragedy lost in the military archives in Whitehall, and who really cares? No damn shit, that's who. As for Love and Hate they disappeared into oblivion, not to be seen again till now." He again leaned over and began whispering. "I was fucking shocked when I saw them again, I can tell you. Those two villains are unscrupulous bastards and for the right wad of money they would kill their own mother, bury her and dig her back up to sell to science."

Hamer straightened his posture and resumed in his normal tone. "The person responsible for bringing their employment to the streets of London, is obviously well aware of their reputation"

"So who employs that calibre of man?"

Hamer waved his fork in the air. "Have you ever heard of McClusky's Irish-American import and export and storage?"

I shook my head. "I can't say I have."

"Neither have I. The question is why? "

"How certain are you they work for this, McClusky character?"

"Nothing conclusive, yet when you have the privilege of using government equipment, especially highly sophisticated computer stations that hold confidentiality that even the Prime Minister does-n't know about, it's surprising what it throws out when simply feed-ing in a car registration such as the one your friends absconded in last night. It was registered to the McClusky's business, but don't get your hopes up, it wouldn't surprise me if the vehicle has already been crushed to a cube at a local scrap-yard. They might even say it has been stolen."

"Obviously you checked to find out if it had been stolen?"

"Nothing has been reported."

"Have you checked McClusky himself?"

"He's clean."

"Then how come I'm at the top of everyone's Christmas list?"

"Well I thought that was obvious. Apparently you have the knack of pissing people off!"

"The only people I piss off are usually authoritarians, and I must confess I enjoy *that*."

"Something I already know, Mister Speed. A certain Detective Constable Stevens rang the ministry to ask if we had an ongoing investigation on you."

"So where do I fit into your investigation? That's why you're here, isn't it?"

"Naturally, only this is no more than a preliminary investigation. I'm interested in what connects a stolen identity with a recently exhumed world war two Spitfire fighter plane, and your involve-ment, Mister Speed!"

That got me a little agitated. "As I already told the police, I per-sonally know nothing about it, other than I knew the farmer who owned the land."

"Yes, I did speak to Mister Bickermass when I went there to observe the salvage operation. As I recall, he was a very pleasant chap. I must confess he didn't mention your presence."

"Maybe it had something to do with the fact I wasn't *there* at the time." I reminded him. "Do you know he died in mysterious cir-cumstances?"

"Yes it was brought to my attention that there was an unfortunate accident."

There was that frigging word again, 'accident'. I could have eas-ily argued my view on how he died but I suspected it would only fall on deaf ears. I drank some coffee to calm down.

"Please understand, Mister Speed, I'm not here to persecute you.

It's your help I really sought."

I struggled to refrain from laughing in his face. "I'm listening."

He wiped his mouth with a napkin, and said, "I don't know how much information you have nor am I interested in any active part you had in the entire episode-."

I was about to protest my innocence when he hand gestured my silence. "Please hear me out." He waited for my nod of approval. "Thank you, Mister Speed. What I am trying to say is I suspect that you actually found the wreck. I think you allowed Mister Bickermass to take the credit, a nice gesture Mister Speed. I suppose the number of arrest warrants you accumulated over the years for non-remittance of treasure trove obviously accounted for the deviation from the truth. How am I doing so far?"

"Have you ever thought of taking up writing fiction," I said calmly. "And you've obviously had a long chat with Stevens."

He ignored my remarks and pushed on. "Okay, the plane is found, exhumed, and the pilot is given a military funeral. After cross-referencing, everything is logged and stored in the archives for eternity. Sounds so simple, don't you think? (I never acknowledged) But no because questions are being asked by the local police and a retired M.o.D. official has had his name used by criminals, all because of a piece of wreckage and a military uniform full of bones.

"Unofficially I decided to reopen the file on Flying Officer Derek Rowland, whose remains were recovered from the crash site. Interestingly, he flew a Spitfire mark one. A wonderful machine so I'm informed. I had the wreckage we exhumed carefully re-examined and discovered that the similarities ended there. What we had was the wreckage of a super marine Spitfire class and Rowland never flew one.

"Derek Rowland was officially stationed along with the Americans at Burtonwood airbase in, Warrington, Lancashire. Now according to records no Super-marine Spitfires were ever stationed there. So the intriguing question is how did Rowland get into the wreck in the first place?"

"Someone made a mistake," I said conceitedly.

"Maybe so, Mister Speed. And if that is the case it can be rectified. But I have a problem, the files are missing. *Must have been misplaced,* is the only reply I receive. Does that not seem very strange to you?"

"Not guilty," I said, and promptly wiped my plate clean with a slice of cold toast.

"I'm not looking for a confession just a bit of inspiration, because if someone in the department is trying to cover up facts then it can only be done by higher ranking personnel than me. Now that worries me. Why should someone want to go to all that trouble to hide information about a body found in the rusting wreck?"

I shrugged my shoulders. "It beats me, you're the detective."

He frowned upon my deliberate evasiveness. I could ease his mind and tell him the name I saw on the tags, but why should I strangle myself by admitting to being there at the scene because that would lead to other accusations.

"I feel that you are taking all this as a big joke, Mister Speed. You obviously don't care as your deliberate nonconformity means I'll be conducting this investigation alone." There was suppressed anger in his tone.

"Old Tom could have told you, but he's dead; an accident so everyone tells me."

"So you obviously don't think it was an accident?"

"You're damn right I don't. Winston proved that. You saw his reaction to those two thugs. He was old Tom's dog, and as I said before, he detests anyone harming his friends, especially his master."

"Can you prove any of this?"

"That Love and Hate killed old Tom? Yes if I can get the dog to talk."

"Being facetious won't help matters, Mister Speed."

"Well I couldn't convince the local police to investigate. Their brains concluded an accident, so what's the point of pursuing the matter."

"Would you like to prove the police wrong?"

"I'm a revengeful type of guy and nothing would please me more. The problem is I'm hardly in a position to take the law into my own hands."

"But would you like to?" His expression was serious.

"Damn right! As for playing detective, I'm just a simple commoner dragged into the entire mess. I wouldn't even know where to begin."

"Simple, really, Mister Speed! Tell me everything you haven't told me. Tell me what you saw at the wreck site that has got people spooked enough to hire killers."

At that point I must admit I lost control and became a little hostile. "I've already stressed I wasn't there. Inside the ministry you probably carry a lot of whack. Outside in the real world you're way out of your jurisdiction. If you really want to be a good detective, you might try convincing the wonderful policemen scattered around good old London that there are two unscrupulous characters roaming the streets bothering people with the intention of wanting to murder them." I stood to leave. "Good day, Detective Inspector, and thanks for the wonderful breakfast."

"I must warn you, Mister Speed, it's far from over. I'd rather you reconsider working alongside me. Those two brutish fiends are still a great threat to you. All you have achieved is to stand on the tail of a couple of rattlesnakes. They will want retribution. They will strike back, and they might be successful next time. I can't protect you unless you help me. You're treading a dangerous path. Hand your problems over to the professionals who get paid for dealing in danger."

I smiled confidently. "Don't fret. I'm a big boy. Must get back or Winston will start tearing my place apart in search of food."

I began to turn away from the table, checked my stride, and said to him: "Ever heard of Operation Huggermugger?" I could tell by his expression he hadn't. "Well as payment for a splendid breakfast, look it up in the archives, it's very interesting. World war two, I do believe, R.A.F. Duxford, carried out operation."

I thought he deserved something for his troubles, and hopefully, they might realize their mistake and bury Craven under his own name with full military honours. As for my own investigation, the right direction had me heading towards McClusky's which I located at Greenland dock in Greenwich.

The dock gate was bustling with activity that no one noticed or challenged me as I slipped through using the blind side of a long wheeled based lorry trundling through the gate. When I reached the warehouse, a large structured concrete building with an array of warning signs indicating a fragile asbestos roof, and looked through the large opened steel doors there wasn't much happening. A solitary bucket loader was shovelling piles of grain into sectioned bays. I decided to return when it was dark, perhaps bring along a selection of tools to break-in.

*

I was back at McClusky's just after mid-night dressed in black combat type clothing, a bomber jacket and soft soled shoes. I considered a balaclava a little excessive. I parked the car down the road and took a leather bag, something similar to a doctor's bag, from the boot and walked fast-paced to the main gate and past the security gatehouse with unimaginable ease. I suspect the lapse of disciplined security was duly down to the attitude of the two guards within the gatehouse, who probably decided that first class security requires first class pay and the pittance they were to be paid didn't warrant the effort to get off their backsides in too much of a hurry, such consideration only served to make my task simple.

Moonlight flickering through the night clouds lit my way sufficiently to scamper across the compound, clutching the leather bag tight to stop the tools from playing a metallic jingle as I bounced along. I checked everywhere was clear at the front of the warehouse before making my way to the rear. It was there I saw a light emitting from a lower window underneath a steel stairway that led to a first floor doorway.

I angled across and away from the building and pushed my back tight against a large steel container while I looked around for possible guards. There were none, at least there were none I could see. I still had to be careful as I circled the container to check the other side. There I found a lorry tarpaulin covering a vehicle. When I lifted the corner of the sheet the momentary flash of moonlight lit up, 'wash me', on the backdoor of a white van. Things were looking promising.

I let the sheet fall and tip-toed across to the window under the stairway and crouched, carefully placing the tool bag down. I peered in. I could see people shifting large wooden crates by hand pulled hydraulic trucks. I counted five men. They were five men too many for me to handle. I eased back and away from the window, gripped my tool bag and began to stand up. That was when something struck the back of my head. I didn't remember the pain.

CHAPTER EIGHT

The thumping inside my head woke me.

I lifted my head. The stiffness in my neck cracked and the first attempt to open my eyes I quickly abandoned when the incoming light felt as if it was splitting my eyeballs. What fraction of feeling I still had in my body made me realize that I was still upright but slouched in some sort of harness. I had a dull pain in my crutch region and all my limbs were a mixture of aches and pins and needles. With half-open eyelids I stood the few inches required to support my own weight. I tried to move about to get the blood circulation going through my body, but all I could do was to squirm as the harness held me fast.

I opened my eyes fully. The harness wasn't a harness as such. Some sick bastard had nailed every conceivable part of my clothing to a wooden stanchion and I was pinned there in the form of a crucifix and no matter how hard I twisted, turned, or pulled, I wasn't going anywhere, indefinitely.

I got a strong whiff of damp as I looked around what appeared to be an attic room. A single light pendant hung from the rafters, its clear glass lamp coated with specks of fly excrement. In the corner of the room, abandoned on a small stool, I spotted the nail gun that had attacked my clothing, and that was about all the furniture there was.

The attic had no skylight. The only way in or out was by a narrow, panelled door. In all honesty, I couldn't visualize much hope of escape, until I heard a bout of laughter and voices drifting from the other side the door.

I attempted to make myself heard but, disappointingly, it came out as a pathetic squeak because my throat was dry. Gathering what saliva I had left in the crevices of my mouth, I swallowed painfully and tried again.

"Is anyone listening?" I bellowed the best I could.

The response was quick and direct and straight away I knew I was dealing with a non-negotiator.

"Shut your fucking mouth!" The voice belonged to an arrogant piece of shit with a strong Irish accent.

I've always detested having a conversation through a closed door, but I'd no choice. "I need a piss!" And neither was I lying.

"Piss down your leg," came back a different Irish voice.

"You might enjoy standing in a pool of stinking fluid but I happen to have far more class and a lot more dignity. Now stop being a frigging selfish bastard and show me the bathroom."

Ten seconds later I heard the clatter of boots scaling a creaky stairway. I watched in anticipation as the latch lifted with a metallic clap and the door squeaked open. A tall, young man, in army fatigues, reluctantly shuffled through the door. He had a spotty complexion and scraggy medium length hair. As he approached I noticed he had a mouthful of disorientated teeth that a dentist would have ripped out and started again.

More appropriately, he had brought the bathroom to me in the form of a dented metal bucket that had seen a lot of action on a building site and by now should have been well and truly delivered to the nearest scrap yard instead.

I said, "How nice, personal service, I see!"

He scowled at me.

"Why am I being held?" I asked sharply. "Who the frigging hell are you?"

He seemed surprised I didn't know but he never answered.

I assumed he was the youngest of the bunch to earn the right to be handed the task of errand boy and by his sour expression he hardly cherished the responsibility. He placed the bucket down on the floor in front of me.

Super-imposing a stare of astonishment, I glanced down at the bucket, then to him, the bucket, to him and said, "What am I suppose to do with that?"

Again he expressed surprise. "It's for you to piss in!"

His Irish accent differed from the other voices that had shouted through, so that accounted for at least three warders. I said, "You're not too bright, are you?"

Puzzlement etched his face. "Meaning what, Mister?"

"You might not have noticed, but as the present situation goes, your production of a portable toilet has all the hallmarks of being a sheer disaster. I'm not renowned for any magical attributes, so I'm going to find it rather difficult to unzip my flies and direct my dick towards the centre of the bucket. Catch on?"

The apparent brain in his head suddenly clicked. His face reddened in embarrassment. "If you think I'm holding your prick over that bucket, you can get fucked, you gay bastard!" With that outburst he quickly left.

"Touchy!" I said, as he disappeared through the door.

I overheard Spotty-face moaning strongly to his comrades about the audacity of my request followed by the roars of laughter. They might think it was a big joke but I was still desperate and struggling to avoid wetting myself. I shouted through again. "I still need a piss!"

The response was swift, although I was a little shocked to see it was a woman with short boyish style auburn hair, wearing tight dark pants and a black T-shirt that clung to the mould of a carefully crafted body. She approached me, anger distorting her pretty face. Her sparkling green eyes stared straight into mine and without flinching she unzipped my flies, rustled around inside my pants and flopped out my dick with staggering speed, reached down for the bucket and tucked the cold steel rim against my scrotum, the entire procedure done without moving her eyes from mine. Now this was a woman with talent and dominance, I thought.

"Piss, Buster! I haven't got all day!" she ordered. Her accent was American.

My sack was so full and bursting at the seam that I had no time to be embarrassed or protest, but I did struggle to piss at first especially when someone is watching. To help things along, I said, "What's all this about?"

She eyeballed me but said nothing.

"I don't know what I've done, but surely we can work something out."

Her silence annoyed me and interrupted my flow.

"Kidnapping is against the law," I said.

"Just concentrate on your bodily functions, Buster."

"I've got a right to know!"

"The only thing you need to know is wet me and the bucket sits upside down on your head."

I finished and she put the bucket unceremoniously down and

was just as fast in putting my dick back into my pants and caused me to flinch when she zipped up my flies. Catching the skin of your scrotum in your zipper can be excruciatingly painful.

I think she knew that when she flashed a false smile and tapped the front of my pants. "Happy now, Buster?" she said.

"I'll be happy when you tell me what the frigging hell is going on? Why am I being held against my will?"

She slid the bucket across the floor with her foot. "You'll know everything when the interrogation begins."

I felt my eyes popping out of their sockets. "What interrogation?"

Before I had the chance to ask why I should need to go through the possible trauma of violence, she'd left and closed the door behind.

What did she mean by *interrogation?* Does that entail torture? The thought of it made me feel tacky. I wondered what nasty things could be inflicted on the human body. Or was I perhaps jumping to conclusions about the form of interrogation to be conducted. One thing I was certain of, I was no longer at McClusky's warehouse because any impending screams courtesy of the inflicted pain upon my body would be heard so we had to be miles from anywhere.

Then it occurred to me. What were they waiting for? I was awake and in prime condition to crack under extreme pressure but they weren't pushing ahead with the questioning. Why? Were they expecting me to worry myself to death?

No, because they were waiting till someone arrived. That had to be the reason. But who were they waiting for? My body tensed and I swallowed hard. They were waiting for Damian Love and Theodore Hate. I had a panic attack as I pictured them in my head eagerly climbing the stairs in anticipation of slicing lumps out of my flesh.

Frantically I began jerking my body forward in an attempt to free my clothing from the nails, twisting and pulling and wasting energy. I didn't want them enjoying their revenge. I don't mind being hit providing I'm in a position to defend myself and give back as good as I got. Yet I don't think such callous killers would give me the chance.

Again I was jolting about like a madman in a straight-jacket, but all my efforts for freedom were useless. The clothing was too tightly nailed to get a good pull and all I achieved was to exhaust myself into submission.

I didn't have to wait too long before I heard the clattering of heavy boots storming up the stairway. The door flew open and bodies piled in. Stood in front of me were the woman, Spotty-face, and two bulldogs in the form of brutish looking Irishman in fatigues who moved towards me menacingly. Both men stood over six foot with bulging muscles, short cropped dark hair, and round deep set brown eyes. You couldn't tell them apart but for one of them having the mangled and battered face of a pugilist. But there was no sign of Love or Hate and I wondered if I'd been reprieved.

I said defiantly. "Have I done something to offend you? Only I'm not usually that bad it warrants being trussed up like Jesus frigging Christ!"

"We'll soon find out how bad you've been!" The deep Irish voice I heard came from behind the group and when they fanned out, a grey haired, bulbous nosed middle-aged man of medium height and supremely smart in army fatigues, stood there rigid, chest pouted, hands behind his back holding a short cane. He had all the hallmarks of a proud man who took considerable care about his appearance, everything that should have shined did indeed shine, combat boots and the buckle on his belt.

Big-nose, (since he didn't introduce himself, I'll refer to him by that name) walked slowly towards me, purposely clumping down his boots on the wooden floor boards with every step, his hands still clasped behind his back.

As he neared, I said, "Great! Now perhaps you can tell me why I'm trussed up playing frigging Jesus?"

His final steps quickened and he stopped approximately a foot away and his grey-blue eyes pierced mine. "Do not take the Lord's name in vain," he said meaningfully. His breath smelt of peppermint.

"It's just a name to me. I'm an atheist," I said, and regretted the remark as he suddenly whipped the cane from behind his back and rammed the tip into my throat, which left me gargling for breath.

"A dead atheist if you speak out of turn again." He removed the cane and repositioned himself to one side of me. Instinctively my eyes strained to follow his every movement in anticipation of another assault.

"Now let us begin by establishing that you are one of McClusky's men." Big Nose told me.

"I knew it!" I spurted out with relief. "I'm afraid you have the wrong man,"

"You was there guarding the rear of the warehouse." Big-nose retorted.

"The hell I was! I was spying through the window."

"Lies won't save you." I noticed the frustration beginning to build in Big-nose's face. "You are one of McClusky's men!?"

"And again I deny it!" I said cockily.

I wasn't cocky when an object smashed into the wooden stanchion just inches from my left ear. My head jerked round and I saw Spotty face stood there displaying his horrendous bulk of teeth in a twisted smile, holding two darts in his hand after embedding the first close to my face with threat. Through clenched teeth I said, "That isn't necessary, you creep!"

Big-nose pointed his cane at me. "Admit it. You are one of McClusky's men?"

I was looking at the dart in Spotty face's raised hand. "No, I'm an innocent bystander."

No sooner had I finished my denial, Spotty-face threw the dart into the fleshy part of my right hand. I grimaced with the stinging sensation and quickly examined the damage. There was no blood oozing where the dart embedded, just a blob of white pulled skin as the weapon dangled. I threw Spotty-face a revengeful glare because given the chance I was going to ram those darts down his throat and pull them out of his arse.

Then something horrible happened and I couldn't control it. The pain increased in my injured hand, a feeling of burning as if the dart was attempting to bury deeper into my flesh.

Big-nose was quick to explain my situation, "You are no doubt feeling the intensified pain now as each dart tip is coated with a solution of muscle distorting serum ZX 34, originally created in Russian laboratories by bored chemists. Heavily administered in the prison camps in the Middle Eastern countries, and gradually found its way to the shores of Ireland for use in nail bombs during the campaign for freedom. For the purpose of interrogation, the serum is usually injected into a chosen muscle with a syringe," he snorted a smirk. "But our way is far more fun."

I began to feel sick, and Big Nose was beginning to enjoy the occasion.

"Now for the intriguing part of the exercise, the muscle goes into spasm. The feeling of tightness and pain and I believe, although I have never experience the devilish stuff, it is equivalent to having

74

your muscle squashed in a mechanical vice and the handle won't stop turning. The suffering probably lasts approximately one minute, but whose counting. Exciting isn't it! There is, of course, an antidote. Correct answers to simple questions."

I just hate that moment when the tormenter proves to be right. I did feel precisely what he told me and it hurt as if it was being put through a mangle. I couldn't even move my fingers. The pain intensified to excruciating. That invisible vice wouldn't stop turning and there was nothing I could do.

Mercifully the pain eased and I was gasping for breath, but Big-nose was relentless and began tearing into my mind again.

"What is McClusky planning?" he bellowed in my ear.

"How the frigging hell should I know! I don't even know him."

"Talk, now!"

"I don't know."

Big-nose gave a hand signal and out of the corner of my eye I saw Spotty-face unleashing another dart. My body tensed as it smashed into my left thigh with a sickening thud. I arched and squirmed, clenching my teeth in readiness for the oncoming blast of pain. I soon realized that the bigger the muscle, the more intensified the agony and I was hurting inside. When the pain eased I was dripping with sweat and I couldn't stop my body from shaking.

Big-nose was at me again. "What is McClusky planning?"

"I've got no frigging idea! I don't even know who he is."

Another dart penetrated my right thigh.

Big-nose came close to my face. "Is it wise to suffer for a mere piece of information?"

I had no time to plead as the pain ripped through my entire body. I think I was screaming. I wanted it to stop, but I had to endure the pain. I had to show these bastards I'm not easily intimidated despite what they did to me. And the more I held on the more Big-nose was pissed-off.

Spotty-face still had that horrible grin when he approached me to retrieve the darts dangling from my body. The bastard deliberately retracted each dart slowly as he watched me wince with each pull. He took particular interest when removing the dart from my hand, enjoying the spectacle with vampirism asperity, fascinatingly amused as the blood oozed from the wound before he returned to his starting position. I tensed when he produced a second set of darts and waited eagerly for the signal to strike again.

Big-nose went on, "Be brave, as we have all the time in the world to break your resistance. Now tell me what devious plans McClusky is concocting and I assure you the pain will stop?"

"You're going beyond the extremes of stupidity, Mister! I don't kn-."

I never got another word out as two darts, almost simultaneously, rammed into my left and right breast muscles. The build up of pain was unbearable. My chest felt as if it was on fire and caving in. I had trouble breathing and between my agonies Big-nose was shouting quick-fire questions in my face.

"Tell me what McClusky has planned?"

Through the hurt and gritted teeth I fought back. "I don't...know," I said weakly.

"How many men does he have at the warehouse?"

I shook my head.

"Tell me the strength of their armaments?"

"How many...times...do I have...to say, I...don't know!" I gasped.

"You will tell me now!" he ravaged my eardrum.

I found some strength from somewhere and flew into a short rage. "Frigging ask him yourself!"

The dart that penetrated my left shoulder muscle put me in deep trouble. Now so disorientated that for a moment I couldn't even scream. I screwed my eyes so tight to fight the onslaught. I didn't even feel the stinging force of Big-nose's cane as he slashed it against the side of my face, in a burst of uncontrollable rage.

"Talk you scraping of scum!" he ranted "What deviousness is McClusky contemplating in his sick mind?"

As my suffering eased, I said, "Aren't you the one that's sick, using me as a pincushion. Asking questions I can't possibly answer. How many times do I have to say, I don't work for McClusky."

In a remarkable change around Big-nose was calm again. "You have an incredible resistance to pain, and such loyalty to a scum-bag like McClusky. Obviously you don't know him as we do or else you would be squealing like a pig to tell me what I want to know. So big hero, what is your name?"

"Does it matter who I am? I still don't work for McClusky."

Big-nose quickly raised his hand to stop Spotty-face from throwing another dart. "Your name or the pain continues."

For awkwardness, I said, "Noddy!"

Suddenly he slashed his cane across my mouth. I howled obscenities, feeling the instant trickle of warm blood leaking from my throbbing split lips.

He gave a quick smile and said, "Strange Mister Noddy how the details we found inside your wallet match the name Shackleton Speed. That either makes you a liar or a thief."

It was out of habit that my wallet followed my change of clothing, I thought. "I still don't work for McClusky!"

"I will be the judge of *that.*"

"Ask him. He might even tell you how he tried to kill me; twice."

"Kill you!" Big-nose scoffed. "Why should he do that?"

"How should I know? I might have found out but someone decided to smash the back of my skull and drag me away."

"What were you hoping to achieve at his warehouse all alone?"

There seemed no point holding back any longer. "My intentions were to break-in. I needed to know what I was up against, see who my enemy is. I didn't think it was wise to introduce myself at his door, mainly as a precaution to prevent him blowing my frigging head off. He's already proved his ruthlessness when he murdered two of my friends. I'm trying to gather evidence of his guilt so I could and pass it onto the police."

"You should have mentioned all this earlier."

"How could I when I never got the frigging chance. I was battered unconscious, kidnapped and trussed up as if I was a trophy. And then you had one hundred and eighty over there displaying his future darting ambitions upon my body."

Big-nose showed no remorse. "It'll teach you to stick to whatever you do best. Now why should McClusky want to kill your friends?"

I shrugged my shoulders or at least tried before remembering nailed clothing is impossible to move. "I can't be sure."

"Perhaps you were treading on one of their operations?"

"I hardly think that's the problem. Until a few hours ago I'd never even heard the name McClusky. Not till two of his henchmen came harassing and threatening me."

"What did they want?"

"It's a long story."

"Going somewhere, Speed?"

As only a fool would take unnecessary punishment for the sake of a slice of truth, I told them everything that had happened, that was, everything they needed to know to convince them I was no threat. I went through the entire episode from the discovery of the plane, through to my untimely presence at the docks, though I did make a few alterations along the narrative route, a few white lies to protect the innocent and wisely left out the submarine and gold. When I'd finished I waited for their reactions.

Big Nose didn't seem to be convinced. "I can't see McClusky making all that fuss for a piece of rusting wreckage and a few broken relics."

"Well that's all it was as far as I'm concerned."

"What did you intend to do with crap?"

"Sell it of course! People are willing to pay for unseen war memorabilia, even a war museum."

"Good grief!" Big Nose's voice exploded angrily. "Is that what it's all come to? We have succeeded in capturing a grieving metal detector enthusiast, hell bent on revenge whose single purpose in life is to make a dishonest profit." He looked me sternly in the face. "Honour and greed don't mix, I can assure you. As for lurking around McClusky's I think you fell lucky to drop into our hands rather than his or you'd probably be mixed up with animal feed and fed to the pigs."

Frigging hell I nearly burst out laughing. *Lucky,* after what they'd inflicted on my suffering body. Given the choice, I think I would have seriously chosen a bullet to the brain.

The girl edged forward in military fashion, stood straight almost to attention, hands behind her back, eyes forward, not looking directly at her commander. "May I speak, Sir?"

Strange as it might sound I did notice on a couple of occasions, when I came under attack from spotty face, that beneath her hard exterior I thought I glimpsed a softer side, a slight squirm when the dart penetrated my flesh. I did, of course, change my opinion when she smirked afterwards.

Big Nose urged her through.

"I have heard the name, Shackleton Speed before," she said. "This guy is headline news in Europe and America, regarded as renegade by treasure trove officialdom. Many historical artefacts that have illegally left British shores are down to him alone. There were two accusations I recall. One concerned a medallion reputedly lost by Oliver Cromwell while in battle, which turned up in an American museum. It didn't please the English heritage who regarded him as nothing but a criminal."

78

This woman had some memory, I admired. I said in my defence, "Speculative nonsense. Nothing was proven so less of the criminal."

She ignored me and went on. "And only last year, a jewel encrusted broach belonging to Mary Queen of Scots, which she apparently lost on a coach journey to London mysteriously turned up at New York jewellers. I've seen the jewel. A magnificent piece displayed in such grandeur. Again the blame linked to the name Shackleton Speed." She looked me accusingly in the eyes. "Do you deny that?"

"Categorically I do! I'm a man of honour. I would never sell a lady's jewels for money."

She went on. "Roman coins in abundance and Saxon gold bracelets. The list is endless. This guy is your modern day marauding archaeologist whose historical value on items he finds means nothing more than making money."

Big Nose said, "So you're nothing but a fucking thief and a useless commodity to us."

"Thanks," I said under my breath.

"It's apparent you were in the wrong place at the wrong time. That is unfortunate. It's a pity you couldn't tell us anything about McClusky."

As Big-nose turned to leave the room, I said sharply, "Surely you're not intending to keep me here, only I'm in need of medical attention. And I'm frigging hungry!"

Without warning the girl struck me twice across the face and rammed her knee into my groin with such power and precision it sent my balls splaying at different angles inside my pants.

"Speak when you're told to, Buster," and she meant it.

I tried to say something else. "I'm only-."

But she cut me off by ramming her clenched fist into my solar plexus with some considerable power for a female, leaving me gasping for breath. "Shut your fucking mouth up!"

Big-nose smiled thinly. "That's my girl," he said with satisfaction.

I guess Big-nose was in a pretty agitated mood as he left, something I defined by his continual slashing of the cane against his thigh. The others followed silently. The door shut and I was left alone in a state of discomfort, breathless and with throbbing sore muscles. I was also concerned about what was going to happen next.

That didn't mean I had given up any hope of escaping as I had made some solid observations. I knew the door wasn't locked and I worked out that only the top two treads of the stairway squeaked. My only real problem was freeing my clothing.

At least I had something to smile about when I heard Big-nose bawling at his troops, calling them incompetent imbeciles for capturing the wrong man. He finished by stating their entire escapade was a diabolical shambles and a disgrace to the regiment. I wondered what regiment he meant because I was unsure if terrorists did have regiments. I did suspect they were IRA but I quickly changed my mind because I was still alive.

Things went quiet downstairs. I heard a car door slam and an engine started and drifted away. The moment worried me.

Straining my ears listening, I finally heard light footsteps climbing the stairs and the girl entered. I had reserved feelings as she approached carrying a tray of food and drink. I didn't dare ask if it was the last meal for the condemned man in case she threw the contents straight into my face and punched the hell out of me again.

She said, "Do you want some food and coffee?" She obviously saw suspicion in my eyes because she added, "Don't worry there's no poison."

On a matter of principal I should have refused the offer, but the rumble of hunger had my stomach thinking my throat had been cut. To be truthful, I was that hungry I would have eaten a scabby donkey between two slices of mouldy bread, but I was quite content with the plate of greasy fried chicken.

I nodded my approval for the food and said, "How about a little freedom while I eat, it's uncomfortable in this position."

"Not permitted, Buster."

"I promise I won't run off."

Suddenly with gunslingers speed she had drawn a handgun from somewhere and bent my nose with the nozzle, all skilfully done without disturbing any of the contents on the tray, not even a spill of coffee. She said confidently, "How far do you think you would get?"

My Adam's apple rippled as I gulped and I was relieved when she replaced the gun into a holster strapped to the side of her leg and then she promptly rammed a chicken leg in my mouth. I took a bite and chewed. My jaw ached.

"I heard a vehicle drive away," I said, trying to avoid spitting food, "Has the big boss gone?"

She tapped my nose with the chicken bone. "You ask too many questions, Buster."

"I enjoy riveting conversation when I'm eating. Which terrorist group are you?"

She shook her head in disbelief. "Never give up, do you?"

I swallowed. "Are you a splinter group from the IRA?"

"Does it matter?"

"To me it does."

"Why?"

"I like to know which terror group intends to kill me so I can haunt them in hell."

She smiled. "Are you afraid of dying?'

I was thoughtful, but the answer came pretty quick. "I guess not."

"Extremely brave you are, Shackleton Speed."

"Not really. I work on the positive assumption that you never remember being born-so you never remember dying. You can't fear something you don't remember."

"Then it matters very little you knowing anything."

I made no attempt to decipher what she meant. I said, "Do your kind of terrorists eventually release their prisoners?"

Her eyes narrowed. "I dislike the term *terrorist*. Fighting for freedom from tyrannical rule is not terrorism."

"Whose eyes are you covering up?"

"Obstinate cretins like you who don't understand what we are trying to achieve."

I pulled a disapproving expression. "I've heard all this frigging bullshit before, fighting for a unified Ireland. Throw out the repressors and the frigging rest of the compulsive crap scraped together."

"Spare me the boring lecture."

"I'm a shit lecturer. I'm more confused by the necessity for so much destruction. Ireland is a beautiful place, including Northern Ireland. People like you fuck it up with your trumpet for freedom. And you all miss one important fact."

"What's that?" She sounded bored.

"Well, have you or any other of those self appointed gladiators ever considered asking the people of Ireland if it was what they wanted? I doubt very much. Why, because you are all nothing but a bunch of Irish gangsters using the excuse of a campaign against tyranny to gain power and supremacy by intimidation and brutality. What you have running about is a regime of self proclaimed degenerates pretending to fight the good fight and hiding behind democracy to prolong their greed to accumulate wealth. No. I'm afraid terrorism doesn't come into the equation, just greedy gangsters accumulating a mass of money."

I think I actually managed to prick her conscience because she didn't strike me with anything. But she was still verbally aggressive.

"You sound just like a politician!" and promptly rammed another chicken leg into my mouth forcing me to frantically chew or choke to death. "Have you finished criticizing?"

I tried to eat quickly and half swallowed.

She didn't wait for an answer. "We don't operate on that pretence." She said proudly.

I managed to gulp down a large proportion. "You blow up innocent people."

"Unfortunately, casualties of war are inevitable."

"How frigging reassuring is *that* to the families of those victims."

"Listen, Buster! Instead of blaming us, try blaming the cowards that run the British government."

My eyebrows arched. "I suppose that makes you sleep easy at night?"

"I don't have a problem sleeping."

"Well how nice for you," I said sarcastically. "But if it's attention you seek, why don't you try a different approach and chain yourselves to a steel fence, you might just convince the good people of Ireland that there is another alternative than murder."

"You think you know it all," she scowled.

"I know enough that true gladiators fight in the battlefield and not behind a remote controlled detonator far away from the destruction of a shopping centre full of women and children, without a soldier in sight."

"Then the quicker the politics are sorted within Ireland, the better!"

"I'm in total agreement. Yet there is one slight problem within a terrorist policy."

"Being?"

"Gangsters don't want an end to the proceedings. They don't want peace because their source of income would dramatically shrivel to nothing. No income means their comfortable lifestyle of luxury would diminish and the poor bastards would have to work for a living."

"You're not exactly high on God's list of achievers." She retorted angrily.

"At the back of the queue, I should imagine, but at least I would be in the queue if I wanted to be."

She paused into some serious thinking, snapped out of it, and rammed another piece of chicken in my mouth. She said, "You talk too much."

I managed to devour three pieces of chicken. The lukewarm coffee I hardly tasted because the aftertaste of chicken fat doesn't compliment coffee and to make matters worse some of the chicken fat had dribbled down my chin. No sooner had I bit the last piece of chicken from the bone she threw everything back on the tray and left the room without a word. With my mouth still full of meat I never got the chance to thank her. At least I could belch without any embarrassment.

Probably half an hour had passed when to my surprise she returned carrying a bowl of water and a towel over her arm. She no longer looked like the warrior I'd got use to. She was now wearing a black silk bathrobe that clung to her damp skin, but her combat boots hardly graced the occasion.

What I did notice when she got closer was the hostility had gone from her face, though I wondered if that was a bad thing or not. She was unpredictable as I'd already experienced, and there's nothing worst than an unpredictable woman.

"No doubt you'll appreciate a wash?" She said.

"Am I beginning to smell so bad?"

"Yeah, it might attract rats."

"It has already." I said sullenly. "Am I then to be sold into slavery?"

"Don't be so ridiculous, unless you think you're worth anything?"

"I like to think I am."

She stepped closer. She smelt sweet. Even without a lick of makeup on her face, she was pretty. She began gently washing and drying my face. For a girl who displayed such a brutish attitude toward me she had a soft touch when it came to playing nursemaid. I'd no complaint. This was far more rewarding than having, Spotty-face, pin my skin to the stanchion.

Yes, her hatred had definitely mellowed. Yet when she began to scrub me down I became suspicious as it actually swayed more towards seductiveness. I think I blushed, because my face flared. At first I thought she might be making a fool of me, deliberately teasing, but there was something about the way her fingers walked down the front of my torso and stopped at my crotch. Hell, this girl wasn't teasing, it was blatant foreplay and I wasn't in any position to do anything about it.

She nibbled my ear lobe and whispered. "Isn't this nicer?"

Hang on a minute, I thought. I recall this bitch was part of a consortium to hurt me badly and I had no intention of playing along.

I said, with a sudden hoarseness in my throat. "What's to become of me?"

"Wait and see." She said softly.

"I want to know now!"

"Be quiet, I hate interruptions when I'm busy."

And before I knew what was happening she had the front of my pants undone and the flannel was down inside my boxers. She kissed my face and lips as she carefully moved the flannel around my dick.

Well I wasn't having any of it!

Non-responsive I intended to be so I kept my lips rigid to the movement of hers but I still felt the warmth radiating from her. Hell, I wanted to respond and kiss those pouting luscious lips. I nearly did but my biggest problem was keeping my manhood limp.

To occupy my mind, I said, "Does this clean up mean I'm going to be released?"

"Hey, wake up dumb-ass! This is the captor's prerogative. To do what they want with their prisoner. There are no rules to abide. I want a fuck it's as simple as that."

"Why don't you go and pick on one of your studs downstairs."

"I'm picking on you! I fuck who I want to fuck. Beside, they have all gone."

Stupidly, I said, "I might not want to participate."

"You're not exactly in a position to argue."

"It's sexual harassment."

"So report me, Buster!"

"I'm going to play hard to get."

"Please do, I like a challenge."

The contest ended when she began caressing my dormant bulge. Despite my resistance I wanted her but on my own terms, not strapped to this stanchion like a side of beef. I had to defy her advances by thinking negatively. I thought of horrible things about her to distract from succumbing to her delicate advances. Clap, came to mind. She might have syphilis or large ulcerating scabs around her vagina? I sighed heavily. It was useless. She was too good for a feeble mind like mine. She knew how to handle a man and my resistance was dramatically failing.

She looked me in the eyes. "Fighting me are you?"

Then she went down on me and my fate was sealed. I'd lost the battle of wills because she discovered my ultimate weakness. It was probably every man's weakness and without doubt the oral sex finally mellowed my resistance. No man in this entire world can resist the warmth of a woman's mouth as she sucks and moves her warm lips up and down the shaft. My dick swelled hard in her mouth. She knew that the way to man's heart isn't through his stomach like most women suggest. She knew differently. She knew it was how a woman performed and she was exceptionally good.

She got to her feet, and said, "Now that didn't take long."

She untied her robe and let it fall open. I never got the chance to look her over properly as she put her arms over my shoulders and the stanchion and raised herself onto my erect manhood, slowly lowering herself, softly groaning in my ear as she clung on. I didn't have to do anything. I couldn't respond, though I wanted to. By her own strength she moved herself up and down rhythmically, squirming side to side, finding her love spots that threw her into spasms of ecstasy. Her groans became frantic jerky screams as she thrust her hips up and down, the speed increasing with ever hip movement until she suddenly squeezed tight into my body and bit my neck vampire style. I grimaced. I felt the hotness of her juices explode as her vaginal muscles squeezed against the girth of my erection. Then hard and furious she bounced her hips to reach the ultimate orgasm. I was extremely glad that her nails dug into the stanchion rather than my flesh as she held on, exhaling huge gasps of air with every spasmodic jerk of her body, before she gently slowed, panting, catching her breath and deeply satisfied. Then to my horror she got off. Hell, I hadn't finished! She frigging left me there unfulfilled, on the verge of eruption and put her robe back on. I was frantic with the frustration of not being finished off. I couldn't even thrust myself off. How could I while I was trapped.

"Are you frigging kidding?" I yelled.

She had a surprised look. "What's wrong?"

"*What's wrong?* Are you blind woman, a huge hard on, no end product. That's the problem!"

"On the contrary, Buster, you've just been had. Used is a better term. It's called womanpower, full control of the situation. How does it feel to be used and left dissatisfied? Fucking awful, I hope!"

"I should have filled your mouth with semen when I had the chance." I retorted defiantly.

"Naughty! And if you had have done, I'd have spat it back in your face."

By this time my erection had all but gone, hanging limply, defeated. She glanced down at my useless piece of dejection.

"Lost interest?" She said, as if it really mattered.

"What do you think?" I snapped.

"Suppose I should put it back into your pants, wouldn't want it to get cold."

After zipping me back up, to add insult to injury, she patted my dejected lump and said, "Better luck next time, Buster."

"There's going to be a next time?" I said.

"Depends?"

"Oh!"

"Depends on whether or not we decide to kill you."

She picked up the towel and bowl and left the room with a swing in her step, leaving me in a state of shock. Frigging hell! I was furious with myself for being weak-minded. Now I've been raped by a girl whose name I don't know and now she wants to kill me! But how might they dispose of me? A firing squad came to mind and since I was already trussed up and ready, then it wasn't fair. They could at least untie me and allow me to die with honour, maybe allow me to fight and die like a Viking, with a sword in my hand even if it was a wooden one.

It was then I heard a vehicle approaching the building, the crunching of tyres on a gravel driveway and I guessed I would soon find out.

CHAPTER NINE

I wasn't exactly grovelling when the big terrorist with pugilist features came at me brandishing a claw hammer and a huge commando knife because my heart was somewhere in my mouth. As the condemned man I considered I deserved at least a dignified death. A bullet to the head would be simple and painless. When he raised the hammer the natural progression was for me to shut my eyes and wait for the first fatal blow and the blade digging into my stomach.

Of all my expectations none of it happened. I dared open one eye to see the big guy pulling the nails from stanchion and what nails he failed to pull he simply hacked at my clothing with the knife until my aching body drooped with every disconnection. My weak legs failed to hold me. The big guy caught me easily, yanked me upright and literally carried me out of the room, down three flights of stairs and out into the pitch dark of night where he effortlessly threw me into the back of a large van. Just before the van doors slammed shut I caught a fleeting glimpse of the moon lit country house that held me prisoner. Then we drove away at speed.

Within the confines of the blacked-out van the American bitch and the two big guys were sat there in comfort while I rolled about the floor like a steel ball in a pinball machine. There seemed to be a frigging hurry to get somewhere.

We were approximately ten minutes into the trip when an array of armoury came magically from nowhere and a sequence of metallic clicking began. The way they handled their weapons in the dark strongly suggested that this wasn't their first venture. Military precision requires time and a meticulous training schedule. This sudden response of loaded weaponry clearly indicated they weren't intended for me, a simple silenced handgun would have concluded that matter. We were heading for a battle.

I guessed we had been travelling twenty-five minutes before we came to a stop. Someone in the front of the van got out. I heard the rattle of a heavy chain followed by a heavy clunk. The sound of grinding steel indicated a huge hinged gate opening. The person got back into the van and slowly we drove off. Within a minute we had stopped again and the engine was switched off. The American bitch (yes I was still angry with her) got out of the van and one of the big guys dragged me out with him. If I wanted to make a run for it I didn't stand a chance. My legs were still so weak I could hardly stand up straight. Frigging hell! I was in lousy shape. I ached all over. The dart wounds were aggravatingly sore, and I wanted to stand there until the strength came back into legs, but the sight of the handgun waving in my face prompted me to ignore my hurt and I reluctantly headed towards a familiar building. We were back at Mcklusky's warehouse.

The big Irishman frogmarched me to the rear of the building, distinctly using me as a shield from any surprised attacks. I didn't appreciate him using my shoulder as a rest for his machine pistol. He pushed me up a flight of steel stairs, along a short gantry and then held me back before we reached the door. There was no ceremonious knock on the door, pugilist features lifted his size twelve boot and effortlessly kicked the door open and before I knew what was happening, our entourage had burst through the doorway.

We were all stood in a large plush office threatening three startled men sat round a large oak desk. Or at least the others were doing the threatening because I was then shoved out of the way while Spotty-face dug his gun into my ribs.

A large man with thick, bushy grey hair and a fat beer gut, who I presumed was McClusky, stood sharply upright, knocking his chair back with the momentum. I considered him extremely brave to be making such dramatic movements with four sets of guns cocked and ready to fire. I thought he was extremely foolish when he began ranting and raving.

"Damn fools! Put those guns away!" He pointed an accusing finger at no one in particular. In fact it seemed to be directed at me. "Are you mad? We can't be seen together. It's too dangerous. You'll get us in trouble."

Big-nose retaliated. "The only one in trouble is you, McClusky. You were paid in advance. You failed to complete the transaction."

McClusky was sweating. "I had to change plans at the last minute."

Big-nose's blood pressure went up. "You put my men in danger. Two hours they waited for the merchandise and you couldn't be bothered to even inform us of a change of plan. You put us in the precarious position of being arrested by the Garda."

McClusky gestured with his hands. "Calm down, calm down, the goods are complete and in a safe haven."

Big-nose sneered. "Don't worry, beer breath, I am calm or else this office and you along with it would have been disintegrated without any need for explanation. Why the hold on delivery?" he demanded strongly.

"I received orders from the Master General. There's been a major –."

Big-nose interrupted McClusky and ripped into him like an angry wasp. "I don't follow such orders! If you thinking of double crossing me, think again. Or maybe your Master General would like to hear of your secret arms deals behind the organizations back."

McClusky's hands went into a prose of pleading. "I assure you its safe. I can't take the chance of moving any of the merchandise until the all clear has been given."

"Your problems are not my problems. You had the money up front, as we agreed. Now I've no weapons and no money. I want my money back so I can take my business elsewhere."

McClusky went white. His eyes widened. "I-I don't keep that much on the premises."

Big-nose gritted his teeth. "It's fucking bullshit!"

"It's the truth!"

"You're a crook, and all crooks have plenty of money stashed away for a rainy day. And it's pissing down outside."

No one looked to see if it was raining outside.

"I'll get it for you tomorrow. I promise!"

Big-nose shook his head. "Tomorrow is too late."

"I'll get it as soon as the bank opens."

Big-nose raised his automatic and aimed it at McClusky's head. "You're a double crossing piece of Irish shit. Let's try again, two hundred thousand pounds, on the table, now!"

McClusky's hands shot up in defeat. He gulped hard. "Okay! Okay! Calm down. The safe is downstairs, in the warehouse."

"Lead the way McClusky," Big-nose ordered, "along with your merry men. No tricks or I'll splatter your brains all over the walls."

We went out of the internal door and down a flight of stairs.

Nervous eyes watched each other. We all followed McClusky as he angled across the dusty warehouse floor. He stopped beside a broken fridge and from inside the freezer department produced a bulk of money. I noticed his hand shaking as he gave the wad to Big-nose who in turn snatched the money from his grasp and then rammed his gun into McClusky's grovelling face.

Big-nose was spitting as he talked. "You don't value your fucking life do you McClusky?"

"I-I said I don't keep that kind of money on the premises. There's two grand, that's all. Take it as collateral. I'll get the rest tomorrow, I promise."

Big-nose was frustrated beyond frustration as he tossed the wad over to Spotty-face. It was then McClusky looked suspiciously at me, if anything he used me as a distraction from his imminent death.

"Who's the rag merchant you've got there?" He asked carefully.

A mysterious hand shoved me to the front.

Big-nose said, "Ah-yes, an associate of yours."

Still confused, McClusky said, "Associate?"

"Actually, he's more of a vigilante. He wants to know why you had his friends killed."

McClusky frowned as he tried to think who I was. "I've never seen this man before."

I could no longer keep my silence. "No but your murdering heavies have. You ordered them to kill an old farmer and a photographer for no reason at all, you frigging bastard!"

Big-nose laughed. "It seems everybody knows what you're like, hey McClusky?"

McClusky's face slowly expanded into shock. His eyes widened as he realized who I was. "He is the metal detector man. How come you have him?"

Big-nose beamed with confidence. "We simply whisked him away from under your pathetic nose."

"I want him!" McClusky flustered. "You must hand him over!" McClusky had amazingly found some courage.

"You're in no position to demand anything," Big-nose snarled. "Why is he so special?"

Fear returned to McClusky's face. "I-I'm not certain. I just know he is."

"Okay, McClusky. I'll give you the chance to sort out the mess you've created. The money or merchandise by tomorrow and I might forget you tried to double-cross me, and I'll hand over, Mister Special here, as a bonus."

"I've already explained, I can't move the merchandise, I'm under strict orders to delay transactions."

Veins popped from Big-nose's forehead. "You're not listening, McClusky."

McClusky pointed at me. "I can't do anything because of *him!*"

Big-nose gazed at me, a cunning smirk on his face. "Why are you so special?"

I shrugged. "I guess I'm just a popular guy."

To McClusky, Big Nose said, "Who's so desperate for the metal man?"

"Does it matter who?"

"Of course it matters you fucking imbecile! I'm down by a cache of weapons, and you still have my money. Just maybe, your employer might satisfy our demands in a more professional manner rather than the amateurish spectacle of your feeble attempt."

"I just need more time," McClusky pleaded.

"I haven't got time. I've been forced to come to London when you should have arrived at the appointed rendezvous. The blame is entirely with you, McClusky, no one else."

While they were squabbling, a moving shadow caught my eye. My heart missed a beat. I instantly knew that this get together wasn't going to be resolved in an orderly manner when I saw Damien Love and Theodore Hate and three other machine-pistol packing thugs easing their way down the stairway from the office we'd vacated and General-bodge-up-Big Nose had failed to cover his arse.

I had only seconds to react yet I was in two minds what to do. But as the menacing assailants positioned themselves behind wooden crates in readiness to open fire, I'd no hesitation when I screamed out a warning.

"Look out! Machine guns," I shouted while scurrying for a place to hide.

Then all hell let loose. Indiscriminate firing came from all directions. Bodies dived for cover including me as I found temporary sanctuary behind a pile of dusty sacking before scrambling for the metallic security of a bag-stitching machine. As I spat dust from my mouth I decided there and then that the first chance I got to run there would be no hesitation: women and children first and me at the front. The only problem with my plan was finding the right moment to move and in what direction.

As the bullets flew I huddled tighter with my hands covering my ears and trying to focus on the mayhem. I saw bodies fall, riddled with red spots, but which side they belonged I couldn't tell. I began drastically looking for a way out.

Then stupidly I took a risky glance around my shield to assess the situation and suddenly a screaming attacker hurtled towards me shooting at everything that protected me. Splintered fragments of wood struck me in the face. Bullets ricocheted off the metal stitching machine and all I could do was cower behind the sacking pile in hope someone would hit him before he reached me.

Instead a handgun slithered across the floor hitting my legs and before I realized the consequences of what I was doing I had the gun in my hand and I was randomly shooting at the oncoming assailant.

I knew the bullets had hit him because his upper body jerked back a couple of times and he dropped to his knees before keeling over into a slow spin and lay there spread-eagled just in front of a sack bale, his eyes wide and motionless. I was horrified as I looked down at my first kill. Then I realized my gun hand was shaking.

I quickly ducked behind the sacking for protection, trying to steady my nerves. That was when the deafening explosion shook the building, scattering debris everywhere. I was covered in wood fragments and dust. Whatever was inside one of the wooden crates, it had exploded. Through the cloud of dust and choking smoke I suddenly became aware of street lighting beaming into the building from where the explosion occurred. I saw the gaping hole in the wall where a door had been.

There was no hesitation as I made my escape. I'm not sure how fast I was travelling when the line of bullets peppered after me as I made the mad dash for freedom, but I survived with no injuries. Into the night air I ran. I kept running towards the main gate as two security men trotted hesitantly in my direction. Surprised expressions as I shot pass them.

I suppose to any passer-by I must have appeared as if I'd taken the brunt of the explosion judging by my tattered clothing flapping in the breeze. But I was far more concerned with running like a frightened rabbit and as I ran it suddenly occurred to me the possibility that I could stand trial for murdering a man even though he had tried to kill me. And to make matters worse I still had the gun gripped hard in my hand and in a panic I wondered if the security guards saw it. The thought only increased my anxiety and made me run faster and I didn't stop running until I'd reached the Roadster. Then I had to get rid of the weapon but I couldn't just throw it in a river or even bury it because it had my fingerprints on it and in the all the right places. I quickly slipped it into a pocket that hadn't been ripped.

Frantically I searched my rags for the car keys before remembering the terrorists had pillaged all my possessions. I flexed my foot, felt the metallic movement of a spare key at the bottom of my sock, which I hastily retrieved. No one had tampered with the car and I was glad of the growling power of the Roadster as it pulled away from the kerb.

CHAPTER TEN

I definitely remembered turning off all the lights before leaving home that night. They were on now. I collected the house keys from the glove compartment and tip-toed to the door and quietly slipped the key into the Yale-lock, eased the door open and crept inside, stopped and listened. I could hear faint crunching noises. I moved along the hallway again on tip-toe. I only got halfway down when Winston started barking, the echo coming from the lounge. I knew I was safe.

I was only mildly surprised to find Hamer sprawled across my leather sofa feeding my guard dog with crunchy dog biscuits. I made my feelings known.

"D.I. Hamer you're trespassing-," I began, but was promptly put out of my stride when he burst out laughing

When he finally sustained a straight face, he said with a splutter, "Did someone drag you through a hawthorn hedge a couple of times?"

I did look a sight, but I wasn't to be distracted.

He went on, "What happened?"

"Never mind what happen to me!" I said angrily. "Breaking into my home is a criminal offence. Or have you perhaps a piece of legitimate court paper allowing you the privilege to help yourself to my goodies?"

"I didn't break in, if that's what you're thinking. If you examine your property, you'll observe there is no sign of a forced entry."

The smug bastard, I thought.

"Well I'm sure the dog didn't let you in! You got in somehow?"

"It's a particular skill of mine." I didn't like his conceited attitude, and he infuriated me even more when he carried on bragging. "I could quite easily break into the Queens bedroom, kiss her on the

94

cheeks of her arse and get back home without any disturbance."

"So you're an expert sneak, congratulations. And I see you've got Winston eating out your hand, too. Is that another specialist job, stealing guard dogs?"

Hamer patted the dogs head. "Once he remembered me from the other night he gave me no problem. He certainly has a fondness of doggie biscuits. Did you know a dog won't bite the hand that feeds it?"

As if I cared but I glared at Winston and told the mutt what I thought, "Traitor!" The dog understood what I meant as he whined and hung his head in shame.

"If it makes you feel ant better, Speed, I did actually knock on the door first. The dog started barking, you never answered. With two killers on the loose, I panicked, thought maybe they'd returned. You may have been hurt. Hell, Speed! I was only doing my job. I swear."

"It is still trespassing,"

Hamer pulled a sour face. "You're such an ungrateful fucker, aren't you?"

"Yes. But only to people who specialize in burglary."

"I didn't think I was doing any harm, so I'd appreciate it if you drop the Mister angry face. I can see you've had a rough ride-."

"A rough ride-," I burst in and almost broke into a laugh. "-are you kidding? I've only been shot at: physically abused: mentally tortured: been used as a pin cushion: shagged: ridiculed: kicked: thumped, and not necessarily in that order. Then I come home to find you enjoying the comforts of my graft and drinking my cans of hard earned beer. Yes, you might assume I'm in an angry mood. But please don't concern yourself on my behalf."

I took a beer can from the coffee table. "Don't mind if I help myself!?" Pulled the ring pull and swallowed a mouthful of beer. It was slightly warm. It told me he had been here for a while.

Hamer suddenly sat upright. "You went to McClusky's warehouse!"

I wiped the back of my hand across my lips. "Prove it!"

"No wonder you're in such a state."

"Then if that's what you think, I suggest you get down to McClusky's with some proper policemen and arrest him and his two goons, Love and Hate."

Hamer looked shocked. "They were there?"

"Damn frigging right *they* were!"

"Well there's no rush now. The police are already swarming all over the warehouse. No doubt you already know?"

"Know about what?"

"McClusky is dead."

"I didn't know."

"His warehouse was blown up. Police suspect gang warfare among the Irish contingency."

"Were there any other casualties?" I asked carefully.

"I heard there were two fatalities and three taken to hospital with serious injuries."

"Any names mentioned?"

"If you're thinking like I am, you hope Love and Hate are the two fatalities."

They were the last two that crossed my mind.

"Can I associate the carnage as your responsibility?"

"No. And don't even try. I've had enough excitement today." I cocked a suspicious glance at Hamer. "Incredible isn't it how news travels fast. How come you know already?"

"The power of radio news bulletins, that's how, Speed. We no longer use the spirit of the 'Pony-express'. Radio waves travel much faster."

"Rather puts a different complexion on the matter," I said.

I sank the remainder of my beer while I thought, crushed the can and tossed it into a waste bin near the fireplace. My line of enquiry rather expired when McClusky died.

"So are you going to tell me what happened when you got to the warehouse?" Hamer had a serious expression.

"Is this the detective side asking?"

"Of course, it is part of my job."

"Well you're wasting your time. Which directs me nicely to ask, what the frigging hell do you want?"

"There are two issues I want to take up with you."

"You only have two?"

Hamer ignored my interruption. "First. I found no documentation regarding, 'operation huggermugger'. Something you made up?"

"No. You did check the mission was conducted from Duxford air-field?"

"Damn fucking right I checked. I double-checked and nothing even remotely relates to 'huggermugger'."

"There's always the possibility it went under a different name."

Hamer smiled thinly, "Are you aware that within the archives of Whitehall, there are millions of documentation I could spend a lifetime searching."

"Give in too easily, Hamer."

"Okay clever arse. Tell me what you know about 'huggermugger'?"

"If I knew the answer, would I be asking?"

Hamer's face reddened. "You're so fucking awkward, Speed! Why do I get the feeling you're holding back on me."

I smiled. "And the other matter?"

"Ah-well now, Speed. This is the real laughable bit. My superior wants to meet the indelible, super sleuth, Shackleton Speed, with the assumption he can personally convince you to work alongside us. Really pathetic, don't you agree?"

I stopped him right there. "I've no intention of entering any government building to be interrogated, whether it is done over a cup of tea, or by cruelty."

"Scared we might not let you out?"

"It's a phobia I have."

"Well don't fret, Speed. We can find a suitable place, so the hairs on the back of you neck don't stand up."

"Who is this superior of yours?"

"His name is Morgan. Commander Harris Morgan. He's okay, a little bit of a pompous git but he will be our chief negotiator if we require the assistance of the Metropolitan Police. He knows enough principles to pull the right strings."

"He sounds as if he is a chap you can depend on."

"Can I relay back your acceptance or not?"

"It really depends on what he wants to talk about?"

Again Hamer's face maddened. "Don't play the innocent with me, Speed. It concerns the plane. It concerns Love and Hate. It concerns you!"

"I've already explained. The plane wreck has nothing to do with me."

Hamer was getting agitated. "Are you not a little intrigued to hear what he has to say?"

I thought about it for a moment. I had nothing to lose by accepting other than time. Perhaps he might relay information that would be useful to me. I would, of course, be defying my strict rules of non-engagement with authority. Yet I had to think positively. The more back-up I had, the better my chances of staying alive.

I nodded in agreement and said, "Why not."

Hamer jerked back in shock. "Fucking hell, are you feeling alright? You actually accepted something!"

"I accepted breakfast from you."

"That was different. I was paying."

"Well, as long as it doesn't cost me anything to meet Commander Harris, then I'll listen."

I turned to leave the room. Over my shoulder, I said, "On your way out, Hamer, shut the door properly. I don't want another burglar or vagabond thinking my home is an open invitation."

I headed for the stairway. I wanted a shower and some rest and the need to be alone, so I could think clearly. My head was fuzzy and confused. I had a lot of questions that I couldn't put answers to.

I heard the front door close and got into the spray of the shower. I shut my eyes as the water powered against my face. I instinctively thought of the girl. I pictured her face. I didn't recall seeing her again once the mayhem started. I wondered if she got out alive. Strange, I rather hoped the bitch did escape.

CHAPTER ELEVEN

The dramatic news coming from the car radio talked of an explosive battle between Irish gangs at London docks. Blah-blah-blah, it went on. None of the story resembled anything I was involved in. I blamed the mix-up on the conflictive statements given by the two dock security guards, who strangely, had seen a lot considering their sleepy confinement inside the security hut. There was one part of their story they did get right. They witnessed an armed scarecrow running away from the premises.

On route to the meeting with Hamer, I made a detour and stopped at the Imperial College where I left a large brown envelope at the reception for the immediate attention of Professor Cyril Squires, before continuing my journey to Hyde Park and the Italian Gardens.

I found Hamer in deep discussion with a tall, lean chap with flaming red hair, wearing a dark grey suit and chomping on a Cuban cigar as he talked. They ceased talking when they saw me. I must admit I was a little tense as I approached them, but by the time I'd reached their position I was rock solid and ready for anything.

The stranger's hand reached out to shake mine and with the cigar clamped between his teeth, he said: "Commander Harris Morgan," he said sharply and precise. "I appreciate your attendance at short notice, Mister Speed."

"Hello Commander," I said.

Commander Harris Morgan had a vice like grip, deliberately imposed to show I wasn't dealing with a powder puff desk clerk but a man whose strengths had powered him to the position he held. I could only admire him for that. He was probably in his middle fifties and on closer inspection his suit was immaculately tailored and expensive as was his leather shoes.

Morgan removed the cigar from his mouth and twirled it through his fingers. "You have an extraordinary occupation in metal detecting, I believe?"

"Hardly extraordinary," I said.

"I should imagine it's not exactly a riveting enjoyment shared by many."

"The fewer the better," I said.

"Oh! Why is that, Mister Speed?"

"Then there's more for me to find."

Morgan smiled. "Naturally there is, and being an outdoor man, how do you find these surroundings for our meeting, suffice I hope?"

I looked around pretending to be interested. "Relaxing providing no one suffers from agoraphobia."

"Good gracious! It's a good thing you don't Mister Speed, it would certainly prove a stumbling block on your outdoor pursuits."

Then Morgan changed his tune and his eyes probed deep into mine. He certainly possessed the skill to make a person suddenly feel uncomfortable. He said, "No disrespect, Mister Speed, but D. I. Hamer informs me that we're actually dealing with nothing more than a crook, who despises paying his taxes amongst other eventful cases of improbity. You just don't look that type."

I gave Hamer one of my searing glares that made the two-faced coward redden. I calmly said, "We are all entitled to our opinions."

Morgan clamped the cigar in the corner of his mouth. It distorted his speech. "Quite right too, Mister Speed. As a matter of fact we all despise paying our taxes. I admire your stand against fattening the coffers of the treasury. I despise their continued misuse of funds. They're worst than crooks, I'd say."

I stopped him right there. I still felt as if he was having a go at me.

"Let's get one thing straight. I'm not a crook!"

Morgan quickly removed the cigar from his mouth and blew out a cloud of cigar smoke. "Of course you're nothing of the kind, Mister Speed, crooks are sent to prison."

I didn't care for the way he said that, either.

Morgan pressed on. "Regardless of your alleged reputation, Mister Speed, I feel confident I can trust you will not divulge to anyone what I am about to relay to you." He paused. (I think he was waiting for my reassurance to stay quiet, but I didn't give it.) "Let me explain," he took in breath. "Within the walls and corridors of Whitehall a serious situation has developed. Certain items have gone missing.

Correspondents regarding war operations at Duxford airfield during 1944 have disappeared. Not a scratch can we find. Initial enquires has produced a blank. Naturally, we would prefer the reason for the paperwork's disappearance to be misplacement rather than deliberate. But we intend to discover the truth. And we will!

"Then there is the other problem of the two murderous cretins, Damien Love and Theodore Hate, who have mysteriously surfaced in London posing as ministry men. And even more baffling, their interest in a crash plane, and their connection with an entrepreneur by the name of McClusky, who we know little about. Now it has become apparent McClusky has been killed after a bloody battle at his headquarters. We hold little explanation on all these concerns."

"You're going to be busy for a while," I said.

Hamer chirped in. "Is that suppose to be funny, Speed?"

I stared Hamer hard in the eyes. "The truth isn't hilarious." I looked back at Morgan. "But I'm the wrong person to be asking for help. Why don't you liaise with the police involved in the McClusky affair, they might offer some answers."

"I'm afraid it doesn't work that way, Mister Speed."

"I can't see why not."

"No, no, Mister Speed. Our first duty is to conduct all ministry investigations before liaising with other forces. We simply cannot have outside intervention on internal affairs no matter how difficult the task ahead. Yet that doesn't mean we can't involve a neutral outsider."

"Meaning yours truly, me?"

"Precisely what I mean, Mister Speed. Now, with regards to your situation, there has to be a good reason why Love and Hate paid particular attention to *you!*"

"I was under the impression they wanted to kill me!"

"Yes, yes! I'm well aware of what they intended." Morgan was getting agitated. He threw his cigar butt into the Serpentine. It hissed loudly as it hit the water. "They are cold-blooded assassins who follow orders. But why did McClusky want you dead?"

I shrugged my shoulders. "I've no idea. I would have asked him but now he's dead too which only complicates things"

"Well! I have some more disappointing news. I made a few discreet enquires regarding the incident at McClusky's warehouse. Love and Hate were not among the dead or injured. They are on the move somewhere."

"They are probably running back to their rat hole, now their pay-master has perished," I said confidently.

"Ah! Mister Speed. That is were our ideas differ. I don't think they were hired by McClusky, more the reverse, I think they were controlling him. If McClusky wanted to be nasty, I'm sure he would have hired a number of Irish thugs to do his dirty work for him. No! I'm sure Love and Hate are still in employment and are now doubly dangerous. I think they still want you for some despicable reason."

"I certainly attract the wrong people."

"It does seem that way, Mister Speed. Have you not wondered why you have been targeted?"

"Not really. As far as I'm concerned they're just a pair of aggravating bastards victimizing the wrong man. They made a mistake."

"I thought you mentioned to D.I. Hamer that you think they killed your friends?"

"It's what I believe."

"And you stick by that?"

"I've seen nothing nor heard anything to suggest any different."

"Then I can't imagine them making any mistake in coming after you, Mister Speed."

I shrugged.

"What exactly did they want?"

I wondered how long it would take him to implement my involvement in the entire affair. I calmly said, "Has Detective Hamer not filled you in with the details? I was accused of tampering with the wreck at Berkshire at least that was the excuse they used when they came knocking on my door."

"Oh yes! Which you categorically denied having any involvement?"

"Yes!" My tone was hard and precise.

"Obviously your denial was insufficient to convince them otherwise. Now what I would like know is what has intrigued them to pursue a treacherous campaign over a pile of junk and a dead pilot? And why can I no longer find the documentation concerning that particular crash site? And even more terrifying, where the hell has Love and Hate gone?"

"As I said before, you're going to be busy, Commander Morgan."

"Not just busy. Our investigation takes on a different variation than normal. Since nothing can be verified and I strongly suspect an insider in Whitehall is deviously covering-up, D.I. Hamer and I will be conducting an unauthorized investigation. Rather secretive-hush-hush probe."

"Secretive?" I said. "Can you do that without attracting attention to yourselves?"

"We damn well have to, Mister Speed! There is something sinister going on. I'm afraid it's 'ears to the wall' and 'nose to the ground' for us until we can establish the truth and expose the culprit operating inside our department. We are taking is a big risk and our careers and very large pensions will be on the firing line if we balls it up."

"Highly commendable," I said disinterestedly.

"Now you know our plans. In the meantime we have to find Love and Hate before they cause us any more problems, and hopefully they will lead us to their employer."

"Well, when you eventually find them, you have my permission to throw them in the Tower of London and squeeze the truth out of them in any way you redeem to be acceptable."

"Something I would enjoy immensely, Mister Speed, only we are British. We have morals to maintain. We're not a third rate country so we can't simply snatch them from the street and throw them in prison before a question is asked. We have to stick to European guidelines. Hard proof is required for the D.P.P. to even sniff at the case. An incident that happened ten years ago in Cyprus doesn't warrant an instant arrest on two men who have no criminal convictions. No warrants for their arrest. No jack-shit!"

"They attacked me. Get them arrested on those grounds."

"That would be a suitable solution but there is one rather large block. I see little evidence on your person of any kind of assault, and from what D. I. Hamer told me, it was the viciousness of yourself and dog that were the aggressors and victors. A top barrister would have a field day with us."

"Got your work cut out then," I said.

"Not if you are willing to assist us. With your valuable help we can penetrate the problem. Naturally, what you decide to divulge to us will be treated with the strictest of confidentiality. The discovery of the Spitfire hides a story, Mister Speed. It has resulted in some very serious events and I feel you can help us uncover that story."

I sighed. "I seem to be having a lot of trouble convincing people I know nothing of the crashed plane other than what I've read in the papers or been told."

"You will be well rewarded, Mister Speed."

"Oh!"

"Further more, any involvement you may have had concerning the matter, you will have my guarantee to be free from any form of prosecution, in writing of course, in return for adequate information. We can't have ruthless villains posing as M.o.D. officials and causing havoc. Unfortunately we lack the valuable information to make those appropriate apprehensions."

"So there's not much hope."

"There is always hope, Mister Speed. Now it has come to my attention that there are certain aspects of your life that had involved you in a slop-pot of deceit. I suspect you know a lot more than you're willing to tell. Basically, Mister Speed, I want you to work with us, not against us. We get the right convictions and you will be adequately paid for your efforts. That means money in your bank account and no questions asked. Does that sound tempting?"

I smiled. "Sounds more like a frigging bribe."

Morgan's forehead deeply lined. "I do not bribe people. As I readily explained, you work for us, we pay. Do we have a deal?"

"I'm not certain I have anything of value to offer you, Commander."

"It all began somewhere, Mister Speed. Start by explaining the reason why so many infuriating criminals are interested in a metal detector enthusiast who has gained a renowned notoriety for selling antiquities on the black markets of Europe."

I shrugged. "Might have tread on a few disapproving toes."

"Have you something they want?"

"I've already told you, it's my life they want."

"Yes we know that, Mister Speed. Perhaps you have something that belongs to them?"

"No!" I said decisively. "But I know what they deserve, a right hook and a kick in the crutch."

I noticed that Morgan was beginning to get frustrated. "I suspect years of elusiveness from the law has somewhat dampened your enthusiasm to cooperate. Nevertheless, we still require your help to round up these monsters."

"I don't really want to get involved," I said strongly.

Morgan's face muscled tightened. "Whichever way you look at it, Mister Speed, you are involved, whether you want to be or not."

"And if I choose not to help, what then?" I thought I'd better ask the question.

Morgan smiled falsely. "I'm sure it won't come to that."

"You sound confident?" I asked warily.

"We have methods of persuasion."

"Torture chamber, you mean?"

"That's the primitive alternative, Mister Speed. What I was actually getting at borders more on the victimization side of life. To put it bluntly, help us and we won't consider putting you on trial for vandalizing a war grave and stealing the pilot's personal equipment."

"You'll never make it stick, Commander," I said calmly.

Morgan attempted to brush-off his bullying tactics. "It's pitiful, I know. But we are desperate, Mister Speed, and additions can be arranged to strengthen our case against you. Not that we would wish to."

"And you're supposed to be the goodies," I scoffed.

"I would think very carefully what is on offer as we can make your life very difficult, Mister Speed."

I didn't doubt Morgan's threats nor was I surprised by them. And normally I don't surrender to threats. Yet I have to be honest with myself, and if I am to progress further I was certainly going to require help and who better than the government themselves.

So I told them straight. "If you want to use me as bait, I want written immunity from prosecution first, information of what I know after."

"That can be immediately arranged," Morgan announced, and began reaching into his pocket for a pen. I stopped him there.

"It has to be presented on official government paper, signed, stamped, and sealed, so I can arrange for my solicitor to hold it in storage just in case, or there's no deal."

Morgan's face tightened. "That's damned impertinent, Speed!"

"No, Commander! That's damned sensible on my part."

"This is preposterous! I'm honourable enough to offer you immunity from spending time in prison, and you fail to take me on my word. Good gracious, you philistine! What do you take me for? Do you realise it entails a trip back to my office! Time is of the essence. We need to press on. We can't allow two murderous villains to abscond a second time"

I stood my ground. "Without official documentation there is nothing. If I'm to get involved in something dubious I want to be in a position where I come out unscathed." I shuffled my feet in readiness to leave. "It's up to you."

I could tell by the frowns on their face's they detested my cockiness. I rather enjoyed watching Morgan bite his bottom lip as he relented.

"Very well Mister Speed. I shall deal with the matter the moment I return to my office. Where can we contact you?"

"D.I. Hamer knows," I said.

As Morgan turned and began walking away in a huff I cheekily asked Hamer if he could locate the whereabouts of Sir Dillon Deveron for me. I did rather expect a volley of questions as to why, or even a tantrum of retaliation, especially as I hadn't exactly been cooperative myself, only he took me completely by surprise and nodded agreeably. I could only assume he was under strict orders to fulfil any demands I made in order to get me to cooperate. I actually found that amusing. Yet I had no doubt the questions would come later, as in my opinion he was too much of a nosey bastard not to.

CHAPTER TWELVE

I returned to the Imperial College in search of Professor Cyril Squires. I found him where I expected him to be at three o'clock in the afternoon sat in his office because that's when he finishes his tutorial sessions and has his lunch. I knocked on his door out of respect and waited for him to answer. His slow, articulated voice said, "Enter."

As I went in he was at his desk seated in his favourite well-worn green leather executive type chair with a napkin on his lap catching the minute crumbs falling as he ate a triangular cut wholemeal sandwich. His bulging round eyes watched my every step as I approached him.

He had grey, wiry hair, kept in place with a wet comb, and his high brow gave his face the appearance of being long. He was sixty years old but to his credit his clean and healthy complexion made him look younger. His long, thin forefinger directed me to the chair opposite him. I made myself comfortable.

He swallowed what he was chewing and said, "Nice to see you again, Shacks. Been keeping away from trouble?"

"I've built a steel wall around myself," I reassured him.

"That's not what I've heard!"

I ignored his remark and pressed on. "Did you get chance to look at the photographs I left."

Professor Squires expressed alarm. "Are you in a hurry, Shacks?

"Well, yes. I don't want to be caught in the rush-hour traffic." I lied. The traffic has never bothered me.

He sighed and shook his head as he carefully laid his napkin on the desk, stood, and went over to the filing cabinet in the corner. As I watched him plod across there was one thing that struck me about old Squires, his inability to be a classy dresser, which was more noticeable as he walked because his dark brown trouser bottoms had lifted ankle height due to the tightness of his braces. He wore a matching brown checked tweed jacket with leather patches sewn on the elbows which certainly didn't compliment the green shirt underneath. He returned with the envelope I had left earlier.

He re-seated, pulled his chair closer to the desk and spread the contents of the envelope onto the desk. "Hmm," he muttered, then put on a pair of square rimmed spectacles and selected one of the reconnaissance photographs.

Besides being an excellent tutor in metallurgy, he knew everything about rock formations that a person could know, and despite it being the most menial of subjects that a person could sit and read about, the rock formations is precisely what I wanted know about.

He sipped in a mouthful of water, flushed the fluid around his mouth, this he does regularly to dislodge food particles in his mouth, and swallowed. When he spoke his eyes appeared to quiver. It was something I had never noticed before. "Well, Shacks, looking at these oldies you do have high expectations of my ability to establish answers from incredibly disorientated water marked photographs."

His negativity disappointed me.

Professor Squires scratched his brow and glanced up to view my expression before continuing. "It's a good job I'm not a quitter, and it'll take a lot more than crap photography to dampen my enthusiasm. Are they something you found or stole? Or should I not be asking?"

"Both and don't ask," I said.

He didn't flinch because he knew me well.

With sharp indrawn breath, he went on: "These are interesting rock formations, but as I stated the quality of the pictures does rather hinder the process of their true locations. Yet challenges I thrive on, and I detest defeatism."

I said, "I do know it's a part of the West side of the British Isle, if that helps any."

The Professor's eyes lit-up. "Ah! So you have learnt something worthwhile?"

"No. Information received pointed me in that general direction, I just took the persons word for granted."

Professor Squires was not amused. He said solemnly, "Shackleton Speed, (he always called me by my full name when he was annoyed), you greatly disappoint. If you had taken the time to attend my lectures with a bit more regularity and commitment to learn, you might have achieved the ability to be in the same position as I am. It pays handsomely well, and you don't have to get your hands dirty."

"I like to get my hands dirty." I said seriously.

"Less of your arrogance, and pay attention to someone who knows what he is doing. Oh! Before I forget, you still owe me a liquid lunch for verifying to the police that you attended one of my lectures when I know damn well you were in Berlin attending-what was the excuse you gave me-ah yes-a seminar in structural engineering. Utter bollocks! More like a slice of the black market caper. You're damned lucky I'm on your side or else you would have had a lot of explaining to do."

"I did thank you for it," I corrected him.

"Verbally is insufficient! You can thank me by taking some weight off your fat wallet and buy me a ticket to the opera instead. Now let's return to the necessities."

Professor Squires meticulously packed away the remnants of his lunch into a briefcase and resumed his study of the photographs. He coughed to clear his throat then began his speech as if he was lecturing a class.

"The sweeping angle of the waves hitting the coast is most definitely a western one, as you rightly suggested," he said while looking at me.

He picked up a magnifying glass and repetitively re-scanned the four pictures with equal amounts of time. His studious silence had me drumming my fingers on my thigh with no rhythmical pattern as I grew impatience.

Finally he said, "These rocks don't relate to any United Kingdom shorelines, that I'm certain. No. I'd be more prone to suggest that the distinct contours of the rocky shorelines actually directs to the South coast of Ireland."

"That's still a fair amount of coastline," I said disappointedly.

The Professors head lifted alarmingly. "You have the patience of a Wildebeest spooked by a stalking Lion, Shackleton Speed!" Then he was down to business once more studying the photographs.

Without looking he drew closer to himself a large map of what I assumed to be of Ireland. He began flitting from the photographs to the map as if he was participating in a game of bobbing for apples.

I had to wait a further two minutes before I saw the smile of contentment on the Professors face. Then he infuriated me by flitting through for a second opinion, map-picture-map before he lay back in his chair and clasped his hands behind his head in a gentle stretch.

"Well?" I probed anxiously.

"Without doubt the South coast of Ireland. And in a straight line I estimate a fifty miles stretch of coastline between Cahirciveen and Skibbereen. I'd like to speculate more but without actually attending the area, and considering the amount of water damage on the photographs, it's the best I can do, Shacks."

I smiled. "You've done more than enough, Professor. Thanks."

"My pleasure, Shacks, though I don't issue freebies, so I'll add the consultancy fee to the drinks bill when you decide to honour your debt. Now be off with you! I'm very busy and whatever you're looking for, good hunting!"

I took back the photographs and went home. I poured myself a beer, dug out a map of Ireland, and began scrutinizing the South coast. The professor's estimation of a fifty miles section was filled with bays, crevices, inlets, and rivers, which would take a multitude of time to explore, but I intended to finish what I started until I could make sense of everything that had happened to me.

I threw some belongings into a small travel suitcase, shaved, showered and dressed into suitable driving clothes. I fed Winston with a hearty meal of diced best steak mixed with biscuit cereal and while I watched in amazement as his slobbering jaws devoured the contents, the telephone rang. It was Professor Squires.

"Glad I caught you before you left."

"Who said I was going anywhere?"

"Just say, I'm a good guesser and I know you too well. Now, pay attention! Forget my previous prediction on the location of the rock formations. I've narrowed the distance between Kilcrohane and Baltimore. If you require a more sporting chance, my money puts the rocks around Roaring-water Bay. Don't forget to send me a postcard!"

Reluctantly I decided to leave Winston at the home of an acquaintance of mine, a nice girl called Judy, while I was away. Okay the mutt had been a marvellous ally but I hardly thought rock climbing or snorkelling would be suitable for a dog. Besides I couldn't possibly concentrate on his welfare and mine too especially now the minefield had widened considerably. I'm sure that if they were willing to kill me they wouldn't think twice about shooting a dog whose acquired reputation of taking no prisoners in battle had become legendary.

I took the M4 to Swansea where I caught the next available night car ferry. I was too late to book a cabin so I found a comfortable chair and slept a few hours. There was one important thing I promised myself, whatever happens in the following days I would have to be back for Len's funeral even if it meant sharing his coffin.

CHAPTER THIRTEEN

Dawn broke as the ferry sailed into a rain lashed Cork harbour. After docking and disembarking I eased the Roadster along the N71 coastal route to Skibbereen. From there I wasted no time in touring the estimated mileage given to me by Professor Squires. It turned out to be a disappointing day searching, as mile after mile, I pinpointed nothing significant. None of the landscapes or coastline matched any in the photographs and I should have anticipated the inevitable structural changes done over sixty years. Overall I was getting nowhere fast and due to my impatience to find something of significance, mixed with hunger and tiredness I was also beginning to get irritated. Dejectedly I went to find the hotel I had booked previously as there was no point in pushing myself beyond exhaustion.

The Baltimore Harbour Hotel was busy and perfect to blend in without attracting too much attention to myself. After dinner I went out to familiarize myself with the area, it also gave me the opportunity to double check if I was being followed. I didn't expect to be, and I wasn't, but to be sure I called into a pub named Bushe's Bar, ordered a Guinness and sat at a suitable table with my back against a wall so I could watch the entrance while I listened to lively tunes and Irish songs.

During a short intermission from the music I took the opportunity to pester Detective Inspector Hamer. I rang him on my mobile and kept it blunt. "Got anything on Deveron?"

Naturally, Hamer was pleased to hear from me. "Oh Speed, so nice of you to surface from your hiding place! I've been searching London for you."

"Why?"

"I have your required documentation stating immunity from prosecution over the matter of Ministry property, signed, sealed, as you asked for. Remember?"

"Yes I remember."

"So how the fuck do you expect me to deliver it when you elect to disappear?"

"Well don't bother breaking into my home. Post it!"

"You have the gratitude of a male spider being killed after mating. Where exactly are you?"

"I'm in a safe place. Now did you locate Deveron?"

"Not exactly, he retired from the Ministry fifteen years ago."

"I know *that!* Where did he go?"

"No trace of him."

"I thought you chaps were good?"

"Shut it you facetious swine. Anyway, the old bastard is probably dead. What's so special about Deveron?"

"I don't know till I meet him."

"Well I hope you have better luck than I did trying to find him. Now are you going to tell me where you are, Speed?"

"I'm on holiday."

"Oh! A pleasant place is it?"

"Are you asking or probing?"

"I haven't decided."

"Well, when you have decided let me know."

Hamer began to mutter some obscenities over the air-waves but I cut him off and switched the receiver to the answer phone.

While I was replacing the mobile back into my pocket I noticed a rugged looking man in a flat cap and knee length coat, staring in my direction and making me nervous. I sipped some Guinness to steady myself, watching his distorted shape through the rim of the glass. He moved towards me. I put the glass down onto the table in anticipation of trouble.

He had a determined look in his eyes but I soon sensed he was no danger to me. Anyone preparing for a fight wouldn't have had a clay pipe clamped between their front teeth and carrying a glass of beer. I pretended to be minding my own business but very wary of his approach.

On closer observation the man was of medium height, portly and had red veined cheeks associated with someone who had spent a good deal of life in the open air. I could tell even before he spoke he was touting for some relevant business and as he hovered over me I got the distinct smell of fish, it rather narrowed down the options of what he did for a living.

When he removed the pipe from between his teeth and smiled at me I could clearly see the arch shape chipped away in his tobacco stained upper two front teeth where the pipe stem fitted perfectly.

"Hullo dhare, Sir!" He said in a jolly voice.

I acknowledged half heartedly with a false smile and a nod. To be honest, I wasn't really in the mood for small talk as my mind had yet to clear from the disappointments of the day, but the Irish fellow was persistent.

"Is it the work or pleasure dhat brings yer to these shores, Sir?"

"Just the relaxation," I said, dully.

"Yer're wouldn't be one of those poets looking for a bit of inspiration, would yer be, Sir?"

"Not really-Mister-ah?" I like to know who I'm talking to.

"It is I, Sir, Shamus O'Malley, at yer service, and owner of a pleasure fishin' boat. Are you, perhaps, in the pursuit of fishin', Sir?"

"Hell no I just eat fish not catch them," I said.

The glint went from his eyes in disappointment. Not that I was bothered, but it gave me an idea.

"How big is your boat?" I asked, thoughtfully.

"Tis very big, Sir. The finest in Baltimore harbour, and she's in readiness for a fine customer like yerself, Sir."

"I told you I'm not interested in fishing," I said assertively. "But I may want to hire it later in the week."

"And why would dhat be, Sir, if it isn't for fishin'? I don't do smuggling, Sir!"

I actually smiled. "If you really must know, I'm a journalist searching for material on the possibility of an attempted Japanese invasion on these very shores in 1944. An excursion around the Bay could reveal some relevant details. " I thought that piece of concoction would confuse him enough and perhaps he'd leave me alone on the presumption that I was crackers.

I was wrong. He didn't rate me as an escapee from a mental institution because he began to rub the grey bristles on his chin while delving into the depths of his brain in search for a speck of information to extend our conversation. Then he took me by surprise.

The Irishman raised a forefinger. "I may just be able to help yer on dhat one, Sir," he said, calmly.

114

I couldn't be positive, but I think I gave him a vacant stare before my mouth clicked into gear. "May?"

"Indeed, Sir!"

He put his glass down on the table, removed his hat and sat down. I didn't argue about his uninvited gesture, but I did notice his clay pipe wasn't lit. I suppose listening to ramble from the old Irishman wouldn't do me any harm, though I was perhaps being a little harsh on calling him old. He was probably in his middle fifties, yet his weathered face and stubbly chin definitely did him no favours in age comparison. He had deep set, grey blue eyes, thick, unkempt greying hair and bushy eyebrows. By the time he'd told me everything about his tale, we had drank a few Guinness's.

"It's an incredible story, Shamus. Can you verify any of this?"

The Irishman's eyes narrowed. "Yer wouldn't be tinking, Shamus O'Malley was to be telling yer lies, would yer, Sir?"

"I'm sure you're not, Shamus, because no one could create a story as yours. And I'm sure you can prove it?"

"Indeed I can, Sir," he announced proudly. "Take yer to the graveyard where the body is buried."

"So tell me the story again but leave out the intricate details."

Shamus slurped down a mouthful of Guinness. Ran the back of his hand over his mouth and began, "As I said, Sir, strolling along the beach at Gollen. Dhat's where I live, Sir, a beautiful place. So dhare I was, Sir, collecting wood from the beach, a young boy as I was, head in the clouds dreamin', when I saw the ghoulish thing washed up on the rocks. A real mess it was, Sir, and badly battered by the sea smashing the body against the rocks. Squinty eyes it had, Sir. Dhat I'm as sure as being sat here with yer holding our empty glasses."

I got the hint and ordered more Guinness. I was going to suffer with a frigging bad head the following morning there was no doubt about that. Go on!" I pushed. "You can clearly remember that?"

"Clear as a twinkle in me Mother's glass eye. Isn't the sort of memory yer can forget, Sir, as a lad. Scared me dhat much I was shaking for days after."

"Did anyone know how the body became washed up on the rocks?"

"I don't know dhat one, Sir. I never asked and I was never told. I thought it better to leave the dead to those who deal in death. I was to hear later dhat the Americans had sunk a Japanese submarine out in mid-Atlantic, and the body had probably drifted this way on the currents."

"So what happened to the body after being retrieved from the water?"

"It was buried, Sir."

"What, straight away? No autopsy, no coroner's inquest?"

"Not dhat I know of, Sir."

"Can you remember where the burial took place?"

Shamus raised his finger in the air. "Indeed I do, Sir."

"Can you take me there tomorrow?"

"Well, Sir..." He began slowly. "...I'm a very busy man, indeed."

"Naturally I expect to pay for your time."

There was a sparkle in the Irishman's eyes. "Well, indeed, Sir, a mere mention of those immortal words is enough to send a leprechaun running for his golden pot to be filled. Is dhare any particular time in the mornin', Sir?"

"Don't make it too early, I've a feeling I'll have need for aspirins."

"Yer disappoint me, Sir. A few pots of the black magic and you've a hangover before getting one. What yer need, Sir, is to drink a glass of Irish water before yer go to bed, and you'll be as fresh as dew on the morning meadow."

I got to my feet. "I'll speak with you tomorrow, Shamus. Goodnight!"

The night air hit me when I got outside and some of my steps needed urgent readjustment as I headed back to the hotel. The walk refreshed me, gave me time to think, though the night-staff on my return to the hotel were not impressed with my insistence for a pot of coffee being sent up to my room, not that the sobering ingredient of the Columbian bean helped me one bit but it was good while it lasted. I stripped naked and fell into bed. The room spun and so did the thoughts in my head before I sank into a quagmire of nightmares from which I thought I would never return.

CHAPTER FOURTEEN

The spear of sunlight pieced the crack in the curtain and hit me directly in the eyes. As for the expected discomfort of the dreaded hangover, thankfully, it never developed. I felt so good I managed a good traditional Irish breakfast consisting of rashers, grilled tomatoes, sausage, black and white pudding slices and potato cake, all washed down with a pot of coffee. I had just finished when Shamus O'Malley arrived.

"Top of the mornin', Sir!" he said cheerily. "Tis a fine day to wander the beautiful lands of Ireland, it is."

"I hardly regard stomping about in a graveyard as a charming excursion." I reminded him.

"O' no, Sir, I meant the views on the way dhare."

"I'm not here for the views," I said sharply. "Let's go!"

Outside Shamus proudly showed me the battered remnants of his Land-Rover, which was also in desperate need of a damn good wash.

I said, "Is it roadworthy?"

Shamus was astonished. "O' don't be fooled by the looks, Sir, it's a fine, fine runner, indeed."

"I'll take your word for it. But before we move on, I have one little complaint."

"And what may dhat be, Sir?" His eyes bulged in anticipation.

"For goodness sake, please stop calling me 'Sir' every five minutes. You can call me, Shacks, okay?"

"Tis a fine name, Sir, a fine name indeed. Shacks it is, Sir!"

I shrugged my shoulders in defeat. I was surely wasting my time trying to change this Irishman's vocabulary.

Shamus O'Malley drove with the same perception as a learner driver with pace. I shouldn't moan as it's not often I have the privilege of being chauffeur driven. As we drove along the country roads there were two noises that I found to be horrendous to my hearing. Shamus's constant crunching of the gears combined equally with his crunching on pieces of dried pork morsels. I've seen a pregnant sow scoffing slops from a bucket eat more quietly.

From Baltimore we took the same scenic route I'd taken the day before until we reach Ballydehob, then onto to the R592 and passed a mushroomed topped mountain as we headed in the direction of Schull. Keeping right as we went through the village, Shamus veered the vehicle off the road and headed down a narrow country lane until we approached a derelict church minus its roof. At first I thought Shamus was taking me on a site seeing trip to liven the day, but he wasn't.

"We're here, Shacks Sir." He announced as if introducing me to something fantastic.

I stepped from the vehicle, stretched my legs and followed Shamus through a broken oak gate hanging by one rusty hinge and along a grassy stone pathway to the rear of the church.

"So what's the story of this sorrowful place?" I asked as we went along.

"O' tis a shame, Shacks Sir," he said over his shoulder. "A violent storm in the twenties ripped the roof clean off, so I was told."

Shamus stopped and swept his hand in an arc to show the area where I assumed the body was buried, but he refused to go any closer. I saw nothing but overgrown vegetation and total neglect.

Bewilderment on my face, I said: "This is the graveyard?"

Shamus nodded once. "It is, Shacks Sir."

"Where are all the headstones?"

"O' well, Shacks Sir, the church was never actually used for burials in his time."

"Then what are we doing here?"

"The body from the shore is buried here, Shacks Sir, just over dhare."

I followed his outstretched arm to a particular clump of long grass. I said, "Hardly distinctive as a grave."

"O' believe me, Shacks Sir. I swear on my own Mother's grave it is. If you squash the grass down you'll find it dhare. I'd do it myself, only I'm a rather superstitious kind of man, and the thought of leaning over another mans grave only heightens me fear of being taken before me time."

I looked blankly at him, "Am I to believe you're scared, Shamus?"

Shamus appeared embarrassed. "Scared?"

"Of the ghoulish hand suddenly shooting from the ground to drag you down into Hell?"

Shamus wasn't afraid to own up to his phobia as he nodded his head slowly. "Dhat's precisely what I'd be tinking, Shacks Sir." And he immediately made the sign of the cross on his chest.

Even I hesitated before crouching down in front of the supposed grave. I parted the grass and found the evidence that proved Shamus was right.

"There's no headstone of any type," I bellowed over to him. "But there is a wooden plaque. It's faded, but I can only read part of the inscription."

"What does it say, Shacks Sir?"

"Let your God-something-something-soul: rest-something-something; probably rest in peace."

It was hardly an impressive piece of writing and proved nothing to confirm this was the last resting place of a Japanese sailor. I got to my feet while contemplating the possibility of hiring a couple of gravediggers to exhume the body for verification, but there's a law against doing that without the proper paperwork and to be accused of grave-robbing didn't really appeal to me.

"Are you sure this is the grave, it has been a long time?"

"As sure as me name is Shamus O'Malley," he said seriously. "Though I'm not sure how the plaque got dhare."

"Why was the body buried here at the ruins, some Irish custom?"

"O' well, yer see, Shacks Sir, the priest at the time, Father Brady, O' he was a fine man, indeed, though a devout Roman Catholic who wouldn't allow a non Catholic to be buried on sacred ground. I'm afraid Father Brady wasn't quite prepared for the religions associated with the Far East, so it was decided dhat this forgotten church would be sufficient until the body was claimed."

"Very thoughtful, only it seems nobody bothered to pass that information on."

"O' tis an awful thing, Shacks Sir-," again his fingers shifted across his chest as he made the sign of the cross, "-time simply passed by. No one came looking. No one remembered, until now. Is it helping at all?"

"Not for me directly, but I should think the Japanese will be grateful."

"Does dhat mean the forgotten soul will be going home?"

"No doubt the Japanese government would want the body returned immediately. They are very honourable with their hero's. Send them a shoe and that's sufficient for a full military honour."

"Dhat'll be a fine, fine thing, Shacks Sir, a fine thing indeed."

"Yes, but not just yet, Shamus. Shall we move on to the part of the coast where you discovered the body?"

Back onto the main road, Shamus eased the Land-Rover through a sweeping bend that took us into Toormore Bay. We had small talk as we drove along, Shamus did all the talking and I just pretended to listen. My head was too full of 'ifs, buts and why's.

We left the vehicle in the car park, made our way down to the beach and walked along the waters edge until we came to a piece of rocky beach. Shamus stopped and looked about as if he was lost, moved perhaps two metres, muttered something, turned, took another two steps and stopped. He didn't exactly fill me with confidence when he began scratching the back of his head and looking rather perturbed.

"Is there a problem?" I asked.

"O' I do indeed, Shacks Sir, I'm having a little trouble on which side of the large rock the body was washed up."

"I hardly think it matters, Shamus." I assured him. "Can you recall what state the body was in when you found it?"

Shamus gave me a strange look. "O' it was dead, Shacks Sir, very dead indeed."

"No! I meant the condition of the body. How did it look?"

"It was battered to a pulp as I told yer last night, Shacks Sir."

Just then a huge wave smashed into a number of large rocks a few metres out and sprayed me with saltwater. It didn't distract me. "No I meant did the body appear bloated?"

"O' no, I distinctly recall a skinny little runt with squinty eyes."

Skinny little runt meant the body could never have travelled from mid-Atlantic without suffering such deformities as severe bloating and rotting flesh. The body had to have surfaced from a closer venue.

Excitedly I said, "How deep is the water around Roaring-water Bay?"

"Dhat would depend on your intentions, Shacks Sir."

"I've suddenly acquired the urge to go fishing, Shamus."

He almost broke into an Irish jig. "I knew yer were a fisherman the minute I first cast eyes on yer. Is it the big fish that appeals, Shacks Sir?"

"Sort of, Shamus. How big did you say your boat was?"

"The biggest in the harbour she is, Shacks Sir, and ready at a special price to you."

"Good because I hope you don't mind fishing for submarines."

Shamus gave me a long look. "Submarines, Shacks, Sir?"

"Yes Shamus. We are going hunting for a frigging great big metallic Japanese submarine which I'm absolutely positive went missing while on a secret mission, here in Roaring-water bay."

"O' yer, be pulling me leg, Shacks Sir? The devil yer are."

"I'm too serious to be pulling your leg, Shamus. My sanity is riding on the hunch."

"O' it's a hunch, is it, Shacks Sir?"

"A bit more towards probability actually."

"O' well, yer see, Shacks Sir, I don't want to disappoint yer, but I've been sailin' and fishin' these waters a long time now. I'm rather proud to say me expertise on these waters is as equal to any seafaring mariner. And apart from the odd rumour of old sunken galleons, I'm afraid, dhat a Japanese submarine never quite reached me imagination, if you know what I'm sayin'?"

"My hunches have in the past have been noted rather spectacular."

"I tink you're a crazy Englishman!"

"Yes, Shamus, but this crazy Englishman is paying frigging good money for the privilege of being crazy."

"Dhat's very true, Shacks Sir. A crazy mans money is as good as any other crazy mans money. Hunting submarines it is!"

"I'm glad you understand, Shamus. Now let me explain about the body you found. You described the condition of the Oriental after being dragged from the sea as skinny. There was no sign of bloating so it hadn't been in the water long. Does that not arouse some suspicion that maybe the body came from a closer source?"

"As a young boy, Shacks Sir, the sight of the dead had me running for help faster than a whippet. It wasn't my job wunderin' how the man died. I'd terrible nightmares for months afterwards, I did, Sir." He half smiled, "Have yer never thought it rather strange how bad things tend to stick in the mind longer than good things."

He had a point there!

I took the photographs from the inside of my bomber jacket and showed them to Shamus. I said, hopefully: "It's a Japanese submarine in a lot of trouble somewhere off the coastline in this area. Any of the rocks look familiar to you?"

He took the pictures and flicked through them with a negative shake of the head.

"I've had an authority on the subject of rock formations pin-pointing these parts as the area on the photographs," I assured him. "He's pretty damn good at his job."

"O' I don't doubt the integrity of the person Shacks Sir. But the pictures are more angled towards the coastline, so I tink we'd be better out dhare on the water."

"Frigging hell, Shamus, I can't venture out there on the open seas!"

Shamus had a concerned expression. "Why? Does the ocean bother you, Shacks Sir?"

"Not at all, but going without lunch does. This sea air is playing havoc with my stomach. You can choose the eating establishment, and I'll pay."

I didn't expect Shamus to disagree with the offer, and he didn't disappoint me. Though, something did start to bother me, a cold feeling at the nape of my neck, as if someone was watching my every movement.

*

When Shamus and I returned to Baltimore, we lunched on oysters and Guinness. Afterwards I went back to the hotel to change into appropriate clothing to combat the inevitable cold wind whipping across the Bay and when I entered my room that apparent bout of paranoia I kept experiencing extended to a bout of panic when I realized my belongings had been searched. Not by a ferocious raving lunatic with intent to throw the clothing all over the room in frustration, but a calculated neat person whose expertise in such matters called for only minor movement of my clothes. None-the-less there'd been enough movement for me to make the connection.

I quickly looked for a weapon to grab and picked up a statuette from the coffee table, not at first realizing I was manhandling the Virgin Mary by her breasts, holding her aloft club-like, alert and ready to strike. I definitely knew I'd a heart inside my chest because it bounced against my ribs with the sound of a bass drum, a dead giveaway of my presence to anyone in hearing distance. With hiding places pretty limited to spring an attack in the main bedroom, I crept across the room to the en-suite, took in a deep breath and rushed in wailing like a banshee hoping to frighten the lurking assailant, which I did to great effect as the lone fly buzzed about my head with extreme confidence until I shattered the annoying insect with a flick of a hand towel.

I felt rather foolish as I wandered back into the bedroom, but I soon exonerated myself because as I replaced the statuette on the table I caught a distinct smell of perfume, not too strong, just enough of the aroma to realize I'd smelt it before somewhere, but I couldn't recall the occasion. I noticed the bed had been made more efficiently than I'd left it, and accepted my intruder was no other than chambermaid attending the room. I shrugged my shoulders, changed my clothing into a cream coloured thick roll-neck jumper, jeans, suitable boots and a decent jacket, then down to the harbour which was clogged with an array of yachts and cruisers and buzzing with people.

I located Shamus. He was busy on his boat at the quay preparing for the sea journey whilst whistling a lively Irish tune. I had visions of him wearing a pirate hat and a black patch over his eye, not that I thought he was the type to rip me off.

The name 'Muff' highlighted on the bow of the boat had me wondering its origin. I was tempted to ask but finally decided against it. The "Muff' was no different than any other boat in the harbour and had obviously been part of a fishing fleet at some time. Underneath its lick of blue and white winter maintenance paint the exterior of the boat showed all the signs of taking a battering by the Atlantic swells. Still, it appeared seaworthy and I doubt Shamus would risk his reputation of providing an un-seaworthy craft because I assumed he valued his own life far too much to take unnecessary risks.

As I neared he was going through a meticulous check of the equipment, and testing the instrument panel was fully operative.

I shouted to him. "Ahoy there shipmate have I permission to come aboard?"

By his look to the heavens it was plainly obvious my maritime quip was originality long past its sell by date. He gestured me aboard, and when I had scrambled on deck, he said, "Changeable weather approaches the Bay, Shacks Sir. Possible rain too, But don't worry yerself, I've a Sou'wester or two and waterproofs aboard ship.

123

Dhare's cold Guinness in the fridge down in the Galley, or yer might want a Paddy's Irish whiskey dhat'll warm the toggles of yer heart. We set sail in ten minutes."

I was looking across the harbour. "Lot's of activity, Shamus, what's with all the yachts?"

"O' dhat lot, shacks Sir, tis for the regatta next week. Tis a good thing we've taken to the water this week as the harbour will be teeming with amateurish sailors who sail their shiny vessels but once a year and annoy the locals. But it's not all glum and disorientation, dhare's the extra revenue it brings in."

I didn't need telling twice about the beer. I de-capped two bottles and put one into Shamus's large leathery hand. He promptly gulped down half the bottle, placed it on the chart table and resumed his radio check, informing the harbour master of the intended journey around the shorelines of Roaring water Bay and return expectancy before dusk. With a final check the 'Muff' slipped her mooring and I suddenly developed a strange surge of excitement that was a mixture of apprehension and delight.

My anxiety disappeared once the first wave smashed into the bow of the boat with the effect of being driven back rather than making progress. I had sailed rough seas before but I had to confess today's conditions had me gripping every conceivable piece of boat to prevent falling flat on my face.

I said, "Whoever named this bay wasn't kidding."

"O' yes Shacks Sir, a rough Bay she is, just like the Irish, tough and beautiful. If yer're tinkin' the boat can't handle the conditions, don't concern yerself, Sir, she's sailed these waters endlessly for thirty years."

"With a Captain like you, Shamus, handling the helm expertly, I've no qualms."

"Dhat's very kind of yer Shacks Sir."

"So where are we heading?"

"I thought we'd start where the body washed ashore and follow the shoreline back to Baltimore. If no success and time Is still with us, we'll circumnavigate the Islands."

"It sounds good to me."

I'd no reason to contradict Shamus's knowledge of these waters, the way he conducted himself proved overwhelmingly his passion for the sea. I placed the photographs in a position where it was beneficial for the two of us to counter-observe against the shoreline and hopefully we would find a match, but to my eyes each shoreline we neared looked the same.

There was another thing Shamus excelled at, his ability to understand the changeable Irish weather. What began as reasonably bright day, the weather suddenly turned and smacked the 'Muff' with a bout of heavy rain, which, inevitably, was always accompanied with a gusty wind that howled and whistled through every nook and cranny of the boat. Add the creaking sound of twisting wood with the added edition of the window wipers flicking side to side and with careful listening, the entire accompaniment had the makings of an orchestral beginning.

I soon discovered there was one disadvantage to the pounding rain lashing against the window pane. It made viewing of the shoreline a lot harder to see so I was forced, or for a more correct application, encouraged by Shamus to venture from the wheelhouse whenever we spotted a place of resemblance. On my first venture out into the elements I ignored Shamus's advisory words and didn't bother with waterproof protection. A good drenching remedied my ignorance that the next time I ventured outside I was better equipped to resist the weather, and more importantly, I'd wipe that grin from Shamus's face.

Apart from the cheap entertainment I provided for Shamus, and some hairy moments close to the shoreline when I thought the boat would be dragged against the rocks and smashed to pieces, overall, it turned out to be another long frustrating day.

"As I said, Shacks Sir, the photographs don't give a clear picture. The landscape has changed dramatically through the years. I tink we're wasting our time. I tink we should get the photographs enlarged? See things a little more clearly."

"That sounds a sensible idea." It had never occurred to me to think of such an easy solution. Then Lens Lazerow drifted into my thoughts. If he had still been alive he would have certainly made the suggestion.

"Have you somewhere to take them, Shamus?"

"Indeed I do Shacks Sir."

"Okay, let's get back."

With the 'Muff' securely anchored, I went ashore. I said to Shamus, "Don't lose the photographs. They are the only ones I have."

"Shacks Sir, you can trust old Shamus to be very careful."

"How long do you think it'll take?"

"It'll not be done today, Shacks, Sir. Is tomorrow morning okay?"

"Fine, I'll be at my hotel. I need to rid the taste of sea salt it doesn't half grabbed the throat."

On entering the hotel I was diverted to the lounge bar by reception informing me one of the new guests was waiting for me. Understandably my approach was cautious and when I caught sight of the man sat there at a table with a grin on his face, I quickly ordered a stiff whiskey, swallowed a mouthful, and with great reluctance I crossed over and sat down opposite Detective Inspector Hamer. I think my expression of displeasure was justifiable.

I said, "You following me?"

"Naturally, I missed your presence in London."

"I prefer my own company."

"So I can see!" Hamer said, directing a stubby finger at my glass "Drinking alone, too. Or do your pockets go deeper than a Scotsman's?"

Smarmy bastard, I thought, accusing me of being tight. I looked him sternly in the eye. "No, my pockets are tight so no light fingered person can penetrate my pants without my knowledge."

"You've lost me, Speed, what are you implying?"

"I'm not implying I'm accusing you of sneaking around my hotel room earlier today rummaging through my belongings."

"What are you drivelling on about?"

"Don't deny it, Detective Inspector, you went into my room."

Okay, maybe the perfume I smelt in my room didn't match his aftershave, but I still considered the accusation a fair one as he had done it before.

He shook his head. "Not me," he said positively. "For fuck sake, Speed, what do you take me for, a common thief?"

"Every hotel has a local looter," I said accusingly.

Hamer's face reddened. "I'm too handsomely paid by the government to warrant such lowness," he retorted angrily.

I never intended to slam the glass down on the table so hard nor attract a few stares. "Don't give me that frigging verbal claptrap. Maybe you're not Raffles, gentleman thief calibre, but you're a frigging expert at breaking into property, you proved it once already. What were you looking for?"

Hamer snorted a laugh. "Yes I *went* to your room, I can't deny that. But I swear I never went in. I knocked, got no reply and left. To be honest I thought you were shafting a bit of skirt. I gathered when you'd finished doing whatever you were doing, you'd end up in the bar sooner or later until the barman told me he'd seen you leave earlier, so I waited. Ask the barman how long I've been here, if you don't believe me; go on!"

I still looked at him accusingly.

"Who's stung your arse, Speed?"

I relented. "I just don't enjoy being followed. It makes me nervous and bad tempered. So where is Commander Morgan?"

"Back at his office digging deeper into every hole he can find. The paranoid fool is totally obsessed his office is bugged. To be honest I think he's losing his mind."

"You sound pissed-off with him?"

"Sometimes I am. He's alright in small doses. I just hate his involvement in my cases. He's better off in the office keeping nosy ministers off my back."

"So what do I not owe the pleasure of your company?"

"Isn't that plainly obvious? Remember what we discussed in London, solidarity? Together battling the enemy? Perhaps you might consider assisting the ministry in collecting sufficient evidence to arrest Love and Hate before they kill anyone one else, preferably your arse, Speed. I don't want your decapitated torso providing nasty statistics in my paperwork."

"I take it you haven't located either of them yet?"

"Love and Hate? Gone, they could be anywhere. And since I can't force you back to London, I'm here to watch your back."

"That's very heroic of you, Detective Inspector, but who is watching your back?"

"Nobody, it's not me they want,"

"Well I'm sorry to disappoint you but I don't need help, so you've wasted your time."

"Too late, Speed, I'm here."

"Since you have mentioned *here,* I'm at a loss to how you found me so easily. I could have been anywhere in the world, yet, as you say, here you are. Is it coincidence or maybe you specialize in surveillance tactics."

"Hell, no!" he said, smugly. "We're not M16 skulking around looking in keyholes. We deal in accurate information, expertly gathered."

"Well I definitely didn't leave my destination details on the table for you to read. I certainly didn't tell you. And I don't rate your mind reading ability."

"No-no, Speed, far more simple than that." I think his head began to swell. "I have a device far better than mind reading. The power of a sophisticated computer system can track anything, especially credit card transactions when you pay bills. I could follow a lump of shit from your toilet all the way through the system and out into the cesspit of the sea. It's that easy!"

Smart arse! I thought bitterly.

"I'm not impressed," I said. "But you do have a perverse and distorted mind, Detective Inspector. With such crudity you should put your self forward to present a science programme on the television, I'm sure the viewers would be fascinated how a piece of shit travels through the system, especially the human kind."

"I could take that comment two ways, Speed."

"Take it how you want, Detective Inspector. As for your sneaky tactics to track me down, I think that comes under the human rights category of an infringement of my privacy."

Hamer shrugged his shoulders. "So, sue me! Which leads me to another infringement of your privacy, what are you doing in these parts, hiding?"

"I'm on frigging holiday, convalescing from the rigours of being abused by thugs and picked on by authorization."

"Bollocks!"

"Really, Detective Inspector, show some respect for a man totally burnt out by his recent traumatised experiences."

"It's still bollocks!"

"Okay, I'm doing some research on aggravating bastards who spend their time harassing people."

"You still don't trust me, do you Speed?"

"Is it that noticeable?"

Hamer fumed. "You're an impertinent twat! I'm an idiot extending my generosity for an inconceivable twerp like you, Speed. I might as well grab my belongings and go back to London while you sort out your own problems. Get yourself killed and see if I care a toss!"

"Please don't let me detain you any longer," I said calmly.

"You appreciate nothing, Speed. To think I've sacrificed my time to help, and you treat me like a leper."

"So I gather you're staying?"

"Damn right I am!"

"Not too close is it?"

"Close enough, Speed. This is a splendid hotel."

I expressed surprise. "I'm to have my very own personal body-guard, lucky me!"

"They gave me the Bridal suite, there was a cancellation."

"How lonely it'll be for you."

Hamer's eyebrows furrowed. "What do you mean?"

"It's a big room," I said smartly. "Dinner you said?"

Hamer looked horrified. "I didn't say that?"

I ignored his protest and said, "Restaurant in an hour. They serve a delicious array of culinary delight to please any palate, even a foul mouth like yours. Be good and I might even let you sit at my table."

"Rah-rah for you Speed," he said bitterly.

I finished my drink, got up and left him to reflect on the situation. As for the two fingered salute he threw at me behind my back, I was in two minds if to turn around and grab the offending two digits and ram them up his fat arse until he pleaded forgiveness. I should have but I didn't bother.

But I was bothered about the disappearance of Love and Hate. It rather put a different complexion on proceedings. As for Hamer, he didn't worry me at all, other than annoying me to death.

When I returned to my room there had been no reattempt to breach the boundaries of my room because the small piece of paper I'd wedged between the lower door hinge and frame was still in place and immediately fell to the floor when I went inside, patheti-cally simple but effective. Conscientiously I locked the door, had a shower, shaved, put on a bathrobe and crashed out onto the bed. I closed my aching eyes. Thoughts criss-crossed through my mind, and I drifted into a world of ambivalence and absolution.

*

Judging by the stares I received when I walked into the restaurant I was definitely overdressed for the occasion. I was wearing a tuxedo and to hell with them! I like smart clothes and I felt extremely com-fortable.

I found Hamer sat at a table staring thoughtfully out of the win-dow seemingly admiring the pleasant and absorbing view over the bay. He startled slightly as I approached and sat down.

He gave me a low whistle. "Trendy!" he remarked, which I made no reply.

I quickly attracted the attention of a waitress and chose a meal of seafood, washed down with a splendid bottle of Muscatel, followed by coffee and Cognac. Hamer selected a more hearty meat dinner and an appetite to match as he scoffed the food down in a mannerism that had all the grace of divulging barbarian. We spoke very little while we ate; the odd comment of food satisfaction, a palatable wine. In the meantime I did a good deal of gazing at other diners, especially the three couples sat at a table in line of my view, bragging to each other the size of their yachts and in particular one of the female diners flirtatiously flashing her eyes at me with every opportunity she got.

With his stomach full Hamer belched, but I drew the line with his dry comment: 'compliments to the chef', which was more distasteful than his bad manners.

"I gather it was enjoyable, Detective Inspector?"

Hamer raised a hand as if he was stopping the local traffic. "Let's cut the Detective crap. If we are going to spend time together, (he belched again much to the annoyance of other diners), then you must call me Dan, Much more friendly, okay?"

I'd no qualms. "Dan, it is." I agreed.

"Shall I call you, Shackleton or have you a preferred nickname or something?"

"Mister Speed will be sufficient."

Hamer couldn't control his frustration. "Damn you, Speed. I was warned you were an awkward bastard but there's awkward and there's fucking awkward and you are way beyond any of them."

I smiled impishly, "I'm here to please."

"Well you're not going to wind me just because you don't like me babysitting. So carry on being awkward all you want. I've stop caring."

"Fine," I said. "How close will you be sticking to me, Danny boy?"

He groaned disapprovingly at being called *Danny*. "Very close."

"I'm that important?"

"I'm reluctant to say this, but yes. You are the only target that has survived to tell the tale, to put it bluntly. Without doubt you seriously dented the reputations of Love and Hate and I expect reprisals. They won't savour the mess they left, witnesses are dangerous, witnesses can testify, they'll want to rectify the problem and not with a fat pay-off for you to keep quiet, more of a slashed throat."

"I think I understand without the relevant details, thank you very much," I said sharply.

"Look, why don't you return to London so we can set you up in a safe house and provide you with around the clock protection."

"They won't know I'm here."

"I found you easy enough!"

"Frigging hell, what you're actually hoping is they do find me." I lowered my voice. "Hope to catch them in the act of murdering me so the evidence is presented on a golden platter."

Cunning bastard! I mumbled while pretending to drink my cognac.

Hamer's eyes searched me in a strange way, as if I'd no right to complain. "Is there a problem with that?"

"No, there's no problem, providing I'm given an extremely large calibre machinegun preferably mounted on an armoured vehicle and surrounded with a reinforced concrete blockade. No, there shouldn't be any frigging problem at all."

"There's no need for such waggishness, Speed."

"I take it you're armed?" I assumed he was. A small calibre weapon could easily be concealed.

He disappointed me when he shook his head. "It's illegal to carry weapons under British Law.

"So we don't have any armoury at all?"

"Sorry, Speed. You must show some trust in your partners."

"And you've decided all by yourself to be my partner?"

"Yes, Speed. Does that scare you?"

"I'm trembling at the knees. Yet there is one serious issue to consider before you get too over confident in your assumption that I'm controllable."

"Being?"

"I've no intentions of providing even a scrap of information until I've completed what I came here to complete. By all means, hover like a fly around a bad smell, but don't push me into complying with pitiful requests."

Hamer's eyes flared. "You still can't grasp that there are villains out there who don't appreciate you in the slightest. Mind you, I can see where they're coming from. It doesn't take much to dislike a person such as you, Speed."

"Oh-yes," I said nonchalantly. "And what can you see?"

"That you're an arrogant meddler, with an attitude problem, layered with dishonesty."

"Dishonesty," I said in disbelief. "Show me an establishment of authority that doesn't smell of dishonesty and I'll show my arse in Burton's the tailors shop window all day with my cheeks squashed against the glass."

"There you are, exactly what I'm getting at, attitude problem."

"No, Detective Inspector, that's called self defence attitude and I won't be pushed around by any snub-nosed pin-striped bureaucrat. Now I've no problem with *that!*"

He muttered something which I didn't hear. But his facial expression told me it was something nasty.

That was when I realized Hamer and I had no chance of creating a workable team. There can't be two team leaders within one group. Yet despite my reluctance to have him under my feet and his blatant openness he was playing with my life, I still thought he could be useful to me.

"Okay, Speed, have it your own way. I'm only here to keep you alive. My job is to stick to you like glue."

"That's very courageous of you. And since your mission requires attaching yourself to me where ever I go, I'm going to allow you the pleasure of sharing a cruise around the bay, and the ironic thing about it is, I'm paying."

"That's really generous of you Speed. Spot of fishing, things like that?"

"Yes, deep sea fishing actually. Maybe some sight-seeing and scuba diving. Do you scuba-dive?"

"Hell no, Speed, I enjoy breathing proper air. Preferably I like my head above the waterline with my feet on terra firma. I'm very experienced in paddling. When is this great event to watch you drown?"

"Tomorrow morning. I advise some warm clothing, the chill factor out in the bay is appalling. And if swimming isn't a strong point I advise a check on whether life-jackets are readily available."

Hamer's eyebrows lifted in horror. "Is it going to be that bad?"

"Have you seen the weather forecast predicted for tomorrow?!"

CHAPTER FIFTEEN

Shamus arrived at the hotel bright and early the next morning, full of enthusiasm and with a nasty habit of drooling over my breakfast.

"Why don't you sit down, Shamus. Do you want me to get you something to eat?"

"O' if you don't mind if I do, Shacks Sir. I was a little rushed to bring these wonderful pictures dhat I missed such a healthy start to the mornin'."

"Did you get the diving gear from the boot of my car?"

"Indeed I did Shacks Sir, safely transferred to the boat in readiness."

"Excellent."

While Shamus ate I studied the enlarged photographs with more than a passing interest. On one particular photograph, what I had first thought were just black dots on the hazy originals, clearly showed three small, motorized rubber crafts with at least two men board apparently attaching implements to the side of the submarine.

I interrupted shamus munching his cornflakes. "What do you make of it?"

Shamus swallowed his cereal. "I'd say the submarine was under attack, Shacks Sir. I examined the photos with a magnifying glass. Those people in the dinghies are attaching what appears to be some sort of disc."

"That's exactly what I thought. And I would guess they were attaching limpet mines, it would explain the smoke bellowing from the rear in the other two photographs. In my opinion I think they first blew the rudder control. It would definitely stop the manoeuvrability of the sub. It would be a sitting target."

"Why would anyone do dhat, Shacks, Sir?"

I shrugged my shoulders. "I know Ireland declared neutrality during the war. Perhaps the Japanese thought it was safe haven. It certainly wasn't attacked by the Allies because they were out searching for it in the Atlantic. So why indeed should anyone attack a submarine in Irish waters? I wouldn't mind betting there's nothing in the history books about it."

"One thing's for sure, Shacks Sir. I know the shoreline. If you look carefully at the second photo, just to the top, right side, there's a faint image showing through the watermark. It's a landmark, a piece of rock rising from the water. I've seen it before! If I'm not mistaken, the splinter of rock holds the ruins of an O'Driscoll's fort. Dun an Oir, 'the golden fort'. The historic fortress is on the West side of Clear Island."

"Well done, Shamus! You've just earned yourself a double bonus."

My jubilation lasted all of ten seconds before I caught a glimpse of Hamer strolling across the dining room.

"Ah, there you are, Speed. Christ, did I struggle to sleep last night. I've never known a bed so hard and lumpy."

"Ah-well that's because of the night-prowler syndrome built into your metabolism," I said. "You've probably been walking in your sleep trying to catch the baddies."

His, 'Ha-ha', lacked conviction. "That's very droll Speed. It's far too early in the morning for you to begin bothering me." Then he realized Shamus was part of my team. "Hello, who might this be?" He wasn't being polite just inquisitive as usual, his roving eyes giving the Irishman an investigative once over. "Found yourself a friend, have you?"

"Shamus, meet Detective Inspector Hamer, Ministry of Defence ace investigator whose volunteered to assist us in our quest for fishing for the big one."

Shamus looked worried. "A policeman, yer mean, Shacks, Sir?"

"One that doesn't carry much jurisdiction in these parts, not unless you tamper with ministry property, isn't that right Detective Inspector?"

My remark didn't go down well with Hamer, when I received his second and most definitely not his last, scowl of the day. But he kept calm and leaned over observing the enlargements. "Have something interesting? It's a submarine!" he blurted in astonishment.

"Your powers of observation are outstanding," I scoffed.

"A second world war Japanese submarine, isn't it?"

"You are quite brilliant, Detective Inspector."

"Cut the crap, Speed! Is that why you're here, in Ireland, to find a submarine?"

"I enjoy wreck diving."

"I don't recall such a wreck in these waters." Hamer said, thoughtfully.

"That's the excitement of wreck hunting, no one knows if it's bull-shit or not until it's found."

Hamer snorted a defiant laugh. "Japanese it might be, but obvi-ously you haven't done your homework, Speed. As far as I can rec-ollect, and my maritime history is quite good to being excellent, and the only Japanese submarine to be sunk in this part of the world was out there in the deep blue ocean of the Atlantic. That submarine has already been located by the yanks, pinpointed and recorded. You're too late, Speed, too many years too late to be precise."

"Now you've spoilt my dream, Hamer. It won't be as much fun now when I'm diving."

"More like I've saved you wasted tank air trying to search for an improbability. Let's instead have a nice cruise around the harbour, collect our things and get ourselves back to London to sort out our problems, and then go on holiday!"

I gave him a hard look. "You're trying to be bossy again."

"So I'll take that as a 'no', then."

*

The three of us sailed to Clear Island. I noticed Hamer suffering through the rough voyage as he looked queasy and his knuckles were whiter than a sprinkle of pure flour as he gripped whatever he could in the wheelhouse providing it had no movement. He even refused a beer. Me! I was excited as a child with a new toy, a sub-marine to be precise.

Once we arrived at the proposed diving site, a position which we had calculated from the photographs where the submarine would have been at the time of the sighting, Shamus dropped the 'Muff's' anchor. I then took the time in explaining to the Irishman the impor-tance of conducting a rigorous training session for a surface coordi-nator on line duty and the various pulling signs he must know to communicate and understand the diver below. And I did stress to him that this practice was what a diver's life depended on. Twice I went through the procedure and twice I didn't get the responsive confidence I'd hope for. Just his expression told me he didn't like this type of work. I asked Hamer if he understood the procedure, but he shrugged his shoulders and then quickly threw his head over the side to throw-up his half digested morning breakfast.

I again went through the communication rope signals with him while I slipped into the neoprene dry suit, attached the aqualung (double tri-mix air tanks-air regulator-buoyancy compensator), put on an adjustable buoyancy life jacket, weight-belt, fins and silicon facemask. Checked the rubber torched illuminated, checked the knives were in position on my arm and one to the side of my leg, checked the wrist attached dive computer (calculated depth, temperature and compass bearings).

"Right, Shamus! Listen again! You are the shore and I'm the diver. Okay?"

"I've got dhat, Shacks Sir."

"One pull on the rope by shore indicates, 'are you okay' to the diver. If the diver pulls the rope once, it indicates, 'I'm okay'. Understand?"

"Indeed I do, Shacks, Sir."

"Two pulls by shore, indicates, 'stay still'. Two pulls by diver, indicates, 'I'm still'. Three pulls by shore, indicates, 'go down'. Three pulls by diver, indicates, 'going down'. Four pulls by shore, indicates, 'come up'. Four pulls by diver, indicates, 'coming up'. Continuous pulls by shore, indicates, 'emergency bring you up'. Continuous pulls by diver, indicates, 'bring me up'. Have you got all that?"

"Indeed, I do, Shacks, Sir." He prodded the side of his head. "Tis here, Sir, within the confines of me head."

"Good! Now is the blue flag flying to show other crafts a diver is down?"

"It is, Shacks, Sir, flapping in the wind, it is."

I pulled the goggles over my eyes and put the aqualung mouthpiece in and sucked in some air to test it was working and then made a walk-in dive and dropped beneath the water line, brought my knees up to my midriff and threw my head down, kicked the fins and made my descent into the depths of Roaringwater bay.

As I descended the darker and colder the water got, not exactly a diver's paradise. Visibility was bad, dropping to less than ten metres so I had to revert to the use of the powerful rubber torch. I made routine checks of my depth on the wrist computer until I levelled at forty metres deep. I shone the torch beam deeper to illuminate the bottom vegetation. If a large vessel of any description was down on the seabed, especially a submarine of such a massive length, I was confident I would find the frigging thing, that's if it hadn't sailed away in 1944, as Shamus had already suggested and made the point *if it was here why hadn't it been discovered before now.* But I wasn't to have my confidence dampened by wasteful thoughts so I pressed on regardless as there was a lot of seabed to search and breathing time under water is limited.

In an hour I'd covered a fair section, establishing a grid reference search which took me in towards the rocky shores and back out again, marking the areas on my submersible chart. An hour doesn't seem a long time floating in water but I was beginning to feel tired which wasn't surprising considering the strong currents I swam against. So I decided to surface, going through the surfacing procedure with the utmost of care as the wrong application at this part of the dive would have had me inside a decompression chamber because of the severe bends, and that's not regarded as having a thumping headache, more in line as closer to death. And that I can vouch for having experienced such a terrible occasion many years before, but then I'd no choice on the matter, it was either swim to the surface at an accelerated rate or be gobbled up whole by a great white shark guiding in on my slipstream.

Apart from that one unfortunate incident my competence in scuba-diving was down to being taught under the guidance and supervision of the great Jacque-Yves Cousteau and his simple application: never allow yourself to descend faster than your last bubble seemed suffice to avoid the bends. *Watch the bubbles or you will suffer*, he used to say. It was a vital observation he severely drummed into my head. I only veered from it the once and learnt harshly the realities of scuba diving incorrectly.

When I broke surface, Shamus's large hand was there to haul me aboard. I removed my facemask. Shamus stood there with a cocky grin on his red veined face.

"Is dhare anything of interest down dhare, Shacks, Sir? Anythin' big, that's made of metal?"

"I haven't finished the search yet so take that look off your face, Shamus!" I said, while removing the aqualung.

"O' well, I be tinking how boring it must be lookin' for the mysterious one. If yer fancy a change, I have noticed a shoal of fish off the Starboard bow."

"Sod off, Shamus! I hate fishing. I'll take a two hour rest, change of tanks and I'll make a second dive."

I was back down beneath the murky water in less than two hours. I scavenged the seabed reaching a depth of between forty-five and fifty metres, swimming in a cross-directional search pattern, inter-weaving through the vegetation, playful small fish darting across the torch beam. I checked every large limpet crusted object in-case the submarine had exploded and fragmented over the seabed. Up-turned everything I found, which was very little. I suppose doubt did start to set into my head about finding anything. Maybe Shamus was right after all and there would be nothing to find, just maybe he knew more than he was telling me and left me to my own devices as time pays very well.

But that was negative thinking. I wasn't a quitter. I had to perse-vere and I had this gut feeling, an inbuilt directional finder that something was here. To drive me on I thought of Lens Lazerow and the horrendous way he died. It made my blood boil, and the eager-ness to search was back in my veins.

I swam a few more runs before fatigue began to slow me down and use up the aqualung air. I was about to resurface when I noticed a section of long sea grass vegetation behaving in an abnormal pat-tern. So minute the deviation, that at first I thought it was an optical illusion until I viewed it from three different positions to confirm the phenomenon. The way the grasses swayed differently to the other forms of surrounding vegetation, as if being sucked toward the shore. I swam down amongst the swaying matter, edging closer to the rock face. I began to feel the flow, a kind of slipstream that pulled me slowly. I swam above and around the location of the pull and shone the torch beam in the direction of the surge. I could see an opening in the rock-face, approximately two square feet, far too small for me to squeeze through without removing my tanks and submerged at a depth of forty-seven metres, it would have been sui-cidal to attempt such a daredevil feat. I shone the flashlight into the hole, the beam penetrating four to five feet. It appeared the hole widened out into oblivion, but to be sure it meant entering what could be a very dangerous interstice.

My biggest problem would be to enlarge the gap, preferably with a long, strong crowbar, though there could be repercussions. I had no way of knowing if my actions would cause a rock-fall. I required a second opinion from an expert but that was time I hadn't got. Yet I had a strong intuition about the gap, and if I didn't investigate, it'll plague my mind for the rest of my miserable life.

I studied the terrain intensely, shining the torch beam up and down, following the cracks and crevices of the rock-face. I came to the conclusion that the formation of rock in that particular area had been the result of a severe disturbance, though I was no expert to ascertain when the damage was caused, or by what method. I quickly marked the area on my chart and kicked for the surface because at that precise moment my safety line was pulled four times: come up!

Back on board, Shamus shouted in my ear as if he assumed that being below water made you deaf for a while. "Weather's changing for worst."

I flicked my head toward Hamer sat in the wheelhouse. "So is his face," I said.

"He's never moved since he went in dhare, Shacks, Sir. I don't tink the idea of him coming along was good."

I smiled. "Oh-yes it was," I winked.

I glanced up at the darkening skies. Shamus helped me out of the diving gear. I said to him. "Any charted underwater caves around Clear Island?"

Shamus rubbed the bristles on his chin in thought. "Not dhat I know of Shacks, Sir."

"So you're not certain then?"

"O' no, Shacks, Sir, never dived before to find one. Yer found somethin'?"

"I'm not sure."

Hamer decided to surface from the wheelhouse and yawned loudly.

"Boring you, Detective Inspector?" I asked.

"I came to see you drown, Speed, you're disappointing me."

"Why don't you accompany me on my next dive? Nothing like first hand close encounter to witness a drowning man. If it really excites you, how about holding me under water until I run out of air."

"Fuck-off Speed! Do you think I'm so stupid, how the fuck do I get back?"

I smiled sinisterly. "Another thing you might consider, what if the boat sank before we get back to Baltimore?"

Hamer suddenly turned a peculiar shade of yellowish-white, dashed to the port side and promptly spewed his guts into the sea. I pulled a face of disgust.

I rather enjoyed the return journey, watching the exploits of Hamer as he struggled to cope with heavy rocking of the boat, constantly white knuckled as he held on for dear life when the bombardment of heavy waves challenged the 'Muffs' durability.

We were now halfway to Baltimore when I noticed the large fishing trawler adjacent to our position. There was something about the ship that didn't seem right but at that moment I couldn't quite put my finger on it. I got the binoculars from the wheelhouse and went on deck. There were plenty of other boats and yachts scattered about the bay, but this particular vessel stood out too proudly, catching my eye on a number of occasions since we left Baltimore. My suspicions that we were being observed were verified as I swept the deck of the trawler. I saw someone standing there looking through binoculars directly at the 'Muff'. Although the distance between the vessels made identification difficult, it reminded me of the cold war when Russian trawlers use to stalk Navy ships. I say Russian because the ship flew a Russian flag.

I went back into the wheelhouse and gave Shamus a nudge to distract him from his concentration, shoving the binoculars in hand. "Starboard bow, approximately six hundred metres, what do you make of that trawler?"

Shamus rammed the glasses hard into his deep wrinkles eyesockets. "Not from Baltimore, Shacks Sir. Could be from another port, but she certainly isn't dhare for the fishin'."

"Why do you say that?"

"No nets, Shacks Sir."

I took the binoculars back and looked for myself. He was right. "She's been with us all day."

"Dhat she has, Shacks Sir."

"You noticed then?"

"Wouldn't be much of a sailor If I didn't, now would I, Shacks Sir. Should I change course? Give her a once over."

"What a damn good idea."

Shamus angled the 'Muff' toward the ship on a collision course.

In between swallowing bile, Hamer chirped up. "What about me, I need to lie down for a while."

"There's a bunk below decks for the mentally sick." I suggested.

"Ha-fucking-ha," Hamer said dully. "I want something that doesn't move." Then Hamer twisted and wretched, unleashing a torrent of indescribable fluid that made my stomach tighten, before he slowly slumped into a heap, a broken man.

"You should have told me you suffered from seasickness?" I said to Hamer.

"I've never suffered before."

"Well it's obvious you were too greedy at breakfast."

"Fuck you too!"

"No need to get touchy! I was only saying." So I left him to his demons and continued observing the big trawler as we approached her. I also noticed Shamus had a cob-on.

"What's eating at you, Shamus?" I said.

He flicked his head toward the door. "What's *gut churner* hangin' around fer? The man's makin' me nervous."

"Oh, he feels I need protection from some bad men. But looking at the state of him now, he couldn't even look after himself!"

We came alongside the trawler keeping approximately fifty metres distance from her. As Shamus observantly pointed out she had no nets. Shamus hit the throttle and pushed the 'Muff' along the length of the trawler reaching the bow where I saw her name plate, 'Flying-fish'.

There was nothing special about the ship. Rust battered like any other sea faring vessel ready for its winter lick of paint. However, I did notice the ships boom was in a perfectly maintained operational order, though at that moment not in use. I saw no life aboard the vessel as we passed. I relented from using the binoculars because I didn't want to appear that I was suspicious of the vessel. The person behind the binoculars I saw on the ships deck had now gone.

We angled away from the trawler and headed back to Baltimore. I went astern and found a space to sit and reflect on the entire episode and the strange feeling I had about the trawler. I think it was a good ploy to have the presence of Hamer in our midst, if the need arises for some heavy police support then I would have to look no further than Hamer to produce the necessary muscle when it's required. That's providing I haven't sent him insane before the jobs finished.

*

When I returned to the hotel to collect my room key there was a letter waiting for me at reception. I must admit I was a little uneasy to know that someone else other than Hamer knew where I was as I'd left no forwarding address. Okay Hamer had found me easily enough but I doubt he would have advertised the place if his minor aim in life was to preserve my existence and if anyone hostile wanted to bump me off they certainly wouldn't advertise their presence.

Carefully I studied the exterior of the envelope. My name was on the front, spelt correctly. No address, no stamp or any other mark suggested a personal delivery. Quickly I asked the spectacled chap on reception. "Did you see who delivered the letter?"

"Yes Sir, a very fine looking Lady." He winked at me as if some sort of sexual rendezvous was to unfold. I could sense his mind working overtime as he contemplated a secret liaison.

Snappily I said, "Description?"

He looked into space, lost, confused. "Do you know, Sir, I'm not sure."

"Too busy looking at her tits and arse, no doubt?"

His complexion reddened. His eyes flicking all directions searching for listening ears. "Well they were nice to look at, Sir. Oh, I do recall she was wearing sunglasses."

"Dark glasses no doubt?" I humoured but I didn't smile. "What about the colour of her hair?"

"Blonde! No, no. Reddish blonde, if such a colour exists."

"Now you're performing. What was she wearing?"

"Ah-there you have me, Mister Speed. But a pair of tight jeans comes to mind."

"How long ago was the letter delivered?"

"Quite recently, maybe only half an hour ago."

"Can you still see the lady on the premises?"

"Oh-no, Mister Speed, she definitely made her exit after the delivering the letter. I watched her leave."

"No doubt, every step of the way?"

His eyebrows screwed up as if he'd misunderstood. "I'm sorry?"

"You followed her arse as she left," I said casually.

"Oh yes, Mister Speed, a discreet gentlemanly glance to watch poetry in motion." His eyes lifted as his mind wandered. "Then spell bound you ask yourself, how..."

I jumped the queue. "Something so full of shit can look so beautiful!"

Dream boy looked at me disgusted. "Not quite what I had in mind, Mister Speed."

I moved away from the reception desk and studied the letter, revolving it full circle.

The envelope was made of quality paper, not the thin cheap brand that comes wrapped, twenty for a pound. This letter had class, bought from an expensive store. Nevertheless, my first instinct had me thinking it was a letter bomb and I almost threw it to the floor before remembering letter bombs explode on opening. I began my own version of a counter-terrorist examination of the envelope with applied caution, not that I would have recognized a letter bomb if I saw one. Carefully I fingered the contents for lumps of putty like material, wires, bi-metal strips, things I would have expected to consist of a bomb. I should have been apprehensive but I wasn't. No jangling nerves. Satisfied the letter wasn't going to explode, I open the envelope and removed the folded piece of paper, again the quality of the paper signified upper class connections.

The content of the letter was short and magnificently mysterious not to be ignored.

Dear, Mister Shackleton Speed.

I write this letter of introduction in anticipation of you accepting an invitation to frequent my humble home with your presence. I would have dearly enjoyed the journey to the South of Ireland to meet you personally, but unfortunately due to illness I'm unable to travel. We have a lot to discuss about the past, about the crashed plane in Berkshire, which I know will not disappoint your appetite for the truth, because it is indeed the truth you seek. I know this letter seems strange to be received at your present destination but information received alerted me to your presence in the Republic of Ireland. I will understand if you totally ignore this letter and do not make the journey. I will, though, guarantee that your safety will be reassured if you decide to test the inquisitive side of yourself. I do hope you will join me. Overleaf you will find the times and place of meeting and a return ticket to Dublin.

This is no hoax, I assure you, Mister Speed. Nor can you expect any sort of entrapment. My intentions are honourable and sincere.

Yours sincerely
Chief Air Marshall Sir Dillon Deveron. (Retired)

I should have been asking myself the serious question as to why Deveron should even be aware that I was here in Ireland only I was too hyped up to see that as a problem. I was more livid that he seemed to consider me as some long lost friend who he had upset in the past. To hell with Deveron! He was the last of my worries. I was too busy trying to locate a submarine and he would have to wait.

I was in the process of tearing the letter and tickets into a thousand pieces when it occurred to me that I had somehow been absorbed into the euphoria of obsession. In my lone quest to discover the truth I was falling into the inevitable trap of greed. Gold was bouncing around my brain. Find the gold! Find it before anyone else. Why? I was forgetting people whose lives I'd destroyed because of my mad obsession to seek artefacts.

No, I was wrong to ignore the letter. Deveron had to be dealt with first. If there's gold to be found, it can wait. I can't let Deveron weasel his way out from his guilt. He owes me an explanation. He has answers to the demons inside my head and I don't care how old he is, I'll throttle the frigging bastard till he squeals the truth.

Back into a civilized relax mode I rang mobile to mobile and got in touch with Shamus and told him I wouldn't need him tomorrow. By the sounds he was making when he mumbled down the line, 'hullo', he was obviously munching on a bag of his favourite dried pork pieces.

"Any particular reason, Shacks Sir?"

I sensed he was concerned he was losing a client, and since I knew very little myself, there wasn't much I could tell him. I said, "I'm going to Dublin to see someone."

He didn't pressurize me. "Will it be for long, Shacks Sir?"

"Unsure. Don't worry the payment meter is still running; but if for some unforeseen circumstances that I don't return, feel free to sell my diving gear."

"O' no, Shacks, Sir, I couldn't do dhat. What about your friend, Detective Inspector Hamer?"

"Sell him too!"

Silence echoed through the airwaves.

I said, "What about him?"

144

"Want me to tell him where you've gone?"

"No! Let him sweat."

"Won't he be a little angry, Shacks Sir?"

"Naturally, he operates better that way, having sleepless nights."

"You're bit of a bastard, if you don't mind me sayin', Shacks, Sir."

"Yes, I am rather. And while you're doing nothing, find out information on the 'Flying-fish'."

I hung up.

CHAPTER SIXTEEN

I dressed casual, nothing too impressive, driving jacket, round necked sweater, and a pair of slacks and comfortable shoes. I left no message at reception that I would be away for the day then drove to the railway station at Cork and parked the Roadster on the long stay car park, collected a pre-booked ticket and boarded the train for Dublin.

There was plenty to think about during the journey. Hard thinking that produces the inevitable headache. Here I was hurtling towards Dublin not knowing what to expect and my only source for protection was a letter assuring my safety from a man who I had never seen before. A man who I strongly suspected had some connection with Lens and Tommy's death.

In addition to stepping into the unknown, there is still the strong probability of killers out there searching for me at this very moment and they may even be waiting for me at the end of the track. Yes, it was hard to relax when knowingly going to a place with the same intention of raiding honey from a bee-hive and expecting not to get stung without wearing the appropriate protective clothing; mine should have been a military tank.

As the train approached Dublin I had my biggest worry, I suddenly feared nothing. I should have been twitching with nervousness but I wasn't. Not even a tingle in the stomach region. No apprehension whatsoever. I had adopted nerves of steel, though I probably had always possessed that toughness but had never really noticed before.

When the train pulled in at Tara Street Station, I didn't rush to disembark. I carefully observed anyone who remotely appeared to be observing my presence. No one did. When I was the last person on the train I left the carriage, vacated the station and walked down towards the River Liffey, glancing back a few times to see if I had picked up a follower from the station before turning left into Burgh Quay. I followed the river upstream. After another quick glance over my shoulder, I walked with pace onto Aston Quay until I had reached the painted steel construction of the Ha'penny Bridge arching over to the north side of the River.

I could see the sense in choosing the bridge as a meeting point as it wasn't ideal to spring a trap if I had wanted to. I glanced left and right before crossing the bridge where I stopped in the middle and waited as instructed. Between five and ten minutes lapsed, I wasn't clock watching. I was beginning to get bored looking at every passer-by, expecting one of them to approach me. Eventually I turned my back and lazily leant my elbows onto the side of the bridge peering over the side, convincing myself to be in a trusting mood, yet slightly edgy about the possibility of a knife in the back while I wasn't looking. I stared down into the river, focusing on the reflection of the bridge as it rippled with the flow of water. My mind began to wander back to the rocks below Roaring Water Bay and if I would need any air power tools to dislodge the rock-face. I was on the verge of dismissing the idea when a voice jolted me upright.

"Well, well, well, Shackleton Speed, you haven't changed a bit!"

I spun round to face the woman's beckoning voice and my heart bounced irregularly. It was her again. The American terrorist, the bitch herself! And by the description given at the hotel reception, it was the very same woman who hand delivered the letter from Deveron. My eyes frantically scanned the bridge for her accomplices. She was quick to read my mind.

"If you're worried about certain individuals, don't be. I'm alone."

"Aren't you the confident one," I said bitterly.

"I'm confident on a number of things, Buster! So don't even consider threatening me in any way for whatever reasons you want to blame me for," she said calmly.

It was hard to restrain myself from exploding in anger. "Funny, I had you down for three smacks: one for the rough reception I received when we first met: two for leaving me sexually frustrated: and three for almost getting me killed at McClusky's warehouse."

"You escaped, so what are you complaining for?"

"Yes, but only by the skin of my teeth and the rags on my back!" I snapped.

"You were unfortunate to pick the wrong time to visit McClusky's. That was your fault not ours. So I'd reconsider any scheming retaliation you're planning against me."

"Oh! Why should I?"

"This bulge in my right hand pocket isn't just my hand keeping warm, that's why. It's a small calibre hand gun, Derringer actually, yet sufficient, I promise, to drop a full grown pig."

I saw the clasped hand in her jacket pocket and the extended finger. "What happened to the frigging promise of immunity from death?"

"As promised providing you keep your hands to yourself."

"Oh I intend to for the time being," I conceded.

There was a glint of uncertainty in her eyes.

"I promise!"

"That remains to be seen. Follow me! I will take you to Deveron."

"Suppose you tell me what Deveron wants or is your leader unlikely to divulge such secrets to an underling?"

"I'll leave Deveron himself to tell you." She turned to go.

"I'm afraid I can't go."

She stopped and looked searchingly into my face. "Not bothering now you've seen me?"

"No it's not that. The problem is I was always warned not to go off with strangers. As you have the advantage of knowing my name, how about yours, I can't keep calling you bitch! Can I?"

She took the insult admirably calm. "Shayna Magginty, now can we go?"

"Lead the way, Shayna," I gestured with my hand.

Despite the initial shock at seeing her again I did prefer her presence than that of an old codger. But there was one particular thing I wanted to ask her as we crossed the bridge to the North side.

"Am I such an easy person to locate?"

"Meaning what?"

"Well, taking in consideration the actual size of the Irish Republic and the estimated half a million visitors presently in the South of Ireland, how the hell did you know where I would be?"

"We have powerful connections. No one is untraceable."

"That's all very nice to know, but who do I owe the pleasure of betraying my whereabouts?"

"Does it really matter?"

"Yes, it frigging does!"

"Do you really expect me to say how we operate as an organization? We have a highly organized network of intelligence. It might surprise you, Buster, that Irish people are not thick paddies as some people think."

"You're an American!"

"Irish-American, with intelligence," She corrected me.

"Is that so Shayna? Didn't know much what McClusky was up too, this power of the organization shit!"

She nearly bit my head off. "Different matter!" she snapped. "McClusky is a double crossing bastard, correction, a dead double crossing bastard."

"Yes I know," I said. "It was headline news in every London paper. Dead people left everywhere."

"We took no casualties." There was pride in her tone.

"I'm glad to hear it. Didn't happen to bump off two ugly looking bastards who look like vultures while in your gunfight?"

"We hardly hung about for an identity parade. Our business was concluded, we came straight back to Ireland."

"What about your merchandise, obviously lost now?"

She ignored me.

"Where are your brothers in arms? Especially the spotty face one with the darts."

"Mind your own business! It's possible you might just meet them again." There was threat in her voice.

"Good!" I said defiantly. "I cherish a return game of darts, only I'll have a set too, though I call mine a bow and arrow."

She was impervious to my challenge.

"So how did you get involved in terrorism?" I asked. "Or should I say, what persuaded you to turn into a killer?"

She stopped at a yellow two-seater Mazda sports car. "You ask too many questions, Shackleton Speed."

"I'm interested."

"Don't be."

I nodded towards her car. "Impressive," I said. "Terrorism pays extremely well."

She wasn't amused. "Get in!"

I didn't argue, I clambered in the passenger seat and snapped the seatbelt on just before the engine roared and the car accelerated with awesome power. She handled the car impeccably. She liked racing, I could judge that by the way she drove passionately and didn't care much for road restrictions. We went out of Dublin and headed South along the N11 coastal road. We weren't followed and if we had, I doubt Team Ferrari would have kept up with us. Nevertheless, I enjoyed the thrill, which I know annoyed her because I think it was her intention to scare the hell out of me. She didn't and I could see by the look on her face it pissed her off that it didn't.

I said casually, "Did you find what you were looking for in my hotel room?"

She seemed surprised by what I said. "What gives you the impression I was in your room?"

"Perfume you wear, nice, but a dead giveaway! The smell choked my room."

"Well, I wasn't there, Buster!"

"You came to the hotel to deliver Deveron's letter."

"So?"

"So the letter delivery was your second visit to the hotel, on your first visit you went to my room and rummaged through my belongings."

"Don't be ridiculous. Have you any proof?"

"I don't need proof, Shayna." I leaned forward so I could see the corners of her eyes. "Do you realize your eyes twinkle like two diamonds when you lie?"

"That is a pathetic!" But she automatically tilted and looked in the rear view mirror. "My eyes have always sparkled. It's the amount of vitamins I take."

"Then how do you explain the smell of your perfume lingering inside my room."

"I wasn't in your room, Buster!"

"You're wearing some now. Jean Paul Gautier 'Classique', I believe!"

"So you have a nose for perfume. Been around a few wearers, have you?"

I smiled impishly. "Are you jealous?"

She expressed revulsion. "Don't be ridiculous!"

"Anyway, Shayna, you disappoint me greatly."

She dropped down a gear and eased the car through a sharp bend. "Why is that?"

"Well to have the audacity to sneak into a man's room and not wait in bed for me."

"Your mind is so disgusting!"

"That's frigging heavy coming from you! I seem to recall you taking advantage of a defenceless man, me."

"That's a woman's prerogative."

I jumped up in my seat. "Hang on a minute! If the roles had been changed you would have been crying rape and I would have been clapped in irons."

She shook her head. "Wrong, Buster," and in a flash she had taken the gun from her pocket and angled it at my stomach while trying to focus on me and the road. "I wouldn't be crying rape, I'd be saying this bitch bites back twice as hard as I put a hole in your belly!"

I was unmoved by her actions and said, "I believe you would. Do watch the road, Shayna," I added calmly, and she just corrected the car's path as it nearly collided with a horn blaring on-coming truck. I never flinched.

"So where are we going, if it's not too much trouble to ask?"

"Yes it is too much trouble."

She leaned forward and slipped a disc into the CD player which blasted out a Bruce Springsteen classic. I couldn't hear her singing along but her lips were moving.

'I was...born in the U.S.A...I was...born in the U.S.A...'

I took the hint and slid down into the car seat.

The remainder of the journey lacked any sort of conversation through no fault of mine as she preferred the music. Instead I observed and memorized the route we were taking, as there was the possibility I would have to make an uninvited return in the near future.

We left the N11 at Kilmacanago, took the R755 to Roundhouse, turned into a dirt track road and came to a shuddering halt outside large ornate gates wedged between a stonewall of fortress proportion. A camera scanned our arrival. Shayna pressed the button on a remote control device and the automatic gates began opening. Then with her customary wheel spin we drove down a tree lined drive till we reached a large stone Manor house.

I got out of the car and looked around in disappointment as I did expect at least two armed guards to grab and throw me against the wall to search me for weapons. None showed. Surely I was worth some consideration for being dangerous? And Shayna, by her casualness, didn't see me as a threat either as she entered the house. I followed her through the entrance and into the hall, along a corridor and into a spacious study with a well stocked library. The walls were decorated with beautifully carved oak veneer with a scattering of oil painting hanging there merely for decoration than viewing.

Shayna pointed across the room to a frail, withered old man crunched up on a studded leather chair. She gave me a gentle nudge to make my way over then without a word she'd disappeared leaving me alone with who I considered to be a treble murderer.

My first instinct should have had me dashing across to Deveron and grab him by the throat to squeeze the truth out of him. Yet looking at his frailty he probably wouldn't have survived even a short throttling. And then I couldn't be sure if he had already anticipated the idea and had placed a hidden marksman to stop me.

As for my first opinion of Dillon Deveron, it was hard to imagine him as a world war two fighter pilot, doubling up as a stone-faced killer. His dried ragged facial features showed no hardness of a man capable of shooting his flying comrade in the back, as Billy Slade had witnessed. Though I saw no evidence of him actually smoking, he was wearing a smoker's jacket and a cravat. He didn't rise to greet me.

"Ah! Mister Speed, at last we meet." Deveron's voice sounded just like a Dalek from a television series of 'Doctor Who'.

"Please, please, come closer. You must excuse me for not rising to my feet alas brittle bone disease rather limits my enthusiasm to walk unassisted. Please, sit down refreshments are on the way."

As I sat my eyes never veered from Deveron.

"I can tell by your expression, Mister Speed, you're wondering why my voice has a distorted sound-." He pulled his cravat sideways to reveal a metallic object embedded in his throat, "-throat cancer attacked my voice box, the legacy for my passion of Panamanian cigars. Without this voice-box device my speech would be useless."

"Ingenious invention," I said, not that I really cared.

"Do you smoke, Mister Speed?"

It was a mistake on Deveron's part to allow me to make a point on smoking as an occupational habit. I would have bored him for hours on reasons on why smoking isn't big and isn't clever, but I decided to keep it simple.

"No," I said bluntly. "It smells like burnt wood and, I imagine, tastes just as revolting. No, I prefer drinking myself to death; far more enjoyable. And if you want my honest opinion, smokers are inconsiderate, selfish bastards, who insist on sharing their desire with other non-participating losers. Then they look confounded when people object. If I was to share my bad habit I end up pissing all over them."

Deveron was a little shocked. "Well-yes-I don't think anyone can argue with your opinion, Mister Speed."

"Good!" I said. "Now perhaps you can tell me how you knew I was Ireland."

"I asked Shayna to find you," he seemed nervous.

"Why?"

"So we can talk!"

"Talk about what?"

"Why do I get the impression that you are very hostile towards me, Mister Speed?"

"Because I hate mysterious games," I said. "I also hate being dragged across Ireland for no good reason."

He raised his hand. "Patience, Mister Speed, all in good time. The main thing is you came. Shayna did well to track you down, and she did warn me your temperament might be a little volatile and you have an obstinate attitude." He snorted a small laugh. "She knows her men."

"Look! I don't have time to be messed around. I'm a busy man and busy men get straight to the point."

"Time, Mister Speed, is what I neither have, nor do I have the energy to pursue matters. I'm a dying man. Old age is incurable. But I've had a fair run in life, I cannot grumble."

It couldn't happen to a nicer man, I thought. I said, "Shall we get on with it then?"

Deveron was surprised by my bluntness, but composed himself and went on. "I'm interested in the Spitfire you found, Mister Speed." He paused, probably expecting me to answer. "Shayna told me you'd mentioned the intriguing information while engaged in riveting conversation. (I thought this bastard is taking the frigging piss) It's been a long time since something so exciting had my heart racing. Please tell me it's true, Mister Speed."

In a bored reply I said, "A friend of mine found it, it was in all the papers."

"Please, Mister Speed, don't judge me as being a fool because I'm an old man."

"Is this leading anywhere?" I knew it was, but I asked anyway to prolong his agony, which was nothing more than he deserved in my view.

"All depends if it's *the one*."

"We are we talking about the plane that included the remains of a pilot?"

"Yes, yes, yes, Mister Speed." Deveron spluttered his tinny words.

"Why should it interest you?"

"Let's stop the pretence, Mister Speed!" Deveron suddenly snapped and an echo followed from the throat box as if he had got a back-feed. I had to admit the old man still had an angry streak built inside. "You were captured by a group of ambitious terrorists. You escaped from the utter carnage that followed and the entire episode or your name isn't even mentioned in any of the tabloids. Think of the money the papers would offer for such a story: man escapes clutches of terrorism. Think of the financial contribution to a dwindling bank balance."

"I don't have a dwindling bank balance," I said.

"That doesn't escape the overwhelming fact that you never mentioned a word to anyone about your abduction. Complete silence. No complaints to the police asking for protection. I found it all very suspicious, indeed. Such actions meant the person has something to hide. He doesn't want to share his secret. He doesn't want any police interference. I'm interested to know why? Am I jolting the correct nerve ends, Mister, Speed?"

More like he was beginning to annoy me.

"The only nerves you're jolting are the ones that might just crack at any second and strangle you for sending your goons to extract information from friends of mine before having them killed." I found it extremely difficult to control my anger.

Deveron was puzzled by the accusation. "Whatever are you insinuating, Mister Speed?"

"McClusky for starters, that's an easy name for you to remember."

Deveron had that Alzheimer's look.

I carried on. "Damian Love and Theodore Hate, two hardened killers, they belong to you! Through McClusky you hired them to kill the farmer whose field the plane was found in. Then for good measure they killed a photographer friend of mine. Then they tried to kill me. All because of one mangled crashed Spitfire."

Deveron went white. "I hope this is all a wild story, Mister Speed? If it isn't you are making a terrible mistake. I have had nothing to do with anything so drastic."

"I don't believe a word you say. Those men were hired by you to kill my friends. Isn't that right?"

I noticed Deveron began shaking. He was no longer the confident man he probably thought he was.

"I did nothing of the sort!" his tinny voice echoed in protest. "I'm not acquainted with any of those men mentioned, Mister Speed. I ordered no such instructions. Good god, man! I can't even get out of this damn chair without assistance."

"There is no need to walk to issue orders."

"You're accusing the wrong person, Mister Speed."

"Then why was Shayna there, in London, with her terrorist croakers? Now, strangely, she is here with you. It doesn't need the powers of observation to connect a deceitful bunch of congregating warlords. Two and two make four and you have a team of professional killers from both ends of Europe."

"There is no connection between Shayna's misdoings and myself, I assure you. It is purely a Grandfather and Granddaughter relationship between us and no more. She is my illegitimate daughter's child, a grandchild I never knew of until two years ago."

"Bullshit bores me," I said.

"It is true, Mister Speed! With my reluctance to marry Shayna's grandmother, she went off to America. It was only after I retired from the military that I found out all this. Sadly the daughter I didn't know died giving birth to Shayna. After I settled back in Ireland, Shayna became a regular visitor from America."

"And you let her use your home as a terrorist base?"

"I never once suspected she was an active terrorist till three months ago when a particular bunch of activists began arriving at my home. Friends, Shayna assured me, dressed in military uniforms and playing war-games. She forgot that my life was spent fighting unseen enemies. My eyes are failing but I know terrorists when I see one. I soon dragged the truth out of her. Alas I'm too old to dissuade her from her actions and I certainly won't turn against her."

"Oh-why not, she kills people."

"She is my angel Mister Speed, I can't turn her in. She is the only piece of life I have left in this world. In a way I admire her. She has the same wild enthusiasm I had when I was young, that same wickedness, a chip off the old block you might say."

I had no sympathy. "That maybe all lovely to you, but Shayna and her band of merry terrorists subjected me to some rough treatment and ruined my clothing."

"You can't blame me for that, Mister Speed. My only interest is the plane. I need to know all the exact details of what you found."

Suddenly my world had backfired. Was I right up frigging shits creek! Had I got the wrong man? How could I have been so blind and brainless not to realize Deveron would have had no prior knowledge that the plane had been found by me unless someone told him and that could have only been Shayna after I had told her. Then again the easiest form of defence is to lie through your teeth. No, Deveron wasn't in the clear yet and I would soon spring a nasty surprise on him.

Subdued, I said, "Well actually there wasn't much left of the plane. A smashed cockpit with a skeleton strapped to the seat."

"Yes, I read that much in the papers. The M.o.D. released the name Flying Officer Derek Rowland as the pilot. Straight away I knew there was a mix-up. I knew Rowland. He flew a Spitfire Mark One, so he's still missing."

"I've already worked that out. But I do know the name of the pilot."

"How could you know that?" Deveron sounded annoyed, betrayed even.

"The corpse told me."

"Please, Mister Speed, this isn't a joking matter I appreciate."

"I saw it on the tag around the skeletons neck."

Deveron's eyes widened slowly. "Whose name did you see?"

It was time to put the hang-mans noose around his neck. I was going to be his executioner. "The name was Craven."

Shock overwhelmed Deveron. "Craven," he said slowly.

"Yes, that's right. Wing Commander Craven. Remember him?"

He nodded to confirm.

"You flew with him on the fatal day he went missing."

Deveron looked as if he was about to throw up. He swallowed hard. "Yes, that was the last time I saw him. When I read about the plane found in Berkshire, I went cold, my bent spine tingled. I knew it was Craven. I could sense his spiritual presence. He has returned to haunt me. I shall have to seek forgiveness for not finding him to give him the hero's burial."

"The dead don't forgive, that's left to the living, it's there you must seek your repentance and, I'm afraid, I don't make those arrangements."

A side door to the study opened breaking the intensity of the atmosphere. A rather scrumptious looking maid came into the room carrying a tea tray. She was a stunner. Perhaps growing old isn't too bad after all, I thought.

"Thank you, my dear!" Deveron said to her. "I've changed my mind. Can you pour me a neat, double whiskey, I think I'm going to need one to thin my blood." He turned to me. "Can I offer you one or do you prefer tea?"

"Too early for my stomach, tea is fine."

I thought I caught a lecherous glint in Deveron's saggy eyes as she poured the tea. I was as guilty as hell! She placed a cup in my hand and smiled, crossed the room to a drinks cabinet, returned with a glass of Irish whiskey for Deveron, and quietly left the room.

I swigged some tea with a quick slurp because no one warned me the tea was frigging hot.

"Well now he has been found thanks to you, Mister Speed. Can you believe I have spent my entire life searching for his plane? Always hoping he had survived the crash. It was a hard burden to carry all these years that I never found my dearest friend."

"Is it normal for friends to shoot friends in the back?" I hit him full in the face with the question.

The seizure I expected Deveron to have nearly materialized as his body shuddered uncontrollably. His complexion discoloured to a yellowish white, and if he still had the strength he would probably have crushed the whiskey glass in his hand. Instead he gulped down the remnants of his drink.

"I-I-don't understand your implication!" His robotic tinny voice squeaked.

"Which part of 'shoot friend in the back' do you not understand so I can clarify it for you?"

"All of it! It's preposterous. It's an insane accusation?"

I put my cup down on the table. "Is it?"

"What do you mean?"

"Like some more whiskey?" I asked him.

I never gave him time to react. I took his glass, poured the spirit, and put it back in his hand before he had time to say no.

"Well, Mister Speed?"

"How do I know you shot Craven in the back?"

157

"Yes, I mean, no! It's despicable what you're implying! Good god! I'm a man of integrity, honour. I fought for freedom against the might of Hitler. I put my life on the line in many aerial battles during the war, a veteran of the Battle of Britain in 1940. My entire existence since has been devoted to serving the security of the United Kingdom."

"Oh I don't doubt your courage, old man. Just curious why your Spitfire fired on Craven's Spitfire."

"No! No! It's not true." The whiskey flowed down his throat.

"Deveron, it's the truth. It's what happened while you were engaged in 'Operation Huggermugger'."

Deveron's blood shot, grey eyes shot open. "How on earth can you know anything about 'Huggermugger'?"

"I'm a frigging clever bastard! Operation Huggermugger involved the hunt for a fictitious Japanese submarine I-52. Submarine I-52 number two, that is! Submarine I-52 number one was sunk by the Americans in mid-Atlantic. Apparently, sub number two was never found; conclusion, it never existed. But Craven found it. His reconnaissance camera snapped the big Jap can. He wanted to tell the world and would have done so if he hadn't crashed after you shot his plane from the sky."

Deveron burst into my conversation, pointing his crooked forefinger accusingly in my direction. "You-you thief!" he spluttered. "You took the camera from the wreck! Wait a minute! The photographer friend you mentioned, good god you've had the film developed! You've found what I spent a lifetime trying to locate." His eyeballs nearly popped out of their sockets. He was panting with excitement. "The submarine, it's here in Ireland, somewhere in the regions of Roaring Water Bay. Please tell me it's true?"

"Stop deviating from the truth!" I yelled at him. Frigging hell, I was mad. "You shot down a British aircraft and killed an unsuspecting comrade who put his trust in you to protect him from harm. And don't even attempt to deny it because I tracked down a witness to the incident."

Deveron looked at me with a pathetic plea of innocence. "What witness?"

"A reliable one, with an impeccable memory and he even described the action in graphic detail. It was a brutal attack on a defenceless craft." What a frigging arsehole I'd have looked if Deveron was to actually see illiterate Billy Slade re-enacting what he displayed to me.

"I find it strange you never went to the ministry with your theory."

"No theory, Deveron, the truth and you know it!"

"Am I to be blackmailed, Mister Speed? Money for silence, is that it?"

Anger had me on the edge of the seat. "You frigging smug bastard, Deveron. Money won't bring back the lives of innocent people. Oh-don't fret old man, I'm not about to bring you to justice. I've no intentions of being your judge and jury. You're dying anyway. (I thought I was a bit callous with what I said, but isn't life a bitch) I'm only interested in the bastards that killed my friends and you had better give me a list of names of all who are involved."

Deveron was looking distinctly uncomfortable.

I said, "You're perspiring. I didn't think it was that warm in this room."

"High blood pressure, you will suffer the same when you reach my age."

"Or more like finding it difficult to tell the truth!"

Deveron sighed heavily and put his glass down. His head dropped into his hands, his fingertips sinking into the sagging skin on his thin face. Then slowly he raised his head, watery eyes staring directly into mine. "Oh, dear-it is no use pretending nothing happened. If I'm to die, I want to die in peace and with a clear conscience. I suppose the time for confession is now appropriate. But please believe me when I say I had nothing to do with your problems. I never ordered anyone to commit such a crime against your friends. The first time I heard your name mentioned was three days ago. I acted quickly. I just couldn't let the opportunity pass me by."

"Okay, I'll accept that for the time being. Now get on with your confession, it should be interesting and aren't you lucky I didn't bring a recorder."

Deveron swallowed excess saliva. "I suppose for you to fully understand the actions of a young tearaway, I had better start from the beginning." He coughed to clear his cracked throat. "I was born in Ireland," he began earnestly. "I grew up in a impoverish Dublin, lonely, searching for a solution to avoid the poverty that Ireland seemed to be experiencing at the time, searching for freedom and adventure. I found it in the brutal ranks of the IRA. I was a raw recruit with high ambitions, absorbed into the fascinating world of violence. Yes, Mister Speed, I too became a terrorist and without bragging I was an experienced campaigner with a list of atrocities and it got me recognition. I wanted to stand high amongst the Irish people in the same way Michael Collins raised to infamous notoriety. I dreamed of being the hero. I wanted the adulation, desperate to be somebody."

"That's all very poetic, Deveron. But Michael Collins was executed for his troubles in 1922, some infamous notoriety he had."

"Whatever the outcome, I wanted fame," Deveron snapped, not liking the interruption. "Then the war reared its ugly head, rather spoilt a good campaign. Though Ireland declared neutrality, there always remained the imminent threat that Hitler would invade Irish shores, to dominate Irish people. Rather pointless fighting to have a free Ireland only for the Germans to suffocate us with imperialism.

"I'd been fighting British ground troops for two years so I certainly wasn't about to offer my services to the army. So I elected to fight the Germans by signing up to join the R.A.F. I'd plenty of flying time under my belt. My uncle taught me to fly in a First World War bi-plane and when I showed them what I could do the military were most impressed with my flying skills."

He was beginning to bore me. I jumped in. "Skip the drivel, Deveron, what happened on the day of the operation?"

"You're not exactly renowned for any patience, are you, Mister Speed?"

"No! Get on with it!"

"As you wish," he coughed twice. (I wasn't counting but if he had coughed a third time my fist would have followed his tongue back down his throat.) "The operation was simply routine reconnaissance, the search for the possibility of a Japanese submarine operating off the shores of England. No one actually believed any of the story, took it as some sort of propaganda, especially when there was talk of the submarine carrying gold. As orders were orders you have to follow them. Craven flew the reconnaissance Spitfire and since there was still the threat of a marauding German Messerschmitt operating in the skies, I was appointed his wing protection. During our flight I developed engine trouble, bit of carbon on the spark plugs, I think the maintenance crew later reported. As for Craven, he was like a rampaging bull when he flew, anyone with a decent engine would have had trouble flying alongside his craft. And it was a lot lighter than my Spitfire, because reconnaissance craft required speed and agility and the craft was stripped of every nonessential piece of equipment. Everything that wasn't needed to fly the plane became superfluous. It included the crafts entire weapon system, the radio equipment, all disregarded. Speed was its primary defence. Although the lightened craft had awesome acceleration, it still took a brave man to fly the Spitfire over occupied territory. Most didn't make it back, but Craven always did. He seemed invincible. His exceptional flying skills always guided him through the barrage of hostilities.

"As it turned out on *that* day I lost contact with Craven because of his Maverick style of flying, and when I finally located him he was on his way back to the airfield, all smiles, giving me the thumbs up, his fist shaking in triumph. It was then I realized he'd actually located the submarine, actually seen the damn contraption, he'd captured it all on film. I just couldn't believe he'd found the submarine. Craven signalled to me, we had developed our own hand signals to verify any destruction we had inflicted on the enemy. He signalled the submarine had been crippled and was sinking. Then in a flash it happened. A strange blinding phenomenon came over me. All I saw was an enemy aircraft in front of my sights. A shroud of red mist filled my eyes. I suddenly hated Craven for being the hero he was, taking all the glory. Then suddenly my thoughts returned to the counties of Ireland and the freedom my brothers in arms yearn for. I thought of when the war would finally end. I thought of the gold bullion aboard the Japanese submarine and how it could be used to ensure our battle to free Ireland from British occupation continued.

"In a moment of sheer madness my mind became possessed. Right there in front of me was my dream of greatness. I just opened both guns on the tail of Craven's Spitfire. I couldn't stop myself. I was mesmerised by the perfect line of tracers as the bullets rattled out in cohesion. (I could see by the expressions and concentration on his face he was reliving the moment.) I hit Craven's plane with everything I had, watched his craft go down in a stooping dive. I guess he was still alive as his Spitfire careered out of control because incredibly he was struggling to pull the craft from out of the crash dive. I followed to find where he would crash so I could retrieve the cameras.

"As fate would have it, my own engine began playing up and by the time I'd recovered, I'd lost the flight path Craven's plane took and night was falling fast. The rest is history. I've wasted a lifetime searching."

Deveron hung his head in shame.

I had about as much pity for Deveron as I would have for a wasp that had just stung me, brutally flattened and rip its wings off before throwing the insect into a spider's web. I wasn't about to let him off the hook. I said, harshly. "People had crazy ideas during the war but yours was the pits, Deveron."

"If I had a second chance to relive the moment I might have gone in a different direction, but it happened, admittedly never forgotten. But there is one important point I wish to state, though it probably sounds rather trivial now, I wish to say that in my capacity as high ranking officer in the British military, I never once passed on information to the IRA, or any other terrorist group. I could have quite easily but refrained from doing so. I had good reasons not too, as I discovered after the war. Over ambitious warlords decided the terrorism scandals were very lucrative business, extortion, robberies, prostitution. It became a case of internal feuding as the factions fought over control of the cities. No, Mister Speed, I wasn't going to feed gangsters with information so they could enhance their wealth."

"How noble of you Deveron, although a little too late for redemption." My tone was harsh and deservedly so.

"Dreams of greatness, Mister Speed, that was my guilt. Young, proud, I wanted to be one of the great ambassadors of Ireland, a respected hero to the Irish people, to grace the same pedestal as Michael Collins did. I wanted to enhance to even greater credibility. To be remembered as the greatest fighter of Irish freedom. Yet as the years went by the dream of finding the plane died, almost forgotten until Shayna brought the memories flooding back into my senile world. She told me all about the intrepid, Shackleton Speed and the discovered Spitfire. It put the zest back on my life with the possibility that all my beliefs could finally be true."

"By shooting down that Spitfire you gained absolutely nothing, Deveron. There is no submarine to be found, there never was. You murdered Craven in cold blood because of the greed for gold. Yet the most stupid thing about the entire farce is it was all based on a speculative report by an unknown source in another part of the world, probably the figment of someone's imagination, and you fell for it. That's pathetic!"

By his expression I don't think Deveron accepted a word I spoke.

"Not as pathetic as you think, Mister Speed." I got the distinct impression that Deveron was on the counter attack, the old man was fighting back. There was a sudden seriousness in the tone of his tinny voice. "I have a distinguished guest arriving later for dinner. We are old acquaintances during my time in the ministry. He is an attaché at the Japanese embassy in London. I have persuaded him and his lovely wife to spend some prime time in Ireland. I would very much like you to meet him, Mister Speed. The conversation will be quite riveting and will reveal some interesting facts concerning the I-52. It will be exhilarating to examine the comparisons of information you both have. You will, of course, stay for the remainder of the day, dinner in the evening, and I wouldn't dream of sending a guest hurrying home at night, so there is a room being prepared for you. I hope that is to your satisfaction?"

The mere mention of Japanese involvement had me hooked especially if he can throw some light on the mysterious submarine. It was an invitation I could hardly refuse, but I didn't want to sound too keen.

I said, "Okay, providing that I'm not on the menu for dinner."

Deveron almost broke into smile. "Good! Mister Speed. I was always confident you would."

"Don't be too over confident, all I said was I'll stay for dinner."

"And miss the highlight of the evening, a man of your character! I don't think so. You're a treasure seeker hiding under the banner of metal detector enthusiast. You sell what you find to the highest bidder with total disregard to the treasure act. Come now, Mister Speed, you're as much a criminal as I, only I've retired. I know you're intrigued to hear the story of the I-52 that never was because if you hadn't been I would have expected the Garda arriving at my door instead of you, Mister Speed."

The old goat had a point. In reality he had done nothing harmful towards me, providing he wasn't frigging lying about him not being involved in endangering my life and mixing up my affairs.

"Will Shayna be joining us for dinner?"

Deveron smiled. "Of course she is, and such a beautiful woman, don't you agree."

"No argument on that statement. Dinner it is, then I'll listen to your pack of lies later."

The door of the study opened and the maid returned.

Deveron said, "All the excitement has worn me out. I must leave you, my medication is due. Feel free to wander anywhere about the house. Examine my wonderful collection of old library masterpieces: works from all the great literary writers of our times. Feel free to roam the gardens. They are full, absorbing, tranquil, and most importantly, help yourself to the drinks. Dinner is served at seven. Oh one thing I need to ask you, Mister Speed."

"Yes."

"If I was the man you were looking for would you have killed me?"

"Without hesitation," I said calmly.

Deveron nodded. "I do believe you would, Mister Speed."

I waited until Deveron had shuffled from the study supported by the maid's arm. I decided against the hospitality of the drinks and instead made my way out of the house through the study French windows and wandered into the gardens for some fresh air as the stagnant atmosphere of doubtfulness had stifled my breathing. The walk around the garden would give me space to reflect on my meeting with Deveron. But one thing was certain, for the first time in days I actually didn't feel threatened.

I never planned the route of my walk I just followed my shadow cast by the late afternoon sun until I found my path blocked by the shoreline of a large lake. I was about to retrace my steps when beyond a large bush I heard splashing water. Automatically I followed the sound, quietly moving and then I saw her emerging from the lake, a naked bronzed sculptured goddess that left me breathless.

Shayna's skin glistened as the suns ray caused a prism through the droplets of water dripping from her athletic muscular body. She had primed muscles stretching from shoulders to calves. In comparison she made my body look like a wrecked temple. I went into a cold sweat as I admired her. I could feel her magnetism drawing me towards her. It was difficult not to lust after her and she knew I was watching her even though she didn't look at me directly. She teased me as she dressed. I had never watched a striptease in reverse as she slipped into white lace panties, no bra, white shirt and white pants, but just as interesting, nonetheless.

Still not acknowledging me by eye contact she said to me, "What do you think of my grandfather?"

"Honest opinion?"

'I wouldn't expect anything else."

She ran a large toothed comb through her wet hair in an arcing fashion.

"He's certainly eccentric, possibly crackers and he's a murderer to put it in better prospective."

"He told you then?"

"I left him no option. Did he teach you terrorism or is it built into the genes?"

"Don't try to be clever, Shackleton, or I might rip your head off!"

I smiled cheekily. "Is that a promise?" She knew what I meant.

"Your mind is in very sick condition, Shackleton."

"Friends call me, Shacks."

"I prefer the name, Shackleton, it has that adventurous sound."

"I have been known to get into a few scrapes."

"Walk me back to the house?" she actually asked nicely.

"Sure, I was about to head back anyway."

She slipped on her shoes and we sauntered back with the deliberate slowness of newly met lovers trying to make time last longer. We talked of the beauty of the place, opinions of the weather, general chitchat with a few laughs thrown in, until we reached the exterior of the house when I decided to spoil the occasion.

"You do know Deveron is dying?"

"I've known for the past six months. That's why he was prepared to tell you of his ruthless past. He no longer has anything to lose, can't put a dying man in prison."

"He'll lose you."

"Not really, I'm the sole beneficiary of his entire estate. I'm going to be very wealthy and he wants me to have it all. I shan't disappoint his wishes."

"No good to you when you're dead."

"I've no intention of dying."

"I should imagine the life span of an active terrorist diminishes with every day that passes."

"I might retire."

"Ye you could but I can't quite picture terrorist chiefs leaving you in peace when there's a fight to be won. Can you? Once a terrorist always a terrorists, it simply can't be erased from your record."

"We will see, Shackleton," she said, casually, as if it didn't really matter.

We entered through the kitchen door and back into the hall, where we met a stoutly built woman who I presumed to be Deveron's housekeeper.

Shayna said to her. "Greta, is my grandfather resting?"

Greta, I guessed, was in her middle forties, not pretty, but spoke with such charm that if I were to shut my eyes for a moment I could have quite easily mistaken her for a younger woman. "Yes dear. And the maid has prepared Mister Speed's room as instructed. Shall I take him there?"

"Thank you, Greta, but there's no need. I'll show Mister Speed to his room."

"Thank you, my dear."

She smiled at me as she passed.

I followed Shayna up the stairs and along the landing like a besotted stalker. She could have been leading me into a trap but I didn't care. She stopped outside an oak panelled door, turned the handle and went inside to spring the trap. Like a fool I followed rather hoping that when I entered she would jump on me with sexual starvation, but she didn't and I wondered if my expression gave away the fact I was disappointed with the outcome.

"I hope you find everything comfortable, Shackleton. There are evening suits of different sizes hanging in the wardrobe. All brand new. There's an en-suite through the far door where you will find all utilities: shaving equipment, soaps, cologne bathrobe, pyjamas-."

"I don't wear pyjamas," I said quickly.

"Then don't! Anything else, just ask."

"This *anything*, does it literally mean anything?"

"Within reason, please Shackleton. See you at seven."

She closed the door behind herself leaving me in a room of silence, so still and quiet I heard one of my shoes creak as I began to move. I had a quick nosey around the room wondering if the room was bugged, then dismissed the idea as pretty stupid. Even if the room had any type of listening device, it would be ineffective and serve no purpose as any conversation between me and my sub-conscience was solely restricted in my head as I don't talk in my sleep.

There was no complaint about the standard of the room. I was going to be fed and watered, so what had I to worry about? As in all expensive excursions into hotels I always get my monies worth from the room. Fill the bath to the brim with hot water mixed with relaxant salts and soak for a good hour, which I did, and promptly fell asleep till the water chilled.

CHAPTER SEVENTEEN

I dressed into a crisp fresh Tuxedo and sauntered down to the dining room with the charisma of a person entering a top class casino. The sound of conversational voices drew me to the dining room. I breezed into the room, brightly illuminated by an enormous crystal glass chandelier. The walls were lined with maple veneer below a dado rail with decorated walls above. An assortment of water coloured painting lined the walls, openly displayed by picture lights, the extra brightness creating a spectacular phosphoresce effect.

The large dining table was laid with an entire set of silver cutlery and side plates for five people. Deveron, looking rather more energetically younger than at our earlier meeting, and naturally being the host, he was seated at the head of the table in a comfortable high back chair with armrests. Shayna sat to his right. To his left sat an Oriental couple. The maid began serving punch as I strolled towards the table in such a casual manner I nearly began whistling.

Deveron, his tinny sound prominent, displayed a joyous reception when he caught sight of my approach.

"Ah-Mister Speed, your timing is impeccable. Please, sit beside, Shayna. We are just about to sample a new recipe punch, Japanese style."

Before I'd the chance to sit, Deveron was announcing me to the Japanese couple. "This is the gentleman I told you about, Mister Shackleton Speed. Mister Speed, allow me to introduce a special friend of mine, Shun Tanamoto San, and he adoring wife, Ryoko."

Tanamoto stood and bowed. "It is an honour to meet you, Mister Speed."

I returned the courtesy with a simple nod of the head and avoiding any sharpness in my tone, said, "Good evening. I'm afraid I've heard nothing of you, Tanamoto San." I thought it best to be openly honest.

Deveron went on. "Ah-but you will after the night is over. I better explain that Shun holds a top position at the Japanese Embassy so his status puts him well in contention to assist us in our quest to pursue the truth. Isn't that so?"

"That is indeed, correct," Tanamoto confirmed with another smart bow.

While Deveron ordered the maid to serve dinner, I leaned over and whispered to Shayna. "Wow! Shayna, you look wonderful. For a moment I almost confused you for a sophisticated and posh Lady rather than the brutal bitch I really know!"

She smiled, made an adjustment in her chair and stabbed the heel of her shoe into my foot. I left her alone and concentrated on the two Japanese guests.

As characteristics go amongst most Orientals, he was short in height, had a chubby appearance, with heavy sacs of flesh below both his eyes. His full head of grey hair was smartly trimmed and required no generous helping of hair cream. It was hard to imagine his age was anything less than sixty, but he didn't give me the impression his life had been an arduous one. He dressed immaculately in an expensive silk tuxedo which only proved he wasn't short of money.

His wife, Ryoko, looked twenty years younger. She was dressed in a strikingly colourful traditional costume, a little heavy on the make-up department but had a shapely and appealing figure and well worth a second look any time of the day. Her smile and look reminded me of a shy teenager associating with a boy for the first time. I thought she was cute. Without realizing I smiled at her a little longer than I perhaps should have done, but who cares!

Tanamoto seem to show no animosity towards my gawping stare at his beloved. He sat back down and pulled up his chair. When he spoke the forming of his mouth made him appear to be grinning, though I couldn't fault his English, it was far superior to my Japanese.

"Dillon has told me of your exceptional skills in the field of metal detecting."

"Has he, indeed!" I sat down, feebly attempting to show interest while accepting a glass of punch.

"The subject has always fascinated my curiosity," Tanamoto went on.

I tentatively tasted the punch. It had a delicious kick to it as it hit the back of my throat. "Something you participate in?" I asked.

"Alas, Mister Speed, the patience required far exceeds mine. Obviously there is a secret to success?"

"No secret. Just sheer hard graft and knowing where to look."

It was at that moment Shayna decided to play footsy with the back of my calf. I didn't mind the attention while I studied Tanamoto's puzzled expression.

"What is-ah-this graft, Mister Speed?"

Deveron chuckled and stepped in. "Simple hard work! Shun. Something you and I pay people to do."

Tanamoto laughed. "Ah-yes, now I understand. Perhaps, Mister Speed, you could find the time to educate my ignorance on the subject, perhaps take me along on one of your excursions into the wild world."

I curled my top lip. "I'm a lousy teacher," I said. "Besides, no one can be taught patience."

"Please, Mister Speed, it would be an honour to watch you in action."

"And take pictures, no doubt?"

I think I upset him with that statement.

"I'm not a Japanese tourist, Mister Speed." There was a sprinkle of embitterment in his tone. "Having spent the past twenty years living in London at the Japanese Embassy, I'm rather past the enthusiastic euphoria of clicking camera film in order to transport nonsensical pictures of Europe back to Japan."

Frigging hell, I thought, I must learn to keep my big mouth shut! I was to shrink into my chair when the maid returned with a large electrically heated dinner trolley. She probably never realized her timely entrance saved me from an embarrassing moment, which Tanamoto would be very unlikely to forget.

After dinner we moved to the lounge for coffee and brandy. I eased into a comfortable leather armchair and contently sipped a wonderful French variety. I sensed Tanamoto was itching to resume probing into my life. He didn't disappoint me.

"Have you spent a lot of time digging things from the ground, Mister Speed?"

I shrugged. "I suppose a lifetime wouldn't be far wrong, but time means nothing. Metal detecting depends on the participant's endurance ability. To know the different sound so as to distinguish between a worthless piece of scrap and that piece of history that's liable to line your pockets with money."

"You obviously enjoy the outdoors?"

"It keeps me out of mischief."

"Until you find something that is treasure trove," Shayna scoffed. "Then you're in trouble."

"No, Shayna. Then it becomes a profitable trouble." I countered. "My only concern centres on the intrusion from the intolerable taxman sniffing into my affairs."

Tanamoto chuckled. "I admire a man who isn't afraid to admit his roguish ambitions, Mister Speed."

"Proud of it, too," I said, suddenly realizing the punch, two bottles of white wine mixed with warming brandy was beginning to weaken my brain cells and tongue.

"How do you know where to look?"

"By using the knowledge obtained by others. There's an extensive library in the London museum that relates to every significant piece in English history, whether there is much truth in the writings depends on the findings of dedicated archaeologists, or in my case, a dedicated detectorist who possesses the same acquired knowledge as that of the professionals but with one distinct advantage."

"You have a bigger spade than everyone else?" Shayna sniggered.

"No not quite, Shayna. I possess a bigger and better detector. Far more sophisticated than the conventional type you can spend thousands of pounds on. I designed it myself. It's accurate to a depth of a metre, and in metal detecting terms that is hell of a depth."

"Was it that exceptional tool that got you into so much bother back in England?" Shayna said.

"If you referring to the rusting Spitfire I discovered then yes, but my initial target for that day was to search for a lost bracelet."

"Did you find the bracelet, Mister Speed?" Royko asked, her eyes sparkling like two huge jewels. I had to admit, for an oriental she was tremendously attractive. No wonder Tanamoto looked healthy for his age and looking at her, who wouldn't be.

I said, "Naturally, I'm good at finding things."

I could see Royoko was impressed. "Locating a bracelet in a massive area, how clever?"

"Not really. Dedication, mustered with the energy to scan a pre-planned grid reference of considerable size without boredom setting in. And most important, having an exceptional bionic ear. Add those together, along with I'm good at what I do, then you have a successful sideline."

I noticed Tanamoto squirming in readiness to ask something of importance. "Dillon informs me that you are searching for Japanese submarine I-52?"

"Has he now! Why should I want to search for something that has already been discovered out in the Atlantic Ocean? Wasn't the I-52 was sunk by the Americans in 1944?"

"You know your history, Mister Speed," Tanamoto congratulated me. "Everything as stated in the war archives. The submarine I-52 was on a mission to deliver raw materials to Germany. That was true. Many rumours suggested the submarine carried gold bullion. I can verify it carried nothing of the sort. The Atlantic bound I-52 served a more prominent purpose, Mister Speed. Not just to deliver the raw materials, which would have been a bonus if the I-52 had managed to avoid the attack by the Americans, but the main point of the mission was a diversion. It was vital to lure the Allies away from the main purpose of the operation, to allow a second I-52 to slip through the Allied sea defences."

"An inappropriate waste of lives for a simple diversion," I said cynically. "It seems Japan also have military geniuses for idiots as well!"

"Please understand, Mister Speed, for the existence of a Japanese person, whether male, female, or child, to sacrifice oneself for the security of their country they will. If death is required, it will be given with no concept of preservation whatsoever. As was the selection of the Atlantic bound crew of the I-52. There was no need to ask for volunteers to risk their life, Japanese people insist they are chosen for such perilous tasks."

"I disagree!" The drink was talking again. "It's a natural instinct of man to self preserve. Is it, just maybe, enforced on them by means of mind numbing internal propaganda, that if the Americans land in Japan, they will rape our women, pillage our Cities, string the men up by their testicles from the highest pole, roast their children, unless we fight to last man. Is it anything like that?"

Tanamoto remained calm. "Ignorance to our cultures is understandable, Mister Speed. I can't expect you to understand sacrificial offerings undertaken by a brave crew. Brave Japanese sailors honoured to sacrifice their lives for their Emperor. To serve Imperial Japan and achieve the highest accolade in death."

Tanamoto's emotions were running high.

I said, "Am I to understand you served in the war?"

Tanamoto looked disappointed, I'd go as far as to say, embarrassed. "Alas the honour to die was never mine. The war ended months before my time in life."

To hide his embarrassment Tanamoto hurriedly opened an attaché case that had been there on the coffee table since we entered the lounge. I had assumed it belong to Deveron. He removed a tatty brown paper folder and offered it to me.

"Please, Mister Speed, browse over the contents."

I put down my brandy glass on the coffee table and began glancing through the pages, stopped after three and looked Tanamoto hard in the eye. I said bluntly, "Excuse my term of phrase, Tanamoto San, but are you trying to take the piss? This is all written in Japanese."

Tanamoto smiled. "In Japan we have a saying: for the agitator to prolong ridicule, the agitator must be prepared to take ridicule."

"Is there a purpose for this lesson in verse besides taking the piss?"

"Oh no, Mister Speed, I made it up. As for the documents, it was not my intention for you to actually translate, more so to prove the existence of what I am about to divulge. I'm authorized to allow any of the contents within that folder to be verified by any person knowledgeable in Japanese."

I handed the folder back to him. "Nice! I'll just take your word for it, Tanamoto, San."

"I am honoured to be in your trust, Mister Speed. Now let's press on. The events of the operation, as you saw by the photograph, meant that two I-52 submarines set sail in 1944. Two, one hundred feet long, five thousand tons of Japanese engineering sailing the southern route from their base. Of course, the reason for the numbered deception was to ensure that if either submarine was spotted it would seem to be only one vessel. The commanders of each submarine were of the highest accolade, chosen for the deep devotion to the Emperor and Japan. Extremely skilled submarine Captains each with their destiny. The Atlantic bound submarine played a massive part in the entire operation by screening the second I-52 by sailing above the second submarine, piggyback style, protecting the second I-52 from detection. The plan worked marvellously. At the precise point of separation the second I-52 stopped engines and drifted on the currents while the Atlantic destined I-52 continued to the rendezvous with a U-boat. An hour later the secret I-52 set a course for a rendezvous with German sympathizers in the West of Ireland, at a location in the Bay of Donegal. From there the merchandise, supposedly, was to be transported by land route to the North of Ireland and then smuggled into Germany. As far as the Japanese war department knew, the separation of the two submarines was successful. History foretells the fate of the Atlantic I-52. As for the secret submarine I-52, neither our government nor the Germans ever heard of the vessel again. It became a myth, and probably would have remained a myth till Dillon mentioned the possibilities the submarine could be found."

I must have expressed myself in a strange way because Tanamoto stared straight into my eyes and said, "For a man destined to find things of historical value, I don't seem to have excited your appetite. Perhaps you have already stumbled across the submarine, Mister Speed?"

I said, strongly, "Sorry to disappoint all expectations, but despite what is told, nothing is strictly true. As far as I'm concerned there is no submarine to be found. Besides, I came to Ireland for a holiday to escape the harrowing experiences inflicted on me back in London," and I flicked an accusing glaring towards Shayna hoping she'd feel guilty. I said to Tanamoto, "So where's this conversation heading?"

Tanamoto appeared disappointed. "I hoped towards finding the elusive submarine, Mister Speed. The Japanese Government want to know the fate of their craft and submariners. Relatives, even to this present moment, pray daily to be told the outcome of their love ones. So do I Mister Speed. My father was a aboard the mythical I-52."

"All very poignant Tanamoto San. What about the elusive two hundred million in gold bullion that went with the submarine?"

"If the gold still exists, naturally the Japanese Government would like the return of their commodity."

"That might not be as easy as it sounds."

"Would there be a problem with that request."

"Not if it's found! Yet who is to say the submarine commander thought sod this for playing war heroes and scampered off to some destined land living a life of luxury."

Tanamoto's eyes nearly dropped from their sockets. "It would never happen, Mister Speed! Honour is the highest and only accolade to a Japanese warrior."

"Then there's another slight problem you may want to consider."

"That is?" Tanamoto expressed concern.

"Think of the consequences if word got out that gold bullion was up for grabs. Would you be in a favourable position to prevent an avalanche of gold diggers bombarding every conceivable nook and cranny looking for it?"

"Well, Mister Speed, I wasn't intending to announce the operation."

"I think the Garda Siochana should be informed," I said.

Tanamoto seemed unsure. "They will be, eventually. Our Embassy in London will finalize the authorization. There is one more possible problem that could arise, Mister Speed."

"Oh-what's that?"

"There was a substantial amount of medical aid aboard the submarine that to certain criminally minded individuals could be viewed as a very rewarding package."

"What are you trying to tell me, Tanamoto san?" I was dreading the answer.

"I don't think the Garda Siochana would appreciate the knowledge that half a ton of opium was also part of the cargo. It could possibly, if it became common knowledge, start an avalanche of drug smugglers."

I exhaled a long breath. "Frigging hell, Tanamoto san, you have to be kidding me?"

"I do not joke, Mister Speed."

"That kind of merchandise, well, distributed properly, it'll far exceed what the gold is worth. Are you positive there was that amount aboard?"

"The documents I believe are very accurate."

"Frigging hell, if that ever circulates we could have a drug war on our hands." I looked hard at Deveron. "How do you feel about all this, Deveron?"

"I don't quite follow, Mister Speed?"

"Would you not like a piece of the action?"

"Oh-no, no, Mister Speed, I'm fully behind Tanamoto's proposed intentions- (I'd need a lot of convincing on that admittance) -I'm only interested in satisfying my curiosity, to finally realize such an event was to be proven true. I'm only interested in submarine being found. And to show my allegiance to Tanamoto, I'm willing to finance fully the task to find the I-52. I want you, Mister Speed, to discover its resting place so Tanamoto can relate back only good news to the people of Japan."

I said thoughtfully, "Assuming I did, I'm damned expensive to hire."

"No expense spared, Mister Speed. Name your price!"

"Have I time to consider?"

"No."

"Okay. How does twenty thousand pound's sound, cash of course."

I expected at least a gasp of surprise from one of them, but both were unmoved, expressionless, and they would have trounced me in a game of Poker.

"Per week," I added. "Until found."

There was no disapproval from either of them.

Deveron reacted first and calmly said, "You drive a hard bargain, Mister Speed."

"It's the cost of living, blame the government."

"I want Shayna there with you."

"Why?" I was far from happy with the request.

"Because I can't be there and I want someone there I can trust impeccably. Surely the pay-master has a right to know how his money is being spent. Don't you agree?"

I made no protest and shrugged my shoulders.

"Then that's final, Mister Speed."

Shayna stood and said, "Now that you boys have sorted out your differences, I'm going to retire."

"Same here," I said, getting to my feet. "I want an early start in the morning. I'll walk you to your room, Shayna, if you've no objections?"

She hadn't. We said goodnight and headed for the stairway. I was glad to leave the stench of bullshit behind or at least that was my opinion for the moment. If I was to believe Tanamoto had a relative aboard the submarine, I was going to need a lot of convincing.

"Fancy a night-cap, Shayna?"

"Not really Shackleton, but if you offering me a good fuck your room is the nearest."

There was definitely no subtleness when she wanted something, yet how could I resist such a delightfully blatant request? I looked at her and she looked at me and before we both disagreed we were in my room with our mouths clasped together in a frantic struggle for dominance. There was a rush to undress, both standing there naked, the only exception she still wore her G-string panties. We touched and aroused each other. Firm breasts and hardened nipples poked me in the chest as she fondled the length of my hardened shaft. A few steps back and we were on the bed and I began exploring her body. Kissing and gently biting her neck, gently down over her breasts, licking and gently sucking her nipples, working my way down to the strip of pubic hair that guided me to the intimate part of a woman's love, slipping the satin panties down in one motion as the tip of my tongue penetrated the crevices of her vagina in search of the trigger button and hitting the target when she thrust her clitoris hard onto my tongue. She grabbed the back of my head by the hair, pulling my face deeper into her fleshy mound so hard that I struggled to breath, but I didn't care!

Without even thinking about our actions I was on my back and she was pressing down on my face as my tongue probed, tasting her juices. She squealed with delight, moaning, talking in-between the ecstasy, "Yes! Yes! Yes!" Her hips thrust faster, the texture of her juice changing. "That's how much you turn me on Shackleton Speed. Yes! Yes! Yes! Yes!"

Then slowly she ceased to a few tentative jerky movements before latching straight onto my manhood with her mouth, pleasuring me before I took control, threw her onto her back and penetrated her vagina as she gasped her approval. Sweat layered our skins as if our bodies had been covered in oil. My skills as a lover were tested to the brink as she cried out for more. Positions altered, dominance changed hands, we were inseparable, two desperate lovers in deep embrace, tearing into one another. The more I rived into her, the more she opened to accept my hard thrusting shaft probing the depths of her love. The way she screamed with ecstasy had me consciously wanting to clamp her mouth shut. Yet there is certain words that make you work harder, and she knew the whole vocabulary.

"Fuck me! Fuck me!" She screamed as I probed deep into her fleshy box. "Fuck me like a mad rabid dog!"

So I did.

"Fuck me harder, you big horny bastard!" she screamed.

Then I felt the warmth of her fluid gushing out as I moved inside her.

"Fuck me! Fuck me! Don't stop. Please don't stop!"

The walls of her vagina tightened against the girth of my shaft, her nails clawing their way into the flesh of my back, tearing across, burning and I loved every moment. Still I probed, pushing deep inside her. I could tell she was struggling to maintain the pace, the pleasurable sensations too sensitive to withstand any longer. She was trying to force me off her while still effectively wanting me to drive deep inside her. She pushed and screamed and pulled me back inside her. But there was no way she could stop me this time. I was no longer tied to a stanchion now. My hands were free. I won't be frustrated again, deprived of satisfaction. I was in control and I wasn't about to release my grip around her buttocks, not until I finally exploded inside of her, pumping hard, thrusting, my semen crashing against a torrent of released vaginal fluid. And when I was totally spent I collapsed onto her gasping for air like a sprinter at the end of a race.

Finally catching my breath I rolled off her and lay on my back. I felt the beads of sweat roll down my body to be absorbed into the sheets.

She exhaled a slow long breath. "You were good, Shackleton Speed. No, you're a lot more than good. I've never experienced a man so energetic so forceful and exciting. You've completely exhausted me. I'm shattered."

"I hope that's a good thing?"

She stroked my face, "Wonderful," She whispered, "Absolutely wonderful," before she yawned and faded into a bout of rhythmic heavy breathing as she slipped into unconsciousness. Exhaustion and drink had finally won.

I was knackered myself, but being on edge made it difficult for me to sleep. I still had a lot to think about. Wondering if I could trust my new partners? And Shayna, could I trust her? The more I pondered the more I realized I couldn't trust anybody or anything?

I was still struggling to sleep when I heard car doors slamming. Slipping from between the sheets I crossed to the window and slightly parted the curtains. The Japanese couple were leaving. I hadn't made up my mind over the Oriental guests on whether they were genuine in their pursuit to find lost relatives, or they could see gold flickering from the bottom of Roaring Bay. I got back into bed and put that problem through the blender. I was still spinning on the problem when I finally fell asleep.

At first light Shayna sleekly slipped the embrace of my arms and slithered from underneath the sheets, obviously trying not to disturb me. I said nothing, just peeped through half open eyes admiring the beautifully shaped goddess as she picked up her clothing and shoes and left the room. I felt safe, so I went back to sleep.

*

The silence startled me awake. It hadn't been my intention to sleep so long. I hurriedly showered and shaved, and went down to breakfast with great expectancy, something like a loving, satisfied smile from Shayna. The dining room was empty. I helped myself to bacon, mushrooms, tomatoes, a few rounds of toast and sat down to eat alone. Shayna never arrived for breakfast, nobody did, which, I thought, was very inconsiderate of my host. I wondered if I'd suddenly developed an incurable rash. My isolation ceased when the maid entered the dining room.

"Where is everyone?" I asked.

With a casual shrug of her shoulders, she said, "Gone, Sir."

"Gone where?

"I don't know, Sir."

Maybe she didn't know or she was under strict orders not to divulge information. Since I don't pay her wages, there was no point in pressurizing and upsetting the girl. After breakfast I used the house telephone. I made two calls: the first call went to Judy who I'd given the mammoth task of keeping Winston in order, and to ask her to do me a huge favour. Fortunately for me, she worked in a very large law firm in central London. She was damned good at asking the right questions. I gave her the relevant information she would require and I would ring her when I was ready. The second call went to Shamus to tell him to prepare the 'Muff' for an afternoon excursion. He was quite concerned over my health.

"All the dashing about won't do your system any good fer diving, Shacks Sir."

"I'll rest when I'm satisfied I deserve a rest," I told him. "So until that moment comes I will be diving this afternoon whether you like it or not."

"Well it's your lungs, Shacks Sir. Oh, I thought yer might like to know the ship we encountered is still anchored out in the bay. The harbour master tells me she's on a research programme to monitor the behaviour of underwater currents."

"Believe that, Shamus?"

"I've no reason to doubt dhat, Shacks, Sir, but I gather yer don't!"

"They weren't doing much to warrant such a claim when we saw them so I've a right to be suspicious."

I replaced the telephone receiver.

My head was suddenly full of complications, mixed with the indecision on whether the 'Flying-fish' represented a problem or not. I certainly didn't believe the story of conducting underwater research, well not at this time of year. Besides which idiot would begin such an operation with the activity surrounding the preparation of the forthcoming regatta.

The taxi arrived and took me to the train station. As the train sped me towards Baltimore, I felt with growing confidence, I had nothing more to fear from Deveron, especially now he understood the knowledge I held against him. As for Shayna, I wasn't sure. The brutal side of her rather out swayed her loving side, but then, anyone can be too over confident and inevitably pay the price. I wondered if my lustful thoughts of her body were beginning to disorientate my way of positive thinking, blinding my quest to seek justice. She was certainly a hard picture to dislodge from my mind. I wondered if it was love.

CHAPTER EIGHTEEN

The first person I met when I got back to the hotel was Hamer who was steaming hot under his grubby collar. He was beginning to get on my nerves and paid no attention to other hotel users as he verbally attacked me.

"Where the fuck did you abscond to without telling? And that thick Paddy you have as a friend is about as informative as a fucking gobstopper sweet changing colour in my mouth."

I wasn't in the mood for a verbal confrontation with slap-arsed features so I said calmly, "There's no need to insult the locals just because you've had a bad day. And where I go is none of your frigging business. But if it'll stop you constantly spitting your dummy out, I've been sightseeing in Dublin." I'd no reason to lie. I reckon Shayna was absolutely worth seeing.

He looked surprised. "Why didn't you say you were going?"

"Why should I? It happens to be my holiday."

"That maybe so, Speed. But it would have been nice to know your movements so I wouldn't be hanging about like a prize in a raffle waiting to be plucked from obscurity. Hell I was worried!"

I frowned with surprise. "Worried about me?"

"Is there something untoward about that?"

"Yes, Detective Inspector, you're beginning to act as if you're my big sister."

"Bollocks to you, Speed! Talking to you is equivalent to getting sense out of a snotty nosed hooligan guilty of smashing a window pane with an offending catapult."

Satisfied with his outburst he trudged away towards the bar weighed down by the huge sulk dragging behind him.

I said, as he strode away. "So I can take it you won't be joining us on the 'Muff' this afternoon?" Now there was a statement for the scrapbook, which, unsurprisingly, caused a few heads to turn. As for Hamer, I considered his instant reply of a swift raise of two fingers damned right impertinent.

"What happened to, 'stick to me like glue policy' you were so positive on applying?"

"Go and drown yourself, Speed, so I can go home with a clear conscience."

I left Hamer to decide which part of his dummy he would spit out next and met Shamus aboard the 'Muff'.

For a change the weather was good and the water considerably calmer as we sailed out into the bay, inevitably chaperoned by the 'Flying-fish'. There was no hard evidence that the ship was actually shadowing us, yet I'd be willing to put all my money on it. And if the ship intended to do research then I'd be sacking the crew because they were a frigging bunch of lazy bastards as there was little happening on deck. But as long as they left me alone I was content on continuing my own piece of research.

Beneath the seas and oceans of our planet the water smothers the madness of an exhilarating existence. It's an entirely different world where a person can think. Pace is smoother and more practiced, it has to be. While we are able to breathe air above the water as fast or as slow as we like, beneath the water you're at its mercy. Too fast a manoeuvre and the wrong breathing pattern are all highly dangerous to a human body submerged in deep water. But it's not all doom and gloom. Diving is divine, a world of excitement its peacefulness only interrupted by the gurgling of escaping air bubbles exhaled from my mouthpiece.

Amongst my array of diving tools I took a very long crowbar, heavy even in water and that excess weight took me down to the seabed at a quicker ratio than kicking with fins. It's a good thing you can't get the bends descending or else I would have been in big trouble. At least I would have plenty of reserved energy for working on the seabed. As for Shamus feeding my lifeline into the water, his hands were probably moving ten to the dozen and suffering from rope burns, trying to keep up with my rapid descent.

Again I located the strong current flow between the fallen rocks that I had found on the previous dive. I rammed the tip of the crowbar into the crack of a rock and levered hard while trying to keep my feet steady on the silted seabed. Fragments of rock splintered but nothing significant happened. I chose another crack in the same rock, again the same result, no progress. I persevered. I'd no choice as I hate defeatism. Working on the same rock I shifted the crowbar around its circumference, levering to and fro, jerking side to side. The effort was tiring, and tired lungs use up air at a fast rate.

If the levering failed to work my only other choice would be with a couple of sticks of dynamite, that is, if I'd any idea of using the stuff properly without blowing myself into a thousand pieces. Then the persistence paid off and the rock suddenly gave and rolled down into the silt causing a cloud to explode into psychedelic form as it drifted on the current. I began attacking the next rock with more brute force, which proved just as stubborn before finally giving. Every rock after gave easily and soon I'd created a tunnel large enough to squeeze through.

I dropped the crowbar to the seabed, waited a few moments for the silt to settle before shining the torch beam into the dark void that stretched into oblivion. I expected something to suddenly shoot out of the hole but nothing did. Still I hesitated from venturing into the unknown, wondering whether I should prop the tunnel with appropriate rigging as I entered, but that would have taken more time. I also discarded the lifeline because I thought it could snag as I went in. I tied the line to a rock so Shamus wouldn't panic if he suddenly realized I wasn't attached to the other end. Satisfied, I kicked the fins hard and squeezed my way through the hole, pushing loose boulders aside. At first I swam cautiously slow, apprehensive of what lay ahead in the gloom. I could even admit to being a little scared.

Within a few metres the tight rock surroundings began to widen with every swim stroke, expanding into a larger structure. I would have expected to find a certain amount of sea-life, maybe a few curious fish darting into the torch beam, but strangely, it seemed devoid of any life. I checked the depth gauge. By my calculation and maintaining the direction I was heading, the readings showed I was beginning to rise. At approximately seventy metres into the void I finally broke the surface into a place of pitch blackness and got to my feet.

I shone the torch beam into the darkness to remove any concerns of a monster surging towards me before I removed the aqualung mouthpiece and goggles. There was a strong smell of damp and I wondered if there were any parasites living in this hole that no scientist had ever heard of. I removed the fins and waded ashore. The dry sand was cold as it pushed between my toes before clogging on my wet feet. I dropped the fins and eased the aqualung from my shoulders along with the weight belt and began flicking the beam in different direction in fits of impatience. I suddenly realized someone had been here before.

The torch beam landed on empty wooden crates. There was no lettering or indication of age or era. Then I startled when the beam illuminated an old diving suit complete with lead weighted boots and iron helmet hanging ghost like on the rock-face, and beside the suit a hand operated air pump and coils of air pipe. Everything I saw directed me into searching for another entrance as the equipment had to have been transported by land not by sea.

As I moved forward I stood on something that snapped. I stepped to one side and shone the torch beam down onto the broken object. I was now beginning to get used to the odd skeleton or two popping up from the ground, only this time I was guilty of standing on the hapless skeletal frame and breaking the left tibia in two places, not that the skeleton complained. There was also an implement in close proximity of the skeleton's bony hand which I retrieved from the floor for closer inspection under the light of the torch. It appeared to be a world war two German submachine gun, a substantially lethal weapon in its killing days, now it was nothing more than a rusting piece of steel that not even gallons of cleaning oil could bring it anywhere back to its former glory. I threw it down and continued the search for the elusive entrance.

I came across a sand dusted waxed tarpaulin wrapped around something rectangular and tied with rope. The ropes broke as I pulled at them, and as I removed the tarpaulin I was amazed to find an old diesel generator. Lifting a side panel the fuel gauge displayed a quarter full. Further examination I found two rubber cables that went out into the darkness, each taking a different direction. I ran the torch beam long the cable and came across a lamp-holder still holding a lamp, although from where I stood it was hard to tell if the filament would still burn.

I pulled the flywheel cord to ensure it was free running and hadn't seized with time. It turned. So I located the start switch and fuel on lever and put them into operation. Amazingly everything seemed perfect and moveable. The wax coated tarpaulin had done its job and had preserved the machine well over the time it had been stood. I went for it and yanked the cord hard, it didn't even splutter. I double-checked the switch and lever was in the correct position and tried again, this time when I pulled the cord I got the tune of gurgled strangulation. I needed to be more assertive so when I pulled the cord again I shouted encouragement to the machine, 'kick in you piece of iron shit!', and this time it responded positively. It spluttered and belched a puff of acrid black smoke from the exhaust, a sure sign that my efforts were drying out the spark plugs. This time I went berserk and yanked the cord three times in quick succession and the engine kicked into life, a slow jerk at first before the crescendo of noise built into a roaring piece of hardened machinery. Thick choking black smoke bellowed from the exhaust, the stench of burnt diesel filling my nostrils and burning my tongue as I tasted the atmosphere. Yet more importantly, slowly, as the voltage built up, the cavern illuminated or in this case half illuminated because half the lamps didn't work, yet the wattage produced was far more encouraging than light from a battery torch.

That was when I saw it. I was spellbound. There, half submerged in the water, leaning heavily on its left side, was the biggest rusting submarine a scrap-yard merchant would have been rubbing his hands to get at. The flaking lettering painted on the conning tower showed that I had found the I-52.

Strangely, at first, I felt nothing. No emotions with the discovery, just struck down with an imaginary paralysis and unable to mutter a word or raise a finger in triumph. I don't recall how long I stood there with no elation, nothing but a stare of utter disbelief but eventually I came to.

Out loud, I said, "Wow!" My voice bounced off the cavern walls.

I wondered how the hell the submarine got here in the first place. How did it navigate into the cave? How did it manage to beach itself? Perhaps it had crashed at speed, its weight momentum carrying it through and probably caused the rock fall. But I couldn't see any damage to the submarine to verify my theory. But who cares! I was the proud owner of a submarine and I wondered if I should tell anyone.

As I edged closer I could see four sagging brown rusted steel cables attached to the front of the submarine, dropping into the sand and angling away. I followed the cables to an enormous motorized winch system housed in a steel girder construction which was secured to the rock face. Then it dawned on me. The positioning of the submarine was no fluke but a highly organized operation that would have taken months to set up. This was no overnight impulsion. Extreme strategic planning and organization had gone into this piece of history.

Now I understood the photographs I had in my possession. It all started to make sense. The vessel had been deliberately sunk and literally dragged into the cave. But why the rock-fall, was that deliberate to conceal the submarine? I had to assume it was, and if that was the intention, then there was definitely another entrance.

I resumed my search around the cave walls for some type of access. What I did find was another significant rock-fall. I shone the torch beam through the cracks in the rocks and there, lodged in-between fallen debris, I saw the protruding bones of a right hand curled round what I assumed was another rusting German submachine gun. I could see a ring on the index finger bone. There was just enough space between the rocks for me to reach in arms length and carefully slip the trinket from the skeletal finger.

I blew the dust and dirt from the ring and examined the piece. It had class, a gold signet ring with a cluster of diamonds circling the initials J.M. I put the ring in my waist belt. One thing was certain, that if this had indeed been the entrance to the cavern, it was no longer of any use.

I decided to concentrate on the submarine. I spent a few moments speculating a number of possibilities on how I could climb the side to get to the conning tower but I didn't have to. As I circled the hull, on the other side I found disbanded oxyacetylene tanks and further along I discovered a gaping hole expertly cut into the side of the steel vessel. I shone the torch beam into the dark hole and cautiously entered.

I found more skeletons lining the uniforms of sailors. Distorted fallen figures lay amongst wooden crates, dropped where they had died in what must have been a fierce gun battle judging by the amount of weapons scattered. With careful footing I tread over the bone structures. I found one skeleton half propped against the steel wall of what appeared to be another storeroom. I counted approximately twenty more bodies scattered in and around the storerooms and I had the feeling that the further I ventured inside the belly of the I-52, the more bones I'd find. For a fleeting moment I wondered which body was Tanamoto's father.

There was no question that it had been a massacre and the Japanese submariners had never stood a chance. Blackened walls showed explosions had occurred, along with unfortunate dismembered skeletons caught up in the blasts, all now part of a mixed-up jigsaw puzzle among torn and shredded uniforms. It must have been a sickening sight when it happened.

There were parts of the submarine under water and were impassable, mainly the engine room, and as I recall from the enlarged aerial photographs, that was where the saboteurs had attached their mines. I found more death in every section I investigated, more evidence of explosions. The control deck showed signs that there had been a serious fire, some skeletons still had melted flesh on their bones.

The conning tower hatch was open so I climbed the steel rung ladder. I reeled a little when seeing another skeleton draped over the conning tower defence cannon. Perhaps he had caused the rock fall that had trapped the man at the entrance, managed to fire a couple of shells before he died. Maybe the after tremor brought down the seabed entrance. It wasn't difficult to imagine the scene of battle inside the confines of the cavern. In my head I could hear the battle rage, the sound of bullets splattering flesh, the inevitable screams from dying men. the intense horror of war.

I broke away from the battling ghosts and returned the way I came and out from the steel coffin, glad to escape the imaginary stifling stench of death. Yet whatever cargo the submarine had on board it had now gone, so too, did the theory of gold. It meant my friends had died for nothing, but only I knew that. I could still lure the mastermind behind the operation out into the open. I had to, how else would I get my revenge?

I trudged away from the I-52 in deep thought, the thick diesel smoke making me cough. I was so mad with failure that I would have no doubt missed what I kicked in the sand if it hadn't flicked up a few inches and the glitter of light it reflected caught my eye. Natural inquisitiveness made me pick it up. It was a metal block approximately one hundred millimetres long, twenty-five millimetres wide and three millimetres thick and had three Japanese symbols stamped in the metal. The sand had kept it clean and I knew old gold when I saw it and this ingot brought a smile to my face. I wondered how many pieces I required to become a rich man.

It was moments like these that I wished I had brought the metal detector along with me instead of having to sift gently through the sand with my feet. But after a few crazy minutes I realized I was wasting my time, there was no more to be found. Whatever amount of gold had been available it was no longer in this place of death and probably gone forever. It gave me plenty to think about as I put the ingot into my waist belt.

I had just fastened the pocket zip when over the sound of the generator motor I heard a violent voice which scared the hell out of me. My body juddered and my heart bounced from one side of my ribcage to the other in a returned serve in tennis and probably just as fast.

"Stand still!" The powerful foreign toned voice ordered.

I did.

"One wrong move and you die!"

I quickly located the diver emerging from the water. Though the English was good I think the diver was Russian. He was holding a polythene bag in his hands in the shape of what I assumed was a machine-pistol and it was pointing in my direction. He had already removed his fins and he threw them onto the sand as he came ashore. I thought about running but to where? How far would I have got before he cut me down.

"Hand's high, where I can see them. Are you alone?"

"Well, strictly speaking, no."

"Put your hands high where I can see them, now!"

Reluctantly I did but only chest height.

"Where are the others?" There was anxiousness in his speech now, his eyes frantically flicking in different directions while still trying to keep one eye on me.

I nodded towards the submarine and said, "In that tin can over there. About a hundred or so Japanese crew, but don't fret, they're not here for a beach party, they're all dead."

"So you are alone pig shit?"

I expressed surprise. I said, "Pig shit, how original!"

"Where is the gold?"

I shook my head. "No gold. There are plenty of ghosts, but no gold."

The diver moved closer, pushing his facemask up onto his forehead, and noticeably his jerky reactions told me the person was agitated. I was right.

"Lying English bastard!" he shouted, the echo of his voice bouncing ping-pong across the cavern walls.

"English Bastard I don't mind but I take offence to being called a liar! There is no gold just a rusting piece of scrap submarine doubling as coffin," I said strongly. "Go and see for yourself."

"Move towards the sub," he ordered.

As he had the persuasive tool pointing directly at me, with reluctance I turned back. Even under threat I still felt confident I wasn't about to get a bullet in my back, well, at least not yet. I trudged thoughtfully towards the I-52, talking under my breath, moaning really. Hell I had a right to frigging moan. I am accused of being a lying, pig breathed bastard, and when I get the chance I'm going to shove that gun right up the arse of his rubber suit.

When we reached the hole in the side of the I-52, I caught my first glimpse of the diver, though I didn't recognize the face squashed into the neoprene of his dry-suit.

He looked into the hold, he wasn't happy. "There should be boxes here!"

"Exactly what I told you, there's nothing but corpses."

. "Where are the boxes?"

The corner of my top lip arched. "Give me a break, will you! It's a wreck, that's all. I'm just a wreck hunter. I'm not even interested in the salvage rights."

"Shut it, pig shit!"

"Is pig shit the best you can come up with?" I asked, only for the tip of the machine pistol to fit perfectly up one of my nostrils.

"You don't listen, pig shit!"

I can take an insult once without over-reacting. I can probably take the same insult twice with just a cringe. The third rather out-steps the boundaries of pleasantness, and this piece of frigging arrogance deserved a smack and I was in deliberation of how my plan of action would commence as he pushed the gun nozzle into my spine encouraging me to retreat back towards our discarded fins. I quickly decided on a jumping back-kick and was I just positioning myself for the attack when another diver broke the surface of the water and my strategy needed a rethink damn frigging quick.

The emerging diver pulled his facemask down around his neck. In one hand he too carried a machine pistol in a polythene bag and in his other hand he held a rather fearsome and powerful spear gun. I wouldn't be far wrong in assuming he wasn't after the fish. But I could tell with the smirk across his face the appearance of the rusty submarine impressed him.

"The contraband, it is here?" his deep voice bellowed as he waded from the water, his accent matched his colleagues.

When the other diver shook his head the smile dropped from his face and he began talking into a mouthpiece. Impossible to hear the conversation but the look in his eyes as he talked and listened sort of warned me I was in serious trouble and that rethink of strategy had to mature very quickly.

It's hard to think when you're under pressure. It's doubly hard to think when your life is in danger, and mine was. I could see clearly the spear gun being raised and its pointed projectile deliberately aimed in my direction. I may be lucky and he could be a lousy shot. Could I take the chance? I didn't think so.

Anyone has a right to survive the merciless intentions of a cold-blooded killer, and when death threatens the natural process of human instinct is to either run for your life or stay and fight, despite the odds. I stood my ground in readiness.

In the corner of my eye I saw the sadistic grin appear on the face of the diver beside me, his slight shuffle back to put space between us, and I knew the moment was coming. I concentrated on the man splashing through the water heading towards me, watching his trigger finger on the spear gun, waiting for the finger to curl and pull. That's when I reacted.

With lightening speed I palmed away the tip of the machine pistol that dug into my ribs and grabbed the startled diver beside me and dragged him into the path of the oncoming spear, hearing the sickening contact as the projectile struck him in the midriff, the muffled squelch as it ripped through the neoprene of his diving suit, embedding deep into the lining of his stomach. As he slumped I swiftly grabbed his gun hand and raised the machine pistol, pushing the dying forefinger hard down on the trigger unleashing a line of bullets across the water in sheer panic. I hit anything that moved. The diver in the water, frantically attempting to lift his own machine pistol to shoot, arched back as the bullets hit home, rolled over, spasmodically jerked and lay faced down in the water. I let go of the diver I held and stepped back breathing heavily, looking down at the embedded spear in the midriff, blood pumping from the wound, hearing the last gasps of a dying man and for a moment I was really scared.

The adrenalin surged through me. A sick taste rising from the depths of my stomach and I threw up as I realized it could have been me laid there in a heap. One thing I was certain of, I'd never make any money being a hardened killer, I had too much of a conscience.

Then my brain was functioning again. I dropped to one knee, grabbed the machine pistol from the dead mans grasp and remained alert, watching the water with the expectancy of others. Five minutes I waited and watched. No one else emerged. Nothing disturbed the water with the exception of the Diver's body drifting. Only then did I move and quickly put on my aqualung and fins.

I never even turned off the generator as I waded back into the water but I did commandeer the spear gun from the dead diver as I passed and reloaded a spear. I dived under the water quite prepared to fire the spear gun again if necessary.

I found no more ruthless characters on my journey to the surface and when I bobbed up at the side of the 'Muff', Shamus had the appearance of a praying catholic churchgoer. "O' be Jesus, you're alright!"

I passed him the spear gun and climbed aboard noticing his strange look at my acquired collectable before placing it to one side. Then he was back in panic mode.

"Is everything alright, Shacks Sir? Dhare were two divers from the 'Flying-fish' goin' into the water from an inflatable. I tugged on the safety rope to warn you, I did, with no reply. Yer had me worried."

"I saw them," I said.

"Well, if you did, Shacks Sir, dhen everything is alright?"

"Yes, Shamus, everything is okay, now."

"Well, it must be, Shacks Sir because yer here safe and sound aboard, dhat yer are, Sir."

"Frigging hell, Shamus, whatever you want to say spit the damn thing out!"

"Well, Shacks Sir, I'd be tinking they'd cause yer some bother."

"They did. How do you think I got that spear gun?"

"Yer got into a fight, did yer, Shacks Sir?"

"That's right, Shamus."

Shamus's complexion turned a peculiar shade of yellowish-white. "Dhare wouldn't be anything sinister goin' on, Shacks Sir?"

"Shamus, whatever are suggesting?"

Shamus looked across the bay. "I don't see the other divers returning to the surface."

"I doubt you will, Shamus. I suggest you get the engine operational and get us out of here before the crew of the 'Flying-fish' realize their men won't be returning under their own steam."

A wicked smirk emerged on Shamus's face. "Yer sorted them out for a few hours with a couple of uppercuts to the chin, did yer, Shacks Sir?"

I soon wiped the smirk off his face. "Not exactly, I was forced to be more drastic, I'm afraid."

Shamus looked at me suspiciously. "I'm not quite understanding, Shack Sir."

"It's simple, Shamus, they tried to kill me!"

Shamus went into a panic. "Holy mother of god, dhey tried to kill yer as in stone dead?"

I slashed my finger across my throat. "Permanently, but I survived."

"What happened to the divers, Shacks Sir?"

"Oh-they're dead."

Shamus's eyes rolled skyward. "O' Jesus, be Jesus, I'm an accessory to murder, now."

"Self defence, if you don't mind, Shamus! They were trying to kill me, remember!"

"We'll have to tell the Garda, Shacks Sir."

"Yes Shamus, but in the meantime get the engine started."

Shamus dashed to the wheelhouse and fumbled with the starter. Through the window I saw him muttering to himself. He showed himself to be a totally different character when he became flustered. He looked clumsy, everything he did seem to go wrong. Items were falling to the floor: papers, some charts. He was embarrassing to watch. Instead I got the binoculars and concentrated on the reactions aboard the 'Flying-fish', mainly the deck which was now swarming with men. Binoculars from the 'Flying-fish were trained on our departure, others desperately searching the choppy waters for the two divers. I wondered how long they would wait before their patience cracked and they reacted against us. Or would they bother to react at all considering Baltimore was bustling with activity? I had to think they would, because whoever I was up against, there was no anticipation to kill in order to get what they wanted. More so I'd be interested to discover the person pulling the strings, whom, I imagine, will be very pissed off at this very moment. I didn't want to be about when they did, not yet anyway. I went back inside the wheelhouse.

Shamus finally got the 'Muff' under way while I consulted the sea chart. I calculated that the cavern was below the ruins of Dun an Oir, the fort of gold. I thought that maybe someone had a sense of humour.

"Shamus, is there a land route into the O'Driscoll fort?"

He glanced at me. "On Clear Island, yer mean, Shacks Sir. O' well, dhare was once, only the fort became too dangerous to allow people to wander among the ruins. Somethin' about the castle floor collapsing."

"I want to go there."

"The place is too dangerous, Shacks Sir!" he said stubbornly.

"I still want to go there!"

Shamus expressed concern. "Why, Shacks Sir? We're in enough trouble. We need to get far away from the 'Flying-fish as we possibly can."

"We've plenty of time before they respond. I'm interested in the fort because by my calculations there is a cavern directly below."

Shamus was too incensed that I don't think he heard what I said about the cavern, "Tis foolish, Shacks Sir. It's just a ruin, dhare is nothin' to see."

"I'll be the judge of that, Shamus, just head the boat in that direction."

Shamus mumbled some disapproving words but did as I asked. And I couldn't complain if instead he decided to ignore me and head straight for Baltimore and hand me over to the authorities for crimes committed. But to his credit he sailed the "Muff' towards North harbour at Clear Island as he obviously preferred the money to filling in witness statements. I went below, dried off and changed into walking gear.

Shamus's usual placid sailing skills had deserted him as he hurried the 'Muff' towards land like a man possessed. I was bouncing around as he sped the boat through the surging swell with the bow lifting high before slapping back down. I made a passing comment of the passage being rather rough and all Shamus did was he hit the throttle defiantly harder maintaining a bombardment of glares and scowls at me and muttering under his breath, his lips barely moving as if was practicing a ventriloquist act. As he turned his head away I managed to catch some of his moaning: "just makin' a living," he said, "get dragged into the dirty gutters; me, Shamus O'Malley, accessory to devious mishaps beneath the waters of Roaring Water Bay," and so on he moaned.

To shut him up, I said, "By the way, Shamus, I found the submarine."

His head shot round. "Yer'll be having me on, Shacks Sir?"

"Scouts honour and hope to die if I'm fibbing. But if you had listened to me instead of moaning you would have heard me mention a cavern beneath the fort. I found it there"

"That's truly amazing. Shacks Sir. But then why has it never been seen before?"

"The sub was hidden deliberately inside a very spacious cavern. Remember the photographs showing the sub under attack. That had nothing to do with the war. It was hijacked, sunk, and then dragged into the cavern by a powerful winch where they burnt their way through the big can with an oxyacetylene torch. A gun battle began and the crew were slaughtered and left to rot down there. But something else happened, an explosion I think, and it caused a rock fall which entombed the submarine inside the cavern. As for the body you discovered on the beach it obviously came from there."

Shamus was horrified. He made the sign of the cross across his chest again and said sadly, "O' Jesus in heaven! What a terrible thing to happen, Shacks Sir. Who'd want to hijack a submarine and kill the crew if it had nothin' to do with the war? What reason would it serve?"

I took the gold ingot from my pocket and put it down in front of him. I said, "That a good enough reason?"

Shamus's eyes lit up. He picked up the ingot as if it was a delicate piece of Ming china. "Is it real?"

"Snap your teeth if you bite it."

"All this skulduggery doesn't seem worth the effort for a prize of just one measly gold bar." He gave me the ingot, shaking his head in disappointment. "Not worth dying fer."

"The sub was reportedly carrying two hundred million pounds in gold bullion. *That*, Shamus is only a sample."

I saw Shamus stiffen as he stared ahead, then his lips moved but for a few seconds no sound emerged before he found his voice. "T-t-two hundred million, yer say?"

"Allegedly, mind you."

"All those gold bars inside the cavern?"

"Ah-well, there's a slight problem, I only found the one. We have to assume the hijackers took the gold and disappeared."

"So who do yer tink took the gold?"

"That's the mystery. Apart from the Japanese and Hitler's loyal command no one knew of its existence. I'm rather hoping the Dun an Oir fort can give us a clue if only to reveal how they entered and left. Maybe we might find surplus stock they left behind. There could be some useful information. It might even reveal a name."

Shamus disheartened, the gloom returned to his face. "So we're lookin' fer an entrance and pieces of scrap?"

"You've got the idea, Shamus."

"So yer're still interested in finding the gold dhen, Shacks Sir?"

"Damn right I am, Shamus because I have another reason to find it and it's nothing to do with money."

"Well, I'm surprised at dhat, Shacks Sir. Another reason rather dhan be rich."

"Not when you consider people I knew have died unnecessarily for it."

I noticed Shamus tightly grip the wheel. "O' me mother of god! I not be knowing of dhat, Shacks Sir. Yer never told me!"

"It's not the first thing you tell a stranger, is it Shamus. But it is important I find the gold because it will attract the nasty bastards who I hold responsible for making me bitter."

"So it's all about dhat, revenge?"

"There's nothing wrong with getting even."

"No, dhare's not, Shacks Sir. But aren't yer takin' a huge gamble?"

"On keeping my sanity or finding some killers, yes this is the biggest gamble of my life and I don't mind admitting I'm scared as hell. But it's my fight and I'm sorry I got you involved."

"Then I've a right to walk away?"

"I wouldn't stop you."

"But I'm not goin' to!" he announced. "Shamus O'Malley doesn't run from a fight, so I'll be stayin' if yer don't mind, Shacks, Sir?"

"I appreciate that, Shamus."

Then I remembered the ring I took from the corpse in the cavern. I retrieved it from my diving belt and examined it further. On the inner ring I could faintly make out McCracken, which I assumed stood for the M on the ring face. I showed Shamus the piece. "Found this on a corpse's finger. I think it belonged to one of the hijacker's because a Japanese sailor would not be wearing such jewellery. Seen anything like it before, Shamus?"

He shook his head slowly. "It, be expensive, I'd say, Shacks, Sir."

"The initials J.M. or the name McCracken mean anything to you, Shamus?"

Although Shamus expressed no emotion in his face as I asked the question, I did notice his body tense. "Ireland is an extremely big

194

place, Shacks, Sir, with a lot of people with the name McCracken. Perhaps I should make more effort and meet more people!"

I said, "Subtle sarcasm isn't called for, Shamus. If you don't mind, that's my speciality. Besides, you're not very good at it."

"Well, look at it seriously, Shacks, Sir. It could relate to a number of people, any where."

"Well if we can trace the ring to a family of McCraken's then there might be a pot of gold at the end of the rainbow with a leprechaun to greet us after all."

Shamus scoffed my hopes hastily. "Who'd be dhat lucky, Shacks, Sir?"

"I might just know the person who can help on the matter."

It suddenly occurred to me that the longer I continued this campaign the more I would be in need of a pair of waders to wear because the deep shit I was sinking into was getting deeper, and deeper. As for the death of the two divers I had left behind in the cavern, my only concern was to prove that I had acted in self defence, as no court in the land would believe my story. On the surface, I suppose Shamus must have seen me as a pretty hard and ruthless character. That didn't really bother me. Yet hiding behind my solid and undefeated expression, I knew that I had sunk to a low grade in the credibility status as I reflected on my achievements to commit enough crimes to warrant a lengthy stretch in prison. But if I can bind everything together and produce the mastermind behind all this, a stint behind bars would be worth the anguish and the torment.

We sailed into North harbour as the ferry departed back to Baltimore. While Shamus docked the 'Muff', I gathered a few necessities into a rucksack, climbing ropes and pulleys, hammer, hung a pair of binoculars around my neck, watched Shamus lock the galley door and we set off up the hill mingling with other bird spotting, sight-seeing tourists.

I'd no worries about any sudden attacks from behind because Shamus constantly looked over his left and right shoulder like a man possessed, highly suspicious of everyone that passed. He must have made himself dizzy by the time he gave up his security precautions.

By the time we had reached the heritage centre the more I understood the simplicity to conduct activities on the Island in 1944 without interference. Before tourism the island would have been practically deserted apart from the residential Islanders minding their own business. Overall it presented the hijacker's with the opportunity and freedom to organize to perfection a successful robbery.

When we finally reached the cliff tops I peered through the binoculars. Far in the distance I could see the 'Flying fish' still anchored. I nudged Shamus in the arm.

"There," I pointed out to sea. "Didn't I say the occupants on 'Flying Fish' would be too dumfounded to up anchor without first establishing the non-return of divers."

"Dhat maybe so, Shacks, Sir. Just how do we explain to the Garda about those men, have yer thought about dhat?"

"Not us Shamus. More like, how are the crew of the 'Flying Fish' going to explain the death of their men? I guarantee that they won't be reporting anything. The questions that will be asked would be too complicated to answer."

Shamus thought about it. He smiled and whispered to me, "So I'm not going to be standing trial as an accomplice then, Shacks, Sir?"

"No. Now let's get on looking for a secret entrance to the cavern below Dun an Oir."

Shamus suddenly stood tall, with a confused expression. "I can't see the point of lookin' fer something that ain't dhare, if yer don't mind me sayin', Shacks Sir?"

"Come on, Shamus, start using that Irish brain. There must be evidence of something because lumping heavy machinery is always easier to move while on terra firma. If I wanted to convey heavy material down a cliff side, I'd be unwilling to use a steep one metre wide pathway winding down with an extremely dangerous drop. I'm willing to wager all your money there's a secret entrance in close proximity of the fort."

"Do you really suspect dhat, Shacks, Sir?"

"Frigging hell, Shamus, no sane warrior, man or beast, even in the fifteenth century, builds a fort on a splinter of rock without having a secret means of escape in-case the unthinkable happens. I think this McCracken and his hijacking friends found it or knew about it."

"Exactly what are we looking for?"

"Use your imagination! Focus on the structure of the land, you might get lucky."

Just by his body language I could tell he was struggling to contain his boredom and after ten minutes I began thinking the same way. I tried to visualize the tunnel, anticipating the possible route to take it below the old fort. But I couldn't picture anything that look remotely like the start of a tunnel, or anything that indicated a fall-in. I gave up. I had to assume the possibility that the restructuring of the Island had concealed what entrance there could have been.

I descended the pathway down to the fort for further inspection and possibly locate the entrance from the fort itself. Shamus didn't ask questions, he just followed. It required careful placement of feet down the rocky pathway, one wrong step and a tumble could be very nasty indeed and I did resent Shamus using my shoulder as a stabilizer.

Down amongst the ruins we examined every nook and cranny and found nothing significant. In his frustration, Shamus, his hands dug into his trouser pockets, kicked a small stone sending it skimming across the fort floor, mumbling under his breath.

"Found anything yet, Shamus?"

He looked up at me. "Yes, Shacks Sir. You'll be pleased to know dhare are rocks and more rocks!"

I shrugged my shoulders. "Perhaps you're right, Shamus. Maybe I'm being too over ambitious in my presumption of an entrance. I must admit when I was down in the cavern whatever entrance there was is now inaccessible. I just wanted to satisfy my curiosity."

"Does it really matter, Shacks, Sir?"

"To me it does. I detest incomplete theories of events. And not just that-," I began and stopped, my eyes flicking in all directions when I suddenly realized a piece of fragmented rock had spat into my cheekbone. I grabbed Shamus and dragged him down to the ground, ignoring his squeals of pain as he banged his elbows against the large rock we hid behind.

I never heard the shot but I suspected a bullet ricochet.

"Hell, Shacks Sir, what was dhat fer?"

"Someone took a shot at us," I said, frantically scanning and pointing to the terrain above.

"What the devil are yer're talking about, Shacks Sir?"

He got his answer straight away as another bullet ricochet spat from the rock and Shamus was eating daisies quicker than a magician's turn of hand.

"What the hell is going on?"

Not trying to be funny, I said, "It might just be possible someone wants us dead!"

"O' Mother Theresa, protect my miserable life." He was too flat to the floor to cross his chest.

"Shut up and look for anyone shooting at us."

"I don't wish to sound disrespectful by saying dhis, Shacks Sir, but fer an Englishman yer can attract some unscrupulous shit. Trouble follows yer quicker than sticking your finger in a wasps nest."

I was still focusing hard on the rocks above. "Shamus, shut up! Instead of feeling sorry for yourself, try searching for the bastards trying to kill you."

He looked at me horrified. "Not on yer life, Shacks Sir. Have me head blown off the moment I lift it?"

I gave him a disapproving look. "Coward," I teased.

"Coward is it, Shacks, Sir? Would yer prefer if I was to dive from my cover and pretend I'd been shot? Yer never know it might just flush the blighter from his vantage point."

"Thanks for the offer of heroism, Shamus, but ill advised because the shooter will only put another bullet in you to make doubly sure."

"Jesus, be Jesus! I'd be jokin', Shacks Sir. Do I have suicidal idiot stamped across me forehead?"

I gave the pretence of looking. "You are so right, Shamus, there is something stamped there."

Shamus went cross-eyed trying to look and instinctively touched his forehead.

I shook my head in disbelief and concentrated on finding a route to escape and there weren't many options. I was just summarizing a few details when I noticed it had gone relatively quiet, no more shots. Then I heard voices from above. Lots of voices and I realized the gunman had been disturbed by a gaggle of tourists or locals. It didn't matter whom, I quickly grabbed the reluctant arm of Shamus and made a mad scramble to reach the top before the group of people disappeared. To make sure they stayed there until we reached the summit I shouted out asking for directions to take us to museum.

If the gunman was amongst the crowd I couldn't tell which one was guilty. After a few seconds I was confident the gunman had disappeared faster than a whippet with its tail on fire. We stayed with the group no longer than necessary, and once I verified there was no longer any danger we back tracked to the harbour.

When we clambered back on the 'Muff's deck' I was probably more in a hurry than Shamus as I quickly unleashed the mooring rope while he started the engine. I happened to glance across to a small speedboat moored close by because I didn't recall it being there when we first arrived. And when I saw 'Flying Fish' in black stencil on the boats bow I knew how wrong I had been in assuming their inability to react quickly.

I also made another serious error when we boarded. Neither of us had bothered to check the boat for intruders, notably, failing to notice the galley door had been forced and then closed. A blind person would have fared better than when I went down the galley steps, but I soon stopped in mid-stride and back stepped when the cold nozzle prodded me in the stomach.

Shamus expressed astonishment when I resurfaced from the galley with my hands in the air. He went rigid with shock when he realized the problem but then it was too late for him to react. The gunman, a scruffily dressed, well built man with dark hair, ordered me to stand next to Shamus so he had both of us in sight and we were both staring down the barrel of a silenced hand gun.

Shamus broke the silence. "I thought yer said no reaction? No one would bother us. Hell, Shacks Sir, yer've got me in bloody war!"

The gunman angered, threatening wildly with the gun. "Be quiet you babbling buffoons!"

Shamus was a little upset at being compared to a buffoon, but I was more interested as to why the gunman's eyes kept shifting back and fro towards the main drag up the hill. He was waiting for some one else. I flicked my eyes in the direction the gunman was looking. Yes I was right. I could see two men hurriedly in descent. Though difficult to tell from a distance there was a certain amount of similarity about the two approaching runners, but my brain was already in overdrive arranging an escape to be worried about those two because the gunman concerned me more. Then the chance to escape happened.

Two things simultaneously helped me decide my plan of action. The boat rocked sharply by incoming waves at the precise moment the gunman elected to glance towards the hillside, slightly unbalancing the gun hand. I reacted with the speed of electric current making contact and powered into the gunman's midriff, while grabbing and twisting the gun hand. Two shots plopped into the air before we fell down the galley steps. The gunman's spine took the brunt of both our weights and the fight stopped there as he never twitched a muscle. I took the gun from his limp grasp and got to my feet with a watchful eye. I kicked him hard and I mean hard. I was so mad I kicked him again and again. He still didn't move or murmur. I was slightly concerned the death count had risen until he moaned.

The boat engine fired up and Shamus popped his head down into the galley. "Dhare are two rather mean looking thugs hurtling down the hill, Shacks, Sir. O' Jesus! Is he dead too?"

"Are you bothered?"

He never answered.

"He's out cold!" I assured him and he was, so I dragged his body up onto the deck.

"What yer goin' to do with him Shacks, Sir?"

"I detest stowaways." And I promptly dumped the bastard on the jetty. 'Now you have observed that I'm not the cold-blooded killer you think I am. Now get us out of here!"

Just as Shamus began to steer the 'Muff' away from the jetty, I pumped two silenced bullets in the outboard engine of the motorboat and tossed the weapon into the depths of the bay. It never occurred to me if I'd done any serious damage but I was confident. We gained distance from the jetty and as I glanced back to the harbour a lump swelled and lodged in my throat with what I saw. The decision to incapacitate the launch's motor proved a priceless choice when I caught sight of Damien Love and Theodore Hate trying to start the frigging boat.

CHAPTER NINETEEN

Shamus crashed the 'Muff' through the waves at a top rate of knots. The ride across Roaring-water Bay is rough enough at a casual pace but the speed Shamus sailed sent waves crashing over the bow and the sea spray covered the wheelhouse windows causing momentary blindness. I'd no complaints. I now wanted the nautical miles between us and Clear Island as wide as feasibly possible and Shamus was achieving the feat. As we approached Baltimore harbour, thankfully within an hour night will have descended.

After the sighting of Love and Hate I now feared for Shamus's safety, I didn't want his death on my conscience. With the boat tightly moored, I handed Shamus a prewritten sizable cheque for his services. His eyes widened as he stared at the figure.

"Is there something wrong, Shamus?"

"Dhare is a mistake, Shacks, Sir. It's far too much!"

"Nonsense, Shamus. You deserve it."

"But it's five thousand pounds!"

"And you find that a problem?"

"I don't feel I can take dhat much, Shacks, Sir?"

"It isn't a bribe to keep quiet about my ruthless actions. It's for your support and use of boat, that's all! I know I've kept you in the dark about what has been happening but that was for your own good. The less you know the better."

"The money is still a generous gesture, Shacks Sir, very generous indeed."

"Now get along to the nearest bank and deposit the check into your account before I change my mind." I told him. "When you've done that, keep away from the harbour and find a nice crowded bar and stay there."

It wasn't my intention to inflict fear into him, this seem to be the outcome. "Why, Shacks Sir? We're safe now. Aren't we?"

"I wish I could say yes, but I'd be lying."

"Holy, Mother of Jesus! Who am I to be afraid of, Shacks, Sir?"

"Remember the two men in hurry to catch us at North harbour? They have a degree in unpleasantness. They kill people for fun. Until I can conclude what I began, I want to keep you from any harm. Your safest option is to lose yourself among the tourists in the busiest pub. Now go. We'll meet later."

I dashed back to hotel and asked at reception if anyone had made enquiries after me.

"Only, Mister Hamer," he replied thoughtfully, "He seemed...a little agitated."

"He's always agitated. It took him a lot of hard years to develop the technique."

"No, no, Mister Speed. I mean really truly agitated. I saw fear in his eyes. I think petrified would be a proper description."

"Did he mention anything?"

"No."

"Leave a message?"

"No, Sir, other than ask for you. Then he left the hotel."

"Left, alone?"

"Yes, he booked out."

"He booked out?"

"Yes, Mister Speed."

"Happen to say where he was going?"

"No, Mister Speed."

I thought a moment. What the frigging hell could have scared a man like, Hamer. Perhaps he'd seen, Love and Hate? But then he already knew all about them. I would have to locate Hamer to find out. I said, "If he returns, don't hesitate to ring my room. If anyone else arrives asking for me, tell the inquisitive person I'm out. Then inform me. Okay?"

"Yes, Mister Speed."

The moment I entered my room I knew I had company. The smell told me. Closing the door, I said, "Took your time getting here."

Shayna was sat in the soft leather chair with one leg out stretched over the chair arm in a position of comfort, quaffing a glass of white wine.

Shayna smiled wickedly. "Did you miss me, Shackleton?"

"Where's Deveron?"

"Missing him, too?"

"What part of 'where's Deveron' don't you understand? So I can simplify it for you!"

"Ooh! Touchy! Touchy! He's on business."

"This is the most important part of his miserable existence and he's on frigging business! You can tell him I found the submarine."

"Tell him yourself. He's at the Quality Hotel, Clonikilty." She got up, shoved the glass into my hand, smiled and said, "Pour me another while I use the bathroom?"

I had trouble concentrating while I poured the wine because I couldn't stop ogling at her pear shaped posterior snugly enclosed in tight leather pants that magnified her rear splendidly. She disappointed me when she closed the bathroom door behind her.

Her voice filtered through a slight gap of the door. "Help yourself to a glass of wine."

"I'm ahead of you," I said, and sank two glasses in quick succession hoping it would slow down my racing mind.

All of a sudden things were happening. All the players were beginning to congregate either in Baltimore or the surrounding area, Deveron and Shayna, a ship full of unscrupulous villains along with Love and Hate and me in the middle spinning. The hornets nest was buzzing and I had to silence them one way or the other.

I felt the walls close in around me. The feeling of slow strangulation as the invisible cord tightened around my neck. I glanced at the bathroom door and wondered how far I could trust Shayna. How far can anyone trust a terrorist?

When she reappeared the fear of her pointing a gun at me vanished when I saw she was naked. No modesty whatsoever. No blush of embarrassment, just sheer poetry in motion as she crossed the room. I could only admire the bounce of her breasts and the twitch of her buttocks as she moved. The mouthful of wine I drank went down my throat in a lump. I struggled to keep my eyes focused on hers. More prominently, I was struggling to stop the stiffening projectile jerking in the front of my pants.

To control my wandering mind I said, "Just out of curiosity, how did you get into my room? No forcible damage to the lock. No damage to the door. So which gel-head down at reception let you in? No doubt your charming smile did the trick."

She lay down on the bed, legs slightly apart in an attempt to entice me. "Do I detect a hint of jealousy creeping into your tone?"

"I'm still asking."

"No one let me in. I'm good at picking locks."

"Frigging hell, you don't happen to work with another handyman name of Hamer?"

"I've never heard the name Hamer! Does he pick locks too?"

"Better than you do."

"I might ask him to join our organization."

"Well you can ask him when you meet him."

"A friend of yours is he?"

"He seems to think so."

"I gather then he's not flavour of the month?"

"To describe him in very few words, I'd say he was the most nosey bastard on this planet. Be extremely careful what you say, he happens to be government property in the form of an M.o.D. policeman and just because you don't witness him taking down notes, don't assume he's missed anything."

"What is he doing here?"

"Pestering me, I'm afraid."

"Have you done something terribly wrong?"

"Yes, he blames me entirely for digging up a warplane and not telling anyone. He wants me to admit it so he can string me up by my bollocks and put me on show to the good people of London. And stop trying to change the subject of illegal entry. How did you manage to squeeze past reception without being noticed?"

"Well it's not the most difficult of tasks considering men are all of the same mould. See something that resembles a bit of attractive ass and their eyes are like lumps of magnetic material forcibly attracted to the source. So much perversion goes on in the mind of a man that they send themselves dizzy as they try to watch everything in sight. I just waited until an attractive woman went one way and I went to the stairway."

"A simple application of, now you see me now you don't, is that it?"

"Yeah, that's exactly it. Now are you going to stand there dumbfounded or are you going to take advantage of my vulnerability, like get your kit off and pleasure me senseless, Shackleton. Now would be nice."

At least with Shayna you knew where you stood. There was no need for fumbling hands or whispers of false passion to get inside

204

her knickers. When she wanted sex, she wasn't afraid to demand and I'm all for that positive approach. I never finished the wine. I stripped, instinctively checked my hands were clean and spent the next few hours as if I hadn't a care in the world.

*

I never got the chance to finish my sexual prowess because a huge explosion filled the night air interrupting my rhythm. My head shot up quicker than a jack-rabbit straining to hear. I ran to the window and saw a large orangey-red blob glowing down at the harbour. Something jolted my insides to move fast and I got dressed.

"Is there trouble?" Shayna asked as she dashed to the bathroom for her clothes.

"That explosion was too close for comfort."

"I'm going with you!"

"Please yourself."

We left the hotel and ran down to quayside. A large crowd had gathered to observe the spectacle of a blazing boat; roaring fires always seem to have that obsessive attraction. I found Shamus at the front, his face brightly illuminated by the flames. He had the vacant stare of a man deep in shock having lost everything.

I shook him to gain his attention. "Frigging hell, Shamus, what happened?"

He was still mesmerized by the fire. He stared deep into the flames with a noticeable tear in his eye and said without looking at me. "The 'Muff', Shacks Sir...she just blew up!"

"Frigging hell, Shamus, I can see that. Thank your lucky arse you weren't on it at the time. Insurance fully up to date, I hope!" I wasn't trying to be humorous.

"The boats replaceable, Shacks Sir," he said with a lump in his throat. "It is dhat detective chap...Hamer."

"What does the old fart want?"

"No, yer don't understand, Shacks, Sir. It's Hamer!"

I started feeling a little aggrieved with the Irishman. "What about Hamer?"

"He was on the 'Muff' when it blew-up."

For a few seconds I was speechless as I searched the roaring flames for a burning body. I turned to Shamus and said, "Are you absolutely sure he went aboard?"

"I know what I saw, Shacks Sir. I found meself a nice comfortable seat by the pub window. I saw Hamer walking down to the harbour. I waited a few minutes to see if he was bein' followed. I went to see what he was up to. In the distance I saw him moving about the deck. As I got closer…" He gestured by throwing his hands into the air a huge explosion. "The force of the blast almost knocked me off me feet. Feel me I'm still shakin'."

I wondered if Shamus has seriously thought about how close he'd come to death. I guess he must have. As for Hamer, I should be feeling sorry that he had to die so horrendously, yet, strangely, I felt nothing other than I'd lost my nearest emergency pull cord.

I grabbed Shamus by the arm. "We've got to get out of here and that includes you."

Shamus looked confused. "What about all the mess? What about Hamer?"

I said to him harshly, "What about us, Shamus! That explosion was no accident, no mistake. It was meant for you and me and anyone else associating with us. We were fortunate. Hamer wasn't. We can't change that now other than find enough evidence to flush out whoever is responsible. We can't do that if we offer ourselves as sacrificial lambs to the slaughter. And that will happen if we stay here."

"He's right, Shamus," Shayna backed me.

Shamus looked at me incredulously. "Are yer suggesting we run away from our responsibilities?"

"Yes, but only for a while, until we are free from danger."

"What about the Garda, it won't take them long to realize the boat belongs to me."

"True. They'll probably find a badly burnt body, but they won't know who it is. Well not for the moment. They'll assume it's you, Shamus. We can use that time to finish the job."

Shamus shook his head defiantly. "Sorry, Shacks, Sir, I can't do dhat. I'll only slow you down. I'll stay and mingle with the Garda. I should be safe. After all this commotion I don't tink anyone will bother me while the Garda are involved. Don't worry I'll drag the story along. Tell them I've no idea what happened, just move with their investigation."

"Okay, Shamus, if that's what you really want to do?"

"I tink it be better if I stay."

"Okay but do me one favour, Shamus."

"What would yer want me doin', Shacks, Sir?"

"When this is over and I'm still breathing I want you to find a new boat so I can compensate you for your loss."

"Dhare's no need, Shacks, Sir. They're very expensive. The insurance should cover the cost."

"Nonsense, Shamus! I'm as much to blame for the loss of your livelihood. Collect the insurance, but I insist on knowing the cost. Have you got that? Because there's a man I know most willing to cover the expenditure of the entire venture and that includes the price of a new boat." I turned to Shayna. "By the way, where did you say Deveron was staying?"

I got no verbal response from her apart from an exhalation of air, but her bemused expression rather told the story.

I shook Shamus by the hand, expressed my gratitude for his companionship and loyalty and slipped quietly away from the chaos. I felt bad leaving behind the carnage for shamus to sort out but I had to be free from involvement regarding the inevitable investigation. In the distance I could hear the sirens of a fire engine.

Collecting the Roadster from the hotel car park, Shayna and I headed away from Baltimore, and away from the prying questions, even more significantly, away from the attentions of the 'Flying-fish', at least until I was ready to challenge the crew straight on.

We took the road to Clonakilty to meet Deveron at the Quality Hotel. And for some unknown reason Shayna insisted on telling me, Clonakilty was the birthplace of Michael Collins the founder of the I.R.A., as if I really cared!

*

"Shayna and Mister Speed, it's so good to see you both," Deveron greeted us with a toothy smile.

Shayna jerked her head towards me. "Big hero, here, has found the submarine."

Deveron's expression was one of pure jubilation. "It's definitely here in Ireland?'

My nod of the head had all the hallmarks of boredom.

"Actually seen it?" Deveron was frothing at the corners of his mouth.

"Naturally, since I found it."

He smiled. "Splendid! Splendid! Tanamoto and the Japanese government will be overwhelmingly ecstatic. You might even become folklore in Japan; an honourable guest of the Country."

"Let's not get too carried away," I said.

"Where does she lay, Mister Speed?" The eagerness and excitement was in his eyes, though it was hard to judge with the sound of his tinny voice. "I've got to know!"

"I'll explain later!" That disappointed him but I had been thinking deeply about McCracken and his involvement in the hijacking. I said to Deveron, "Is there truth in the rumours that IRA terrorists helped the Germans during the war?"

He thought a moment. "Yes, there were those that hated the British more than the Germans. Why do you ask?"

I held the ring close to his face so he could have a good look at it without fobbing me off. "Seen anything like that before?"

Deveron's eyes widened told me he had.

"Good gracious!" Deveron spluttered.

"I want to know all about an active IRA terrorist in 1944, J. McCracken. You do remember him? No doubt he was about when you were involved in playing with bombs."

"There is no need to undermine my beliefs at the time, Mister Speed."

"You're talking to someone who doesn't give a frigging toss in your beliefs. Is the name McCracken familiar or not?"

"Is McCracken a link?"

"Why am I experiencing problems in getting a simple answer to a simple question; McCracken?" I reminded him.

"Yes, yes, I know the name. There's not many disgruntled Irishman who were around in the late thirties who hadn't heard of Jimmy 'the merciless' McCracken, Commanding Officer of the Munster Brigade. Realistically he was nothing but a powerful warlord. His contribution to the cause was to victimize loyal Irish people, who ran shops and businesses, into paying money for protection. The money bought weapons. There were some, who dare to speak against him, who suggested it only increased his wealth. Without contradiction, McCracken was nothing more than a common racketeer using the backbone of the I.R.A. to fill his pockets with money."

I quickly looked at Shayna. "There you are, Shayna, exactly what I was preaching to you, born criminals, nothing more."

She pulled her tongue out. It made her look childishly cute.

Deveron butted in. "Can we continue without trivial interruptions." He went on about McCracken. "No, Mister Speed, I'm not saying McCracken didn't commit himself to the cause. He was an awesome fighter. His hatred for the British was brutish. He specialized in bombs. He liked to listen to the sound of the bomb exploding. He would stay in the vicinity to witness his work. He hated the idea of a ceasefire while the war progressed in Europe. Hated the Irishmen who fought for the British during the war, swore he would kill all the traitors if they returned to their homelands."

"He sounds quite a guy."

"I kept well away from him. Has he something to do with the submarine?"

"He made it disappear."

Deveron shook his head. "Then the rumours were true that he collaborated with the Germans."

"Not necessarily, he could have got lucky."

"No, Mister Speed, McCracken hated the British enough to fight against them regardless. But if he was guilty of intercepting the I-52, then he double-crossed the Germans. Now that doesn't surprise me. The conniving rat must have smelt some profitable arrangement."

"He was obviously aware of the gold."

"Absolutely no other reason," Deveron said solidly. "But to be truthful, Mister Speed, I'm glad he stood on German toes instead of Irish ones. Do you know why they called McCracken 'the merciless'?"

I shrugged, "Because he was a nasty bastard?"

"That's exactly what he was, Mister Speed. McCracken invented the suicide bomber. He'd prime bombs to go off well before the bomb planter had time to escape. It was his favourite ploy. The bomb planter never knew, never had an option, that way no bomb disposal team had any chance to diffuse the situation."

"So I guess you didn't rate highly of him?"

"Sheer hatred is more in question, Mister Speed, because he killed innocent Irish people, and that was never part of the cause."

"He doesn't sound welcoming. Where was he originally from?"

Deveron mauled his way through the question. "He was a Corkonian. Is the bastard still alive?"

I shook my head. "Not unless someone else wore his ring. He's buried under a couple of tons of rock, in a cavern beneath the ruins of Dun an Oir."

"Good heavens above!"

"I thought you'd be pleased that he found his own personal coffin."

"A cavern, you say? Beneath Dun an Oir. Isn't that the old fort on Clear Island, the one referred to as the 'fort of gold'?"

"That's the one!"

"How ironic he chose that particular place."

"Nothing ironic about his choice, it was the perfect place and large enough to hide a submarine for sixty years. The cavern isn't on any maps or charts, but McCracken seemed to know the location and used it to his advantage when he hijacked the I-52 in 1944. Only his plan rather backfired. He never anticipated the possibility of the cavern tumbling down on his frigging head."

"So the gold is still there?"

My, "no," was savagely blunt. I suspected he was treasure hunting again.

"Where is it then?"

"How the frigging hell should I know!"

"Do you intend to keep looking for it?"

"Without any doubt, because if you weren't responsible for ordering the deaths of my friends, then some else is, the smell of that gold is going to lure and catch me the culprits."

"Such a deep vendetta might get you killed, Mister Speed."

"Ask me if I care a frigging toss! Oh, while we're on the subject of money and wealth, that promise of unlimited expenditure, I'll probably require quite a substantial amount to replace a fishing vessel that was blown up."

Deveron's eyelids widened. "Good gracious, Mister Speed! You're very clumsy."

"No fault of mine. I think the intention was I should have been on it at the time. Now if you don't mind I'd like to wash for dinner."

"Dinner, Mister Speed?"

"Thank you for offering. Shayna and I are ravenously hungry. And we will be stopping here with you. It's unsafe to return to my hotel due to the probability of awkward police questions or a bullet in the back of my head."

Deveron slowly shook his head. "Dear me, Mister Speed, you have a remarkable knack of landing yourself in a lot of trouble."

"Not intentional, I can assure you."

CHAPTER TWENTY

Despite Deveron's protest that I took Shayna with me, I went alone to Cork City. I parked the Roadster and went in search of the registrar office for birth, deaths and marriages in South Mall. I entered the building and approached the reception desk displaying one of my charming and cheeky smiles to the middle aged woman with a face like a Sergeant Major and built just as solid. I explained my predicament, the importance in tracing the whereabouts of the McCracken family, and were there any living relatives still in the area.

I got a huge smile in return, though her reply was straightforward and typical of a pompous twit.

"It is against company policy to divulge confidential information to any one unless directly concerned. Are you a family member? We would require proof of identity."

"I have no family connections." There was no need at this stage to be dishonest as it would serve no useful advantage. I showed her the ring and pointed to the name engraved. "It's my intention to return this piece to the family of the inscribed name."

She mellowed as she gazed at the sparklers. "Rather expensive looking."

"I've no idea of its value, just interested in returning to its owner."

"I would advise you to contact the Garda."

"I don't think they would be much help on the matter, it's not exactly a missing person's case. I am willing to leave it in your custodial safety if you could guarantee the ring reaches the right owner. I've no other intentions other than an honourably one."

"I'm very sorry, Mister-Ah?"

"Speed, Shackleton Speed."

"I would like to help, Mister Speed, but I can't go against company policy. And neither can we accept responsibility for returning property to the rightful owner."

I had hit an invisible brick wall in the form of stubbornness and I'd no argument over the matter just because she didn't know how to flex a rule never mind breaking one. Our short intimate meeting was cut even shorter when she blanked me to answer the telephone. I made to leave, not wanting to push hard and draw attention to myself, when another receptionist beckoned me over while iron drawers had her back turned.

I got a strong smell of cheap scent when she leaned over the counter. In a whispered voice, while constantly checking she wasn't under observation, she said, "I couldn't help overhearing your conversation. I know a lady by the name of Millie Malloy. Her mother died six months gone. Her mother's surname was McCracken. She might be able to help. Millie runs a craft shop in Corn market Street."

I went there.

Corn market Street, is a tight pedestrian through-fare, all vehicles prohibited. Brightly painted shops gave it a sort of magical avenue. I found Millie's Crafts, a sea-blue painted front shop filled with an assortment of ware. The shop assistant, a red haired girl with a freckled complexion, was far too young to be the proprietor.

I said pleasantly. "Could I possibly speak to Millie?"

"She's in the back baking. Who shall I say wants her?" She spoke with a strong Northern Ireland accent.

"Shackleton Speed. Tell her it concerns a piece of jewellery I have in my possession that belongs to a member of the McCracken family. I believe Millie's nee name was McCracken."

"I'll only be a moment."

"Thank you."

She disappeared into the rear of the shop. While I hummed a tune inside my head waiting for the girl's return, I thought, how nice it was to be in area where trust was highly thought of, since I could have quite easily ransack the shop and till and be on my way in half the time it took her to resurface from the back.

It looked promising when she returned, because she had a smile on her face. Pleasantly, she said: "Come through to the parlour, Mister Speed."

As I entered the room the first thing that struck me was the smell of baking bread exciting my taste buds. The woman I saw washing her hands in the pot sink had long dark hair lined with wisps of grey, all tied back in a ponytail that hung down as far as her lower spine. She wore a white apron over a flowing flowery patterned cotton dress.

She looked directly at me and said, in a soft Irish voice, "Mister Speed is it?"

The suspicion in her tone matched the suspicion distorting her eyebrows. Her grey blue eyes appeared watery. At first I thought she maybe upset, only that notion was soon squandered by the strong whiff of onions that suddenly invaded my nostrils as I approached her.

"Yes. Shackleton Speed, but please, call me Shacks."

She clinically wiped her hands on a towel and gestured me to the kitchen table. "Please, sit down, Shacks. How can I help?"

I sat, took the ring from my pocket and showed the piece to her in the hope she might instantly recognize it. Just by her blank expression I knew she didn't.

She eased into a chair opposite me. "A very beautiful ring, Shacks. What has it to do with me?" She smiled. She had a nice smile, too. "Not proposing are you?"

"Better than that, Millie," I said. "It belongs to a Jimmy McCracken. I believe your maiden name was McCracken and I was wondering if perhaps there was a person of that name within your family."

She looked me unblinkingly in the eye and slowly said, "My father was called, Jimmy."

"Then maybe I've found the right place. Does the ring look familiar?"

She shook her head. "No. I've never seen anything like it before."

"Do you know the whereabouts of your father?"

"No. According to my mother, God bless her soul, he left home one late July morning in 1944 and never returned so she constantly reminded me. He hasn't been seen since. I was four years of age when he went and quite frankly I can't remember him being part of my life at all. They say what you don't have you don't miss! (Her philosophy was right) My mother could have told you more about him, but unfortunately, she passed away a while ago."

"I'm sorry to hear that."

"Just the old age syndrome, wear and tear, happens to all of us eventually. What makes you think the ring belonged to my father?"

"I can't be sure it does, Millie. That's why I need to know more about his background. If he is the right person, then I'm obliged to leave the ring in your possession. I do believe it's valuable."

"How did you come by the ring?"

"It's an extremely long and complex story for you to understand at this time."

"If it was my father's ring, I think I've a right to know!"

"In due course, you will be told everything that you need to know. I promise. You'll have to trust me."

She smiled. "You have beautiful blue eyes, Shacks. I have a tendency to believe people with blue eyes." She thought a moment. "There is an old trunk upstairs in the attic. It was my mother's. She kept all my fathers personal belongings in there. We could start there. Now I've no idea what's inside the trunk, as I've never really found the time to look."

"There's no time like the present." I prompted.

"You're right, Shacks! Follow me!"

We went up two flights of creaking stairway and through a door. She blindly located and flicked on the light switch. The attic was illuminated by two pendants either end of a spacious well maintained storeroom filled with a collection of bric-a-brac, different sized cardboard boxes, piles of neatly stacked newspapers and the inevitable scary headless corpse that doubles as a seamstress's dummy you can always find hiding away in any attic.

Millie crossed to the far corner of the room and dragged out a large hand carved wooden trunk. I marvelled at the craftsmanship, such detailed carvings delicately etched into the wood. That alone was worth a hefty price.

I said, "Did your mother ever mention what he did for a living?"

She opened the trunk as she talked. "Yes, I remember asking as a child, I suppose it was a natural thing to ask questions about your own father."

"Did she say?"

"Stonemason and builder, she told me. I never actually saw any evidence of what he did for a living, but I did see his trade written on their marriage certificate."

"That accounts for it!" I said, thinking aloud.

"You know something, Shacks?"

"Well I did find the ring amongst ruins on Clear Island, Baltimore."

"It still doesn't prove it belonged to my father."

"I feel confident I've found the right place."

"Oh look!" She squealed like an excited child. "There's a pile of journals here."

She removed the black books, ten in all. Each dated. They spanned from 1934 to 1944. She began reading the 1934 journal.

"It's written in Irish," she said.

It had the same unappealing look for deciphering as Japanese. I said: "Do you understand the Irish language?"

She spoke in a different accent and voice. "My mother insisted I learnt and spoke our ancestral voice. It's gaeltacht."

"I don't wish to pry but what exactly did you say?"

She smiled. "I've met a very nice man today!"

I couldn't contradict her. I said, "Thank you!"

She began translating the first page. "It is a motto: I serve no King, nor Kaiser: I serve nothing but a free Ireland."

Frigging pathetic cultural prattle! I thought.

She quickly flicked through the pages, only stopping at certain chapters to read a few lines. Sometimes she cringed at certain paragraphs. Journal by journal she flicked through, again only stopping at certain paragraphs. I also witnessed the odd tear filling her eyes. Then her body stiffened and she couldn't hide her shock.

She said slowly, almost apologetically, "God in heaven! My father was the IRA Commander of Southern Ireland. I always believed he was a good catholic. What did he become?"

I tried to be gentle with her. "A freedom fighter, from what I can gather."

Those tears I saw slowly dripped down her cheeks "A terrorist and a murderer. These journals are confessional submissions on paper."

"It does signify in that direction," I said.

You have to give Jimmy McCracken a certain amount of credit for a man obsessed with murder. He'd been a prolific writer, though I found it confusingly strange why he should want to write the incriminating material down on paper. Then so did many other murderous minds though out history. I suppose McCracken was no different.

I said, "The 1944 journal was obviously his last, perhaps if we read through it properly it might tell us the last moments before your father disappeared. I suggest the last month?"

"Yes." She nodded in agreement, turning to the final chapters in June and continued the translation with fluency.

She began, "Met German spies Harrington and Lodge for the final time." She suddenly stopped and looked at me. "This gets worst."

"Don't concern yourself too much Millie, what we've learnt today goes no further than you and me and this room. I promise. Please, read on."

She nodded with thanks and went on. "I convinced them to switch the rendezvous with the Jap sub to Roaring Water Bay, a mile, South West from Cape Clear. Believed my story the Garda Siochana had discovered the possibility of a smuggling gang operating in Galway Bay. Both, Harrington and Lodge accepted changes had to be urgently made. Once their task was completed, I did them in. My protector, Saint Brandon holds them safe from discovery."

Millie paused and looked up at me. "What does he mean by *Did them in!*, Shacks?"

"I suspect he killed them, Millie." I thought it best to be blunt.

She recoiled with disgust. "My Mother always said he was a good man. Do you think she knew of his terrible background?"

I said comfortingly, "Maybe she did, maybe she didn't. They were difficult times during the early forties. Your father obviously went about his beliefs in the way he thought right."

Millie sniffled back the tears. "No wonder my mother never saw him again, he's either languishing in prison or he's dead."

"I think you'll have to expect the worst, Millie." She gazed at me like a frightened child. "I took the ring from a corpse I found buried under fallen rocks on Clear Island. If it was your father, then I've brought you bad news, which I never intended. I'm sorry about that. But I'm confident his body will be recovered even though the task will be a mammoth operation and will take a major construction job to complete."

Another lonely tear dribbled down her cheek. From the bottom of the trunk she carefully brought out a framed black and white photograph of a group of men in out dated diving gear. She pointed to a man in the centre.

"That is my father. My mother often showed me this picture. It was her fond memory of the man she loved. *He was a handsome devil*, she used to say. Just look at my father's face. Is that the face of terrorist and a murderer?"

"Looks can be incredibly deceiving. It's what goes on in the mind that counts."

Without contradiction, McCracken was a killer. As all religious fanatics and freedom fighters they master the art of death and destruction. We live in a world full of madness, so what's one more dangerous freak? There are many more McCracken's out there in some dark corner of the world itching to start a war because of their beliefs and remedies.

Millie said quietly, "At least I can put Old Willie's mind at rest."

"Who's Willie?"

She pointed to the smallest member of the group of eight divers. "That's Willie. Willie Donahue. Still see him about. He's probably the only one I've ever met from this photograph, which seems strange since my mother always maintained that the eight of them were inseparable companions."

"What became of the others?"

"I don't rightly know. As for Willie it's a real shame."

"Why? He's obviously had a long life."

"A long troubled life is more appropriate. Apparently, something traumatised him many, many years ago. Drink got a hold of him, wrecked his life. Bit of an introvert. Never married and doesn't seem to have any relatives. Someone gave him the name 'Wandering Willie', stuck with him ever since."

"Where can I find, Willie?"

She gave me a suspicious look. "I don't think he could help you with anything."

"It's possible he might be able to piece together your father's movements on the day he disappeared, so we can verify if it's him."

"I doubt that, Shacks. My mother spent many hours trying to talk to him. As I said, lives in a world of his own. Get more sense from a stuffed animal than get him to talk of the past."

I persisted. "I'd still like to try."

She still had the suspicious look.

"Please!"

I could have easily found him myself given the time, but it would be far quicker if Millie put me in the right direction rather than spend hours searching the pubs of Cork City. Besides, I had a feeling my time was running low.

Thankfully, she said, "I shouldn't think he'll mind me telling you.

His favourite haunt is 'The Ovens', in Oliver Plunkett Street, a nice quiet pub."

I noticed a chapter at the bottom of the page in the journal. I said, "Is there anything more in the final chapters?"

She studied the journal. "A piece of redemption, I think. He's written: 'beyond the line of light; when the sun rises and illuminates the Virgin Mary and through her eyes she will foretell my domain of madness: my future life: my dreams of stardom. Again the spirit of Saint Brandon saves me from destruction'.

"Well, that's his final passage. No indication where he was going. His words disappear as he did."

"This, 'Saint Brandon', seems to be a significant part of his life, something special within your family?"

She shook her head. "Nothing I can relate to. Sorry!"

I gave Millie the ring. She didn't fuss. "Better hang on to this. I'm confident the ring has found the right person."

"Thank you," She said, and clasped it in her hand as if it was the most precious thing in her life. "What do you think I should do with the journals, burn them?"

"I'd be inclined to read them through properly before you decide, Millie. Perhaps you may find something in there that doesn't relate to your father's unfortunate side. Your Mother loved him for something. Maybe he wasn't all bad after all."

When I left her, I couldn't be certain if the tears in her eyes were of happiness or sadness.

*

I ordered a Guinness and asked the barman if Wandering Willie Donahue had come in. He jabbed a finger towards the shrivelled old man sat alone by the window, seemingly staring into a glass of whiskey. First observations of the unkempt loner had me agreeing with Millie, he certainly was an introvert and he looked like a tramp. I paid for the drink and wandered across to the sad looking man. He startled when I sat down opposite him.

I smelt his bad body odour as he twitched nervously in his seat. What I first thought to be black lines criss-crossing his face turned out to be dirt ingrained into his deep lined complexion. His confused dark sunken eyes searched mine.

"That seat *be* taken," he said in a low voice

"That's right!" I said.

"Then why don't yer move to another and leave me in peace."

"I don't want to be shouting across the room when I talk to you."

"I'm not in mood to talk to strangers."

"You'll talk to me, Willie, because if you don't I'll pester you all day until you do."

"Yer know me name?"

"Yes Willie. Millie Malloy said you'd be here."

"Who did yer say?" There was a sudden squeak in his voice. "Millie Malloy, yer say?"

"That's right, Jimmy McCracken's daughter."

It was clearly obvious Willie was horrified when I mentioned the name McCracken. Now I had his immediate attention. He obviously thought it was a name that would never resurface again, especially from a stranger. He realised he'd been wrong, yet he attempted to squash the connection.

"I-I-dunno, that name!"

"Which name don't you know Willie, Millie Malloy or Jimmy McCracken?

He scowled. "I've never heard of them."

"There's no point denying the fact, Willie. Surely you can at least remember your old pal, Jimmy McCracken?"

He eyed me suspiciously. "Who might yer be?"

"My name is of no importance."

"Are yer a relation of Millie's?"

"So you do know, Millie. No, I'm a friend. She was most grateful for the return of her father's signet ring into her possession. The ring I took from Jimmy. The one he always wore. The one he was wearing when he went missing. Remember the ring, the one with his initials engraved on the front."

"Yer can't have!" Willie snapped quicker than a mantrap.

"Oh, why's that?"

"Because he's de-," He suddenly stopped, realizing his mistake.

"Dead, were you going to say?"

"How do I know, not seen him for a long time."

"What do you call a long time, a week, month, year, or maybe not since nineteen forty-four?"

"Yer're not going to keep pestering me like Molly McCracken did. (I gathered that would be Millie's mother) Constantly nagging me to tell her where Jimmy was. Nagged me stupid asking if he had run off with another woman."

"She was concerned about him. She loved him."

"He loved her. He told me that."

"Did you ever tell her what happened to him?"

"I told yer I never saw him!"

"You never saw him because you were too busy scampering for your life from the secret cavern, under the ruins of Dun an Oir. Isn't that so?"

By the expression on his face, Willie nearly died there and then. What trace of life he still had in his body quickly drained. His complexion went sickly white, and the blackheads spotting his face were now more prominent. I had got Willie petrified. Understandable when a complete stranger happens to walk into his miserable life and confronts him about a secret he's kept to himself for all those years. That pathetic look on his face told me I was accurate in my assumption.

"How-I-I-don't understand!"

"How I know so much?"

Willie was trembling, his left knee knocking against the table. He said edgily, "Is Jimmy still alive?"

"Only in spirit," I assured him. "Plus the ten confessional journals he wrote."

He leaned closer to me, a concerned expression crumpling his face, his strong breath making me recoil slightly.

"What d'yer mean, confessional journals?" he whispered.

I eased back from the smell of his breath and took in a mouthful of Guinness, swallowed and said, "Nothing incriminating that concerns you or the other members of McCracken's private racketeers."

He ignored my accusation referring to racketeer. "It don't rightly matter about the others, they got caught with Jimmy."

"When the tunnel roof fell in?"

He eyed me with a look suggesting I was thick. "Well, yeah."

"How many men died?"

"Seven, including Jimmy...Hey...hold on a minute! Yer'd have known that if yer were excavating the tunnel."

"Who mentioned anything about digging?"

"Yer found his body?"

"Well I assume it's him. All I found was a skeletal hand with a ring."

"Yer'd have had to be inside the cavern if yer found Jimmy. He was last out. The tunnel was only wide enough for one man at a time."

"I took the sea route. Remember the one, where you hauled a Japanese submarine into the cavern. Have to admit, that was an exceptional piece of ingenuity."

Willie hand gestured his reluctance to go on. "No more talk. I'm saying nothing more. Leave me alone!"

I got angry. "You better talk to me! I'm probably the only person in the whole wide world who can get you hanged. Do you understand that, Willie?"

"I wasn't there! You can't prove I was! Anyway hanging has been abolished."

He was certainly a defiant stubborn bastard for his size. I said, "Depends who the hangman is, Willie. There were a lot of dead Japanese submariners down there in that horrible damp place. They had been slaughtered, gunned down with hardly a fight. I think I could quite easily convince a court of your involvement to murder. Maybe find a trace of your DNA down there."

Willie got himself in sweaty fluster. "You can't incriminate me. I dunno if I could stand all the aggravation of a trial. We were a diving team and made a decent living repairing quays and jetties and run down buildings. That's all! Yer can't make me confess to anything else. So leave alone!"

"I don't believe you know nothing."

"It's the truth!"

"I could come to a compromise."

He was thinking about that one. "What on?"

"You tell me everything that happened on that day."

"Go on?"

"I want to know all about Jimmy McCracken, and I mean everything. And when I walk out of here I'll forget all about ever seeing you. Your freedom guaranteed. Now I can't be fairer than that.

He had that doubtful expression.

I pushed on. "Just the whole story concerning Jimmy McCracken and I promise you'll not see me or hear from me again."

"Why should I trust a stranger?" He threw the palm of his hand towards me in disgust. "Shop me to Garda the moment my backs turned, yer will!"

"Millie put trust in me. She took me into her confidence. She trusted me enough to give me your name, because she thought you could help me."

"Are yer in trouble?" he said slowly.

"Not just me. The lives of countless people may depend on any scraps of information you tell me."

"So yer won't mention anything we said?"

"That's right."

"I have yer word, or God will strike yer down!"

"You have my word!"

"If yer do I'll kill yer, I swear it!"

I stared him straight in the eyes and said bluntly, "Willie I could smash your throat with one punch so less of the threats. I want to know about Jimmy McCracken and then you can sink back into your void of loneliness. Okay?"

He leaned even closer to me with the intention that no one would overhear, which was pointless because there was no one near enough to hear. But I wasn't going to argue.

"It all began one drunken night when the eight of us were having one of our usual benders," Willie's eyes flicked about anxiously as he talked. "Jimmy came up with this crackpot idea of us all becoming rich men. Now we all knew Jimmy was involved with IRA. He thrived on the adventure. He said he was mixed-up with German spies and had heard about a shipment of gold destined for German shores. We were flabbergasted when he said he intended to hijack the gold from under the noses of the Germans.

"Yet the more he talked, the more we listened. The thought of gold had us dribbling. The plan was simple. It was workable, workable yet bloody dangerous. The dangerous part of it I didn't fancy. I tend to flap when the mention of killing people entered the conversation. I wanted out. Wealth I'd tried to achieve later in a more civilised manner. Jimmy wouldn't accept my withdrawal. I'd made the mistake of listening instead of walking away when I had the chance. I always thought Jimmy was a friend. I was wrong. He was a bully, a dangerous bully. I was too scared to say no. He said he would kill me to maintain my silence. I'd no choice but to participate.

"It took us a month to construct everything inside the cavern. He trained us to use weapons. We practiced the attack until we were as good as any commando unit. When everything was in place the plan was executed with unbelievable expertise. I had to hand it to

Jimmy, he was a smooth operator. I had no doubt whatsoever, if he'd managed to escape the mess, he would have made Commander-in-Chief of the IRA."

I was getting bored. "Never mind how good he was, get on with it!"

"Well just as Jimmy had told us. This Jap submarine sat off Clear Island as dusk began to fall. I've no idea where it came from. It was just sat there, waiting to be hit. We moved in and attached limpet mines to the propellers and fins. The sub was obviously leaking water because it sank fast stern first. Down she went to the bottom, crippled and helpless. We secured steel cables to her and dragged the entire submarine into the cavern. Jimmy might have been a murderous, anti-Brit, fascists, but yer can't fault the ingenious piece of engineering skills in the design and building of a diesel winch capable of dragging so much tonnage. It took two days to pull the sub into the cavern such was the gear ratio. Inch by inch she came in. I just couldn't believe what we were doing, but it worked. It worked! It was a magnificent sight, she was a real beauty."

"Well I can assure you, Willie, it's nothing but a rusting relic now. Go on!"

"We had our submachine guns in readiness in case any of the crew tried to leave the sub. We burnt our way through with the oxy-acetylene torch, exactly where Jimmy said the strong room was. When we finally broke through I stayed outside to cover the conning tower and the deck hatches. I heard the gun battle and the explosions. It was a massacre. Submariners don't make good ground troops. Not one was left alive. Jimmy didn't want witnesses to the crime. But momentarily our wickedness was forgotten when we found the gold boxes.

"Apart from seven boxes, we took the rest by handcarts to North Harbour and loaded the gold onto our boat. We also loaded something concealed in waxed material bags, probably the size of sand bags."

"What was in those?"

Willie shrugged his shoulders. "Jimmy didn't say and neither of us was in the right frame of mind to ask a madman, besides we were exhausted, just glad the job was done. Jimmy sailed away alone. He returned ten hours later. It was part of the plan. The gold he took away, he said, belonged to the coffers of the IRA, and would be used in the fight against British tyranny after the war in Europe was concluded. I suspected the gold was his elevation up the ladder to the top of the IRA ladder."

"Do you ever get to know what he did with it?"

"The secret died with him. Anyway-," I noticed that Willie was relishing getting the guilt off his chest, there was no stopping his mouth, "-when he returned, we each took a box of gold as payment for our part in the operation. But the killing didn't end there. Sean, he was always the obstinate one, decided to confront Jimmy. Saying one box of gold wasn't enough payment for the risk they had all taken. I thought he'd an arguable case. Jimmy didn't. Without hesitation or a moments thought, he wiped Sean out. Without any remorse, Jimmy gunned him down, right there in the cavern. Gold bars dropped from the disintegrating box as the bullets ripped into Sean's body. Then, with a smirking smile on his face, Jimmy turned to the rest of us and callously said, 'there yer are lads come and collect yer bonus.' Then he pumped the remainder of the magazine into Sean's face so if he were to be found he wouldn't be recognized."

I said, "Charming character, Jimmy McCracken!"

"I'd befriended a madman and I was petrified. The ironic disappointment concerning the rest of the lads is they accepted Jimmy's offer and filled their pockets with the extra. I declined, said I was happy with mine. Jimmy knew I hated him for what he did to Sean. The stare he gave me had me earmarked as his next kill. I had to get out of that place of death. I was first up the tunnel and I thought the rest were following. Jimmy would have been last because he would have switched the power off and meticulously recovered the generator with the tarpaulin. I suspected he had an insane vision of re-floating the submarine, hoist the IRA flag and use it against the Brits. That's when I heard a strange eerie gargled scream coming from the deep in the cavern. It came from one of the Japanese submariners. I heard one of our lads shout, 'watch out! There's one on the conning tower!' Seconds after a terrific explosion occurred inside the tunnel. It shook the whole place. I could feel the tremors under my feet. I think a submariner managed to fire a few rounds of cannon shells at the tunnel walls. As I looked back I could see a massive cloud of dust heading up the tunnel.

"I didn't hang about to find out what happened. When that tunnel started shaking and chunks of rock began cascading down, I was out of the there. I even threw down my box of gold because it was impeding my running ability and I ran. I ran for my life! When I got out and looked behind all I saw escaping from the tunnel entrance was that chasing bellowing cloud of dust mushrooming into the air. I waited for the dust to settle. Then I saw the tunnel was blocked and no one else had got out."

"What did you do then?"

There was even fear on his face as he was telling. "I kept on running! Back to the boat and back to the mainland. I deliberately disappeared for a month, waiting for news of the accident. Week after week I heard nothing. Week after week, Molly McCracken was pestering me, asking if I'd seen Jimmy. Months went by, still nothing. Months became years, still no word and Molly McCracken's pestering has turned me into a drunken wreck ever since."

"Why didn't you just tell somebody? Tell a few lies. Jimmy and his mates had gone to the O'Driscoll's fort on Clear Island, they haven't returned. A search party would have been formed and you would have been in the clear. No witnesses to say otherwise."

"That's easy to say when yer're not scared shitless. In the forties people were edgy, untrustworthy. Implication in a crime of robbery and murder wouldn't go down very well with the Irish Guards whether the target was the enemy or not. And with Jimmy involved with the IRA, well that definitely sealed my mouth. I wasn't going to spend the next twenty years stuck in a smelly Irish prison. No thank you! Kept the blabbing tightly shut, and went about my business trying to be as normal as possible."

"That's everything?"

He nodded. "There is no more to tell. Now will yer leave me alone! So I get to finish the rest of my horrible life in peace."

"Which I promised would honour."

"Yer won't tell Millie I ran away and didn't stop to try and rescue her father?"

"No point upsetting her more than she probably is now," I said. "One more question, Willie. Why didn't you go back for the gold in the tunnel, it's obviously still buried there under the debris. Think of the wealth it would have brought."

"Perhaps yer haven't heard of the O'Driscoll curse. Back in the thirties people died mysteriously on Clear Island in the vicinity of the ruin fort. I suspected the curse struck again. I'd rather die in poverty than challenge the curse of O'Driscoll. I've never been back to the Island since for either merchandise."

I never realised till much later the slip of the tongue by Willie, as we only talked about gold, yet he mentioned *either merchandise* which in my opinion was a reference to two products. Satisfied with the information extracted, I bought Willie a few pints and a whiskey chaser and made to leave. Then I checked my stride as I remembered something I wanted to ask him.

"Ever heard of St Brandon?"

Willie shook his head as he thought. "No I dare say I don't…Oh! Wait a minute. Yes, Jimmy and I did some roof repairs at a small church. It was called St Brandon. But that was a long time ago, probably the year thirty-nine."

"Where was this church?"

"Now yer're asking something. But it was somewhere around Skibberean."

*

I left Cork and drove back to see Deveron, only he had gone, and so too had Shayna. No message, no jack shit! I headed back to Baltimore as fast as the Roadster could move without crashing. I suddenly sensed danger, but I couldn't put my finger on whether it was my problem or someone else's. I hit the accelerator to the floor and drove hard, burning fuel and rubber at an alarming rate.

I had almost reached the turn-off for Baltimore when the in-car mobile rang. I pressed the appropriate button for two way contact. I knew the number but the voice didn't match the owner.

"Yes!" I answered sharply.

"We have an interfering friend of yours, Speed."

For a moment I was baffled as I had difficulty in distinguishing the mystery man's voice over a heavy roaring sound in the background. To hear it again I said, "I don't have friends!"

"If you hurry, Speed, you may save your sailor companion from a drop to his death. Be at the fog station at Mizen Head. No police, just you, alone. I wouldn't hang about, the tides ebbing and a body smashes nastily on rocks."

The mobile went dead. The voice! I'm sure I knew that voice. The smirking in the tone as he talked. That same smirking sound I'd heard from Damien Love. I panicked as I realized they had him. The frigging bastards had Shamus!

I drove to Shamus's home at Collen. I brought the Roadster to a shuddering halt outside his house and went to check. There was no need to knock on the front door because it had been kicked from its hinges and lay at an angle all splintered and battered. I shouted for Shamus but got no reply. I went inside and looked round. The place had been trashed. I returned quickly to the Roadster and headed for Mizen Head without a contingency plan to fall back on. It was obvious if I show myself, the first bullet would hit me before I got close enough to plea for Shamus's life to be spared, that is, if Love and Hate had allowed him to live that long. My guts churned inside as I raced towards my destiny with death.

CHAPTER TWENTYONE

I approached the car-park at Mizen head cautiously. Stopped the car and looked around before getting out, using the car door as protection from a possible bullet. Again I looked around. The two salon cars parked close by were empty.

They were waiting for me on the white concrete bridge leading to the Mizen Head fog station. I could see Shamus standing in front of Love and Hate. The cowards were using him as a shield. I looked down at the floor and picked up two smooth flat stones and put one in each hand. I slammed the car door to attract their attention and began walking towards the bridge.

Love and Hate were alert as I approached. I didn't have many options to pick from. I should have really told the Garda of the situation and left the hostage negotiations to them. But I think that Love would have killed Shamus the moment they were challenged. No, they wanted me. Now I was here to save a man's life, only this time I was on time. Besides, how could I possibly be accepted through the gates of hell if I was to allow the Irish man to perish without even attempting a reasonable rescue? I can't be an egoistic bastard all my life.

Within shouting distance, I yelled. "Are you alright Shamus?"

Shamus nodded, shouting back. "As fine as I can be-," before he was cut off by a hard nudge in the small of his back with a silenced gun.

"Keep walking towards us, Speed! Love yelled back. "Get your hands up so I can see what they're doing."

As I raised my hands, I slipped the pebbles between the forefinger and middle finger of each hand and gripped so when I showed the palms of my hands the pebbles were invisible from view. They seem satisfied with my hands at shoulder height.

"That's it, Speed, Keep coming!" Love gestured me forward with his gun hand.

Stupid as it might sound, I was gambling on a hunch that I wasn't about to die by the bullet but instead Hate wanted to tear me apart piece by piece and feed me to the Basking Sharks. He wanted me to suffer as he had suffered by Winston's teeth. As much as I wanted revenge on them, Hate equally wanted revenge on me. I could see the fury burning in his eyes as I went through the iron-barred gate and onto the bridge. Yes he definitely had me down for a butcher's death. But if I needed any strong encouragement to take him on, my blood sizzled when I saw the severe bruising and cuts around Shamus's cheekbones and eyes.

"Not in any pain, are you, Shamus?" I asked, keeping a watchful eye on the fidgety movements of Love and Hate.

Shamus shook his head. "I'm Irish, Shacks Sir. Me skin's like leather."

He was also a lousy liar, though I admired his bravery.

"Very chivalrous of you to turn up, Speed, and so pleasant to have your company."

"Crackers more like, but I'm here." I began lowering my hands, sneakily slipping the pebbles back into the palms of my hands.

Love jabbed the gun deeper into Shamus's spine. "Nothing stupid now, Speed, or I'll blow a hole threw the old man's spleen."

"Just tired arms," I said convincingly, "can't hold them aloft all day."

Hate began sneering. His fingers twitched in anticipation to tear me apart and for the first time I saw his recent disfigurement. The half ear was an unsightly mess, a jagged piece of purplish-red flesh that no plastic surgeon could reshape to normality. There were bite marks dotting his face and scratches criss-crossed the bridge of his nose. And then there were the deep purplish bite marks on his hand obviously from his first skirmish with Winston when they had clashed at the farm. *Hell I loved that dog!*

I can't say I was about to enjoy the next exciting encounter when Hate drew a long bladed knife that glinted menacingly when the sun caught it. But after that I never had much choice when he suddenly lunged towards me snarling obscenities. I saw the inflamed madness in his eyes. Spit flew angularly from his mouth as he pounded forward. That was when I struck.

I looked beyond the oncoming Hate and shouted, "Get him Winston!"

My plan worked as Hate suddenly slammed on the shoe leather brakes, frantically twisting with the expectancy of Winston snapping at his heels, slashing the knife downwards where he thought the imaginary dog was. That momentary distraction even distracted Love, as his eyes flicked to find the non-existent beast. Love was the first to realize the deception and his eyes shot back in my direction, horror across his face when he realized he was too late.

The pebble I threw struck him between the eyes, knocking him back against the parapet railings. Blood ran down the bridge of his nose and dripped off the nib. Swiftly I twisted and threw the second pebble at Hate and caught him straight in the left eyeball. As I move forward for the flaying knife in Hate's fist, I got a fleeting glimpse of Shamus, despite his bondage, shoulder charging the howling Love over the side of the railing. I was to reflect later how Love had managed to grab a hold of the concrete bridge support as he fell, which prevented his fall to certain death on the rocks. But he hung in there gamely, swinging and screaming for help, frantically attempting to scramble back to safety, which to Shamus's credit, he marvellously prevented by kicking his fingers with his every attempt he made to climb back onto the bridge. I got the distinct impression Shamus was beginning to enjoy himself as he shouted his own brand of Irish obscenities while lashing out with both feet, who could blame him?

But I had my own battle as I struggled with Hate for control of the knife. The frigging bastard was far stronger opposition than I'd anticipated as the swishing blade nicked the skin of my left cheek. The sight of leaking blood excited Hate as he tried to kick my feet from under me. The fight had us crashing against the parapets like two gladiators battling to the death in the centre of the arena. We were spinning, our feet shuffling for the firmness and grip of terra-firma. Our bodies rolled across the top of the railing, advantage changing constantly. Our knees thudded into each other's midriff hoping for the one fatal blow to gain the upper hand.

Shamus might have been enjoying his domination of Love, but I was feeling the strain and exhaustion, tiring by the second and I needed inspiration quick. I got it in a way I didn't think possible, though I didn't know what possessed me to latch my teeth onto Hate's right eyebrow but I did and I was biting hard into the baggy skin to hang on. I shook my head like a wild animal tearing the flesh of its prey. Hate's screams sounded like a wounded wolf, but I didn't let go until my mouth came away and Hate released me and went reeling back, clutching his face. Blood pumped from between his fingers, running down his cheek and chin. I spat out the offensive lump of hairy flesh to the floor. The ragged piece of eyebrow twitched like a squashed caterpillar.

Hate came at me again with the knife, slashing blindly because the blood from the eyebrow filled his eye and his other eye had swelled by the force of the pebble striking it. As he slashed the blade I dodged easily, waiting for the right moment. When the knife arm came in a sweeping arc I grabbed the hand and carried the momentum round until the knife blade pierced the side of Hate's neck and I carried on forcibly ramming the blade home, up to the hilt.

I managed to pull away from the ensuing mess and gore. Hate began gurgling, attempting to dislodge the blade which angled down from the wound. Even as the blood gushed, Hate still wasn't finished as his fingers fumbled into his pocket trying to pullout a gun. I ran at him and leapt into the air angling my body and executing a solid sidekick into his chest sending him crashing over the parapet railings. Instinctively I tried to grab him but he'd gone over too quick, only inches from my grasp. He dropped to the rocks below, his screams smothered by the roar of the waves.

I quickly released Shamus from his bonds and said, "I can't leave you alone for one minute-eh-Shamus?

Shamus's head lowered in shame. "I'm terribly sorry, Shacks Sir."

"Not you fault, Shamus."

"Took me by surprise, dhey did, Shacks Sir!"

"They're good at that, Shamus."

"Tried to fight them off, I did, just too many."

I patted him on the shoulder. "I'm proud of you, Shamus. I don't have many true friends but you are high on my list."

Shamus smiled. "Dhat I'll always be, Shacks Sir."

Then suddenly his smile had vanished into an expression of shock and I realized Love had scrambled back onto the bridge further back and began legging it towards the fog station. I'd not finished with him yet so I went after him.

By the time I'd reached the white washed building, Love had vanished. He couldn't have ventured far, not unless his high board diving skills outweighed his sense of stupidity because his only escape was perpendicular and a long way down. Exerting extreme caution I circled the fog station, eyes and ears fully alert. Then I heard the faint sound of shuffled feet. I pretended to jerk forward before retracting even faster as the piece of log tried to whack me across the head but instead crashed into the side of the building. Splinters of wood flew but I saw enough of Love's arm to grab and follow up by kicking my left boot into his midriff and sent him splaying to the floor.

Again he was scrambling to his feet trying to run away. I gave chase and caught him up near the cliff edge. He'd nowhere to go now, trapped like a caged animal. He made an instinctive grab for me, grasping a handful of my jacket. I had visions of him attempting to pull me over the side with him so I concentrated on standing firm. Then I smashed my fist into his face. His body shuddered such was the force of the blow. He lost his footing and slipped down the rock, dangling over the edge, holding on for dear life.

"Help me, Speed! Love pleaded. "I'm slipping."

"Fuck off you murdering bastard!"

"You can't let me die. It's immoral. It's murder!"

"No, it's revenge!"

"Help me, Speed. Please, I don't want to die!"

Frigging hell, I was so mad with his diabolical plea that I reached down, grabbed both his wrists and yanked him back to relative safety, well sufficient enough for him to be precariously balanced on edge by the tip of his toes while I held him by his jacket. He didn't struggle knowing only an inch separated his backward return down the cliff face.

"Right you frigging parasite, the name of your paymaster now."

"Go to hell!"

"That's exactly where I'm sending you unless you give me the right answers!"

He snorted at me. "Kill me and that constitutes cold-blooded murder."

"So put me on trial! And even then it would be worth it!"

"You're not designed for killing, Speed. It takes something special to look a man straight in the eye and finish him," the bastard snarled.

I ignored his taunt. "Give me the name of your paymaster, now!"

"Free me first."

I thought that a fair agreement so I pulled him away from the edge. Well then? Hurry my patience is wearing thin."

"Will you let me walk away?"

"That depends on if you give me the right name."

"You know I work for McClusky."

"McClusky's dead!"

"I can't help that!"

"You kill people for money, Love. You don't work for nothing and with payment terminated you'd have disappeared and returned to that stench pit you call home. So you piece of swivelling shit, who and where is your paymaster?"

"Go to hell!"

I shoved him back. "I'd rephrase that statement shit bag! That's twice you've said it. I'm not the one dangling so close to the edge using only toe nails to hang on."

I shook him a little and particles of rock slid down the rock face with great effect.

Still he was defiant. "Let me fall, Speed, and you'll never know!"

"Is your paymaster on the 'Flying Fish'?"

"Nothing until I'm in a safe place." Love was gambling.

I shook him some more. With my teeth clenched, I said, "Talk, you piece of diarrhoea! You've nothing to lose, only your life."

"Precisely Speed, if I talk, I die anyway. It's that sort of situation. And you're just an English scum who has no idea how to murder someone simply!"

"You mean there's a particular skill in killing an old defenceless farmer by drowning him in cow shit. Or perhaps killing a kind faced photographer in London, and burning him to a cinder. They were my friends you messed up."

"You can't prove I'd anything to do with that!"

"I'll have a damn good try while you're rotting in a prison cell."

"You think so, Speed?" I didn't appreciate his attitude. "Okay, I might have a brief appearance in court just to discover I'm nothing more than a tourist being bullied by a madman."

Nor did I like his arrogance.

"You frigging piece of slimy leech, you killed my friends! Yet the disheartening side to your defence is you never questioned the order to kill defenceless people. So you're going down for murder, no problem!"

"You still have no proof. No witnesses to back your accusations. No, metal man, you are the murderer. I witnessed you murder Theodore Hate! So you can go to hell!"

"Is that so? Talking of hell, before you go there, my friends will want a few words with you!"

When I pushed Love effortlessly over the edge I felt nothing. I stared him straight in the eyes as he went backwards attempting a frantic front crawl in fresh air trying to maintain his balance. I wasn't laughing as he fell to his death, nor did I cringe as his screams scared the shit out of the seagulls perched on ledges below, his death screams quickly smothered by the squawking barrage.

I heard pounding feet approaching. Shamus was running towards me closely followed by another man who I assumed was the operator of the fog station.

"What was that dreadful scream?" The man asked.

"Good god! It seems there has been a terrible accident. Did you see what just happened?"

The man peered gingerly over the precipice, concern distorting his face. "Has someone fallen?"

"I think so." I said with a shocked tone. "I was walking along and I saw this figure, well I think he jumped!"

Shamus watched me with astonishment. He knew different.

"I better inform the coastguard," the man said as if the situation occurred frequently.

"I'll leave that in your capable hands, my good man. Come along, Shamus, there's nothing more we can do."

While the man used his mobile, Shamus and I slipped away, at first a casual stroll, which increased to a brisk walk converging into a run.

Shamus said, between gasping breaths. "Oh, God be praised, yer're alright, Shacks Sir. I gather yer did the swine?

"He went over the edge."

"Would that be, on his own accord, Shacks Sir?"

"Accidents do happen!" I said.

"Dhat they do," he agreed breathlessly.

We probably made it halfway across the concrete bridge when something zinged and whipped off the railing an inch in front of me. I dropped to the floor dragging Shamus along with me and stayed flat while I peered around.

"Damn it! Did you see where the shots came from?"

"I never even heard it, Shacks, Sir. I started fallin' when yer did."

There was the faintest of splutters as another barrage of fire chipped the concrete in a dozen places only a metre away. That was when I suspected the sniper didn't have a clear view of our position, so I began to crawl along the bridge on my stomach, scuffing the toes of my walking boots as I pushed. Shamus followed closely.

As we crawled I said over my shoulder, "I think this bridge is going to need a lick of paint after this fiasco."

I heard Shamus's groan and followed that with a mumbled, "I've befriended a complete madman."

He was probably right.

We had made it to the gateway with no injuries when everything went quiet. I listened intently before the shrilling cry from circling seagulls broke the silence. In the far distance I heard the faint sound of a car engine, which quickly disappeared from hear shot.

"I think our sniper has gone."

"How can you tell?"

I stood to prove it to Shamus and I didn't get shot.

"Has that convinced you? Let's go, Shamus."

Shamus got to his feet and rubbed the grey bristles on his chin. "Gave up rather too easily, don't you think, Shacks Sir?"

"The thought had crossed my mind, but I've no time to ponder on fragments of puzzlement, I've a master criminal to apprehend."

It was moments like this when I realized I wasn't getting any younger. My body ached everywhere. My joints creaked and cracked. My elbows and knees had all the evidence of severe abrasions. I definitely knew the pressure wasn't getting to me but I was beginning to feel the pace and regretting it.

I recovered Hate's gun from the floor and tucked it away inside my coat. My steps quicken.

Shamus panting like a running dog, said, "I forgot to mention dhare were three other men with those two thugs."

"Did you recognize any of them"?

"Two I tink were crewmen."

We kept walking, not even looking at each other. I was too preoccupied watching for any more surprise attacks.

"Our friends from the 'Flying-fish', do you suppose?"

"I'd say dhat, Shacks Sir."

"What about the third person?"

Shamus blew out hard. "O' he was a big man. English, and a bit toffee nosed by the way he talked. But he was the one dishing out the orders."

"Can you describe him more specifically?"

"Hardly, Shacks, Sir, not with a size ten boot in my face!"

"It doesn't matter, Shamus."

When we reached the Roadster one of the car's had gone. It was then I had an apparition for disaster. I quickly grabbed Shamus's arm as he was about to open the car door and pulled him back.

Shamus spooked by my action. "What is it, Shacks Sir?"

"Stand clear, Shamus! I've a very funny feeling."

He stepped back slowly while I went down on my hands and knees looking underneath the Roadster and instantly I found a device.

"It's a bomb!" I said.

Shamus backed off horrified. "A bomb, yer say?"

"Well I assume it's a bomb because I didn't put it there and it would explain why the sniper didn't hang about. I think the intention was to pin us down long enough for the sneaky bastard to attach this and then disappear from blame."

"We'd best get clear of the wretched thing before we get blown to smithereens, Shacks Sir."

"And leave my beautiful car to be fragmented across Ireland. Never! It's only a small bomb. It's a simple device. If I keep these two magnetic contacts together and pull vigorously the offending implement, like this!"

Shamus was cringing when I showed him the device, though I was extremely careful not to drop it as I got to my feet.

"Now what are yer supposing to do with dhat, Shacks, Sir?"

"Duck down, Shamus, and I'll show you!"

I swung the bomb high over my left shoulder and dived for cover. My ears went numb when the device hit the ground and exploded sending a shower of rock and soil debris raining down on us. Shamus was furious.

"What in the name of Jesus Christ possessed you to do dhat?"

"Because I want the saboteurs to presume their dastardly deed was an instant success, that's why, Shamus. Hopefully I've convinced people I'm dead. Now hurry up and get off the floor, I've only precious time to lose."

I rammed my way through the gears driving at a ridiculous speed for the type of roads. Driving one handed and changing gears at the same time I fumbled into my pocket and gave Shamus a piece of folded paper. He opened it and peered at me in surprise. "It be a telephone number, Shacks Sir!"

"How observant you are Shamus! When I drop you off at Baltimore, ring that number straight away. And just because she has the sweetest voice you've ever heard over a telephone, don't hang about telling her so. Tell her that, Shackleton Speed said continue the planned operation and fast."

"What planned operation is dhat, Shacks, Sir?"

"Stop asking silly questions and do as you're told."

"Why don't you, ring the number yourself, Shacks Sir?"

"Because, Shamus, I'm going aboard the "Flying-fish' tonight."

"Alone?"

"Yes."

He gazed at me dumbfounded. "Isn't dhat a stupid thing to do, if yer don't mind me sayin' so?"

"Yes," I said annoyed.

"I'd better come with yer, Shacks, Sir!"

"No," I snapped, "Too frigging dangerous. Just ring that number, that's far more important at this stage. And tell her to arrange the rendezvous at that place on the note, urgently. Tell her it's a matter of life or death."

Shamus read the details. "Why that place Shacks, Sir?"

"Because, Shamus, that's where I predict all this shambles finally ends, one way or the other."

CHAPTER TWENTY TWO

I waited until darkness before I made my move along the quayside at Baltimore harbour. As I crept through, in the distance, I saw a motorised inflatable dingy and on closer observation I saw the 'Flying-fish' logo in small white stencil. I was on the verge of going directly to it when I caught sight of a crewman lurking in the shadows, sat waiting. I could only assume it would be a ride back to the ship for Love and Hate, after disposing of me. Slowly, ever so quietly, I edged around and came in behind where he sat. The sole of my left boot stood on some discarded rope, which I retrieved from the ground, held it either end and moved closer to the unsuspecting crewman. I lashed the rope around his neck and yanked him to his feet, twisted my body and threw him, judo style, over my shoulder. He hit the ground heavily. I heard a feeble moan which proved I hadn't snapped his neck with my actions. To silence him I instantly followed with a savage kick to his jawbone. I didn't like the horrible crunch I heard but then I didn't particularly like the crewman. I left him where he lay. I hardly thought it mattered whether he was dead or not.

I clambered into the craft, kicked a blanket to one side, and uncovered a snipers rifle. Frantically I looked around, realizing this particular crewman wasn't waiting for Love or Hate because he'd already witnessed their execution. He was waiting for someone else. Quickly I had the rifle in my hand in readiness, searching through the pitch black with expectancy of an attack. Seconds turned into minutes and nothing happened so I slipped the crafts mooring, started the outboard engine and steered the dingy across the bay towards the 'Flying-fish' anchored out in the harbour. While I steered I kept the rifle handy. I glanced back to the harbour as I left. I saw no signs of any pursuit or any fist waving agitated assassin.

I approached the anchored 'Flying Fish' in a generous arc, mainly to establish if watchmen were present on deck. Then again what had they to fear? All terminations were in progress, so they thought! I steered the craft towards the boarding ladder, switched off the engines and cruised in with the current. After tying the boat to the foot of the boarding ladder and replaced the rifle in my hand with the gun I had retrieved from Hate, I warily climbed the steel stairway, my eyes flicking at every shadow that moved.

The deck was only partially illuminated though I saw no signs of life and all I could hear was the creaking of the ship as it gently rocked. Crouched, I carefully tiptoed along the deck when I suddenly froze mid-step as I got a whiff of cigarette smoke. I checked my stride and pushed my body hard against the steel wall listening. I heard the person suck hard and deep on a cigarette and exhale the offensive smoke. I found his position as the smoke cloud mushroomed from between two mounds of tarpaulin. Inch by inch I crept nearer. So close now I heard the rattling breath of a heavy weed user. Then the red burning stub ejected from the gap and the person moved forward into a beautifully timed right hook that twisted the guards head so violently, he was out cold before his crumpled body hit the deck.

Quickly I dragged him back into the crevice. If he had a gun of any description I never saw it. I continued towards a steel door with a stream of light angling down to the deck. I peered through the gap. It was clear, so I silently opened the door and went inside. There was a stairway. I listened. Satisfied there was no one at the bottom of the stairs I tip-toed down, glad of the cushioned soles of my boots.

Then I stopped when I heard faint voices coming from the far end of the corridor. It seemed the obvious route, especially when I recognized one of the voices. With the gun extended I moved along, passing two closed steel doors until I came to one half opened. I heard the same voices again. Peering through the crack in the door I saw the back of a big man sat comfortably in an appealing leather armed chair drinking from a large brandy glass. I pushed the door open with the tip of the gun, checked through the crack to ensure no crow bar wielding fiend had taken a position behind the door then entered. I expected to find a surprise or two waiting for me, but when I saw her I was frigging mad.

"Now isn't this all very sweet and cosy." I said. "Hello, Shayna! And Commander Harris Morgan, all chasing Deveron's dreams, I see! I hope you're not celebrating too early."

Morgan spun round in his chair spilling brandy on his lap. "Shackleton Speed. Damn you!"

"No one move! That includes you, Shayna."

Shayna had a look of sheer horror. "It's not what it seems." She blurted. "I've nothing to do with this!"

"Shut up, Shayna! I hold the gun so I get the deciding vote on who to trust. At the moment I'm too mad to be trusting. I'll get to you after I've finish with frigging arse bandit here!"

"My, my, Speed such vulgarity! I would have expected a little more decorum when a lady is present and something better than 'arse bandit'."

"Somehow, it suits you."

Morgan casually continued sipping his drink. I must admit it rather infuriated my senses that I wanted to smash the glass from his grasp. I refrained from doing so and remained in position by the door.

Morgan toasted me. "I have to admire you, Speed. You've been a wonderful adversary. You certainly know how to make quite a nuisance of yourself. The worst thing about the entire event is you can't even die gracefully or quietly. It's very upsetting."

"I aim to annoy. I've always been good at that. I couldn't leave this frigging damn forsaken world without saying goodbye to my commissioning employer, who happens to be a conniving, murdering rat."

"Insolence becomes you, Speed. You're forgetting one important factor!"

"Oh-what's that?"

"I haven't personally killed anyone."

"And that makes things alright! You make me puke, you frigging low down parasite. You don't have to pull the trigger to issue orders."

"Don't be such a philistine, Speed! I'm not a murderer. I manipulate people, as I did with you, Mister bumbling amateur. I threw you a few goodies to pursue. Allowed you a little leeway to go hunting for the submarine, and finally draw you back in when the time was right. You were perfect. It's in your nature to find things and admittedly, you're damned good at finding things. So damn good I was confident you wouldn't let me down in finding the Japanese submarine, though I will give you some credit for evasion, and you were damned hard to find on a number of occasions."

"Well you've found me now!"

I was a little concerned as to why Morgan's eyes kept flicking to and fro to the door.

I said, "If you're expecting either of the murderers Love or Hate, forget it! I took care of those two squealing bastards. You know the two. The same ones you were going to put behind bars with a little persuasion from my testimony. That was your intention when we first met, but, of course, that was your manipulating crap, wasn't it. Now reality has taken its course. And I guess, now, this means I don't get paid for my services to the ministry?"

"You're absolutely hilarious, Speed. Yet I suppose you are entitled to that rare privilege of humour. Who am I to argue with a man holding a gun?"

"Yes, I'm renowned for a bellyful of laughs but first I want some straight answers from you."

"Why don't you put the gun down, Speed? Good god man, your hands trembling so much you'll probably wouldn't be able to fire the wretched thing. Have a drink! We can talk, come to some arrangement."

I held the gun firm, accurately. A gut shot a certain outcome and Morgan knew it.

With gritted teeth, I said, "Don't underestimate me. I'm also renowned by many as being a controlled schizophrenic and a man in my state might well just lose grip of that control. You may not think I'm experienced in the art of killing people, but I'm learning fast, no thanks to you. In fact, I'm quite open that I don't even possess a certificate to prove my capabilities of a crack shot and I could easily aim for your body and because I'm not used to the recoil of this handgun, the bullet might just end up in one of your legs or it might even be your head. Either way, I'm not fussy."

I noticed a few beads of perspiration rolling down Morgan's forehead. Now he was beginning to worry. I was enjoying watching him squirm.

I said calmly, surprising even myself. "I've never deliberately set out to kill a man before, regardless how nasty they are. I've hurt a few whose intentions were to hurt me. I've hospitalised a few even and I never send flowers. I could do the same to you shit breath, but I know I would experience horrible nightmares that you would come out from under the gallons of excrement that surround your murderous regime smelling of prize roses; that you'll slip away from justice with terrible ease, to live in a lavish lifestyle." The more I talked the angrier I got. "I can't have that. I could never live with the guilt of allowing you to escape punishment."

I deliberately aimed the gun at him to make him sweat more.

"Don't be ridiculous, Speed! You're not a cold-blooded killer. You'll be killing the wrong man! Do you want that on your conscience for the rest of your prison life?"

"What makes you think I'll see the inside of a prison?"

"For Christ sake man, I'm a government official. You'll never explain my death away!"

"I don't care what happens to me."

I squeezed the trigger.

I heard the metallic click when I shouldn't have done.

For a moment I stood there dumbfounded. There was no explosion from the gun. No kick back knocking my hand slightly. No acrid stench of a spent bullet drifting into my nostrils. I expected all three, maybe even two. I'd be unlucky to get only one, but none at all! A misfire, I assured myself. Again and again my trigger finger repeated the firing motions only to receive the same unproductive results. Click-click-click-click-click echoed in my ears. Each click had my sweat glands working over-time. My body became tacky. I knew an empty barrel when I heard one. I looked at Morgan. He had flinched on every occasion I had pulled the trigger. But now he was smirking.

After the last chamber echoed its last metallic click, all I heard was, 'oops', and it hadn't come from Morgan's mouth.

There was one thing I did prove to myself, I definitely didn't possess eyes in the back of my head or I might have reacted far quicker to the piece of cold steel sticking into the back of my ear.

I attempted to look round but my face was shoved back by the nozzle, which I managed to glimpse in my attempt.

I said calmly, "The miracles of modern science-eh-Hamer? I've got to admire the witch doctor that stitched you back together."

"Shut the fuck up, Speed! When you select a gun, choose one with bullets in."

I broke into a smile. "Why do I get this feeling that you sent out your hired killers with empty guns. Maybe the idea was we'd kill each other to save you the trouble. And last man standing picked off by a sniper or the pathetic bomb trick. I've got to hand it to you, Hamer, simplicity resolved around a cunning and deceitful piece of nastiness."

"Deductions are very accurate, Speed. You've got it in one. Don't even think about using that gun as a club, or even visualize it as a projectile. I do possess a sharp shooters certificate that complements this gun in my hand, so drop the weapon, Speed, now!"

I let go and the gun clattered as it hit the floor. Morgan was up on his feet.

To Hamer I said, "The apparition of your spirit rising from the grave, Hamer, should have me scared shitless. Strange, though, how I predicted your resurrection was imminent."

"So the horrific death on the boat didn't convince you?"

"Nice deception, Hamer. Plant a bomb with a quick timer, slip aboard a waiting craft and sail back to the 'Flying Fish'. You upset poor old Shamus. It made him depressed thinking you had died on his boat. Now that was nasty but then your middle name is *nasty!*"

"You just don't appreciate simplicity, Speed. I had to stop you nosing around the open waves. How did it make you feel, Speed. Sorry to see me go?"

"I'd mixed feelings. Not that your death would have bothered me. Fat bastards like you, Hamer, don't warrant any sympathy whatsoever."

The gun jamming into my head didn't deter me.

"I never trusted you when you first turned up on my doorstep. But then, I never trust a policeman. I tried to, but you always turned up at every inappropriate moment. Whenever something happened to me and you were there. The bullshit you concocted about chaperoning me for my safety. Setting me up more like! When you inadvertently told me about McClusky's warehouse, stupidly, I believed you were relaying useful information, not sending me into a frigging trap to be fucked up by warring terrorists."

From facing the point of a gun, Morgan was confidently rejuvenated. He stabbed his forefinger into my face. "You are absolutely wrong speed. We never anticipated McClusky would dare to double-cross us by selling our merchandise to unauthorized buyers. The idea was for McClusky to capture and scare you enough to drive you into our caring hands for protection."

"It all backfired." I sneered.

"Only for a while till we readjusted our schedule. We are not mind-readers. We didn't contemplate McClusky's incompetence in dealing with simple matters. Then there was the audacity of the Irish gang to abscond with our puppet. It all became messy. McClusky deserved to die in that gun battle. It saved us the problem of killing him."

"How clever you think, Morgan. But what would you have done if I had been killed. Who would you have got to find the I-52?"

Morgan waved his hand in acceptance of his flaw. "With you gone out of our way we would have eventually found the photographs. We'd have ripped your home apart piece by piece until we got what we wanted. But never mind, everything has now fallen magnificently into perspective."

I gave Shayna a hard glare. "What about Miss blabber-mouth over there. Where does she fit into your dream?"

"You have me all wrong," Shayna protested her innocence.

I ignored her.

"Think you're fucking clever, Speed?" Hamer spat angrily.

"Not as clever as I wanted to be. I made a few shocking mistakes along the way like allowing you to tag along. But as always, you know what it's like when shit becomes lodged in the pattern on the soles of your shoes, cleaning is difficult and the smell never seems to leave."

Hamer clipped my ear with the barrel. "Your mouth is full of shit, Speed."

Morgan said, "What exactly happened to Love and Hate?"

"They're both dead!" I said spitefully.

"Was it your doing, Speed?" Morgan asked.

"Well I'm here and they aren't rather answers that! Unfortunately they met me while I was in a bad mood. I didn't like the odds of two against one so I shortened them. Last time I saw them they were holding hands and leaping over the side of a cliff."

Morgan casually shrugged his shoulders. "As you said, Speed, saved us a job and the less there are on the payroll, the better."

"They were supposed to be the best." I assumed Hamer was talking to Morgan. "Hire top notch killers and they can't complete a simple clean up job." He sighed heavily "You just can't buy decent assassins anymore. If you want a job doing, then do it your fucking self!"

I said quickly, "Kill me and the gold goes with me."

"There was no gold," Morgan said sharply. "The submarine was empty of cargo. If there was any gold it has been removed and disappeared and spent no doubt."

"Removed and disappeared, I can't argue about," I said. "But spent…I'd rephrase that assumption."

Morgan gave me a curious stare. "Why?"

I prodded myself in the chest. "Because this so called bumbling amateur at least knows the perpetrator of the entire operation was killed before he'd the time to spend his golden prize."

Hamer buried the nozzle of the gun deeper into my cheek.

"Where the fuck is the gold?"

"Get a life, Hamer! I haven't got the wretched stuff."

"He's a fucking lying bastard!"

"Oh, I might be a bastard, but I'm no liar."

Hamer shook his head in disbelief. "Arrogance right to the end, hey, Speed."

I didn't like the sound of what he said, but I didn't show any fear, nor did I flinch when he began his heavy-handed Morse code on my face with the gun in cohesion with his words. "Where's the fucking gold?"

"So you are deaf as well as stupid, Hamer. At the moment I don't know."

Hamer was getting frustrated and itching to pull the trigger. Morgan was thankfully calmer and finger signalled to Hamer to calm down.

Morgan said, "I'm beginning to find you quite amusing, Speed, and you seem to have a lot of answers to a lot of ageing problems. What disturbs me is the efficiency you have shown as a killing machine, rather strange for just a metal detector man. That makes me highly suspicious. Maybe you're not who we think you are, Speed?"

"Oh, I'm myself alright, with a few inclusions on the art of being callous. Scum, as you are, Morgan, has succeeded in turning me into a machine that I'm not really keen to be associated with. But you chose to mess up my life by murdering my friends which has done more than infuriate me. It has made me realize that my approach to life has been rather boring. I've now this sudden passion to rid dirt like you from the face of the earth."

Morgan grinned. "Harsh words from a man with a gun to his head. A mere click of my fingers and half your brains will be splattered against the wall. Is it your wish to die? Are you brave enough to die for nothing?"

"I take it you mean am I scared to die?"

Hamer pressed the nozzle against the side of my nose. "Well are you, Speed?"

"There's your problem before you start! I work on the principle that you have no recollection being born as you're pulled screaming from that orifice of security: therefore I doubt very much you'll remember dying. Take that into consideration, I can confidently predict I don't fear death. And I can confidently say that with my demise nobody gets to know where the Japanese gold is, and, not forgetting, the one ton of *opium*, all in sizable bags which are easily transported. Now imagine the price of that on the open market of this despicable world."

Somehow greed inevitably cropped up again.

Morgan's eyebrows arched. "What opium?"

"The opium classified as medical supplies."

"There was nothing of any value on the submarine," Morgan said, "I checked everything myself."

I had their attention now. "That's because in 1944 a certain Irish terrorist with a far superior brain than yours, named, McCracken, took the frigging lot."

I was looking at some extremely puzzled expressions.

"Now that you pieces of frigging shit realize I do your job better than yourselves, and I'm an inquisitive genius and not a bumbling amateur, as suggested too hastily. I think there's a call for an apology. But please, don't all rush at once."

"He's fucking lying!" Hamer blurted out, his face red with anger. "He's stalling. Get rid of the bastard, now!"

"Be a little patient." Morgan remonstrated with Hamer. He turned to me. "Where did you extract that information from?"

"A contributor to the arrangement of a daring hijack when they captured the submarine, who, I might add, would prefer to remain anonymous."

Hamer punched me in the side of the head. "Tell me the fucking name?"

My teeth clenched. I said, "Do that again and I'll do more than break your arm."

Morgan made a harsh gesture that Hamer stayed in control of his anger.

"Now if you allow me to finish I can verify that the informant has about as much idea where the gold is, as you two. It seems I'm the only one alive who knows where it is. So it's negotiation time."

"So negotiate then!" I didn't care for Morgan's hurriedness.

"First. Why did you have my friends killed? They were frigging innocent participants."

"Oh, you are referring to the old farmer and photographer? Ah-well, Speed, when you decide to steal government property, you should think more carefully when you get people to lie for you; cover your tracks. Unfortunately, your friends had the same stubbornness you possess. It was you, Speed that forced us to use heavy handed tactics. It was your greed that put your friend's lives at risk, and they paid a heavy price. So don't blame us, just look in a mirror, Speed."

"There was no need to murder them!"

"Yes there was!" Morgan said acidly. We couldn't leave the mess behind. The mess had to be dealt with. Your friends were inconveniences. Therefore it became necessary to eradicate the problems put before us."

I went for Morgan like a raging Rhinoceros. But as I moved the back of my skull imploded in a momentary excruciating pain before subsiding as I collapsed into a void of soundless darkness.

CHAPTER TWENTYTHREE

I realised I was still alive when I tried to curl my toes up inside my shoes. From the swaying sensation and the coldness of steel beneath me, I assumed I was still aboard the 'Flying-fish'. I made the attempt to open my eyes only the blinding pain ripped into my iris's forcing a momentary shutdown of vision. I could still move my hands and feet, so I knew I hadn't been bound or chained. Slowly, I pushed myself up from the floor into a sitting position. Again I opened my eyes. The sharp streak of brightness came from a bulkhead light fitting on the ceiling of what appeared to be a stockade of steel walls and steel bars giving the impression I was in a prison cell you could associate with in any western film on the television.

As I rubbed my stiff neck, I glanced around room, my head spun wildly, throbbed mercilessly and there's nothing worst than a banging headache and no remedy. Though, seeing Deveron and Shayna sat on an old iron bed watching my squirming antics of a waking drunk, did come close to being worst. I was surprised to see both of them in a state of utter dejection.

My speech sluggish, I said, "Seeing your two depressing faces, I guess I'm not in heavenly paradise. Not unless you're both dead as well and this is suppose to be a jokers version of the Garden of Eden and you two are my guardian angels. Now isn't that wild to the imagination, you two a couple of angels!"

Shayna responded first as she spat her dummy out. "Just because you have a bad head doesn't give you the damn right to be an obstinate shit!"

"Oh, while we're on the subject of obstinate shits," I said, "Aren't you two on the wrong side of the cell door?"

"No!" She snapped quicker than a mousetrap. "Actually we wouldn't be in this damn mess if we hadn't come looking for you at your hotel and run into a steel barrier of weapons. Good god, you make enemies really fast and no thanks to you being a selfish bastard, we are prisoners too."

I expressed surprise and said, "Well that does make everything right then! As for being selfish, how about, how does your head feel Shacks, after being banged around? Or should I humbly apologize for taking the blame for something your Grandfather started!"

"Give your anger a rest Shackleton," Shayna said. "So how do you feel?"

"As if a fat bastard called Hamer kicked the frigging crap out of me!"

"He did," she said. "After a couple of crewmen threw you in here he spurted out some obscenities and kicked you in the chest a couple of times. Mind you, I don't think he hurt you much, you were out cold and dumb heads don't feel much pain."

"Thanks for the compliment, Shayna. As for fat boy, I owe him one!"

I noticed Shayna hadn't escaped a beating judging by the severe bruising around her left cheekbone. I still felt a little giddy to stand up so I shuffled back against the steel wall. I said, "Nasty discolouration around the eye, Shayna. What's your story?"

"Nothing I can't stand."

"Step out of line?"

"What do you mean?"

I gestured a full grandeur. "Which murderer or pirates or any other despicable lout did you upset? Perhaps it's Morgan who is as bent as a rejected European commission banana. Or maybe you're all a bunch of terrorist renegades? Then there is poor old Deveron here, who has caused this farcical nightmare we find ourselves involved with."

Her angry eyes lit up like beacons. "Hell, Shackleton! You still believe I'm part of their set-up?"

"It explains a great deal. How everybody seemed to know where I was. How easy people found me."

"I found you because my Grandfather insisted on meeting you. I used the resources available to me to find you. And that basically is it!"

"And I have to be stupid enough to believe that!"

"Yeah, but I know you won't."

Deveron stirred. "You have it all worked out, don't you, Mister

Speed?" (I was beginning to think Deveron had lost use of his tinny voice.) "Yes my actions have brought about the misery we're in. But how was I to know Harris Morgan would continue what I started. When he was a young pip-squeak and a run about errand boy through the corridors of Whitehall, I never explained my intentions to him. He simply worked it out for himself and continued the pursuit. I was absolutely shocked beyond belief when he showed himself at Baltimore. He was always a clever and brash sod when he was younger. The crafty bastard lured us to your hotel with a false message. Now we are here, probably to die in this godforsaken cell."

"It's nothing more than you deserve when you shot Craven from the sky, so think yourself lucky prison has only just caught you up."

Shayna jumped in defensively at that point. "That makes two of you then!"

I stopped arguing with her because my chest was hurting bad and I'd trouble breathing. I wondered if Hamer's boot had perhaps broken a couple of my ribs.

I said to Deveron, "Seems you and McCracken had the same idealistic values. Those futuristic dreams of climbing the Irish pinnacle of power. Of course, where your dreams faded and you became the normal and responsible person, McCracken died as savagely as his dreams. But I just can't make my mind up who took the right path!"

Deveron's face twisted with hatred. "You can be very cynical, Mister Speed. I'd hate the prospect of you running an old peoples home."

"You have me wrong, Deveron. I like old people, especially those with pure hearts. Something you don't have!"

"There's no forgiveness in you, is there, Mister Speed!?" He could get quite angry for an old man.

Shayna quickly drew the finishing line. "Bickering isn't going to find us a way out of this hole!"

With an added touch of cockiness, I said, "Well, Shayna, unless you can produce one of your magic door opening escapades, I can honestly say I'll listen to any sensible suggestions. Don't suppose you have any?"

"We need a diversion." Shayna, suggested half-heartedly.

"Ah, very good, Shayna, you taking your clothes off or should I?"

She wasn't amused with my suggestive proposition, but I didn't care who I upset anymore. I was tired and hungry. I'd been battered, clubbed, and I wanted to kill certain people. So why shouldn't I be annoyed, obstinate, and darn right frigging awkward!

Just as I thought my day couldn't worsen in walked more trouble in the shape of Morgan and Hamer, followed by a couple of armed crewmen.

I said sarcastically, "Well look at this! We have an entire entourage of hotel staff to take us to breakfast."

Hamer had his face to the bars. "Shut the fuck up, Speed!"

"Ah-service with a smile as usual, can't beat it!"

"I should shoot you now, you interfering fuck!"

"Think of the gold, Hamer." I tapped my head. "It's all in here waiting to be prised apart to expose all that wealth."

There was one thing about Hamer which I found interesting, how easy he was to wind up to the height of exploding. Again he had to be restrained by Morgan.

Morgan flashed a forced smile and said, "Is it your wish to die, Speed?"

"Why, is there some other outcome?"

"There is another choice."

"I have an option then?"

"A share of the proceeds, there is enough for all."

"What percentage had you in mind?" I thought I'd ask.

"Equal share with all concerned."

By the look on Hamer's face he didn't approve of Morgan's solution to get me to talk.

"What about Deveron and Shayna?"

Morgan shrugged his shoulders. "What about them?"

"I want their safety guaranteed."

Morgan was blunt. "I'm afraid they are not part of the deal. Now how about your version on where the gold is hidden?"

"Go and frigging stick your head up Hamer's arse! Their safety or nothing from me, it's your move."

Morgan did indeed move but not the way I expected. There was no warning, no verbal threat and definitely no hesitation as Morgan drew an automatic handgun and shot Deveron in the middle of the chest.

Shayna screamed. My mouth dropped to the floor as I watched Deveron slump across the bed, coughing up blood, a red stain seeping through his clothing, spreading out like a twisting kaleidoscopic image.

Enraged, ignoring the sharp pains in my chest, I shot to my feet and lunged towards the bars, spit flying from my mouth as I screamed obscenities. "You frigging spineless murdering bastard, Morgan. There was no need for that. He was no threat to you. He was just an old man who came to end a chapter in his life. I remember you saying you didn't kill people?"

Morgan angled the gun towards Shayna and calmly said, "I lied. Your problem, Speed is you're getting too sentimental. Now I've little time to waste, the girl is next. I wouldn't hesitate too long because if I rid the lot of you all I lose is a fortune. I'll still get my large pension from the government. I'll still reap in money from a lucrative business deal. But all of you will be buried in the confines of a pauper's coffin, and for cheapness, thrown into one."

He had me panicking as I struggled to rethink my strategy.

"Quickly now, Speed! My finger is curling to the point of crushing the trigger."

"Spare the girl she can't harm you, now."

"On the contrary, Speed, she's a bigger pain in the neck than you are! Tell me where the merchandise is, and you might just be in time to stick your finger in the bullet hole and save one of the Royal Canadian Mounted Police's finest undercover operatives."

Confused, I said, "Canadian who?"

Morgan expressed surprise. "Don't tell me the intrepid metal detector, quite extraordinaire, didn't know our lovely Shayna is a damn policewoman?"

I just hate that feeling when some cocky bastard is one frigging step ahead. I considered Morgan as a real slimy bastard and would have told him so if my head hadn't automatically spun round to verbally challenge Shayna only to see her attempting to save a dying man.

With suppressed anger, I said, "Frigging hell, Shayna! Is it the truth?"

She did turn to look at me but said nothing, not that I didn't notice a few genuine tears roll down her cheek as she listened to the last gasps of breath exhaling from Deveron as he died at that precise moment. Hardened I might be accused, and rightly so, as I felt nothing towards his death.

As for Shayna, she had produced more twists and turns in her life that were harder to follow than a roadmap in the dark with no torch. Was she a terrorist, or not? Was Morgan simply shooting shit from his mouth about her being an undercover operative? Regardless of what was the truth I couldn't let her die too.

I turned back to Morgan. "Okay, you win. But Shayna stays with me. I want her."

"Not in the script, Speed."

"Well you'd better rewrite the script. She either accompanies me or you might as well kill us both here and now."

In the corner of my eye I thought I caught Shayna's head jolting round, her face contorted with fear when I mentioned shooting us now, though I could have mistaken her movement.

I didn't mistake Morgan's movements as for one brief moment he was initiating my wishes as he deliberately aimed the automatic in my direction. "Don't tempt fate, Speed. Desperate men take desperate measures. One more death isn't going to make me squeamish in the slightest, nor am I likely to lose sleep over the problem. I have my reasons why she should die. Have you never heard the saying: 'A Mountie always gets their man?' I don't wish to be hiding beneath a stone for the rest of my life. She might have failed on this mission but I've no desire to allow her a second opportunity."

My heart might have been jigging about inside my ribcage, but my expression remained defiant, calm, no emotions of fear. That was me all over, hard on the outside, and soft on the inside.

"I've no interest in the gold, just the girl. I don't want to see her harmed. She remains by my side or nothing. You decide, Morgan."

"There's no guarantee to be any gold at all, Speed. Why should I want to spare her when she intends to see me put in prison."

It was then I remembered the piece of Japanese gold and dipped into my trouser pocket to retrieve it, obviously they never searched an unconscious man. I tossed the gold piece through the bars. Numerous eyes followed the mesmerizing gold flash as it hit the floor with a metallic tinkle. Hamer was quick to retrieve it from the floor, gloating at the piece, a look of desire filling his fat face with delight. Hesitantly he passed it to Morgan.

Thankfully the gun lowered. I wanted to breathe a sigh of relief but that would have only exposed my weakness under pressure, so I held my breath a little longer.

Morgan nodded his head a few times in acknowledgement of my demands. "Your ruthless bargaining powers precede you, Speed. I hope she's worthy of your gallantry. So where's the rest of the gold?"

"Do you think I'd be so stupid and tell you, just so you can pump a couple of bullets into us. Give me some credit, please. Besides, I can't explain exactly where it is, I can only show."

"Okay, Speed, I'll accept that. Just remember no funny business or stupidity or the girl gets the first bullet. So what destination are we taking navigator?"

"CrookHaven. It's on the other side of the Bay."

"Yes, I know of the village. Why that place?"

As much as Morgan and Hamer wanted to see the gold, so did I

"You're forgetting I can only show you."

They turned to leave, presumably to discuss my proposition and if satisfied, raise anchor and reposition the 'Flying Fish' closer to our destination. I'd gained a stay of execution without a doubt. I knew deep down that no matter what I did or say there was no way they would let either of us disappear out of their lives, not unless we were both dead. Just before Morgan left the stockade room, I said to him. "What about Deveron, you can't just leave the man here to rot."

"Of course I can. Dead people are of no use to me, especially a decrepit old man. I'll leave you two to decide which corner you put him in."

I gave Morgan the appropriate middle finger salute and mumbled, "Callous bastard", as his back disappeared out of the room.

Shayna stood away from Deveron. I put the old mans legs up onto the bed before rigor mortis stiffened his aging bones, covered his body with the shabby blanket and moved away. I had my reasons to distance myself. I was no pathologist. I couldn't estimate the time before a body began smelling and attracting flies.

Shayna looked me in the eyes. "No matter what you do for them, they've no intention of releasing us."

I smiled. "I know that."

"How come you're so calm?"

I took her hand and lay her palm over my pumping heart. "Only calm on the outside, as you can feel, Shayna. I can't let these frigging shits think I'm losing my composure. While I continue to keep them interested, we keep on living, it's as simple as that."

"You've obviously got it all planned, Shackleton Speed, what's next?"

"Are you kidding, Shayna! I'm playing this minute by minute. All we can do is let fate take its course."

"That's it?"

"If you hadn't noticed, Shayna, there are bars of steel prohibiting us from doing very little. Besides, according to Morgan, you're supposed to be the professional. What did he say you were, Canadian Mounted Police? Somehow I just can't imagine you in a bright red uniform sat on a very large horse pursuing the baddies through the snow capped Rockies."

"For your information clever-clogs we only wear bright red uniforms on ceremonial occasions. Our uniforms are actually grey."

"So beat around the head with a bush for getting it wrong!"

"Give me a break, will you!" She sat down on the floor and put her back against the wall. "I might come from a different part of the world but I'm on your side for fuck sake!"

I exhaled a sarcastic laugh. "You weren't exactly on my side when you kidnapped me and subjected me to a brand of humiliating torture."

"I wasn't exactly in a position to prevent anything without blowing my cover!" She protested strongly. "Anyway, how was it humiliating?"

"What about the penetrative tattooing over my body? And that reminds me, when I catch up with your buddies, that spotty fucker is destined for my boot up his arse followed by his darts!"

"I must admit I never anticipated that it was going to happen. Honestly! And remember it was on the understanding that I thought you were one of McClusky's men. Anyway, you're still in one piece, I made sure you were spared."

"Well thanks for not very much! I've holes to prove the pain I went through."

"I'm generally sorry you had to endure so much. But at the moment I'm not in the mood for a verbal fight, can we give it a miss?"

"Frigging hell," I said, suddenly remembering what has happened. "I'm being totally selfish and totally disrespectful over your loss of your Grandfather. Let us call a truce, okay?"

Her red eyes glanced at Deveron then back to mine. "I've a confession to make."

I gave one of my suspicious looks. "Oh yes!"

"Deveron wasn't my Grandfather."

"You're a bag of twisted laughs, Shayna!"

"It's the truth."

"He was convinced you were. Frigging hell, I was!"

"I know. To make a good undercover operator, lying through your teeth is top of the quality list. It was an elaborate set-up to get me inside the organizations that received weapons from a gun running operation. Deveron gave me the ideal Irish background to convince the right people of my allegiance to the Irish cause. I'm ashamed to admit, we used the old man. Mind you, when he confessed to me his involvement in the IRA, it was quite a shock. Then you appeared and the whole operation exploded in my face. Eighteen months of lying, deceit and hanging about with a bunch of fanatical hand shaggers, in an attempt to expose the British contact, went right out of the window, no thanks to you. Bet you didn't know this ship is bulging with weaponry destined for numerous Irish groups."

"Frigging hell, Shayna, you're a real dark Sumpter horse with a carrot shoved up your arse instead of in front of your nose. The only sense I can make of your existence is you're on the good side of the law masquerading as a murdering bastard. And as for damaging your mission, if you don't mind, I've given you, whom I suspect are your devious middlemen, Morgan and Hamer, served up on a plate. Just because you end up in the same cell as me, don't be in such a hurry to discredit me. You, Yanks, always so ungrateful."

"Ungrateful Canadian, if you don't mind! At least have the right nationality."

"Whatever! So what was Harris Morgan's involvement on Canadian territory that warranted your elaborate cloak and dagger tactics?"

"In the beginning I didn't know it was Morgan. All we knew from a reliable source of information was we were dealing with a person inside the Ministry of Defence in London. We had no rank, no position of authority, no department, no jack shit! The operation we were investigating involved weapons sold by the Russian Mafia being smuggled into Alaska and Canada. There were a number of smuggling routes being used. Some routes went via America onto Ireland. Some went via Europe. Some went directly to Ireland. There was always a variation, which were hard to pursue. It was if they knew every move we made and countered by switching their operations before we had time to react. We suffered casualties, losing two fine and devoted policemen. Two wasted lives. There was a tremendous strain on manpower, facilities stretched beyond control. It was decided to concentrate on finding the arms buyer, the middleman, which meant pursuing him through the Irish factions that purchased the merchandise. I volunteered."

"Very brave of you," I said. "Obviously you're not married?"

"Only to my job and neither did I expect any medals. As it was we stumbled across Deveron. He was searching for lost relatives. Everything was perfect to give me the cover I required to infiltrate a faction within Ireland. We actually suspected Deveron's involvement at first, but as time went on it soon became clear he was somebody searching for nothing more than compassion and company, though he did spring a few surprises when he told me the true story of his life. I must say he was very repentant."

"They all are when they get older. A little too late to be sorry," I said bitterly. "He murdered a war hero on the speculation there was money to finance a war against Britain. No, I'm afraid I've little compassion for Deveron. He hasn't even paid me for my services."

"You're a heartless person, Shackleton Speed."

"That's good coming from the woman who used the poor sod," I reminded her.

"It's not been easy. There were times when I nearly gave up on the operation. But I just remember the good officers of the Mounted Police who died during the investigation. That drove me on. I was determined to bring their killers to justice."

"At least we have something in common."

"Anyway, Shackleton Speed, you can thank me you're still alive to even get this far."

"Meaning what?"

"At Mcklusky's warehouse, who do you think started the carnage so you could escape?"

"My brain doesn't function under the term bedlam. I wasn't exactly watching. I was trying to survive like every other frigging idiot."

"I fired the first shot. And how the hell do you think you got the gun you fled with, by magic! No. I slid it across the floor to your feet. Still not convinced?"

"You could have confided in me earlier than now?"

"I had to be absolutely certain you were nothing more than just an anti-social chief militant against authority, if you understand what I'm driving at? Besides, you were a civilian for god's sake!"

"Thanks for the vote of confidence in my limited abilities."

"Don't be so touchy, Shackleton Speed, you're making up for it now."

We were both silenced by the clanging sound of the anchor being raised. Morgan was going for it. I'd taken a tremendous gamble in boarding the vessel. I'd survived. Now it was time to bring the nightmare to an end.

CHAPTER TWENTYFOUR

Two heavily armed guards came to fetch us and they were just as heavy when hurrying us along by using the tip of their machine pistols to prod us forward like pigs going to slaughter. On deck the beginning of the day was miserable and daunting but the sea air smelt good especially after being cooped up in the sweat box of a cell. The wind strengthened with the threat of rain imminent within the hour. We left the ship and boarded a launch. We weren't alone. Morgan and Hamer and six more crew were there waiting, all armed to the hilt and all looking as pissed off as I was.

Morgan gestured us to sit. "Make yourselves comfortable and secure yourselves. I don't want you falling overboard and drowning at such a crucial part of the exercise."

Shayna and I sat astern. She snuggled into me, which was pleasant until I realized her intentions were for a more significant reason when she began whispering in my ear. "How long do you estimate we have before they realize there's no gold?"

"Did anyone mention there was no gold?"

"You've seen it?"

I made a gesture with my finger and thumb indicating a fraction of space. "I found one small ingot inside the cavern when I discovered the submarine. While you were preoccupied with Deveron, I showed the ingot to greedy bastards over there. Hamer drooled over it."

"Oh-that's what you threw from the cell. One little piece proves nothing."

"It's there to found."

"How can you be positive?"

"Call it metal detector intuition. We can't see it but it's there ready, in all its glory, to be exposed. And it's our destiny to find."

Hamer caught us talking. "Shut the fuck up, you two!"

I said, "We're flirting with each other you jealous bastard."

Hamer just pulled a face and turned away.

When we reached the stone harbour wall of CrookHaven village you could have thinly sliced the quietness of the early morning. I examined the skies. Perhaps it wasn't going to rain after all. And the sun made an appearance.

Apart from the odd seagull screeching above, nothing else moved. Shayna and I clamoured from the launch under the scrutiny of the guards which stifled any chance to make a run for it. Then again I didn't want to. I was too excited to know if I my assumptions were correct. I was probably more intrigued than the likes of Morgan or Hamer. I wanted to know the outcome just to satisfy the amount of effort I'd put into exposing this bunch of murderous criminals.

Morgan said, "Where now, Speed?"

I pointed in the direction of the stone built church. "Over there, at Saint Brandon's church."

Morgan gave me an incredulous look. He said unconvinced: "Who, in their right mind, hides gold in such a small building frequently occupied?"

"McCracken did in 1944. Anyway, Morgan, I don't know why you're fretting, I've seen bank vaults much smaller."

Before I had even finished talking, Hamer was sprinting towards the church. He moved remarkably well for a fat boy. He also reminded me of a thick dog chasing a stick.

Morgan said, "Remember, Speed, nothing stupid. One false move and the guards have the order to drop you where you stand. Now lead on and tread carefully."

When I got there the church door latch had been broken. Hamer was already inside, scratching around like a rampant rat. He had no decorum whatsoever and probably never dreamed of trying the latch to open the door. Small churches like Saint Brandon don't normally hold the kind of wealth associated with large churches, so they rarely locked the doors. Rather they were left open for people to pray.

Once inside I said to Hamer, "I know this might sound strange for a man of your brutish calibre and limited intelligence but there are other alternatives to gaining entry instead of kicking the door in. Have you ever envisaged knocking for once?"

Though my voice echoed through the church, Hamer ignored me as he upturned everything that would upturn.

"Where is it, Speed?" Hamer's voice bellowed throughout the church. I imagined the dead coming in to complain about the noise. "Where the fuck is it?"

"It isn't likely to be sat on a pew for the last sixty years, you impatient bastard."

Hamer flew at me ramming his gun under my chin.

"You're getting right up my fucking nose with your smart remarks."

"Good!"

"Well, Speed," Morgan broke in, "I hope you haven't brought us here to change our ways because I hate religion."

"It's a matter of being patient," I said, trying to remember the writings of Jimmy McCracken.

I started to recite the words inside my head. 'Beyond the line of light when the sun rises and illuminates the Virgin Mary: through her eyes she will foretell my domain of madness'. I disregarded the words 'domain of madness', as being his hiding place. I concentrated on the line, 'when the sun illuminates the Virgin Mary, through her eyes'.

Through the eyes of the Virgin Mary, I narrated to myself over and over.

I scanned the entire church searching for that one vital piece of inspiration that would lead me to what McCracken meant. 'Through the eyes of the Virgin Mary', I repeated. I caught sight of a statue of the Virgin Mary near the Altar and quickly crossed the church floor to where the statue stood. Without touching the figurine I studied the brightly painted clay figure for a few moments, intrigued by the two feet high beautifully crafted sculpture. She looked radiant and proud holding the baby Jesus. I began circling the statue, not really knowing what I was looking for.

'Through her eyes she will foretell', I mumbled to myself. *What the frigging hell did McCracken mean?*

You couldn't see through an eye because the statute only had painted eyes. I guess I was clutching at straws. I looked around viewing at different angles away from the statue. I pressed and poked different parts of the sculpture in the hope some part of the pottery would give but nothing moved, not even a hairline crack. I even raised the statue from its pedestal to see if there was anything significant underneath. There was nothing. No magical button to press. Despairingly I glanced at Morgan. He still had a wary eye on me and by his expression he had me marked down has an absolute crackpot.

"Better not be stalling, Speed!" Morgan said in a bored tone.

He kept a firm grip on Shayna to show that he meant business in carrying out his threat to shoot her. I hated the moment because he knew I had a soft spot for her and was relishing his power of control.

I broke away from his stare and continued the search, but while I searched I was also looking for an escape route. The contingency plan needed to be in place for when everything went sour. The doorway seemed the only logical means of escape but Morgan had two armed guards blocking the way, as if he was reading my mind. And if I did go for that option the best I could do was to barge my way through. Yet how far would I get before a line of bullets mowed me down in mid-stride. I also considered throwing myself through the stain glass windows but two problems stemmed that idea very quickly. One: the windows were out of reach unless I decided to take up high-jumping lessons: and two, each window had a steel mesh protecting the stained glass against breakage.

I turned my concentration back to the task in hand. McCracken's madness had me stressed. Again I put his words through the grinder, 'the Virgin Mary', why was it so prominent in his writings? It was frigging hard to think when you're put under pressure, and the probing stares from Morgan and Hamer burning a hole in my head didn't help matters.

I thought deeper. *A virgin*, I mumbled to myself: a person who has never experienced penetration within sexual activity. A virgin would be childless. Yet most images of the Virgin Mary show her holding the baby Jesus!

'Through the eyes of the Virgin Mary, She will foretell'.

Suddenly it hit me! The stained glass window! There, in the centre pane clearly depicted the image of the Virgin Mary in magnificent colour. The image highlighted and prominent as the sunshine burst through the glass to spread colourful enchantment around the church walls. But it wasn't the whole image that made me take notice. It was the pieces of green glass that formed her eyes and from them the prismatic image of colour striking down a line of green and hitting a particular point on the floor.

I shifted quickly across and went down on one knee feeling and probing the area of the wooden floor where the light hit. My finger located a hole clogged with dirt. It seemed natural to press, so I did and remarkably a section of the floor lifted with a rusty squeak to reveal an inch gap. McCracken had been deviously clever in his design of a secret floor that I had been invisible to the naked eye. I got my fingers into the gap and lifted the flap to reveal a metre square black hole.

Slowly bodies converged around me. Heads peered over in total shock gawping down into the dark void. For a moment, so did I, until a thick damp musty stench hit me from the darkness making me retreat.

"Anyone got a torch?" I asked with excitement in my voice when there shouldn't have been.

A torch was quickly put into the palm of my hand, and my eyes followed the beam of light as it hit a dusty cobwebbed wooden stairway.

Morgan said, "Do the honours, Speed and get your arse down there!"

"Such kindness," I said with hesitancy. "I mean anything could be lurking in the darkness waiting for an unsuspecting victim like me."

"Stop whimpering, Speed, you're expendable!"

"Thanks you ungrateful bastard," I said and for my insolence immediately got a gun shoved in my back by one of the guards.

I took a first tentative step down onto the first rung, half expecting it to collapse under my weight. I was wrong. Each step felt solid enough for me to confidently go down into a deep cellar. As I reached out to steady myself I unwittingly disturbed a settling of thick dust, choking as it clouded the atmosphere. I coughed and spluttered a few times and got no sympathy.

"Not dying on us, are you, Speed?" Hamer shouted down.

"Not at all, why don't you get your frigging fat hairy arse down here and join me in this wonderful place."

The rest of the entourage followed. Heavy clunking as boots clamoured down, torch beams bouncing off the walls. Some scared idiot let out a screech when my torch beam illuminated the two skeletal frames sparsely covered with the remnants of large deteriorating overcoats commonly worn in the forties. Each skull had a hole in the middle of the forehead.

"Friends of yours, Speed?" Hamer said derisively.

"German spies actually" I said. "Let me introduce Harrington and Lodge, collaborators with IRA sympathizers and murdered by Jimmy McCracken so he could mastermind the greatest hijack in all sea-faring history. To be fair, you could argue that McCracken was solely responsible for preventing the Germans from continuing the war when he looted the I-52."

"Do I look as if I care a fucking toss?" Hamer jabbed me in the back. "Get moving!"

"You should do," I said as I moved on. "Or else you wouldn't find yourself down this hole shuffling up to my backside."

Again Hamer jabbed me forward.

I moved the torch beam around in various directions and since nobody had bothered to clean up for sixty years it wasn't surprising we had to run the gauntlet of the inevitable dusty cobwebs and listen to the varied splutters from unsuspecting recipients as they walked into one.

Someone let out a loud whistle of surprise when they came across the many shelves of armaments. I estimated there was enough to supply a rampaging army and would have no doubt caused British troops plenty of trouble after the war. Now they were only relics, defunct for use. Not even worth the scrap value.

Hamer was blind to the array of weapons as he scampered around the cellar like a man possessed. Pulling off tarpaulins and creating expanding dust clouds. I just stood back until he exhausted himself.

Morgan ordered a guard to keep a watchful eye on us while a mass search was conducted. After about three minutes of frantic disruption someone shouted.

"There's a padlocked steel door over here!"

There was a mad rush towards the voice, including me, though mine was an involuntary momentum as I got swept up with the euphoria and bustled towards the excitement because it was obvious the guard didn't want to miss out and to be totally honest neither did I. A hefty brute of a man began sledging the rusty big padlock from door with an even more rusty iron bar. Even though he had bulging muscles it took him a lot of effort but it finally gave when a crack filled the air.

It took three men to physically prise open the door. It's creaking and groaning steel refusing to give up its secrets. When the door was sufficiently wide enough, Hamer barged his way to the front and shone a torch into the blackness.

"The rooms full with boxes!" Hamer blurted.

He sent one of the crew inside, and moments later he re-emerged carrying an oblong box with Japanese symbols stamped on the side. By the way he put it down on the floor it looked heavy. Hamer took hold of the steel bar and smashed the box apart.

A golden glow glittered as the torch beams reflected off the collection of ingots spewing from between the broken wood. They matched the one I found in the cavern under Dun an Oir. Hamer stooped down and scooped a handful of gold and let the ingots drop back into the box. Speechless men listened to the metallic tinkling as they fell. Wide eyes gloated on the wealth before them. Neither mine, nor Shayna's altered because this was probably the moment when our lives were at terrible risk. The look we gave each other told the same story.

"Right, men," Morgan bellowed. "Get the rest of the boxes. I want an inventory of the amount collected. Anyone found filling their pockets before the count will have a hand chopped off. So hurry and get back to the ship." To me, he said: "Medical supplies, Speed, doesn't seem to be available, perhaps your information was invalid?"

Surprised, I said, "Strange, I noticed some more boxes with Japanese symbols back there."

Morgan shook his head disbelievingly. "Why do I get these speculative notions running around inside my head, referring that you're a lying toad. Please correct me if I'm perhaps being a little over ambitious with my assumption, only I haven't seen one medical box of any description and that includes a two pound fifty pence first aid kit, from any good shop."

I shrugged. "I can't always be right!"

It was the narrowing of Morgan's left eye that alerted me the time of execution had approached. With lightening reactions I twisted, grabbed the nearest guard and threw him into everybody else close enough to cause a human pile up. I grabbed Shayna by the arm and dragged her towards the stairway. Instantly a crescendo of bullets followed our stride in perfectly formed lines either side us as we ran.

I heard Morgan scream out, "Stop shooting you idiots! There are unstable high explosives all around us. Do you want to blow us to smithereens? Get after them!"

I didn't hang about as I pulled Shayna out of the hole and we ran from the church. We ran fast and hard heading in the direction back to the jetty. I had no immediate plan and struggled to even think of one. The only definite situation I understood was my energy being exhausted at an alarming rate. Bullets chased our every step, zipping off the ground at different angles. More disconcerting, Shayna slowed me down, she might be a dynamist in the sexual energy department but she couldn't run. My strength alone pulled her along before she dramatically fell down as if tackled by a fifteen stone rugby player which only served to knock me off balance. I presumed she'd stubbed her toe on a raised stone. I jerked her back on to her feet and again we were running only when we approached the jetty we had to dodge another volley of sub machinegun fire coming from the direction of the motor launch we arrived on.

Quickly we diverted right, running along the rugged terrain, heading for nowhere in particular. I glanced back to see two in pursuit of us. One was Hamer, huffing and puffing as he gave chase. The odd bullet whistled past.

I suddenly realized we were getting no where fast because Shayna had lost the will to run. Her legs were tiring rapidly as she struggled to skim over the rocky terrain. We were in the open and now an easy target. It didn't require the accuracy of a marksman to 'spray and play' with a machine pistol. I looked for hiding places which were far and few and when I saw large rocks to one side, we headed in that direction and sank behind them.

I peeped out between two of the rocks. Hamer had obviously seen our place of refuge because he was hand signalling for the goon to sweep around in one direction while he went the other. The situation made my mind up for me. It was pointless to run any more because the bullet in the back was ominous. I had no immediate plan swirling in my head other than I certainly wasn't going to die in any cowardly fashion. If I can take one of them with me at least I'd have gone down fighting.

Constantly checking both sides of the rock the goon was approaching the fastest. I would have preferred Hamer but beggars can't be choosy. I had one positive chance. If I can disarm the goon quick enough at least I would have a crack at Hamer. Maybe get one clear shot before he got me. I climbed the rock a metre high, anticipating the goon would assume I was flat to the floor in hiding. Patiently I waited, controlling my breathing. Then I saw the shadow of a head inching round the rock. He was definitely surprised when I pounced and the first thing I grabbed was the machine pistol he held, knocking the weapon downwards, bullets firing into the ground as we grappled for supremacy. We hit the ground, rolled and twisted. Dirt flicked up into our faces, mouths and eyes. Then the machine pistol went off again and we both stopped struggling.

I never felt a thing. The goon's eyes slowly widened as he stared at me. Soundless as his body stiffened. I became aware of a sticky substance running into my fingers where they had clamped the machine pistol. I was eyeball to eyeball with the goon, the stench of his breath getting heavier and more rapid before he finally flopped down on top of me. Dead people strangely become heavy. I quickly threw him off while trying desperately to wrench the machine pistol from his tightened grip and get to my feet. But I was a second too late when Hamer shot me.

Dead people don't feel pain and I was in agony as I crumpled to the floor clutching my left shoulder. Then I felt a severe burning sensation as if some sadistic torturer had shoved a red-hot poker into the bullet hole because that was exactly the pain I got. I grimaced, my teeth clenched with both the hurt and anger. Hamer stood over me smirking. He had Shayna by the throat as he stood behind her. She looked groggy and she was bleeding heavily from a cut just above her eye. Hamer had been brutal when he smashed his gun into her face to slow her down.

His gun was aimed at me. "As predicted, Speed, professionalism outsmarts the amateur. But before I kill you I would like to thank you, from the bottom of a sceptic tank, for finding our golden future. I'm glad I didn't kill when I'd the chance in London, or else we'd probably never have found the gold. Alas, Speed, death comes at a price and fortunately I'm to become rich."

"You won't get away with it!" I spat my threats.

"Yes I will!" Hamer said with confidence. "And while I'm soaking up all that nice sunshine at some paradise location, you'll be getting lowered, along with Miss Loser here, in that pauper's grave we promised."

I managed a defiant blast of words. "Don't count on it Hamer! I'll haunt you from wherever I am, you murdering bastard!"

Hamer's smile broadened as his finger bent over the trigger. I flinched in readiness for the bullet exploding from the barrel. But as I cringed, from the corner of my eye, I saw a black shadow suddenly engulf Hamer just before a huge fist crashed into the side of his face that sent him plummeting sideways, making him release his grip on Shayna. He dropped to the ground in a heap, blood trickling from the side of his mouth.

I couldn't believe my ears when I heard Shamus's angry voice.

"Dhat, you obnoxious granite of English shit, is for blowing up me boat!"

Shamus looked at me. He said, "Hullo dhare, Shacks Sir. I didn't want to miss all the fun."

Then he promptly spat into Hamer's hair, (which I thought must be some sort of Irish custom) then he kicked him in the midriff. "And dhat, English bastard, is for givin' me friends a rough and unpleasant time." He looked at Shayna with an apologetic expression. "Excuse me dreadful behaviour, Miss. Tis very unusual for Shamus O'Malley to conduct himself in such a disorderly manner in front of a Lady."

Shayna threw herself into the Irishman and hugged him. He was slightly embarrassed by the emotional ordeal. She said, "You were magnificent, Shamus!"

I could only marvel at Shamus's brilliant timing as he had saved my life. He helped me to my feet, took my weight, allowed Shayna to loop her arm through his, and we headed wearily back to the church.

All of a sudden the place was swarming with heavily armed men. A helicopter flew overhead heading for the 'Flying-fish'. Motor launches skimmed across the water. Uniformed men ran past to collect Hamer.

In a panic I said, "Did you see Morgan?"

Shamus looked puzzled. "Morgan? If he was inside the church then he's trapped with no escape, Shacks, Sir. I was too busy runnin' to stop Hamer pulling the trigger."

"Frigging hell, Shamus, what if you hadn't made it!"

"O' dhare was no need to worry about dhat, Shacks, Sir. Dhare was a sharpshooter on standby ready to take the bastard down."

A senior Garda officer angled across to us. With a salute, he said, "Chief Inspector, Micky O'Connor. I presume I'm addressing, Mister Shackleton Speed and Miss Shayna Magginty?

Shayna nodded. I could only grunt.

"You'll have a lot of explaining to do. When you've rested I'd appreciate urgent cooperation. Now apparently we have to wait for a number of Japanese officials who are flying in." Then he noticed the blood soaking my jacket sleeve. "Good grief man you're injured. Medic!" he shouted. "This man requires attention."

Alarmed I said, "What about Morgan?"

"We have in custody, Sir. He's ranting on about how he tracked you down, Sir. That you're a thieving and murdering misfit and it should be you we put in handcuffs and not him."

I panicked. "You didn't believe him?"

"Not in any way, Sir. He tried to shoot one of my men!"

CHAPTER TWENTYFIVE

The private helicopter that flew in circled and landed sending a gush of violent back draft smashing into us. Two Orientals emerged from the cockpit. I recognized Tanamoto instantly. It was apparent he hadn't heard of Deveron's death because he looked too happy. I considered it wasn't my place to tell him. Chief Inspector Micky O'Conner met them from the craft. They talked for five minutes.

In the meantime the medic finished patching my wound and put my arm into a sling. Luckily the bullet went right through with minimum damage, perhaps a chipped shoulder blade. Then Tanamoto and his companion hurried towards us, all teeth with huge smiles, with the Garda officer dragging in their wake. Bowing once they reached where I was being attended.

"Ah, Mister Speed!" Then his smile dropped. "You've been hurt!"

"Just a flesh wound." I assured him.

"I wish you fast recovery." He gestured to his companion. "Let me introduce to you, Haisi Yoshimoto, military attaché, Japanese consulate in London."

Yoshimoto bowed. "It is a great honour to meet you, Mister Speed. The entire people of Japan will be greatly indebted to the man who found the I-52."

"News travels fast but I'm glad to be of service."

Again their heads bowed and Yoshimoto said, "It is a service that will be truly honoured, Mister Speed."

I said to O'Connor. "There's a cavern you might want to visit below Dun an Oir on Clear Island. That's where you will find the sub and the bodies of the submariners. There are two entrances and both have a degree of difficulty for entry: one by sea but you'll require diving gear: the other by the fort itself only you will require excavation equipment to remove tons of rocks. Under those rocks are the bodies of seven Irishmen. They are responsible for the hijacking of the I-52 in 1944, and for the murder of the Japanese crew."

With a well rehearsed suspicious tone, O'Conner said, "How did you discover all this, if I might be asking?"

"I guess I was just damn lucky."

Yoshimoto reached inside his coat pocket. He produced a white envelope and bowed while he handed it to me. "Please accept our humble thanks, Mister Shackleton Speed."

I thanked Yoshimoto and tucked the offering into my pocket.

Tanamoto said, "We shall leave you to continue your medical treatment, Mister Speed."

When they had gone with O'Connor, Shayna whispered to me. "Well they got back their submarine and gold but what do you think happened to the opium?"

"I haven't clue! I don't think even McCracken knew either. But I know a tramp called Willie. He knows where it is, because I suspect while he had nothing to do for ten hours, he went nosing around a submarine and found the so called medical supplies. Probably had knowledge of its importance and stashed the stuff away to collect later. It wouldn't surprise me if all seven were in on the conspiracy to keep the knowledge from McCracken. But circumstances changed Willie's way of thinking. He was too frightened to return to the Island to collect."

"So it's still there, on the Island?"

"I guess so!"

"What are you going to do about it?"

"I'm going to do nothing but hope it's rotted away. If that much opium hit the streets, well just think of the epidemic of drug users."

"I have another infuriating question to ask?"

"Being?"

"What was in the envelope you slipped into your pocket?"

"This envelope, you mean?" I tapped my pocket as I spoke.

"Yes that one!"

"Ah-well that's ex gratis, of course."

"Yeah how silly of me, but remind me again in layman terms?"

"It's a letter of authority from the Japanese Government allowing me salvage rights to the gold."

Shayna had a confused look. "Salvage rights?"

"That's right. I'm not stupid. I negotiated a payment of two percent of all the recovered gold. The fee was kindly agreed by the Japanese government in respect of my honourable disclosure of their property."

"You took a chance. They might not have wanted to pay out."

"Ah yes, I did point out that minor probability to them. Then I would have had to apply, 'finder's keepers-losers weepers-giving back is stealing-and frigging lucky they got it back-policy'. But you have to respect the Japanese for their upholding of promises. I knew they would agree. Now that they have the submarine and the gold back, they'll be a happy bunch back in Japan."

"Shackleton Speed you annoying manipulating two faced son of a bitch!"

"Less of the annoying if you don't mind!"

Her face lit up. "Jesus Christ! That's probably two and half million Yen."

"No, that's two and half million pounds sterling."

"You're one lucky Limey bastard!"

"No, I'm a rich lucky Limey bastard!"

"There's no need to brag."

"Not all for me, if you don't mind! As a matter of decency, I shall be sharing out a good proportion certain families. And I promised Shamus a new boat."

"I've got to hand it to you, Shackleton, you've proven to be one hell of a guy."

"It's nice to be appreciated at last. Shall we go and spend some money?"

"What have you in mind?"

"Somewhere quiet, away from all this mess. Does the Caribbean sound nice?"

"Is that an invitation?"

"You're not busy, are you?"

She laughed, "I'll find the time. But just imagine if you had kept all that gold."

"The thought had occurred to me, Shayna. But friends died because of it. There would always be a pang of guilt burning in my head if I did."

"Isn't the salvage money not in the same category?"

"No! I earned that by risking my life."

For a moment I looked away from Shayna when I caught sight of the handcuffed Morgan and Hamer being thrown into the rear of separate vehicles. As the motorcade departed I imagined Hamer quietly sat there mentally sharpening his knife in the desperate hope he could still silence me forever.

The End

Printed in the United Kingdom
by Lightning Source UK Ltd.
114864UKS00001B/1-24